ASSAULT
BY FIRE

D0029808

...LT
BY FIRE

A TYCE ASHER NOVEL

H. RIPLEY
RAWLINGS IV

LT. COL., USMC (RET.)

PINNACLE BOOKS
Kensington Publishing Corp.
www.kensingtonbooks.com

PINNACLE BOOKS are published by

Kensington Publishing Corp.
119 West 40th Street
New York, NY 10018

All Kensington titles, imprints, and distributed lines are available at special quantity discounts for bulk purchases for sales promotions, premiums, fund-raising, educational, or institutional use. Special book excerpts or customized printings can also be created to fit specific needs. For details, write or phone the office of the Kensington sales manager: Kensington Publishing Corp., 119 West 40th Street, New York, NY 10018, attn: Sales Department; phone 1-800-221-2647.

PINNACLE BOOKS and the Pinnacle logo are Reg. U.S. Pat. & TM Off.

ISBN-13: 978-0-7860-4706-2
ISBN-10: 0-7860-4706-2

First printing: October 2020

10 9 8 7 6 5 4 3 2 1

Printed in the United States of America

Electronic edition:

ISBN-13: 978-0-7860-4707-9 (e-book)
ISBN-10: 0-7860-4707-0 (e-book)

To my wife and children—
Home Team: It's time to taste some of that
freedom we've defended all those years!
—Lieutenant Colonel Dad

ACKNOWLEDGMENTS

Inevitably, when someone sits to write a novel, they have people behind them, to their front and on the sides to thank. Unfortunately for me, I have a whole army (and perhaps a Marine Corps, Air Force, and Navy, too).

Special thanks to: my wife and kids for enduring and encouraging me through the creative process; my mother, who is my second editor, bickering pal, and constant source of candy for the grandchildren; Mark Greaney, my mentor, confidant, and good friend; authors and friends Marc Cameron and Mike Maden, for listening to me drone on with ideas, then providing sage advice in return; the indomitable Gary Goldstein, my Kensington editor, who put up with a lot more than an editor should have to and never once lost his smile; the whole Rawlings and Felger families, for their patience and kindness; my spiritual allies, the Dastur/Haksars, Westbrooks, Cerritellis, Tellerias, Smiths, Pinions, Papases, and Burts; the queen pharmacist and her Elden Street Tea Shop; and many, many others who will remain nameless to protect their innocence in having anything to do with this novel.

*Se un infortunio deve essere fatto a un uomo,
dovrebbe essere così severo che la sua vendetta
non ha bisogno di essere temuta.*
(If an injury has to be done to a man, it should be
so severe that his vengeance need not be feared.)
—NICCOLÒ MACHIAVELLI, *The Prince*

PROLOGUE

When Premier of the Soviet Union Joseph V. Stalin died in 1954, the Russian Executive Command finally received permission from the presidium to alter the grand Soviet national military strategy from one focusing on the defense of *Rodina* (Mother Russia) to something completely new—one that could be summed up by saying that a series of lightning offenses are the best defense in the modern, nuclear era. In these new war plans, a successful invasion of Europe was given as a foregone conclusion. Russia was completely confident they held the upper hand on the Continent.

But the invasion of the continental United States, without the use of strategic nuclear arms, remained a vexing problem for Soviet military planners. Three major obstacles prevented the generals from supporting an invasion.

The following pages are an excerpt from the original Soviet War plan.

Union of Soviet Socialist Republics

War Plan 90X-54 (Invasion of the United States)
Combined Assault of America
by Russian Ocean and Air Forces

Para 18-01

1. Invasion of the contiguous forty-eight United States by sea is determined by the leading Soviet naval planners in Leningrad to be impractical at this time. Achieving our doctrinal and desirable five to one troop ratio via undetected large transport ships and across the Atlantic/Pacific oceans is not feasible with current technology.

2. Invasion of the United States is <u>unlikely to be sustainable</u> due to wanton and massive U.S. practice of private firearm ownership. The American Second Amendment means conflict within the continental United States will devolve rapidly and inevitably into a bloody house-to-house conflict. Insurgencies will consist chiefly of remnant military interspersed with willing, patriotic, and well-armed civilian insurgents—who will arise shortly after (or during) the planned Soviet "Assault Phases" and after our forces' initial seizure of the U.S. coast(s).

3. The U.S. policy of Mutual Assured Destruction (MAD) means an invasion would be <u>costly,</u> as any surviving U.S. nuclear force command and control architecture will retaliate with strategic nuclear weapons.

SOVIET MILITARY EXECUTIVE COMMAND
CONCLUSIONS

<u>Para 18-02</u>
Any invasion of the U.S. will be cost prohibitive in both materials and personnel, and any estimates for victory in a land invasion of the continental United States offered to the Supreme Soviet in War Plan 90X-54 should remain marked as merely "feasible," until the three listed factors can be removed or mitigated.

Finally, it is the estimate of my entire staff that invasion should only be considered in the event of an existential threat against Mother Russia herself.

Signed,
Colonel General I. V. Magyv
Soviet General Staff Headquarters
Offensive War Plan 90X, April 1990 Revision

CHAPTER 1

Twelve years ago
Fallujah, Iraq

He was being dragged backward into a building by the scruff of his flak jacket. As his heels left marks in the sand and dirt, he dazedly stared up and admired the beautiful blue-grey smoke eddies in the air. The near-constant fighting had left a cloud of swirling gas from the guns. Still deafened by the explosion, Lieutenant Tyce Asher looked around, bewildered. His face and hands were singed and burning in agony, but he couldn't remember why. He scrambled to his feet, wobbling and taking in his surroundings. His Marines had taken up positions at the windows. As things became clearer to Tyce, he could feel a thumping, a dull pounding against his face and chest, the bass of booms and pops reverberating through his body even in his still mostly silent world. Nearby, a machine gun was going full bore out a narrow window.

Good! The men are letting them have it, he thought, somewhat proud of himself for making his first coherent thought through the haze in the room and the fog in his brain.

Three grenades had been used to clear the room of militant fighters, and now the formal, antique-style office furniture was ripped and shredded. Charred and torn, the filing cabinets leaked Iraqi government paperwork out onto the floor. A painting of Saddam Hussein, sliced by shrapnel, hung off-kilter on the wall.

Tyce was starting to remember the detonation that had torn up and through the bottom of his Marine Corps Humvee. Shards of searing-hot steel shrapnel had spiraled through the air, slicing and tearing everything in their path. The two Marines in the front seats were spared the hell of being chopped into a hundred pieces by the ricocheting metal: Both were vaporized, disappearing in the fireball that engulfed the Humvee.

The shock wave from the underbelly IED had blown out all four doors, catapulting Marine Lieutenant Tyce Asher from the back seat and out of the vehicle. His heavy body-armor-clad frame was ejected and thrown in a somersault. He landed on his head with a sickening crunch.

He had lain in a heap atop a twisted Humvee door. His brain pounded, displacing all rational thoughts. Sitting partially upright, he fixed his gaze on the vehicle he'd occupied only a moment before. Now flames roared out the top and sides of the contorted wreckage. It took a major effort, but with a shaky hand, he reached up to his head. His helmet was gone, splintered on impact with the concrete. Thankfully, it had done its job—breaking into pieces so his head didn't.

He'd sensed a shape next to him—Sergeant Dixon kneeling over him. Tyce could see the sergeant's mouth moving, but no sound seemed to be coming out. There wasn't even a ringing in Tyce's ears, just dead silence. That and the feeling that every inch of his body had been beaten with a lead pipe.

After a few seconds of screaming in his ear, the sergeant had given up and dragged him toward a nearby building by the handle built into the back of his flak jacket. Tyce's legs kicked weakly at the baking-hot noonday pavement, his body automatically trying to assist even in his near-insensible state as he was manhandled across the street.

Emerging from the memory, Tyce grabbed his platoon sergeant by the shoulder. He pointed at the building down the street, presumably the one from which the enemy had initiated the IED. Tyce motioned for him to assemble a squad and follow him. Deaf or not, the time had come to take the fight to the enemy. His platoon sergeant looked him up and down and seemed to be saying something, probably telling Tyce to go get checked out by one of the navy corpsmen. Tyce just shook his head and told him to hurry up. Or at least, Tyce hoped that was what it sounded like. He still couldn't hear his own voice.

Not long after, Tyce was leading the squad out into the acrid air, past the still-burning wreckage of his Humvee. He picked the middle of the group. A good place from which to lead—he could see everyone and contribute to some accurate fire, if need be. Tyce was an expert marksman with both his rifle and his service pistol.

Youngish by most standards, but considerably older than most of his men, Tyce was twenty-six. Taller than average, about six-three, lean and with sandy blond hair. Marines used every tactic in the book to maintain order and discipline, but the most important of all was respect. And that could only be earned. Tyce had done pretty well in the eyes of the men over in these last months in practically nonstop combat. He never shied away from a firefight and never ordered his men to do something he wasn't personally willing to do himself.

When they reached the building, the men hoisted each other up through two blasted-out corner windows.

Never clear a building through the front door. Tyce recited the maxim to himself, then thought, *or any door, for that matter.*

He'd learned that in his first fifteen minutes of combat. Anyone who didn't went home in a body bag.

Once the men's eyes adjusted to the gloom and smoke inside, Tyce pointed at each squad leader, directing them to start clearing the building from room to room. Rifles short stocked, up and at the ready. Grenadiers in the middle, machine gunners bringing up the rear. Adrenaline and blood pumping.

Each squad received some quick instructions from their sergeants, then raced off to different parts of the building. Tyce dashed a note onto a scrap of paper for his radioman to transmit back to their company commander.

As the squads passed by on their assignments, a few men gaped at him openly. A few minutes before, they had seen him blown clean out of his Humvee, and here he was, standing tall and issuing orders. Tyce waited next to his radio operator in the empty room, weapon at the ready and every muscle tensed and straining for any sign of action from the squads.

Five blasts from upstairs. Even in his deafened state, Tyce felt the concussions.

Corporal Clausen's squad. He bounded up the stairs after his men, realizing as he did how foolish he was to do so without anyone to assist.

No time, he thought, *gotta attack. I'll just have to rely on my other senses.*

Bullets and fragments of wall skittered by him as he ascended the stairs. When he got to the top, the smell of gunpowder was strong—and mixed with something else. He smelled the air. In his deafened state his other senses were already taking over.

Cooking oil and cardamom? he thought.

Dull, pumping sounds of adrenaline-fueled blood rushed through his ears.

As he reached the top of the stairs, his heart sank. In a flash, he realized he'd sent his men into a trap. No one had survived. The small room was a bloody scene of death, booby-trapped. A veritable kill zone.

Holy shit . . . my orders killed them, he thought.

Two flashing shapes caught his eye. Two figures moving at the exact same moment. In a heart-bursting instant, he made a decision born of combat experience to target the one he assessed as more dangerous.

He chose the terrorist at the door, balancing an AK-47 assault rifle against his hip and blazing away at full auto as he tossed a grenade into the room with his other hand. Directed by instinct, Tyce pulled the trigger twice. Accurate and controlled, both rounds met their marks. The man fell in a heap, motionless.

The choice was a good one, but out of the corner of his eye, he saw another movement down by his feet. A wounded terrorist with a knife. Tyce swung his carbine around—too late. He felt a searing pain in his leg as the terrorist's wicked blade cut deep into his calf. The wound and his body armor brought him crashing heavily to the floor. The fighter jumped on top of him, weighing him down, trying to drive the deadly knife into Tyce's neck. Tyce blocked it and tried to reach for his own Marine Ka-Bar fighting knife.

This was the wrong move. By shifting one hand, he was rewarded with a wicked downward slash across his face.

He had reduced the threat from two to one, but now he was in a death struggle on a floor slick with blood, battle-field debris, and cooking oil. And somewhere in the smoke-filled room, a hand grenade ticked silently.

Tyce had to do something—anything—or he was going to die. In one swift, calculated movement, he wrenched the wounded terrorist fully on top of him like a shield. It was the right move. The man kicked and clawed at Tyce, but it was too late. The grenade exploded in a huge blast. Shrapnel filled the air of the small room.

Tyce went deaf again.

Twelve years ago
St. Petersburg, Russia

Colonel Viktor Kolikoff paced up and down his large, new, oak-paneled office, lost in thought. He'd worked twenty-two years to earn this place in the army head-quarters building in Saint Petersburg. Twenty-two long, in-dustrious years.

The best years of my life, he thought, and he felt he'd earned this corner office, one with enormous floor-to-ceiling Empire-style picture-frame windows overlooking the Moyka River. It afforded him wondrous views of the Bolshoi Theatre and the Fabergé art museum.

The building was once a grand palace of Tzar Nicho-las II. Kolikoff had occasionally tried to guess what the office had been used for, just about a hundred years ago. It was his now, along with his vaunted new title, Chief of Staff of the Western Military District, and all the duties at-tendant to that position.

As one of the Russian army's quickest and brightest rising stars, Kolikoff had made full colonel in less than twenty years—a meteoric rise only achieved by less than one percent of all Russian officers. He was absolutely certain of himself, and certain that he was destined for greatness.

That is, he had been . . . until just that moment.

At a slight squeak of over-polished shoes behind him, Kolikoff tore his gaze from the beautiful views and equally ripped himself away from any remaining thought of grandeur.

Everything had changed in the blink of an eye a few hours before. With just a few words, the general had placed him in charge of the worst assignment Kolikoff had ever heard of. Hell, worse than he could dream of. He couldn't think of a more career-killing project if he tried.

He pivoted sharply about and glared at the three lieutenants standing at attention, as if they were to blame for spoiling his grand dreams of climbing to the very top of the military ladder. "A fucking computer?!" he shouted.

The officers stared blankly back at him from the same spot on the worn red carpet.

Colonel Kolikoff didn't bother waiting for an answer; he continued his tirade. "The Victory Day parade is one month away. Every military district will come with their fighter jets, tanks, troops, all polished to the last brass belt buckle"—he inhaled deeply and boomed again—"and quite literally, you *fools* have nothing to show for your *months* of preparation except a stupid computer?"

Of course, Kolikoff knew basically what this computer was. The so-called SPETS-VTOR computer. In the closing days of World War II, the Soviets had gone out of their way to capture a bunch of Nazi computer scientists, just as they had captured German rocket scientists for their missile program. Ever since, some of these scientists had been toiling away with first Soviet and now Russian Federation computers to make them do something. Well, finally, they were supposedly doing something

Sighing heavily, Kolikoff resigned himself to his fate. He lowered his voice and spoke slowly. "Okay . . . go and issue the order. Every man below the rank of major will march in the parade. I want every baker, cook, and mechanic in this command to polish their boots, clean their rifle, and drill every day from now until then." He went back over to the window, trying to gain some solace from the view overlooking the bourgeoisie—*Just as*, he thought, *maybe the Tzar did.*

His anger rising again, continuing to stare at the bustling streets of Saint Petersburg, he shouted, "Ev-er-y day!" Then, simmering down, he said, "And last—and most importantly—I want something big on that computer. Something enormous. If we have nothing but this *stupid computer* as our centerpiece, I want it to calculate something immense in scope and grandeur."

One of the lieutenants opened his dry mouth, about to ask a question.

Kolikoff interrupted before the junior officer could speak. "Have it calculate the plans . . . the battle plans to invade the United States of America." And with a wave of his hand, he dismissed the men, who gladly hurried off.

Kolikoff suddenly noticed that the huge windows he'd been looking through so proudly—windows that framed a view he'd admired immensely these last few months—had iron bars on them. The converted Tzar's palace was just a pathetic, worn-out army headquarters. As drab and confining as all the other offices he'd had before.

CHAPTER 2

Twelve years ago
Fallujah

Tyce tried to push the dead man off him, but he was drained, almost completely out of strength. The adrenaline rush was ebbing. He felt a sharp pain in his face and a dull steady throb below. He inched his hand down his leg. His fingers felt nothing but a sinewy mess below his knee where his leg should be.

The grenade had shredded the insurgent, killing him instantly, but apparently Tyce had left a small section of himself uncovered by the man's body. The explosion turned Tyce's leg into a mass of exposed ligaments, flesh, and blood vessels. Through blood-clouded vision, he saw movement at the stairwell and fully expected another enemy fighter coming to finish him off. Instead, his captain ran forward, towering over him. Tyce tried to read his boss's words as he dragged the dead enemy off him. The captain looked at Tyce's bleeding cheek, then down to his missing leg. The captain smiled in a reassuring way and Tyce saw the words, "You'll be okay."

A navy corpsman appeared. He slapped a four-inch gauze wadding on Tyce's cheek wound. Elevated his head from the debris. Put a tourniquet on his leg. Stabbed him in the thigh with two morphine auto-shots. Dipped his finger in Tyce's blood and wrote "M-M" on his forehead, then ran back down the stairs to attend other casualties.

Tyce watched, detached, as a machine gun team entered the room. Stepping over Tyce, they ran to the window. Brass shell casings poured from the Fabrique Nationale M240G 7.62mm machine gun in a downspout, mixing with the blood, rubble, and remains. A second Marine machine gun team took a position at another window and began firing.

Tyce yearned to help, to get into the fight alongside his boys, but another corpsman arrived, pinned him down, said something, checked the tourniquet, and pointed to his leg while shaking his head. None of the words were clear.

Tyce's vision started to tunnel. His chest began to feel warm, and he could feel his heartbeat, slow and arrhythmic. Everything was getting fuzzy, but the pain was receding. The double morphine shot was taking effect. He smiled as a Marine Shoulder-Launched Multipurpose Assault Weapon, or SMAW, anti-rocket crew moved to the window pushing a machine gun team aside. The displaced machine gunners in wild-eyed dismay now took a moment to look at him, prone and bleeding on the floor.

The rocket gunner fired. The big 83mm rocket let loose a sharp crack.

Tyce felt rather than heard the brief but massive red flame of the rocket's backblast. Heat, body parts, brass casings, dirt, and battlefield detritus ricocheted around the room, peppering him.

Hmm . . . we're all gonna die because of my stupid orders. But that doc, thought Tyce, *was totally hardcore . . . I gotta remember to tell him he's doing a great job under fire . . . Real pro . . .*

Tyce was vaguely aware of another massive, bright

red flash. More debris flew through the air, like stinging hornets. His world was starting to go black.

And then . . . nothing.

Twelve years ago
Siberia

Two AK-47 rifle barrels thrust into the truck bed, lifting the canvas flap and revealing the five dirty, half-frozen men hiding beneath. The early morning light reflecting off the heavy snow outside blinded them. The back of the large troop truck was cramped and stank from the men's foul odors.

Two men with thick, almost guttural Siberian accents, their AKs still pointed forcefully at Colonel Viktor Kolikoff and his officers and the scientists, ordered them all gruffly and immediately out of the truck. They all rose up stiffly, joints aching, eyes watery and fatigued.

Kolikoff pulled his grey army greatcoat around him, trying to gather some semblance of the proud officer he had been only a few days before his great fall. The shoulders of the large coat had kept him from dying of cold but were now bare where the shoulder boards of a colonel had once been.

Kolikoff painfully threw a leg over the side of the truck and clumsily dropped to the frozen earth, losing whatever dignity he had so far maintained in front of the Siberian enlisted men. They laughed at all of them as the others tumbled roughly off the truck after him.

The prisoners gathered in a cluster, blinking—their eyes still stinging in the glaring winter sunlight. They glanced around, anxiously wondering what came next.

A Russian army captain in a dirty overcoat and worn

black leather gloves spoke out of Kolikoff's earshot to the armed Siberian soldiers, then quickly gave a shout for all the prisoners to walk over to a deep pit forty yards away in an open field.

Three other trucks were being unloaded, too, and a long line of terrified, gaunt prisoners—tied together by ropes—trudged through the deep snow joining the rest over at the pit. A heavy military tractor idled nearby, the engine sputtering, thick diesel exhaust rising into the sky. The rock-hard Siberian ground hadn't yielded much to the tractor; Kolikoff noticed the shallow scrape was only a few feet deep.

Kolikoff watched as the other roped-together prisoners were hustled and lined up next to the pit. All the men's eyes grew wide as they realized what was about to happen.

This was an execution!

There was no other conclusion to be drawn. How could this have happened? Kolikoff thought he had achieved a true breakthrough with the computer. But the presentation had been dismissed as an enormous waste of Russian resources and labeled as "treasonous" by his commander. He'd become the scapegoat for his entire command's failure to impress Moscow. It must have worked, because he next day his boss was still in command, but he, Dr. Vogel, and the rest of the team received orders that read simply, "Upon receipt, report immediately to the commander, Transbaikal Regional Headquarters. Further instructions upon arrival at said new duty location. Transportation will be arranged. Failure to report will be considered a crime of disobedience of orders." Getting him out of the way clearly prevented any protestations or chance for disloyalty.

As Kolikoff eyed the men lined up along the long pit, a sense of utter betrayal slowed his walk. His lieutenants and scientists, coming to the same realization, halted with him.

Three soldiers raced over and kicked Kolikoff and his men roughly with heavy boots and jabbed them with the barrels of their rifles toward the end of the line of prisoners. Everyone was lined up on the near end of the pit.

This, Kolikoff presumed, was so their bodies would fall back and make it easier for the bulldozer driver to cover them over. Efficient.

He glanced down the line: they were on the far end of about forty men in total. With only a dozen rifles, the execution was going to be a mess.

I could do this better, he thought. His arrogance briefly flared up, an almost out-of-body feeling. Then he remembered that he, too, was one of the condemned men, and shivers of fear ran down his spine.

The heavy snowdrifts crunched underfoot as the firing squad lined up opposite Kolikoff and the prisoners. *A group of boys, really*, he thought.

Kolikoff looked out at the frozen snow-covered hills past the trucks, staff cars, and small assembly of men. In the distance, the mountains and evergreen forests beckoned. He contemplated making a run for it, in spite of his ice-numbed knees and joints. But any time to run had come and gone; even if his legs were able to comply, his mind was unwilling, and the distance was too great.

Ten paces, and I'd be cut to pieces.

He sighed and hung his head. Considering his life, he inhaled deeply, filling his lungs with the cold air. A life of hard service, late nights to make himself look good in the eyes of his superiors. Days of hard training as a young man, given opportunities by Mother Russia. A system that gave him advantages, one he had trusted. All in vain . . . it had only gotten him here, at the point of a dozen rifle barrels. Not even enough rifles to do the job in one volley.

A sergeant came around, tying the men's hands and

ankles together with metal twine and pulling hoods over their heads. The sergeant grinned when he got to Kolikoff. He smiled as he pulled a thick burlap sack over Kolikoff's head.

After what seemed an eternity, Kolikoff heard the sergeant's footsteps crunching back over the snow toward the firing line. The commands came fast.

"*Zaryazhay!*" Load.

Kolikoff heard through the hood the sounds of men weeping, sobbing hysterically.

"*Tselya! . . .*" Take aim.

Kolikoff recognized the sounds of safeties clicking off and the clatter of bolts as a dozen AK-47 rifles chambered rounds. He heard some of the prisoners fall to their knees and pray.

"*Ogon!*" Fire!

The crack of a dozen rifles rang out crisply, followed by a dozen heavy thuds as the men fell, and then the sound was lost in the vast emptiness.

"*Ogon!*" Another volley and more thuds, these directly adjacent to Kolikoff.

However, this time he heard a new sound. A howl began down the line, like a wounded animal. One of the shots had clearly failed to hit its mark, and a wounded man was gagging and gurgling on his own blood.

Bastards, he thought. *Can they do nothing right?*

"For God's sake, put him out of his misery!" Kolikoff heard himself shout, though he was surprised by his own courage. The crunch of snow. A single pistol shot, and the howling ceased.

The crunch of more snow, and someone stopped directly in front of him. He cringed slightly, awaiting the bullet.

So they saved me for last. Typical, he thought.

Then, to his great surprise, the hood was lifted. He squinted against the bright daylight. The rising sun once more warmed his face.

In front of him, a general's shoulder boards. The Trans-baikal region's commander—General Grigor Tympkin, he remembered from his briefing on the SPETS-VTOR. Though his stomach still churned, he chanced a glance down the line at the dozens of bloodstained bodies lying in the snow.

General Tympkin's face was grim, lined from years of service and fighting in Afghanistan and Chechnya. He raised his fingers, making a pistol, and stuck the forefinger against Kolikoff's forehead before snapping down his thumb.

"Bang," he said, a wry smile on his face.

Kolikoff flinched, his knees wobbling from the sudden release of fear, and he collapsed to the ground.

"Welcome to Siberia, Major," Tympkin said. "Now you and that computer work for me."

General Tympkin let it set in a moment but remained staring down directly into Kolikoff's uplifted eyes.

"We will await our chance, then we are going to make history. You, me, and that computer."

CHAPTER 3

Two years ago
Washington, D.C.

Tyce was sweating through his Marine Corps Service Alpha uniform more from the worry than the overly heated old Marine Corps building. Outwardly, his uniform was sharp, pressed with a perfect row of combat ribbons across his chest. One of them represented his greatest honor but also the grim reason he was here today. The Purple Heart.

His nerves were at their end, but today was the day. A Marine sergeant, likewise dressed in the Marine Corps dress uniform, ushered him inside the outer office.

"Sir, you are to knock on the hatch and then report directly to the colonel of the board." said the Marine, using the naval term for a door. Even when not aboard a sailing vessel, Marines and sailors used the old nautical terms. "Hatch" for a door, "bulkhead" for a wall, and "porthole" for a window.

Tyce knocked, then strode in, trying his level best to disguise his limp. The room was cavernous, its ancient wooden walls bedecked with oil paintings of navy and Marine Corps battles. In front of him, a Marine colonel sat at the center of the table. Beside him were two lieutenant colonels and two U.S. Navy commanders with medical insignia on their collars.

Tyce walked to the middle of the room, snapped to attention, and barked out, "Captain Tyce Asher, reporting as ordered."

"Okay, Captain," said the colonel, rummaging through the stack of papers on the desk in front of him, "You know why you're here, right, Asher?"

"Affirmative, sir."

"Alright, then. Please tell the board, in your own words, why you believe the government should retain you on active duty."

"Well, sir—"

The colonel interrupted, "Oh, and, stand at ease. I mean, as best as you can with that leg."

Tyce's face flushed as the colonel's words reinforced the nature of his appointment here before the Naval Medical Retention Review board. Lumped in with several other officers who had spotty records and others who were sick or lame, like himself. Feeling a lot like he was in a pile of rejects, and worse, he now had to prove to the Marine Corps personally why he believed he was still fit for service.

Tyce cleared his throat and began again, this time with noticeably less gusto than before. The colonel's offhanded comment had all but fully let the wind out of his sails, "Well, sir . . . um, gentlemen . . . if you all have read through my record, you will see I can now pass a first-class physical fitness test—"

"The modified PFT though. You do a rowing machine or something, right, Captain?" interjected one of the Marine Corps lieutenant colonels.

"Yes, um . . . yes, sir. I can do everything any other Marine can do, all but for the running."

"So . . . not quite everything a *normal* Marine can do," said the other one of the Navy docs, indicating quotation marks with his fingers.

"Correct, sir. It's all in my file," said Tyce, his voice began to betray his frustration.

"Okay, yes, yes. We've looked over it all. But tell me *why* you want to remain," said the colonel.

"Sir . . . the Corps is, is . . . is my life. I want to continue to serve our nation's defense."

One of the navy doctors spoke up, "Fine, Captain Asher, but in reviewing your files, I see you were also subjected to a very large blast. Um . . ." He picked over the paperwork one sheet at a time until he found it. "A roadside bomb . . . blew you out of your Humvee." He looked up, a little incredulously. "How are your cognitive skills?"

"Fine, sir," Tyce said stiffly. "No different than anyone else who got bumped around over there."

"We call that more than a *bump*, Captain. It's called a traumatic brain injury."

"I do *not* have TBI, sir. I've been tested and I'm fine." His voice grew testy.

The colonel intervened before the situation got worse. "Look, we're just not sure why you don't want to go home, Captain Asher. Settle down. Take a break, you know? I've looked over the compensatory offer from the government, and you have a very nice retirement and disability package being offered to you."

"Sir, I never joined the Corps for money."

"OK, Captain Asher . . ." The colonel's look became more serious, "I'm going to level with you. The Corps really wants to have all our wounded warriors *off* the rosters . . . you know, it looks like we're back to fighting in the Middle East, a nd we need to keep the Corps free from . . . well, in any case the Corps values your sacrifice. You have earned it. But maybe it's time to finally hang up the sword, Marine."

"Respectfully, sir, I disagree. I want to remain on active duty."

"Okay," said the colonel, drumming his fingers on the table and looking up and down the table. "Unless there is an objection from the navy medical personnel or any of the other officers of the board here, I'm going to go ahead and stamp approval."

Tyce felt a sense of immense relief and tried to conceal the beginnings of a smile.

"But," the colonel continued, "with the recent hostilities in Iran, we only have one spot available for someone with breadth of expertise and, ahem. . . your type of disability. We're going to send you over to train with the reserves and the National Guard."

Then, sensing Tyce's agitation, the colonel held up a hand. "You will remain on active duty, but we really do need experienced personnel, *combat* experienced personnel, training the weekend warriors for our mighty gun club."

"Sir, I—" Tyce began.

"Captain," snapped the colonel, "that's all this board will entertain at this point."

The old colonel sighed, compassionately, but obviously resigned to what was best for the service. "You are dismissed, Captain Asher."

With that, Tyce wheeled about and marched back through the open hatch. His shoulders slumped, and the usual Marine Corps perfect posture was now a little less erect.

CHAPTER 4

Two years ago
Moscow, Russia

"**G**et them here tomorrow."

"Mr. President, I really don't think it's possible . . ."

There was an air of extreme urgency in the Russian capital. Just the day before, the president had fired the rest of his cabinet. The official Russian news reported they had all resigned, but everyone knew that wasn't the case. They had been sacked, down to the last man, and quite a number of them had gone missing overnight.

"You heard me," said President of the Russian Federation Kryptov to his newly minted Minister of Defense. He was looking through the *Annual Analysis of External Threats to the Motherland.* A Russian intelligence product the Minister was well aware of. This year's analyses included quite a bit of new material.

President Kryptov dropped the file back onto the desk, leaned back in his large, overstuffed office chair, and pushed the gold-rimmed reading glasses down his nose staring over them at the Minister. If the look wasn't enough to chill a man's blood, the knowledge of the President's recent, savage purge certainly was. The world had known this President as one willing to excessively interfere in global affairs. An old-school Russian warmonger, but one who also wielded immense power, and there had been few to oppose him. Even fewer this morning.

"Tomorrow, I want them here in Moscow briefing everyone."

"All of them?" asked the Minister.

"General Tympkin, this SPET-VTOR computer and that colonel . . . what's his name."

"Kolikoff, Mr. President."

"Yes, the same. I want to see it all for myself and meet the people who are behind this supposed wonder weapon. And I want to test out Tympkin's and this colonel's device . . . and their plan."

The new Minister of Defense would beg for more time and perhaps plead for reason, but even as he prepared his thoughts, he did so with the recognition that he was merely put into this position to be a "yes" man. One to align the remaining less-militant members of the inner circle.

There was no hope for peace with the West. Years of American intervention coupled with years of immense Russian economic losses and now, new and even bolder predictions from this General Tympkin and his discarded crew of misfits. Before, the SPET-VTOR computer and its analyses had been labeled as audacious military lunacy. But, over time, the data from the computer and the team had become increasingly accurate and was now included in the annual intelligence reports. Moreover, its many predictions and doctrine had grown in the hearts of those who favored action over the dribs and drabs of diplomacy.

In dire times, lunatics will rule the stage, thought the Minister.

But now, the military theorems had been like a bomb. A bomb dropped directly into Moscow at exactly the right moment. The President and his loyal supporters had been searching for solutions to regain Russian dominance for years, and now they had fixated upon this plan. It was clear Tympkin had timed things perfectly.

"Comrade President, if I may, there have been some discussions, amongst . . ." he was about to say "what's left," but halted himself. "Some members of the general staff. They think there is wisdom in perhaps, taking a step back-

"We have." the President interrupted, "For ten years in this office, Comrade Minister, and the twenty years in the FSB and KGB before it, I have watched as the West picks us apart little by little and greedily laps up what we have lost. We are a shadow of our former selves. America is, and remains the most existential threat we have ever faced, and I include Nazi Germany in that judgment. In fact, America is worse than the Nazis. We have lost more to America than we ever did to Germany. Every day, every month, and every year we have been forced to our heels and cast one step closer to hell."

The President paused staring into the Minister's eyes, "In any case, you are already beginning to sound like your predecessor."

The Minister blanched, and a cold sweat trickled down his back.

The President leaned forward and pulled out a file, this one with the Minister's picture and name across the front. He spoke while he thumbed through it, "As long as America exists, we will never be as we are meant to be. Because of their dominance in the world, we live in *their* construct of freedom, not ours. Or as Comrade Lenin put it so aptly, 'Freedom in capitalist society always remains about the same as it was in ancient Greek republics: Freedom for slave owners.' We've been handed a golden opportunity, and I intend that we take it. Russia will lead the world into the next age."

"Comrade President, Tympkin's plan is just one of many. I . . . I still see another path forward."

The President pulled a photograph of the Minister's family out of the file, sighed heavily, and continued, "But I do not, Comrade . . ."

CHAPTER 5

Tomorrow . . .
Aboard the cargo ship Shujaa

The weather-beaten, black-hulled ship slipped into the crowded mix of tugboats, oilers, bulk cargo ships, and others steaming through the predawn twilight. She flew the flag of Ethiopia, but her actual port of origin was on a continent away. Plumes of thick smoke rose from her twin stacks as the ship plowed from the dark blue Atlantic Ocean swells into the calmer, green-brown waters of the Chesapeake Bay.

Her unremarkable name, *Shujaa*, was stenciled in faded red lettering across her stern. She passed directly in front of the bristling guns of an outbound patrol cruiser, USS *Normandy*, and right under the nose of the ancient guns on Fort Wool just outside Norfolk, Virginia. The fortress island had been built to keep U.S. waters safe from foreign navies, but the fort was not much more than a roost for seagulls now. Its heavy, 1812 iron cannon was long rusted, and even its World War II artillery pieces had been removed, along with any concerns that the mainland U.S. would ever be invaded again.

Three hundred miles north at the headquarters of the U.S. Coast Guard Vessel Traffic Service, a state-of-the-art radar and satellite monitoring system sent a message to U.S. Customs and Border. A cargo vessel named *Shujaa* had just entered U.S. territorial waters, on time and in accordance with the sailing plans filed by her parent company, a supposedly reputable shipping firm in North Africa. In reality, it was a shell company that existed only through some paperwork and a mailbox.

A tired, "wee hour" watch officer glanced at the new blip among the thousands of others in U.S. territorial waters. Since 9/11 it was required by law that a federal agent verify each ship entering and exiting the U.S. at least digitally. A monotonous job, given the sheer volume of ships.

He confirmed *Shujaa* was steering toward her listed port of landfall, Baltimore. Her cargo was listed as coffee and timber. Everything looked legit. He forwarded the data to the Baltimore customs station. Finally, he clicked the ship icon on the livestream map, changing the vessel's marker from a red icon that read "UNK status," designating it as unknown, to the yellow abbreviation for Routine Maritime Merchant Traffic, Inspect After Arrival: *RMMT-IAA*. Just as he'd done for the sixty-four other vessels he'd tagged that morning.

Then he flicked the computer screen controller and went back to browsing the Internet. He cupped his cold hands around his third coffee of the morning, blowing on it.

"Chief, can't we turn up the frickin' heat?" he said as his boss walked into the control center. The boss just shook his head, and the watch officer went back to absently thinking about the one hour of watch he had left before his replacement arrived and he could finally get some sleep.

* * *

Aboard *Shujaa*, the crew, cargo, and activity were anything but routine.

Upon entering Chesapeake Bay, a klaxon alarm brought the ship to general quarters, the navy equivalent of battle stations. Loudspeakers barked out strict orders for all hands to remain belowdecks. All watertight hatches were to be securely dogged down and confirmed with the bridge. No exceptions were permitted.

Heavy steel louvers lowered with a clatter over the bridge's glass windows. Overhead, fluorescent lights were shut off and electric battle lanterns snapped on, bathing the ship's combat information center in dark red light to preserve the crew's night vision. Two dozen men sat still at their control stations, their eyes reflecting the red glow back like the eyes of a pit of vipers.

Several powerful vibrations shook the thick metal bulkheads as the loud hiss of six hydraulic pistons elevated the cargo container missile launchers to a precise angle of thirty-three degrees—the optimum firing angle to avoid the coastal U.S. missile radar. Heavy blast doors were flung open to reveal the launchers' contents—six Scarab, SS-21D intermediate-range tactical nuclear missiles.

This type of missile had never been deemed a threat to the U.S. through fifty years of U.S. and Russian strategic arms talks. The missiles had too short a range to reach the continental U.S. That is, unless the missiles were sailed across the Atlantic and Pacific Oceans up to the U.S. coasts, packed and disguised inside ordinary cargo ships.

Shujaa's commanding officer, a Captain 2nd Rank of the Russian Navy, watched through the half-light as the army missile technicians added last-minute updates to the radar and launch computers. The men and their electronics were a tight fit in his makeshift control room. The bulky cargo ship was not originally designed as a warship, only retrofitted as one. She definitely wasn't built to carry troops or missiles, but that was indeed the Russian captain's cargo.

For the past three weeks *Shujaa* had followed precise routing, slipping unmolested through the regular shipping lanes of all ordinary civilian cargo ships of her class transiting the Atlantic. Even if a coastal patrol had boarded her for a cursory check, they wouldn't have spotted the carefully concealed missile racks and probably wouldn't have noticed the hinged bow, which could open to launch landing crafts disguised as common sightseeing boats.

Any coast guard or navy inspection would, however, have noticed three hundred fifty elite Russian special forces crowded into an area converted from cargo bays. The atmosphere among these men, the Spetsnaz, was electric, alive with last-minute preparations. A few heavy gunners cleaned their machine guns. Small unit leaders inspected handheld rocket launchers, while officers confirmed objectives and routes in low tones over Russian maps of the U.S. East Coast.

But no one had gotten close during the ship's entire 2,400-nautical-mile journey. The captain and her crew had ensured that. In fact, the mission depended upon secrecy and perfect timing.

The Captain didn't know the names of the other approaching attack ships. He was fairly certain that five other dual-purpose missile and troop ships were committed to the U.S. East Coast. Like seagoing Trojan Horses, though carrying a much deadlier cargo than their Greek counterparts had two thousand years before. But their purpose was really no different: a decisive, surprise invasion and utter destruction of their enemy's centers of power. Each captain was meant to be unaware of the others in case of a compromise.

The internal alarm was silenced, and the loudspeakers came alive with a final countdown in Russian.

"Pyat'... chetyre... tri... dva... odin... pusk!"

On the final word, *"pusk,"* the missile men turned their launch keys. Outside the command center, six sequenced pops of ejection charges were followed by a shrill screech as the rocket motors ignited. For a brief moment, bright light burst under and around the steel blast louvers. The brilliant white flash bleached the otherwise darkened red room. Men covered their eyes or squinted. The bridge shook, rattling teeth and sending some scrambling after skittering pens and coffee cups. In moments, the Scarab missiles roared to their top speed of Mach 5.3—just over one mile per second.

Then everything was silent. Green lights came on in the pilothouse indicating "all clear." An announcement over the loudspeaker confirmed it: *"Vse chisto."*

The Captain pulled an iron lever to open the hatch to the outside. His senior men followed him as he stepped into a thick fog of rocket propellent exhaust. The dirty grey smoke billowed into the bridge, carrying with it a noxious odor. The stench was a mix of spent booster fuel, ammonium perchlorate, and acrylonitrile acids. Altogether it smelled like kerosene and dead fish. Some of the younger sailors gagged, bringing smiles to the faces of the Russian army soldiers, who were well used to the sights, sounds, and smells.

The Captain's expression remained stoic as he looked over the railing of his ship. It was hard to discern anything in the dim light and smoke, but he took confidence in the fact that he'd accomplished the first part of his mission: launching the missiles inside the U.S. radar security network. Now it was time for the next phase of the invasion.

As the smoke cleared, he and the senior officers watched the bright yellow missile trails. The missiles were now well over the banks of the Chesapeake, bound for strategic targets. They didn't look much different than a few bright stars twinkling through a misty night's haze. But each of them and hundreds of others were now launching across the U.S. east and west coasts. Each missile signaled the first invasion of the United States homeland in modern history.

He stepped back into his bridge through some lasting haze and announced loudly, "Helmsman, come to zero-one-five degrees. All engines ahead full."

Then he grabbed the loudspeaker handset and continued. "This is the captain speaking. All stations, stand down from launch. Damage control parties are released back to their divisions. Combat division, man all weapons systems. Deck department, prepare to launch assault landing craft at my command."

He turned to face his first officer. "XO, break satellite radio silence. Signal fleet command, 'Launch complete. Commencing assault phase.'" Then, after a second of consideration, he added, "I want you in the well-deck to supervise launch of the landing craft."

"Aye, aye, Captain," said the second-in-command, moving off to execute the order.

He pulled back his braided officer's cuff and squinted at his watch in the smoky green gloom. He noted the time. *Three minutes before impact.*

CHAPTER 6

Navy Commander Victoria Remington and three of her friends from the medical staff at Bethesda Naval Hospital jogged past the Lincoln Memorial and down Independence Avenue, chatting freely, their breath forming ghosts in the cold December air. The four women made a point of closing their respective offices for a few hours once a week to get some exercise together.

Victoria had her long, raven-black hair pulled into a tight high ponytail. Her pale blue, almond-shaped eyes, gave Victoria a natural look of aloofness—an unfortunate trait of which she was only too aware. Most people initially misjudged her, assuming arrogance behind her magazine-cover good looks and natural voluptuousness. Or, all too often, assuming brainlessness. She tried not to let it bug her. The few close friends she had loved her for her single-minded loyalty and stinging wit.

The four women stopped, panting heavily and resting at their usual midpoint spot at the Martin Luther King, Jr. Memorial. They paused to enjoy the views of D.C. and catch their breath before round two of the hour-long run. They conversed, as close friends do, about disgruntled coworkers and callous bosses.

A male military officer jogged by, probably from the Pentagon across the Potomac River. He stared at the girls and slowed down a bit, probably hoping the women would talk to him. When none did, he picked up his pace and trotted off.

"Victoria, a hot Westie just eyed you up."

"I'm not into military guys right now," she said as she sipped water from a bottle strapped to her wrist. The women were close; they spent free time with each other and sometimes had drinks together. So they had codes for men from the two sides of the Potomac: Westies for men from the Pentagon, and Easties for Politicos.

But something had caught Victoria's eye out on the Potomac. Three boats were speeding up the waterway in tight formation. They looked like dinner-cruise or double-decker booze-cruise boats. The type that had enough room for a full restaurant below, a separate, upper bar deck, and plenty of space for lounging or milling around—a common enough sight. But not at the hellbent-for-leather speeds at which these three were traveling.

The lead boat was the longest, with second-story glass observation windows and a bulky suite of electronics on a topmast. It was riding extremely low in the water. Victoria had spent over sixteen years as a U.S. Navy surgeon, most of that aboard navy and Marine support ships, and she noted, with deepening curiosity, that the radar and electronics atop the boats were military grade. Or maybe it was the men on deck who looked out of place. They wore uniforms inconsistent with any U.S. gear she knew of, and they looked to be carrying firearms.

Tough to make out the uniforms at this distance, she thought as they neared. *Maybe just dining staff uniforms?*

The two smaller boats peeled off from the first and

headed west. One entered Four Mile Run, right next to Reagan National Airport. The next boat followed, but then quickly darted into the Pentagon Lagoon Yacht Basin. The largest veered sharply east, passing the Pentagon, and increased its throttle, jetting up a heavy wake that dangerously rocked several small pleasure craft. The boat just barely passed through the open art deco gates into the Washington Tidal Basin directly in front of the women.

Victoria held up her hand to silence everyone, stood up from the bench, and pointed.

The boat was plowing through a shocked cluster of rental paddleboats, tossing them aside before its massive hull like matchsticks, and heading directly for them.

It was close enough now for all to hear the engines' angry growl as they were jammed into full reverse. Brown mud churned up from the bottom of the basin, but it slowed the speeding boat very little. A few nearby onlookers abruptly stopped their dog walks or jogs and stood aghast, watching in horrified fascination, like watching a train about to collide with the station.

"It's gonna crash!" screamed one of Victoria's friends, cupping her hands over her mouth in horror. They all stepped closer together as they watched.

With a ghastly metallic crunch, the bow of the boat plowed into the decorative cement steps. The steel bow crumpled back into itself like a crushed tin can. But without a moment's hesitation, the men on deck slammed a large metal ramp down and onto the grass only a hundred feet from the women.

"Is this a drill?" someone nearby asked no one in particular.

Victoria could see the men's faces clearly now. They

were younger Caucasian boys. The name stenciled on the side of the dinner boat read *Aurora*.

Civilian boat, Military guys . . . but not U.S.

Affirming that likelihood, dozens of men armed with rifles stormed off the boat, down the steel gangway, and began halting cars on Independence Avenue. The top of the boat opened like a clamshell, and five armored vehicles drove up and out of the now-open interior. Some of the men vaulted up onto the armored vehicles, weapons at the ready and pointed menacingly at the shocked crowd of onlookers. Then the vehicles raced off toward the Capitol Building.

Victoria thought, *This is what our Marines look like when they practice an amphibious assault.*

She turned to her friends. "Get your shit together. There is some real bullshit going down, and we need to get the fuck out of here and back to the hospital, ASAP!"

The other women nodded silently but stood motionless looking off in the direction the men had disappeared. Just then, gunfire erupted from the other side of the Potomac, shaking the others from their momentary stupor and underscoring Victoria's orders.

"Move it, ladies. . . and I mean *right fucking now*!"

A heavy explosion thundered from across the river near the airport, followed rapidly by another, then another. Thick plumes of black smoke billowed from both locations, and a great red spout of flame flared up the sides of the Pentagon.

Without another word, Victoria raced off to commandeer a ride back to the hospital, the others following closely behind.

Two minutes before impact . . .
Morgantown, West Virginia

U.S. Marine Major Tyce Asher's Humvee bumped along the gravel and brush, pulling to a halt just off the shoulder of Interstate 79. He grabbed the radio handset from the dash and thumbed the mic to radio his platoon.

"All stations, this is Dragoon-six. I'm pulling off before the bridge to get a headcount of the convoy. First and second platoons, pull off with me and do engine 'hot checks.' Gunny, stage the headquarters section behind me." He then switched to the Army National Guard radio and spoke into the mic. "B Troop, you're clear to continue back to base. Your colonel should be getting close, and you can detach from me and head back to the 150th."

"Aye, aye, sir," said the soldier, cheerfully slipping in some Marine jargon.

"Good to go, Lieutenant Zane. Looks like we'll make a Marine out of you yet," said Tyce, eminently aware that the entire West Virginia National Guard convoy of military vehicles were all listening in on their back and forth.

"Not if Colonel Nepo has anything to say about that, sir." It was a rare form of disobedience, but no one, least of all Major Tyce Asher, liked the bald-headed and scornful Colonel Nepo, commander of the 150th Cavalry Regiment and the boss of everyone who'd been involved in the monthlong Ridge Runner maneuver exercise.

In solidarity with the boss, and being the acting executive officer of the combined Marine and National Guard troops, Tyce was about to tell the lieutenant to behave when Gunny interrupted over the radio. "Dragoon-six, this is Gunny. We copy, sir. Pulling up on your six o'clock now and need to talk to you ASAP."

"Roger," said Tyce simply. Then he opened the Humvee door and stepped out into the overgrown grass, wobbling unsteadily. A Marine Corps LAV pulled up behind him. The LAV, short for Light Armored Vehicle, was a big, eight-wheeled armored car with a 25mm cannon turret. People often mistook it for a tank with wheels, but they were the mainstay vehicle of Tyce's Marine reconnaissance unit.

Tyce was still straightening himself up, a pained grimace on his face, as Gunnery Sergeant Chaz Dixon jumped out of the LAV and walked over toward him, the rest of the men stepping off, too. The unit's military working dog, Trigger also leapt out and happily followed Gunny. The pooch skillfully clambered out and down the front of the LAV. His tail wagged faster and he picked up his pace upon spotting Tyce.

"Leg bothering you again this morning, sir?" asked Gunny.

"Yeah . . . I guess so," said Tyce.

Trigger smashed against Tyce like a furry tornado, then forced his way between Tyce's legs in a zigzag, knocking him further off balance. Tyce braced himself against the attack by holding the top of the Humvee door for balance. Trigger plopped down on his haunches in front of Tyce, a drooling tongue lolling out as he looked up at him earnestly. Tyce reddened, slightly embarrassed at being caught in a moment of weakness in front of his troops. He knew it was foolish to be ashamed of his prosthetic leg, and he was also aware that most already knew all about it. But he practiced almost every waking minute walking and moving just like a normal Marine, and he hoped some of the troops might never know.

Once Trigger's greeting had simmered down, Tyce knelt

down to pet him, then absently scratched at his own leg, the prosthetic one. He glanced up and caught Gunny staring at him with a puzzled look.

"Ha!" chuckled Tyce. "I do that like five times a day still. The docs call it a 'phantom limb' itch. Your brain plays tricks and still thinks there's a leg there."

Tyce turned his attention back to Trigger, his hand out flat, palm down in a command for Trigger to sit. He did so, though his tail and butt now wagged even more fiercely in anticipation of what inevitably came next. Like most dogs, Trigger knew who fed him—and also knew Tyce was a total softy. Quick obedience to Tyce's commands meant one of several treats Tyce always carried in his drop pouch. Tyce reached in and pulled out a sticky mess of lint-covered gummy bears.

Gunny looked at the dirt-covered treats, then back to Tyce, "Sir, you're going to make that mutt sick."

Tyce brushed off the comment, but both men couldn't help smiling as Trigger greedily guzzled the gummy bears down in one gulp, licking his chops, then gave a hopeful expression that begged for more.

Trigger was a trained Belgian Malinois, and he had been with the unit for more than three years. He'd made two combat deployments, one to Iraq and one to Afghanistan, during the worst of the ISIS and Taliban battles, and had come out relatively unscathed and even more attached to his Marines. He'd even been promoted to corporal. This wasn't just an honorific title for the Marines, who had been promoting dogs and horses in their ranks since the famous battles of Belleau Wood in World War I and Okinawa in World War II. Tyce had watched Trigger jump on more than one occasion at the sound of a car backfiring and wondered if dogs got PTSD.

Trigger genuinely loved his Marines, but he always felt most at home with the body-building, machine gun–toting section leader, Staff Sergeant Alejandra Encantar Celestina Diaz-Perez. As he looked back at four more LAVs from the convoy pulling off the highway and getting in line behind Gunny's vehicles, the short but buff female staff sergeant came up to join the pair. "I overheard headquarters' last radio comms check," she said, a thick Bronx Spanish accent coloring her words and mannerisms. "The colonel is at Exit 155." The woman's muscled biceps practically burst from her rolled uniform sleeves. She hefted a medium machine gun over her shoulder as she spoke.

"Thanks, Staff Sergeant Diaz," said Tyce, "but do me a solid, leave the firepower in your Humvee." He pointed at the machine gun slung over her shoulder and then back to her vehicle. "It scares the natives, and last I checked, we're still in West Virginia, not Al Anbar in Iraq."

Then he pointed to the traffic jam they were causing.

North and southbound civilian traffic on Interstate 79 was rubbernecking as they slowly passed the menacing Marine Corps armored vehicles. A few kids stared at the convoy, cheeks pressed against the glass as they peered with childlike fascination at the unusual military hardware.

Gunny interjected. "Can't be helped, but we don't need—"

VROOOOM.

Four jet fighter planes blasted over low and fast, directly over the troops.

The roar of their engines was intense. They passed no more than a few hundred feet off the ground, racing up the valley. The clustered troops collectively ducked, some dropping to the ground, so unexpected were the powerful planes' blasts.

"What the fuck was that?" said Gunny Dixon, echoing everyone's thoughts as they all watched the jets continuing up and hugging the valley.

In seconds, with throttles wide open, the four jet fighters pointed straight up, streaking skyward and gaining altitude rapidly. Only now did everyone notice what the jets were aiming for: a formation of nearly a hundred jets, over 40,000 feet high, their long, white contrails marking their silent progress westward.

Diaz slid closer to Tyce and Gunny, who were both still staring up. "*Dios mío!* What the hell is that, Major?" she asked.

"I'll be damned if I know exactly, Diaz," said Tyce. His voice contained awe of the spectacle, but he couldn't conceal a note of concern. "The lower jets, the ones that passed right over us, are ours. Interceptors. Pretty sure they're F-16 Fighting Falcons. Probably scrambled out of North Carolina. There's a reserve fighter squadron down there. Though from the looks of things, that's only a handful of 'em." Some other fighters also streaked up from adjacent valleys, but it didn't look like more than ten or twelve total. "Wonder where the rest of their buddies are?"

Tyce's ominous words resonated, leaving everyone wondering and worried.

"What about those?" Diaz pointed. "The ones way up there?"

The two sets of aircraft now looked as if they were about to intersect.

"I don't know exactly, Staff Sergeant. But I do know we would never fly that many of our own bombers in formation over the nation. If that's even what they are . . ."

"Bombers?" Gunny and Diaz both said, shocked.

"Pretty sure it's against the law, or a U.S. code, or something," Tyce continued.

Suddenly, there appeared two bright red plumes, puffs of dirty grey, then bright white smoke trails. Two of the big aircraft fell out of formation and started a long, slow, steady death spiral toward the ground. Another red flash, then a third big aircraft followed the other two, falling and tumbling like a leaf from a tree. The delayed sounds of explosions met their ears, like distant thunder. No one moved. Even the traffic on 79 stopped. Everyone was transfixed by the unfolding aerial dogfight.

Tyce was the first to react, grabbing Gunny Dixon by his shoulder and pivoting him sharply.

"Gunny, get on net. Radio everyone. Maximum alert. Take our HQ and the Guard's B Troop back to base immediately. Break speed limits—just get everyone back to Morgantown ASAP."

"Sir, what the hell is going on?"

"We're under attack. No time to analyze."

Gunny turned to go, but turned back. "How about you, sir? You gonna be okay?" He pointed at Tyce's leg.

"I'm fine, Gunny." Tyce waved him off. "I'll take my section back to protect the colonel. See you back there as soon as we can rope everyone up. But hey"—Tyce's expression darkened—"lock and load, 'kay?"

"Got it." Gunny ran to his LAVs, Trigger racing next to him with his tail tucked. Intuitively, he knew something bad was happening.

Sergeant Diaz turned to Tyce and pointed toward the south. "Hey, look, sir. Look at that. More of our fighters headed to take down those others?"

Diaz was the first to spot another long line of high-flying

aircraft: four visible specks, low on the southern horizon. A pair of thin, white trails with yellow halos dropped below the dots and started to spiral in a lazy corkscrew fashion, growing larger by the second.

Tyce's brain knew inherently what was coming, but none of it made sense here in the middle of West Virginia.

"Get down!" he yelled. "Everyone get down!" His shouts were met with stares all around. The battle in the sky, although fascinating, seemed detached from the grunts on the ground.

"Incoming missiles!" Tyce yelled.

The last words had the desired effect. Everyone scattered off the highway, diving headlong into the grass, flopping onto their stomachs and clutching their helmets tight on their heads. Some had experienced Iraq or Afghanistan and knew the same thing as troops who had engaged in all foreign wars: that laying flat and sucking your body into the earth was the only defense for what was coming next.

Two of the inbound missiles struck, but both were wide. One detonated in the trees, the other in the river below the bridge. The third and fourth missiles, however, struck their intended targets with a flat, earsplitting *smack*. Tyce and Diaz rolled onto their elbows and watched as a blast of fire tossed enormous chunks of concrete and twisted steel bridge spans into the air, which then rained down with a crash.

The center and southbound lanes of the bridge fell away completely, leaving a third of the bridge dangling but intact. Tyce and Diaz watched in horror as three passenger cars and the last LAV in Gunny Dixon's section plunged into the void that opened down into the Monongahela River below.

"Holy shit, sir," yelled Diaz. "That was Sergeant Monroe's vehicle!"

"I know," said Tyce, standing up, his eyes taking in all the destruction. Small pieces of debris that had been vaulted high into the air were still falling. A shroud of grey dust hung in the air. "Go back and get your platoon. Tell everyone to get over here. We need to help." Tyce looked to the south and saw headlights approaching. "And we need to block traffic. We don't want anyone driving into that blasthole. I'll see if I can get the colonel on the radio."

Tyce walked over to his vehicle and picked up the radio. SSgt. Diaz looked about for the Marines and soldiers she was going to utilize to cordon off the site. Just as she was yelling for a few of the non-commissioned officers, or NCOs, to come over and help, a bright blue Porsche sped up. She turned to yell for someone to stop it, but it deftly carved its way around the halted traffic and dodged the Humvees moving to block off the blasthole.

Tyce saw what was happening and dropped the radio handset, pointing at one of the nearest men. "Quick, stop that guy!"

Two men moved to intercept the fast-moving car, but the Porsche dodged the men, skirting them and onto the shoulder as it accelerated toward the bridge. Tyce pulled a flare off his Humvee, pulled the igniter, and ran toward the Porsche, waving the flare over his head. Either the driver didn't see him or didn't care. The Porsche accelerated right past Tyce and out onto the bridge. The driver never even had time to apply the brakes.

Everyone watched helplessly as the car disappeared over the edge. From below came a crunch and the sound of glass shattering.

Tyce stood motionless for a moment, then walked over to the blasthole.

"Shit," he said to himself. "It's all happening again. People just keep dying around me."

Tyce peered through the bridge's caved-in asphalt and severed steel spans that yawned back at him like the maw of a giant beast. Below, not a soul moved, but the wrecks of the three passenger cars, the upside-down Humvee, and the blue Porsche on top of it were all burning in a heap of carnage.

CHAPTER 7

One minute before impact...
The White House, Washington, D.C.

The President sipped his coffee while watching his favorite morning newscast. A hair and makeup crew worked on his face and nose. Another attached a microphone cord behind his tie and smoothed his jacket's lapels. The news broadcast was out of San Francisco, but the basic content was all over the other channels that morning. A ghastly report. A killer had run rampant through a day care with an assault rifle.

The President's press secretary stood in front of him and flipped through her notes, "OK, this a.m. we have one obvious change. You'll have to give condolences for the kids and their families first." She said.

"Yeah. Figured," said the President, still absently glued to the set as the news anchors now handed the broadcast over to a field correspondent in Saudi Arabia. In the top corner a video played of a line of U.S. soldiers getting off a plane, tanks rumbling off ship's ramps and Army Apache helicopters flying in tight formations. It was stock footage. The President had deployed the troops six months earlier and they were already up on the borders to Iran where it still looked like the Iranians might invade Iraq any day. But the message was clear. The U.S. was back in the

Middle East, and in great numbers to attempt to stave off Iran's most recent aggression.

The makeup man pushed a little plastic wheelie-cart around to better apply powder and cream on the President's nose and forehead, blocking the TV in doing so.

The President growled, "Look, can this wait?" pushing him gruffly aside.

This part of the routine was immensely annoying, but all his PR personnel told him that every time he began speaking in earnest, a bright sheen broke out on his forehead. Couldn't have that.

"No, Mister President. You're live in minutes. Let them do their jobs. Just do me a favor and stick to the talking points today. Don't go off script. Condolences first, then to teleprompter and the Iran and global peace stuff."

"What about the Russia stuff?"

"Mister President, we've spoken about this. If you talk about Russia, then the mainstream media will just chalk up more wins to Russia's unilateral disarmament and then go into our own, slow disarmament in response."

"Yeah, but we *are* disarming. We're right there on the world stage doing what's right."

"You know that, I know that, but the narrative is still that Russia started a global peace dividend and America is now not a leader, but a follower in global nuclear security."

"With over ninety percent of our stockpile already neutralized, I'd say we're at the front, damn it." The President was so unsettled he sloshed a huge splash of coffee. Fortunately, it all went onto the makeup bib and the makeup crew quickly snatched it up before it leaked all over his shirt and tie.

"Ninety percent is not the same as the Russians' hundred percent."

"Yeah." Said the President, conceding the point, "Just

make sure the Veep's team is saying the same things. Where is he today?" he sighed heavily as he contemplated whether to sip the remains of his Starbuck's mocha latte or call for a new one.

Both the Iran situation and Russia's latest attempts to unilaterally disarm nukes were huge setbacks to his plans. Plans that included a second term next year and maybe more important for his legacy, his dreams of a Nobel Prize. The thoughts of losing a shot at an everlasting legacy, a piece in the history books, seemed to be slipping away, so he just fixed his attention onto the tone of the broadcast.

That morning's news was a genuinely sad affair across all broadcast networks. There was no footage of the massacre yet, but it was still like a bomb across the news and social media. Images of children killed would eclipse all other news, and all just as he needed good press for the Iran situation and a spotlight on his own nuclear disarmament achievements. Almost all of the U.S. nukes were in some stage of decommissioning.

"At least it underscores my policy to decimate all these assault rifles." He said, hoping she might change her mind, "Can't I mention that in the opener?"

"No, sir. It muddies down your condolences. It makes it look like you are somehow stealing credit. You don't want to mix messages today, Mister President."

"Hmmm . . ." he grumbled.

He flicked around the channels to see if anything else was popping up. All of the newscasters made a business of feigning sentimentality that morning, and he needed to get into the right "mood."

He caught a popular broadcast midstream, "So, my question Joe, is just how did this madman, this—this—assassin get ahold of these weapons. Weapons that should only be used in war."

Another anchor chimed in, "They're still out there. Loads of them. Buried in people's yards. The Bible Belt is clinging to them. Fringe extreme elements, you know. But here's my question, Martha: Why is it taking so long to get them off the streets? Six months ago, the President and Congress promised action after the last attack. But we've exposed, right here on our program, the six months of utter incompetence his administration has faced trying to round these things up. We need the National Guard to get off their collective butts and do the job they were assigned. Clean our streets."

Another talking head chimed in, "And, if the President can't get the job done, we need to get rid of him."

The President flared up and turned to his press secretary with an angry look. Having his usual favorite newscasters throw him under the bus was going to hurt with the Millennial demographic.

She put her hand up, "Mister President, calm down."

The President roughly pushed the makeup guy aside. The man then gave an exasperated look toward the press secretary. She gave him the signal to finish up quickly. They'd just have to deal with the dreaded sheen.

The President calmed down, though only slightly as the news continued, "Ok, all that and more on this morning's show. Next, over to Bob where we are awaiting the President's presser. Time to get some answers."

"Indeed. Additionally, insiders say today he may announce a troop surge to the Middle East. Maybe even a call-up of the Guard and reserves."

The President turned back to his press secretary, "God damn it, Jane, how do they get this shit in advance?"

He needed more caffeine, and he needed to stop the leaks from his own cabinet. In a few seconds, the last bit of powdering was done, and his press secretary glanced his forehead over, then gave a thumbs-up. The bib came off, and the President headed toward the Oval Office.

Video cameras followed as the President walked confidently through the large, oak door into the Oval Office saluting the two Marines who proceeded to close and secure the door behind him ceremoniously. The bright lights from the TV cameras practically blinded him as he entered, but he remained sharp. His face unemotional, with maybe a twinge of sadness but still exhibiting determination. One of the items that had gotten him elected was his appearance of coolness under stress. At least in public, said his critics.

His press secretary had told him he looked more commanding taking his desk, rather than starting any address already sitting. If nothing else, he had a commanding presence. The President strode across the carpet and sat, pulling his chair forward and tucking his legs under the *Resolute* desk. He made a big show of opening his speech folder. All of this was carefully choreographed, of course.

He began, "People of our great nation. I speak to you today at a period of great triumph, but also at a time of immense tragedy."

In the back, the press secretary smiled. His tone and pitch were perfect that morning. It really didn't matter to her if he had any genuine concern—he rarely did—as long as it *sounded* like he did.

"I have read the initial reports from California and . . ." the slightest pause and the hint of a sniffle, but still sounding strong. "I am stricken with grief. Later today, I have phone calls lined up with several of the victims' families." He lied.

The last note was not on the teleprompter, and the press secretary blanched a bit, but she was reassured: it sounded convincing, even if it wasn't true.

"Thanks to my assault weapons ban, we can at least count on less of these tragedies than in the previous, gun-loving administrations."

The press secretary rolled her eyes in dismay, then gave a slashing motion across her throat to the President to carry on with the speech. He got the hint but seemed more than a little pleased he'd gotten his own point across.

"We will have more on that topic later. Much more. But this morning, I need to talk about the great week, in fact a tremendous month and even year as I've led the world in mitigating the dangers facing us across the globe."

More digressions from the teleprompter, but at least he was roughly back on target.

"We've had an unprecedented year of peace. We're on a path to total denuclearization. We've made great strides toward removing assault weapons, as I mentioned, and we have made immense steps toward preventing the recent aggression from Iran toward their neighbors."

Behind the President and outside the Oval Office window, a column of thick, black smoke rose silently into the sky. Set against the grey winter of D.C. it was clear even though it was miles away. No one in the Oval Office seemed to notice. Since no one was allowed to have a cell phone in the room, the small gathering of press and staff remained uninformed of any happenings. Everyone remained silent and fixed on the President's words.

"Iraq, the newest of our global community of democracies, and I'll underscore, Iraq *is* now a democracy, has come a long way thanks to our and our allies' great efforts. But now, today, they are threatened with a total reversal.

The situation must be addressed. I have called upon action from NATO and our partnered forces. I have called upon the UN Security Council. In the absence of their leadership, we must take our own actions to combat threats abroad."

Behind the President, a second black smoke column appeared. Now, a cameraman noticed. He pulled away from the camera's eyecup and squinted at it in bewilderment. The two Secret Service members detailed to the room turned toward each other, eyes widening. Their earpieces went into overload. None of it was clear, information was coming in too fast for them to understand.

Sensing something amiss in the room, but unsure what and unwilling to turn around on a live broadcast, the President cleared his throat and continued. It was after all, time for his big whammy.

"So, I am authorizing the immediate call-up of additional forces. Select National Guard and Reserves will go and join our most ready active-duty forces in the region. The call-up will start with the rest of the Eighteenth Airborne and the as-yet-undeployed portions of the 1st and 2nd Marine Divisions. America will not tolerate—"

A muffled explosion from inside the White House interrupted the President. But there was enough sound padding throughout the Oval Office that most in the room just looked around with curious expressions. Was it just something heavy being dropped upstairs or in an adjacent corridor or room? Then came six or seven dull thuds against the large entry door. The two Secret Service men pulled opened the doors. Immediately the shouts, wails, and screams from below assailed everyone's ears. There was utter panic in the White House lobby and outer offices.

With the door now open, sounds of a second and third

explosion entered the room like thunderclaps. Everyone, including the President, ducked down to the floor.

For a brief second, everyone; several reporters and cameramen, the two Secret Service men, the two Marines and the press secretary all stared at one another in confusion.

Then, the sound of fully automatic gunfire sent the cold chill of panic through the room. This was no mere accident; the White House was under a determined and coordinated attack. One of the reporters crawled over and behind a Secret Service agent and clutched at him. Both agents had taken up positions on either side of the door and now drew their pistols. They tapped at their earbuds, but they had gone silent. No one responded to their constant calls for a situation report.

One of the Marines pulled open a cabinet door, revealing a small armory of rifles, pistols, and grenades. He grabbed an M4 carbine and tossed a second over to his buddy, who was crossing the room to meet him.

Just then, a third Secret Service agent raced into the room at a full sprint, his black sports coat flapping, his pistol up and at the ready. He didn't get far. A barrage of automatic weapons fire blasted into the room behind him from down the adjacent hallways. In a sickening series of smacking sounds, both the agent entering the office and the Marine crossing it were caught by several dozen rounds. The agent's momentum kept him going, and he rolled off to the side. The Marine was not so fortunate. Unlike the agent, who wore a bulletproof vest, the Marine had no body armor and fell in a heap right across the entryway.

An agent and the remaining Marine grabbed the man by the arms and dragged him inside so they could kick the door shut. The Marine's body left a slick and glistening red streak across the ornate POTUS-seal carpet. An agent secured the heavy-duty locks and returned to get a rifle and grenades.

A reporter shrieked as the wounded agent crawled over toward her, his immobile legs dragging across the floor, foamy blood gurgling from his lips. His vest had done nothing but slow the armor-piercing rounds and perhaps prolong his life. He was sure to die of blood loss in another few minutes.

One of the agents shoved the reporter aside and came over to try to hastily interrogate his wounded buddy, "Max, what's happening?" but a bullet had pierced the side of his neck above the body armor, and he could only clutch at his wound and mouth unintelligible words, blood pouring through his fingers.

Both Secret Service agents nodded to each other. It was time to put into effect the security protocol to get POTUS the hell out of here.

"Dasher, Dasher!" one of them barked into the mic. No indication whether it was received, but it was protocol to broadcast it so everyone would know to provide all assistance to the POTUS in escaping the White House.

One rushed over to pull the President from behind the desk. The other opened a secret door leading into an ante chamber and a hidden escape route. But they didn't get far.

BOOM!

A huge explosion blew the double doors off their hinges, spraying wood and metal debris like a shotgun into the room.

Sustained 7.62mm machine gun fire immediately followed, killing the dazed reporters and camera personnel who weren't already blown flat or peppered into moaning red heaps by the shrapnel. The remaining Marine, a large splinter from the oak door sticking out of his abdomen, his face and arms covered in pockmarks of blood, put up a gallant last fight. He pumped suppressing fire toward the blown doors at dim shapes through the smoke he had to assume were attackers. But his magazine quickly went dry, and, amid the smoke and dust, his muzzle flashes were now a beacon for incoming fire. Riddled with bullets, he fell to a sitting clump against the *Resolute* desk still clutching his M4 carbine.

Behind the heavy and ancient wood desk, the last remaining occupants of the Oval Office alive rubbed their eyes, choking from the smoke and trying to figure out a next course of action.

One was chosen for them. In a sustained and withering hail of bullets, the beautifully carved desk, a gift from the Queen of England and built from pieces of the HMS *Resolute*'s heavy oak timbers, was torn to pieces. Timbers that in their day were meant to take a cannon's blast now saw hundreds of rounds of 7.62mm which blasted chunks away until the ornately carved piece of history could no longer protect the men behind it.

Cameras from two major news networks were blasted back against the wall but remained rolling throughout the siege and continued to broadcast the Oval Office's last stand live to the entire world.

CHAPTER 8

Impact
AAF Tank Museum, Danville, Virginia

"Have fun. Your entrance fee covers any four tanks you want, except the two in the far corner," Lawton Custis said as he winked at the three kids who looked like they were about to burst out of their hides to jump onto one of the tank displays. "You wouldn't want to crawl around in those two, anyhow. They're still full of mud and dirt."

The kids' father paid Lawton the entry fee, and the three raced over to the Russian T-62A tank. Lawton smiled, but seeing the parents happily snapping pictures and not minding the kids, he felt the need to add, "Hey folks, please stick with the little ones. We had one fall off a tank last year and break her arm."

"Wow," the kids' mother said. "Where did you learn about tanks and stuff?"

"Well . . . I'm retired from the army."

"Yeah? My cousin is in the army, or maybe it's Marines . . . I get them confused. What rank were you?"

"One-star general," said Lawton.

She took a step back. "Oh," she said, eyeing the short old greybeard up and down with some disbelief. "How come you're working here?"

"Keeps me busy. Besides, the old lady makes me march here to work every day to keep fit."

She was about to ask more questions when a familiar face over her shoulder caught Lawton's attention, "Excuse me, please." He turned to the new arrival. "Hey, Bill."

"Hey, *Yo-negg*," said Bill, using a derogatory Cherokee term for "white man."

"We grabbin' breakfast?" asked Lawton.

"I have to go back to the chicken coops first. Judy forgot her cell phone in the car."

Lawton informed museum security he'd be gone for an hour or so, and both men headed out to Bill's old Ford. As Lawton got in on the passenger side, the rusty door creaked.

"Bill, one day this thing is just going to fall apart."

"I got wheels, don't I?" said Bill.

"I swear, you're the worst mechanic. You never fix your own car."

"Can't. Too busy repairing other people's," said Bill.

A few minutes later, they arrived at the big chicken farm where Judy worked. Lawton hated the smell, but it didn't seem to bother Judy or Bill anymore. Lawton could never understand how they both could handle it, but between the chickens and Bill's work as a mechanic, the two seemed to enjoy a decent living.

"Okay, wait a second. I'll run the cell phone in," said Bill. "Be right back."

Lawton hopped out of the car to stretch his legs while Bill ran in.

There's only one thing worse than the stench out here, thought Lawton, *and that's the noise.*

Inside the long, low, windowless buildings, thousands of hens clucked in an endless cacophony. It sounded wretched, almost violent to Lawton's ears. It was incessant, and even from his spot by the road, more than a hundred meters from the buildings, he could hear them clucking away.

What a noise . . . and what a stink.

Then, in a heartbeat, a deathly calm came over everything and shrouded Lawton in silence. Birds in the trees stopped moving. The usual buzz of the southern cicadas was still. Even the chickens in the coop went completely silent.

For that millisecond, Lawton thought he was having a heart attack.

Instinct told him to turn, and he had a moment to glance back toward Danville.

That's when retired U.S. Army Brigadier General Lawton Custis, who had survived ten deployments to foreign lands and countless dangerous missions in Iraq and Afghanistan, saw a part of warfare that even he had never experienced. And he was so taken by the sight, he stared straight into the face of modern war's deadliest demon: the white-hot core of a nuclear blast.

CHAPTER 9

Near Morgantown, West Virginia

Colonel Nepo pulled his Humvee right up beside where Tyce and SSgt. Diaz were conducting their recovery efforts at the bridge. He joined them in looking down into the jagged hole created by the missile.

"Jesus . . . What the fuck is going on, Major?" said the colonel. His tone sounded almost accusatory, as if Tyce himself were responsible for the blast.

"It's an attack, sir," said Tyce, too busy to look up at the colonel.

Tyce had a handheld radio in one hand and was attentively watching the men below as they recovered the bodies and weapons. Two Humvees and an LAV had lowered steel ropes from their towing winches, and both below and above, troops were maneuvering the ropes into place to move the stack of vehicles to get to the survivors—or, more likely, the bodies—in the lower vehicles.

The colonel peered over the edge and watched the men working for a moment. Two were wading through waist-high water and picking their way across bridge debris. Two more were kneeling atop the blue Porsche, staring upwards, their arms held up and wide to snatch big hooks dangling on steel cables from recovery vehicles that were being slowly lowered down. Once they grabbed them, and satisfied the two men were secured from falling into the freezing river, Tyce turned his attention toward the colonel.

U.S. Army Colonel David Nepo was the joint forces commander for their exercise in the woods and was therefore Tyce's boss. At least temporarily. For the past several months, they'd trained together in a Joint Interoperability and Readiness Exercise, which really just amounted to Tyce's Marines being added to the ranks of the West Virginia's 150th Cavalry Regiment.

It had been a great opportunity on paper, but Nepo was an egotistical boss who bristled at every slight—real or imagined—from the Marines. Several of Nepo's National Guardsmen confided to Tyce that the daily anguish, harsh leadership, and generally unsupportive atmosphere all stemmed from David Nepo's narcissism. Still, Tyce had risen to the task and was serving as the interim executive officer, called the "XO" and who was second-in-command. It put him under Nepo's gun on a daily basis even more during the exercise but also put him in a spot to keep the training exercise flowing, and to keep both U.S. National Guard and U.S. Marine Corps troops happy and gainfully employed.

"Sir, we need to get you back to Morgantown," Tyce said matter-of-factly. Right at that moment, he couldn't have cared less about the colonel; he was more worried about the remains of the men, yet to be recovered from the pit at the bottom of the bridge.

He continued. "Back at your command post, you can prep and issue orders. I sent the forward half of the convoy back already, before the bridge collapsed." He glanced below. "All except the one LAV that . . . didn't make it. The rest are on their way, and I instructed them to get comms with your headquarters before approaching

Morgantown. No telling what might be waiting for us back there after this surprise attack. I'll remain here to supervise the recovery of our fallen and to intercept the rest of the regiment as they come through the hills. Then we can join you at the Morgantown reserve center."

The colonel's eyes widened, and he stared at Tyce. "To do what, exactly, Major Asher?"

"Fight back, sir. Defend our homes, I guess. Maybe see if there are any orders waiting for us at headquarters." Tyce remained stone-faced.

"From who? What orders?" The colonel looked as if his mind was spinning out of control. His eyes glanced furtively from side to side. He removed his helmet and clutched at his forehead with his fingers.

"Sir, I have no idea at this point. Right now, we need to gather our fallen. But the next thing is to take stock and prepare our troops."

"Prepare for what? With what?" The colonel glanced around at the mixed unit of Marines and soldiers, then down at Tyce's prosthetic leg. "The rest of the regiment is just as unfit for any real combat duty, Major. And if what is happening is what I think is happening, we need real gunfighters, not reservists."

Tyce's narrowed his eyes a bit. Any of Tyce's 4th Light Armored Reconnaissance men, or even the guys from the 150th, would have taken exception, but it was clear the colonel was practically out of his wits—and certainly out of his depth. Tyce had seen it before, in Afghanistan and Iraq. Some leaders' initial reactions to unexpected combat situations were not exactly Hollywood's version of heroism, all bravado and testosterone. Tyce himself had felt it before, that sudden rush of anger and confusion. A spike in adrenaline, the realization that all decisions rested now with you—and the men's eager but chaotic anticipation of orders, awaiting basic directions to provide purpose, order, and calm.

Tyce decided to switch gears to get his boss back on track. "Hey, sir," he said, letting the anger subside and gesturing around him. "We are none of us ready for whatever this is. But you are in charge, and we trust you to figure out our next course of action. If you and the Headquarters companies can head back to HQ, I think we'll all feel a bit better that our leadership is where it needs to be to best make sense of all this and issue the proper orders. Besides that, if it is a full-blown attack, we have a duty to the citizens of Morgantown . . . to all of West Virginia, for that matter."

Tyce's words seemed to have the desired effect. "Yeah," the colonel said, looking around a bit uncomfortably, still clutching his forehead, squeezing and contracting the skin into wrinkles with his fingertips.

Tyce thought, *He may only now be realizing his position and the effect his momentary stupor could have on the troops.*

"Yeah, that's what we're gonna do," said the colonel slowly. "I'll get the HQ company back to base." He stopped squeezing his forehead and looked down at his helmet. He ran his finger almost lovingly over the black eagle on the brim, the rank insignia of a full bird army colonel. He stood up straighter, lifted his chin, and seemed to regain an air of authority as if seeing the symbol of his rank had reminded him who he was, or at least who he needed to be.

"Asher, I need you to remain here. Then I want you to get everyone back as best as you can." The colonel basically repeated Tyce's words, his voice still sounding a bit distant. "And I'll have your assignment waiting for you."

The colonel put his helmet back on, pulling the leather chin strap down. Then he seemed to realize there was more to be said, especially given that Tyce was clearly the person in charge here and was doing well, dealing with some of the colonel's own casualties. "Umm, good work in taking charge of the rescue. Carry on, Major Asher." He seemed to be waiting for something. Tyce came to attention and saluted.

The colonel saluted back. Then he turned to his Humvee and climbed aboard, and he and his section of twelve Humvees headed southwest toward the longer but safer route back into Morgantown.

SSgt. Diaz came over to Tyce. She had been standing a respectful distance away from the two officers—an old trick used by the senior enlisted. She'd not been quite close enough for the colonel to notice, but just close enough to hear everything.

"What the fuck was that?"

Tyce sighed heavily. "SSgt, you were in Fallujah back in the day, right?"

"Yeah, so what?"

"Do you remember your first day of combat?"

"I've tried pretty hard to forget that shit."

"Well . . . this is the colonel's first real day of combat. Might be the same for lots of the men from the 150th. But they are a solid regiment with a long and storied history dating back to the Revolutionary War." Tyce looked solidly into SSgt. Diaz's light brown eyes, punctuating his next statements by speaking in a slow and measured tone. "He needs us, you and me, *all* his combat vets, to keep everything in order until he has the time to . . . bring everything into focus."

"Hope he doesn't barf," Diaz said, shifting her machine

gun with a grimace to the other shoulder. "Or worse . . ." She smirked and winked at Tyce.

Officers played a game of undermining their leaders, but generally not so for the Staff Non-Commissioned Officers, or SNCOs, like Diaz. Basically, these lifers among the enlisted troops had been through enough bullshit in their careers that they were much more interested in getting the job done than posturing.

Tyce couldn't suppress a small smile. The senior enlisted troops in both the army and Marines always spoke the truth. Even when officers couldn't or didn't because of an unwritten code of decorum between the ranks.

His smile quickly faded, though, as he watched the soldiers and Marines pull out the first waterlogged and mangled corpse from the vehicle on top of the heap, the blue Porsche. It was a female. Probably in her fifties, as far as Tyce could discern.

And now, once again, things were real.

CHAPTER 10

South of Morgantown

It was a full four hours before Tyce finished recovery operations below the bridge. Civilian and military bodies lay nearby in body bags, some badly mangled beyond all recognition. Twelve in all. He carefully handed the civilians over to a fire rescue crew, who had arrived in the meantime. Gunny Dixon also came back with his LAV section and a bundle of body bags. They respectfully sealed up the fallen men.

When quizzed, Gunny Dixon didn't know anything new about the situation. The colonel made it back successfully with his headquarters company, but the National Guard HQ was just as much in the dark as everyone else. TVs were out, cell and landlines were out. No one really knew what was happening. As he was leaving their HQ, the communication section had been trying to set up a radio and satellite shot to get some communications, or comms, with higher headquarters—or anyone outside of Morgantown, West Virginia, for that matter. So far, no luck.

Tyce halted the vehicles in his unit. His composite regiment in total wasn't more than 200 men. Comprised of eighty Marines from Company D, of the Marine 4th Light Armored Reconnaissance, and one hundred and twenty National Guardsmen from the 1st Squadron, 150th Cavalry. Their sum was barely big enough to even field an active duty battalion, let alone the regiment they were supposed to be on paper. They had spent two months training in the woods together. Soldiers and Marines had taken turns being both the attacker and the defender, fighting with blank ammunition. In the second month, the units joined forces for a final graduation field exercise: a huge attack on a heavily defended and entrenched enemy. All simulated, of course, but involving an exceedingly difficult series of tactical battlefield tasks, with mortars, artillery, machine guns, and enemy snipers. The troops had given it their all and were covered in mosquito bites and completely exhausted.

By all accounts from their higher headquarters, the Army and Marine Corps reserve evaluators, the two units had performed admirably. More importantly to Tyce, they had gained a mutual respect for one another. It was true that none of the men or women were active duty, the frontline troops that lived and breathed Army or Marine Corps every day. No, these were what the active duty folks called "weekend warriors," a group made up of men and women who held other jobs but stood in readiness to fight if the need arose. They had all sorts of other jobs, some even very lucrative in industry or business, but each had felt a calling to do a little more for their country. So they generally served one weekend a month. That is, until several recent crises and rising global tension—all stuff well above their heads—had caused a flurry of orders to activate the men and women and send them to "shake the rust out," as most of the troops called the exercise.

At first, it had seemed like one big joke, but the veterans mixed within the ranks of both the army and Marines swiftly took charge of critical ranks and ensured they had a good exercise. At least the American taxpayers could be proud of spending the nearly $450,000 they had budgeted for the reservists to go out and play in the woods. They had fired pretty much every weapon in their shared arsenals, requalified almost every soldier and Marine on the basics of rifle and machinegun marksmanship, and remembered once again the things that had drawn them to serve. Camaraderie, brotherhood, a love of country, and the joy of being outdoors instead of caught up in some rat race, stuffed into a cubicle farm. After a few weeks, the troops started to look the part. Orders were efficiently followed. Rivalries between services, though ever-present, were alleviated by a newfound respect.

Now, evening was falling, and the troops were fighting a battle against sleep and fatigue as Tyce pulled them onto a hilly rise in the waning sunlight near Morgantown.

These were the thoughts floating through Tyce's head as his Humvee, the lead in the column, wound its way toward Morgantown along 79. It had been an arduous and emotional recovery, but the feeling of satisfaction for performing his duty and recovering those killed, however grim the task, was strong. That feeling faded instantly when he spotted two dark columns of smoke looming over the town. One was directly in the center of the town, the other in the vicinity of the reserve center. Tyce called over the radios for his leaders to come up to his Humvee. As he waited the few minutes for them to arrive, he pulled out his binoculars and scanned the town.

Gunny Dixon and SSgt. Diaz arrived first, soon followed by First Lieutenant Chad Zane, the B Troop commander, to join Tyce in staring across the valley. As they watched, a series of planes flew overhead—big, lumbering prop planes. Behind them, dozens of parachutes opened up.

"Holy shit, sir." SSgt. Diaz was the first to speak up. "What is it?"

"Paratroopers," said Gunny Dixon. "But judging by the dark olive color of their chutes, those are not ours. They look Eastern Bloc."

Tyce pulled away from the binoculars and looked at the gathered leadership. "Okay, bring it in." Tyce motioned for everyone to gather close around him. "Look, this is it. If you don't have a sense of dread in your gut, you're not a real soldier or Marine. I think we all pretty much get what's going on, and it should make everyone's short 'n curlies stand on end."

A few troops looked about to interrupt, but Tyce held his hand up. "We've been hit. We've been invaded. Whoever it is has just hit several bridges and is invading our town." Over the town, more parachutes opened and drifted toward the ground. "We have to get moving. It's not safe here in the open. But I want hasty consensus. I want to hear from you, briefly, but then we need to act."

SSgt. Diaz was the first to speak. "We need to attack these fuckers, sir. No mercy. Whoever them bitches is, we kick them the fuck out of America."

A few shouts of "hell yeah" and "that's what I'm talkin' 'bout," erupted from the gathered leadership.

Gunnery Sergeant Dixon spoke next. "Sir, by my math counting 'chutes, that's about a regiment, maybe more. That's a full-fledged combat organization. If you look in between the men coming down, see those large grey cylinders, those are full of heavy weapons and ammo. Those guys are here to stomp some ass, and last I checked, we have next to zero ammunition."

Emphasizing Gunny's point, the staccato of gunfire erupted across the valley, with tracers arcing across the sky in different directions.

Everyone turned to watch, but Gunny Dixon continued speaking. "We turned in everything besides a few mags for the security of the convoy. Pretty sure we don't have any heavy ammo at all." He paused as everyone's attention turned away from the gunfire and back to him, "We need to head for the hills, sir. Restock, rearm as best as able, and attack this problem like the legit operation it is. If we run into that"—he pointed back to the town—"willy-nilly, we are gonna lose a whole lot more men than those who perished at the bridge. At this point, and up against a regiment, I don't think many will survive, and I don't see what we could gain."

"Why we standing 'round talkin' about it?" exclaimed one of the army sergeants.

Tyce ignored the outburst. "Okay, who else has something they want to say? This is a heavy decision. We're ignoring our own base in Morgantown and running. I want to hear from others." Tyce looked back now to the sergeant. "And I want calm and reasoned ideas. Not panic." Tyce's sharp words told the story: no time for nonsense.

"Is this leadership by consensus?" Lieutenant Zane asked. "That's not the army way. Besides, I think we're all just ready to do whatever you think we gotta do, sir. We are out of time and out of Schlitz. I'm still trying to take stock of what happened along the route as my guys arrive, but the best reports I have say I lost almost all my armor.

My Bradley Fighting Vehicles got wiped out in that initial missile attack."

This was news to Tyce, and he and others looked on with shock.

"The men are mostly okay, sir. Thank God they were in the trucks, or we would have lost them, too. I'll get a firm report and let you know once I have the details." He looked around, "But I agree with the Major. We need to get out of Dodge and assess the situation." He looked at Tyce, "Besides, sir, we've watched you in action for the past couple o' months. We know what you're capable of." It seemed like he couldn't refrain from looking at Tyce's prosthetic leg as he continued, "We know about your combat experiences in Iraq, too. Know you've been there, done that. Lead us, sir. Just don't fuck it up."

Tyce frowned, fighting the mixed emotions of pride in the trust he'd been given but deeply concerned about the reports of losses.

At least most of the men are okay, Tyce thought, *but for how long if we linger.* He felt like a cursed man. Death and bad decisions followed him like virus.

"Okay," he said finally, "Here's what we're going to do. First, we need to get off the road and into the trees. It's been a while since I've seen any U.S. aviation, and if my guess is right, we no longer own the skies."

Tyce pulled a map from his flak jacket's cargo pouch. "Second, we take to the hills. Travel in small groups. Squads and vehicle sections of no more than about four vehicles. Any larger than that and we'll attract a lot of attention. We're a juicy target, and I'm sure once those . . . *enemy* get their shit squared, or demolish the Morgantown HQ, they'll go hunting for other targets.

Tyce pointed to the map. "Here. The city of Parsons." He'd never been there, but it looked far enough into the valley, but not so far that they couldn't return if they got reports that might force a return.

Like civilian casualties, thought Tyce.

The men nodded, and Tyce continued, "Once I'm done talking, get your men into the woods, break out your maps, and pair up with someone who knows the area. I want one senior leader, staff sergeant or above, with every vehicle section. You figure out how to make that happen, but do it quickly. Stay up on your radios at all times, but no chatter. We don't know who else might be listening."

"Is that wise, sir, splitting up?" asked another NCO.

"Yes, we're a target together. A big, fat target with no ammo to defend ourselves. Got it? Thant's the mission for now. Pick covered routes through the forest, and we'll rally at the city of Parsons for more orders. You all are big boys and girls—I trust you to make it happen."

"Time line?" asked another.

"I'd say about five hours from now."

"What then?" asked another.

"We make a longer-range plan." Tyce was done. Any more Q&A was likely going to become counterproductive, "Everyone copy? Understood?" He looked around at their faces ready to turn and go, but one of the sergeants—a kid he remembered from Canfield, another local town— blurted out, "Sir, those are our families down there. We can't just . . . abandon them!"

Now it was Lieutenant Zane's turn. He answered angrily before Tyce could. "We're not abandoning anyone, soldier." he growled, flashing an angry look. "We're taking a calcu- lated, tactical step to higher ground. Getting to a position of advantage to take stock, gain some intel, and then strike with precision. We do no one any good rushing in. As a weapons section leader, you should know how important prep is before combat. And you heard the major. We're not racing in to get everyone killed on a fruitless, hasty assault. We're living to fight another day. Then we can knock these bastards out of Morgantown. Our town."

"Don't you mean retreating, sir?" The man responded to Lieutenant Zane, but the comment was clearly leveled toward Tyce and his decision to take to the hills.

Damn it, thought Tyce. *The men are on edge and are apt to speak frankly now.*

Not a bad thing ordinarily; he was trying to gain confidence through a difficult decision, they were all volunteers, after all. But it gave Tyce a terrible sinking feeling of doubt coupled with self-loathing that he was once again dooming his men.

"How about you shut your fucking trap and follow orders!" barked Lieutenant Zane.

Tyce was thankful for the support, but the timing wasn't perfect. Using force to keep everyone in line wouldn't last long, and he knew it. His order was a huge ask. With many of their homes and families threatened, he needed reason and willingness. He needed to give them a solid plan. Something to believe in.

Still, Tyce's stomach sank as low as ever, and he started to remember what he hated most about military leadership. Responsibility for men who were going to get killed or wounded once again rested on his shoulders. He set his misgivings aside and spoke in a clear and consistent tone meant to settle the debate, at least temporarily.

"Okay, look, I know as well as you do that there are thousands of innocent civilians down there. Families and friends. But I also know that the likelihood of the enemy waging war against civilians is less than zero. That means *we* are the target. Or more likely, our HQ. We get to Parsons, we reorganize, and we come back and kick these mother-fuckers' asses."

Tyce normally tried to steer away from too much pro-fanity in front of the men, it made his talk cheap, but it seemed appropriate, and the men needed to know he at least believed in what he was saying.

Tyce looked to Gunnery Sergeant Dixon, "I also think I know how I can get our hands on some ammunition. Gunny, pull your section into the trees with mine. After everyone's headed out, I have another mission for you." He turned back to his leadership. "The rest of you, stay up on your encrypted radios, but don't make a call unless it's urgent. These guys look like a modern army, and I'm sure they'll have direction-finding gear. We link up at Parsons in five hours."

The men all raced off to their unit, and Tyce turned to the Gunny.

"What about the colonel?" asked the Gunny, half under his breath, "By now, he and the Headquarters company have made it to the reserve center. Directly under that cloud of paratroopers." He pointed to a black plume of smoke rising from the vicinity. More gunfire echoed a deep stac-cato in the distance.

"The colonel will have to hold his own. He didn't make it to colonel for nothing." Brushing the point aside, he pulled out his map again, "Gunny, did you see that gun store a bit back—the one near the city of Anmoore?"

"Which one? We passed like five of 'em."

"Okay, you pick, then. The largest one, I guess. I want you to do a raid on the local gun store. See if they have any hidden firearms left over from the assault weapons ban that we can . . . um . . . commandeer."

"Ha! I thank God we live in West Virginia. Can't go ten miles without finding a gun store."

Tyce's Humvee drivers and many others had already gotten wind of what was up and pulled off into the woods. Gunny followed Tyce over where the two unfolded the map on the hood of Tyce's Humvee and formulated a plan to confiscate some civilian ammunition.

CHAPTER 11

Dulles International Airport, Washington, D.C.

The giant Ilyushin Il-76 four-engine Russian jet shook violently on landing. The wet brakes squealed, but the brand-new tires stabilized the big, overloaded aircraft and plowed cleanly through the slushy snow. The engines whined into reverse, and the large plane turned and taxied to the Dulles airport service apron, stopping at gate A6. Every few minutes, a similar aircraft touched down behind them.

A newly and hastily promoted General Kolikoff raised the window shade from inside the jet and surveyed Dulles International Airport.

Is it a perk of finally being in the right camp at the right time? he had thought when Tympkin had produced the one-star shoulder boards just before their flight departed. The promotion had done little for his station or even his future outlook. Plus, he was still flying in with little fanfare and absolutely zero of the creature comforts he'd imagined were afforded to a general.

Barren. Cold. Not much to look at, he thought. It was just the airport, after all, but this was his first time to America, and he had been expecting something different. *Something . . . more.*

Rows and rows of neatly parked civilian airliners sat quietly at odd intervals, abandoned at their gates. He scanned the terminal building for any signs of life. There must have been some shooting involved when seizing Dulles, because Kolikoff could see that a few of the large windows were shattered. Four grey shapes passed rapidly by his window going in the opposite direction. Kolikoff immediately recognized them from their tail fins: Mikoyan MiG-35 Russian jet fighters, probably headed out to intercept more remnant U.S. Air Force. He'd calculated they'd be a nuisance until they greatly diminished their numbers, but they were now operating scattered and without any centralized authority.

If everything was still working according to his and the SPETS-VTOR computer's plan, there would be even more heavy air transports arriving carrying attack helicopters that would give them more of an edge on the ground while the fighters took care of the skies. Right now, the Russians on the ground would still be attacking American military centers. The infantry had need for more than the multi-role attack aircraft that had just passed. Kolikoff had arrived in the middle of the pack, the third wave. There were fourteen more waves yet to come, and until they had everything on the ground, he was nervously watching for signs the plan or its interwoven time lines were slipping.

No matter, he thought. *This is proof that the plan is working, and we now have command of the American skies.*

With most of America's active forces still fighting overseas in Iran, the surprise invasion had caught America with little but home defense units, the National Guard, and the not-yet-mobilized reserves.

"A disorganized rabble of weekend warriors," he had explained to the generals in the planning rooms back in Moscow.

Kolikoff had spent most of the eight-hour flight over

the Atlantic rehashing the timetables. He had most of the major moving parts memorized. During the trip, he'd lain awake, restless and fretting over the smallest details in the exacting deployment schedule created by the SPETS-VTOR. Kolikoff and his men had calculated things to the last detail, but they had relied heavily on the timing recommended by the SPETS-VTOR. Much more than his neck was on the line now. But his mind was more at ease now that they had landed. He might soon get radio or other comms confirming that timings were on track.

He knew that literally several armies' worth of men, about three hundred thousand, were swarming toward the United States from greatly dispersed locations by ship and by air. By now, all critical U.S. air response aircraft and missile batteries should have been killed on the ground, allowing these follow-on Russian waves to penetrate. Confusion and surprise were Russia's best friends on the battlefields today. Overwhelming the enemy's system was a function of Koilikoff's plan, but it also left many parts vulnerable as they infiltrated the U.S. borders. He would fret over that part until they got the word that their precisely targeted attacks had successfully demolished this scattered defense system.

America is just too wide and too broad to defend, he thought, *a thousand little attacks sow the seeds of confusion and shock, and gradually the door opens.*

These were, after all, locations where no one had really seen an invader for over two hundred years.

Surrounded by hundreds of sleeping soldiers, Kolikoff was eminently aware that while the men slept fitfully, he, as the central planner for the American invasion, had been struggling to get even a few moments of rest without being awakened by his racing mind.

He stared through the window as they taxied some more. There was no more time to worry; he knew better than most that, right now, time was of the essence. He needed to get the computer hooked up as soon as possible. He stood up uncomfortably from the mesh cargo seat and stretched aching muscles, then went to the back of the aircraft. There, his three majors were sleeping in a jumble on the steel floor and partially on the boxes that housed the SPETS-VTOR PKS, the portable version of his big-brained computer. He envied the majors their utter lack of concern or even awareness of the massive undertaking going on around them. He shook them roughly awake, pushing them with his boot.

The portable system was not exactly portable according to most people's understanding of the word. It consisted of three large military cases, each about the size of a large refrigerator. This smaller version of Kolikoff's wonderwork combat computer would provide necessary battlefield predictions in the short term until they could set up a satellite uplink. Once established, the system would communicate with its bigger pal back in Moscow and could harness every bit of the powerful mainframe.

The heavy transport aircraft's back ramp lowered, and bright morning sunlight broke into the still-darkened space. A gust of bone-chilling winter wind entered the cabin along with the bright morning light. Everyone aboard grumbled loudly as they came awake.

A Russian airman's voice boomed above the whine of the jet's still-spinning turbofans, directing everyone to stand aside. A forklift appeared behind the big Russian air force sergeant and banged noisily up the plane's ramp. Two men ran aboard the aircraft and unhitched the SPETS-VTOR computer system boxes, and the big forklift proceeded to lift them and head back down the ramp.

At the same time, the front entrance opened and a hard-edged, dirty, and battle-weary Russian army officer squeezed into the crowded compartment. He looked around the plane, holding up a photo and scanning the faces of all the soldiers.

Spotting General Kolikoff, he pointed at him. He shouted above the noise, "You are to come with me, General. Immediately." He signaled to someone outside the plane's forward hatch, and four soldiers boarded quickly, grabbed both Kolikoff's and his majors' military packs, then raced up the Dulles jet bridge.

"How . . . I mean, what is your mission with me, Captain? Am I under arrest?" asked Kolikoff with some trepidation. This was not in his plan, and he still had a deep-rooted fear from his days in front of a firing squad. The entire aircraft was now focused on him.

The captain stared at Kolikoff for a moment, thoroughly puzzled. Then something funny seemed to register, and the captain started laughing. Judging from the dry, caked mud on his uniform and streaks of dirty sweat across his brow, he looked like he hadn't laughed in a while. He turned back to the front of the aircraft, still laughing, and said, "Sir, just follow me. I'll explain the rest as we go." The words didn't exactly settle Kolikoff's still air-sickened stomach.

Together, they all followed the captain through the mostly dark Dulles terminal. Past several lobbies with closed fast-food and pizza eateries, wine bars, and even some fashionable clothing stores. All were darkened and closed. Kolikoff spotted two blood-stained bodies in blue uniforms. From the look of it, they were airport police officers. Probably didn't even have weapons, just looked official as the first wave of Spetsnaz seized the airport. You didn't have to be military to die in a war, just look like you might be an official and they'd take you out. Spetsnaz didn't take chances. It was the first sign to Kolikoff that he and the men had entered not just a war zone but a battlefield to boot. The differences were not subtle.

Down the rest of the Concourse, Russian soldiers scattered amongst the gates were working with vast arrays of communications equipment and hastily cracking open boxes from transports backed directly against the terminal. Long lines of weary Russian soldiers spilled out of arriving passenger jets and into the terminal. They were bleary eyed from their flights but likewise looking around curiously at the terminal with the interest of kids in a new playground. As each soldier entered through their gates and into America, they were directed toward a neat line of logistics officers standing next to the broken-open wooden crates. Each one handed the men a rifle and machine gun ammunition, rations, grenades, and various other equipment. Washington's Dulles airport was back in business, just not in the manner intended by the former occupants.

Once they were outside the front of the terminal, the cold wind whipped the faces of Kolikoff and his three majors to a bright red, and they all squinted and blinked in the bright winter morning's sunshine. This was their first good look at America. They didn't seem impressed.

"This is it?" said Major Quico, careful to keep his voice low so Kolikoff wouldn't hear him. "It just looks like Russia . . . I mean, where are the discos and the girls?"

"They are not here at the airport, you idiot," said Major Pavel.

"But where is the Statue of Liberty?" asked Major Drugov.

"Idiot!" said Pavel. "That is in Boston."

A large, black SUV was waiting for them. They stowed their gear and took a seat. Inside, they were greeted by a full bar and big screen TV. The captain had clearly commandeered the best vehicle he could lay his hands on. Pavel reached toward the bar, but received a quick slap from Kolikoff, whose look was enough to get the major to immediately sit back down.

The SUV drove off, and finally the special forces captain spoke, "General, I am Captain Shenkov. I am a special forces commander. We seized our objective and exceeded the time line, but I lost most of my men. They sent me and what's left of my unit to be your personal bodyguards."

Kolikoff was beginning to get the picture of what his operation looked like on the ground. A lot of personal sacrifice. A lump swelled in his throat, "How were you able to seize it so quickly?" he heard himself say.

"The resistance was smaller than we expected. I guess they never really planned for a full and determined attack. We exploded into their midst; they were not ready for us. Still, it was a very bloody fight. We only just completed mopping up."

Kolikoff knew by heart which Spetsnaz forces he'd assigned to which targets in the invasion order for the American capital of D.C. But, in his sleep-deprived state, Kolikoff hadn't thought to look at the patch on the captain's uniform before they got into the SUV.

"And what was your objective, Captain?" asked Kolikoff.

"We came ashore yesterday aboard one of the phony cargo ships—*Shujaa* was her name. Our objective was to capture the Pentagon."

CHAPTER 12

Parsons, West Virginia

The drive to the city of Parsons, West Virginia, had been hair-raising. Radio silence was broken more than was comfortable to Tyce. Some of the reports were from scouts spotting Russian forces and seemed legit; while others were just ghosts called over the radio by skittish men broken into the new realities of war. The sky was littered with an ever-growing mix of aircraft. A mix of small attack jet fighters and larger, high-flying aircraft which were presumed by most to be assortments of heavy lift transports. For the last part of their journey, every fifteen minutes or so, the men spotted or heard something new overhead. Because of the bumpy roads and with parts of the route through deep woods, no one was really certain who the aircraft belonged to. So they bolted for forest cover when any aircraft was spotted.

A few sky battles raged overhead. The men watched from under cover as fighters and bombers fought in winding and looping spirals. The fighters chased higher-flying aircraft; then other fighters joined the mix. At any other time it would look like a wonderful aerial display of the modern flying age. But the men watched as a dozen or more aircraft were shot down, falling toward earth in flaming, smoking heaps. Missile launches scratched at the sky with long white streaks. Many of the battles started in view, but the ultimate fates of the pilots often occurred out of sight and over the horizons. Without any of the specialized, ultra-high-frequency radios needed to communicate, they couldn't talk to any of them, or even really guess who was winning.

Then a lone aircraft appeared, making regular sweeping patterns from north to south. A drone. A high-altitude, wide-wingspan reconnaissance drone, they speculated. Likely fitted with the latest in surveillance gear to see in the infrared and ultraviolet spectrums. The men remained relatively defenseless against it all. It was all enough to make the infantry and reconnaissance men's hair stand on end.

It was on this rare occasion that Tyce broke radio silence when they appeared and instructed the troops to go into deeper cover and remain there until it was gone. They were almost certainly reconnaissance aircraft looking for any surviving American troops.

Five hours later, Tyce's Humvee pulled up to the Parsons town hall. Several of the other four-vehicle Humvee groups had made it and were parked in distributed areas under trees or under the bank and fast-food restaurant overhangs to hide from further aerial observation.

Tyce spoke briefly with the few men assembled outside the town hall waiting for him, then sent word for Gunny and SSgt. Diaz. The city's municipal building was an old, well-constructed two-story red brick building with a four-story clock tower that commanded a view of the town and valley.

Tyce directed four men to go up into the tower to keep a lookout. He and Gunny were discussing what to do next when SSgt. Diaz's Humvee pulled up and she hopped out, her machine gun over her shoulder and Trigger at her side. The dog's expression—tail sagging, quiet but alert to the slightest movement or noise—seemed to mimic that of the troops. His eyes glanced around constantly, and his ears changed direction at any new sound, even the ones at frequencies above human hearing.

"Gunny, how much ammo did we end up confiscating?" said Tyce, petting Trigger as they spoke.

"Some." replied Gunny.

Tyce grimaced, understanding only too well the implications. "Okay, look, here's what I want to do," said Tyce. "Let's see if we can find the mayor and let him know we're here for some rest and preparation but don't intend to stay. Civilian authorities are going to be wary of any kind of troops in their valley."

"I think we'll be lucky if we don't find them whimpering back in their homes," said SSgt. Diaz with a smile.

"Yeah, well, tell the men to stay sharp, and let's head up and see who's still around at their posts and doing their jobs. If we're lucky, they won't be interested in us and we can commandeer some fuel and food."

The small group followed Tyce up the stone steps, passing a large copper sign that stated the building was both the Parsons city hall and also the seat of the Tucker County government. The building was old, but clearly was a proud monument to the city and county.

Two large oak and etched-glass doors creaked open, and they caught a glimpse of the men Tyce had dispatched racing up the wide wooden stairs to try to gain access to the clock tower. Tyce pointed out old black-and-white photos adorning the walls of packs of scruffy boys gathered outside the courthouse through the ages. It was not until they passed several that Tyce realized they were pictures of mountain men from the community who had just volunteered and were being sworn in to head off to World War I, World War II, Korea, and Vietnam.

Many of them didn't come home, thought Tyce.

Tyce and the rest headed up the stairs, looking for someone in charge. After they had climbed to the top, a heavyset, mustachioed man in a grey and blue uniform with a sheriff's badge halted their progress. He had his pistol drawn and was holding Tyce's men at bay. In turn, they were looking back at Tyce for instructions. It looked to be a bit of a standoff, but Tyce quickly assessed the situation and defused it.

"Hi, Sheriff. My men are under my orders to get up into your clock tower and keep a lookout. If we can get your permission, that would be helpful."

"Permission *not* granted," said the sheriff, now leveling the pistol at Tyce.

Tyce signaled for his men to lower their rifles, and he ascended the last few steps two at time. "Sheriff, I'm not certain if you know just what's going on, but we need to keep a watch over the roads leading into the valley. We've . . . that is, America has been invaded." It sounded completely odd coming out of his mouth, enough so that his voice even wavered a bit, making it sound less believable still.

"So you say." The sheriff still didn't lower his pistol. "You the guy in charge?" He asked, looking down the stairs past Tyce and his small group. "Or is there someone else more important coming?"

"No. I'm Major Tyce Asher. I'm in charge." Remembering he was just in charge temporarily until the colonel could be found, he added, "For now . . ."

"Okay, then come with me." The sheriff holstered his pistol and indicated a door with the word "MAYOR" emblazoned across it. "Send your men back down. There's no guns allowed in the county courthouse. And when you're done, go talk to the chief of police. I don't work with any federal government ninnies."

Tyce and his men stared at the sheriff, a little taken aback by his boldness, but proceeded.

Maybe this wasn't a good idea after all, thought Tyce, but he and Gunny gave SSgt. their weapons and nodded for her to lead the men back as Tyce and Gunny followed the sheriff into the mayor's office.

Inside, they found an old, traditional, but comfortable waiting room. The walls were lined with framed children's drawings, obviously from some contest to decorate the mayor's office. An interesting touch.

A mayor of the people, Tyce thought. *I'll be able to work with this guy. He'll want to protect his community.*

The sheriff knocked on the next set of doors.

"Mayor, you have some visitors."

The door opened revealing a middle-aged, well-dressed, and shapely red-haired woman. She gave a half-smile but narrowed her eyes when she saw Tyce and Gunny. With a quiet Southern accent, she said, "Why, hello there, boys," waving them into her office. "We're mighty busy, but why don't y'all come on in and have a seat?"

Tyce was not interested in tying up any more of his time line with local bumpkin politicians, even beautiful ones. Before anyone was even seated, he impatiently began, "Okay, ma'am—"

"Honorable Mayor Susanna Holly of Parsons works," she interrupted in a forced but patient monotone, pointing to the words on a wooden name block on her desk: MAYOR SUSANNA HOLLY.

She smiled as she returned behind her desk, sitting

slowly and deliberately, smoothing her skirt and making a teepee with her hands, "Or sometimes just *Susanna* . . . once folks get to know me a while." She winked.

Then her smile faded a bit, "Now, what can Tucker County do for our brave men and women in uniform?"

"Yes, Mrs.—er, Honorable Mayor . . ." Tyce tried to restart his address to her.

"Why don't we start this way, Major," Susanna said, quickly recognizing his military rank. "You all have come to our fair city and county in the mountains because the Russians have taken over Charleston and Morgantown. You and your boys are looking for a place to hole up while you figure out what's going on, and the little town of Parsons looked like a damn fine spot from your maps."

Her eyes scanned between them both, then settled back on Tyce. Underneath her Scarlett O'Hara Southern charm, it was obvious Mayor Susanna Holly was an exceedingly intelligent woman, and likely a very cunning politician. Things were starting to come into perspective for Tyce. He wasn't about to march into town and provide instructions or even make demands of the local civil authorities—least of all with *her* at the helm.

Tyce tried to recover. "Yes . . . that about sums it up. I will add something, though. If we don't do something about these . . . Russian invaders"—the word *Russians* still sounded surreal to Tyce—"your authority here in Parsons may not last." Till now, Tyce had suspected, but hadn't known for sure it was Russians, "I'm not sure how long they'll let you keep on being mayor."

"Well now, Major, you let lil' old Susanna worry about that. If they even make it up this far," she said with a grin.

Her small attempt at humor, small though it was, made the men smile.

"Meanwhile, you have my permission to grab some fuel and food for your troops. I suspect that's your ulterior motive, isn't it?" she winked again, "I'll see that they open the McDonald's across the street for your boys. Maybe you can do some planning with my police chief. We can bring in some of the local boys who live up in the hills. They'll give you tips on places you can hole up until you can get yourselves straight."

Tyce was waiting for a "but." Something told him Mayor Holly was just too shrewd to let the opportunity of Tyce owing her a favor pass her by.

"Well, that would be a real help. We may have to stay in the hills a little while. At least a few days. We really need to find out just what the Russians are up to." Tyce scratched his head. Russians. Why in heaven's name would they be interested in invading the United States?

Susanna didn't skip a beat, making Tyce even more sure she had just played him like a fiddle. "Okay, Major, it's a deal. You all can use our gas and get some local facts." Her lips curled up into an alluring but deadly smile that didn't quite materialize through her unblinking eyes. "But let's just make sure you remember that when our little old town needs some help. We might have to call on you for some little favors . . . From time to time."

Great, now he was in for *more* than one favor. Well, he supposed it was the right thing to do in this crisis. Work with the civil and duly elected officials. Tyce and Gunny stood and followed the sheriff out. Tyce looked over his shoulder and saw Susanna's gaze following them, her arms across her chest, and her signature charming but disarming half-smile playing on her lips.

CHAPTER 13

The Pentagon, Washington, D.C.

Kolikoff was rushed through a number of dimly lit corridors. In several spots, blast marks on the walls told the tale: the Pentagon had not given up without a fight. Overhead fluorescent lights had been knocked down and some sparked, giving the otherwise modern and well-organized hallways an eerie look. Kolikoff was not really used to the sights and smells of combat. He noticed an acrid mix from explosives or gunpowder and the stink of burning plastic. The heavy odors instantly turned his and the majors' stomachs.

Debris was scattered everywhere. Flags of the U.S. military—Army, Navy, Air Force, and Marines—were strewn across the floors, and men rushing to and fro trampled over them with seemingly little concern for aught but whatever mission they were on. The area must have been some kind of ceremonial entrance or planning area for high-level personnel. Important-looking papers and dossiers stamped with SECRET or TOP SECRET littered a floor covered with spent shell casings and broken glass from display cases.

Kolikoff hoped someone was looking through the documents; there were probably valuable secrets they could use. Right now, the fighting Russian soldiers had little regard for the preservation of documents and computers. Kolikoff supposed soon enough Russian intelligence officers would be combing through it all. All part of processes that happened well below his and the SPETS-VTOR's strategic level of war. He had only drawn up the higher-level plans. The so-called "big blue arrows." Individual units were assigned to their sectors and would have a host of tasks that he wasn't privy to. Still, it was odd to be racing along on foot, well below the tactical level. He had a pistol on his side, but he'd been told there was little need for it now. He hoped that was true, because he wasn't a very good shot. Much better at politicking and staff work than any actual soldiering.

As the small group continued deeper into the Pentagon, he heard and saw Russian troops running on adjacent corridors. At one point, their security detachment leader, Captain Shenkov, held them up while he spoke into his squad tactical radio throat microphone. After listening for a moment, he held up his hand and indicated for Kolikoff and the majors to kneel as he put his rifle to his shoulder and aimed down the corridor.

"What is it, man?" hissed Kolikoff ducking behind Shenkov, and with the three majors ducking wild eyed behind him for cover.

A few bursts of gunfire from an office farther along the hallway. Now Kolikoff understood the reason. Clearly, a few holdouts had barricaded themselves in some of the smaller, tertiary offices. *Well, you have to give them credit*, Kolikoff thought. The Americans were willing to fight to the death to defend even this giant, five-sided monument to military bureaucracy.

Two dull explosions later, Captain Shenkov nudged them to start moving again. Kolikoff and the majors tried to peer into the office as they passed but could only see the backs of heavily armed Russian Spetsnaz men, their chests heaving from the exertion of the recent battle, standing among detritus and overturned desks. A Russian officer, his pistol drawn, appeared to be about to deliver the coup de grâce to some unseen enemy behind the desks. They passed, Shenkov indicating for them to hasten their pace. An odd feeling passed through Kolikoff as the sounds of two pistol shots echoed behind him.

Finally, after descending three flights of stairs, they were led to a long corridor. The doors at the end had been blasted open with demolitions. Four men from Spetsgruppa V, the badasses of the badasses, who had taken the building, were resting by the massive steel doors in broken office chairs. Two were cleaning their new AK-12 assault rifles as the other two talked and smoked what looked like American cigarettes, obviously a perk of the capture. The men barely looked at Kolikoff; even his general shoulder boards were not enough to impress these battle-hardened men, but they quickly rose and nodded to Shenkov as he passed.

Respect from warrior to warrior in the same unit? thought Kolikoff.

Still, unacceptable behavior. But after a glance at their hardened scowls, he decided it best not to reproach them for their breach in military decorum just now.

Once past the entrance into the room, Kolikoff surveyed his new home: a large, central office surrounded by smaller, glassed-in offices facing the central room. The so-called "Iron Room" in the Pentagon was to be their new headquarters. The command center for the rest of the invasion—and subsequent pacification—of the different states.

A main computer screen and ten or twelve computer workstations. Most of it looked to have been captured intact. He didn't have long to take it in. Six men bustled in wheeling the crated SPETS-VTOR on handcarts. Disregarding Kolikoff, they began breaking open the boxes and installing the SPETS-VTOR on top of the existing computers and monitors and connecting them.

"Do we have a satellite uplink?" Kolikoff asked one of the technicians.

The junior officer glanced at Kolikoff for a moment. "Yes. All is in order. Please keep out of the way while my men get everything installed."

Although the initial phases of the invasion had been completed, America was far from pacified. Kolikoff and the SPET-VTOR had predicted a full six months to destroy organized resistance. During that time, the Russians were vulnerable.

A commotion at the door distracted Kolikoff from his thoughts. He turned in time to see the four *Spetsgruppa* men jump to attention. The two smoking men hastily extinguishing their cigarettes under their boot heels, the other two jumping up, pieces of their disassembled rifles spilling onto the floor.

Five black-clad soldiers entered and looked around briefly, then signaled outside the door. General Tympkin entered behind them. He took the room in quickly and smiled on sighting Kolikoff.

"Viktor! You have made it in one piece. And it is fitting

I find you here, in the veritable belly of the beast." He came in closer, inspecting the technicians who remained at work installing the SPETS-VTOR.

"Good, you are already setting up shop." He clasped a hand on Kolikoff's shoulder. "Listen, Viktor, I am very proud of your accomplishments. Your predictions have allowed us to make gains we could not have dreamed of ten or even five years ago." General Tympkin came in even closer, and his voice lowered. "I must ask . . . are you confident in the next phases? I understand most of the Americans, the civilians I mean, were disarmed of their assault-caliber rifles. But many reports have been coming in that they are still engaging civilians with hunting rifles or shotguns, and in some of the inner cities, they have received murderous fire from pistols and Molotov cocktails."

Kolikoff looked at him with surprise. "Well, General . . . we predict . . . that is we . . . uh, the SPETS-VTOR . . ." he stammered.

"Ah, no matter, no matter. We are well ahead of the time line." He gripped Kolikoff by his new shoulder boards in a fatherly way. "And as I say, the boys are sweeping these dissidents aside with ease. They pose little threat to our heavily armed forces. The invasion's first waves and the infiltration tactics and ruses you invented have been more than effective. The precision targets you gave us have all but knocked out any real military resistance. It seems that little computer of yours has been spot on."

Kolikoff smiled but remained silent.

"Ah, I see you are just fresh from the airport. *Nyet*? I should give you some updates and let you hook up your big brain."

General Tympkin sat in a large, comfortable leather office chair. Kolikoff looked around for another chair, then wheeled it over to the general, who seemed in the mood for a chat. Kolikoff noticed his chair was bloodstained. Several bullet holes dotted the back, and the stuffing was coming out. There wasn't time to appear squeamish in front of Tympkin, though, so he sat down, then instantly regretted it. He could feel the still-wet and sticky blood as it seeped through his camouflage trousers.

"Let me fill you in on the latest happenings. I know you understand the plan in the larger sense, but war is war, Comrade General, and things change once we make first contact." Seeing some shock in Kolikoff's eyes, he added, "Not to worry, the men have improvised where there were gaps in the plan, as our field generals are supposed to."

The slights, both that his plan had gaps and that he wasn't a field commander, were not lost on Kolikoff.

General Tympkin continued, "Reports state the President of the United States has been killed. It is regrettable, but some of his Secret Service agents decided to make a last stand at the White House, and the president was caught in the crossfire. The vice president has disappeared into hiding, or is missing, maybe even dead somewhere. There is still much confusion." The general paused and looked at Kolikoff, judging his reaction. There was none. Kolikoff was more interested in saving his own skin at this point, and he'd grown slightly numb to all the battlefield stimuli.

"I see, General. That is not contrary to our plan."

"No, you are correct. Not our biggest issue at the moment. But we have managed to find the American secretary of state, and she has been more than willing to step up to assume the new duties as president. She has immediately agreed to our terms, as long as it brings about a cease-fire. We suspect she will immediately lodge a protest with the international community. But, since we now control the majority of U.S. communications and news, we can filter out what we don't like. Again, thanks to your careful planning, we have detected very little in the way of public media interference. In most regions, we control what information the people will hear. A very satisfactory initial gain, General Kolikoff. You should be proud."

The general clapped Kolikoff on the shoulder again and smiled a broad, gold-toothed grin. "Now, I must be off. There is a matter of the two nearest bases, Fort Myer and Fort Belvoir."

"They resist?" said Kolikoff. This news truly caught him off guard. Both of the D.C. bases had nothing but support personnel, and no real combat commands.

"Yes, your computer failed to predict a handful of military police and computer experts would put up a fight." He laughed a bit at the last comment, knowing full well the implications for Kolikoff as well.

Having toyed with Kolikoff enough and seeing he'd dampened his spirits, Tympkin chuckled and patted him again. "But Viktor, no one could have predicted a bunch of grave diggers at Arlington National Cemetery would arm themselves and fight to the last man for a handful of old headstones, either. It's no matter . . . we will mop them up, too, soon. You focus on getting your computers running and in premium condition. Use whatever you need from the computer networks you find here. You have my permission."

And with that, General Tympkin strode back out, his protection detail eyeing the damaged room and Kolikoff suspiciously once again. Their AKs had been at the ready the whole time.

The old bastard trusts no one. Even us, his loyal dogs, thought Kolikoff, looking at his computer technicians and the three majors who were still standing in the corner, hoping to remain unnoticed.

He surveyed what was left of the Iron Room—the former core of the U.S. military's might. The command and control center for all U.S. forces, now covered in dangling wires and broken computer screens. Only now did he see four bodies stacked hastily in the corner. Looking closer, they looked like staff officers. None looked as though they were even armed. They all appeared to have met violent ends. One was still wearing his reading glasses. For some reason that angered him.

Kolikoff and his countrymen were now occupiers, conquerors of this land. After so many years of hating and fearing America, he felt a new and completely different sensation. There was no greater power left on the planet. With the overthrow of the U.S. government, Russia was the world's only superpower. In a split second, that wonder turned to terror.

What have we done? he thought. His head was beginning to absorb the gravity of everything and began to swim. Maybe it was fatigue from the last few days of preparation, planning, and flights. *No, no, this is right. It has always been right. As long as I can remember, America has been the enemy. They blocked Russia's natural order in the world with venom and deception for so many, many years.*

But something gnawed at him. Absently, Kolikoff reached behind him. Suddenly he recalled where he had been sitting. Between his fingers he felt the sticky, still-warm blood that had covered his backside and legs. He pulled out a gore-stained hand and realized he was covered in another man's death. He raced from the Iron Room, passing the lackadaisical and uncaring guards. His stomach began churning violently, and he urgently sought out the nearest bathroom before he added vomit to the list of new battlefield sights and smells.

CHAPTER 14

Parsons

Tyce sipped on some coffee, cupping his hands around it to warm them against the biting winter cold. He and Parsons Police Chief Braydon had planned all night and now sat in the squad car, both staring out into the darkness watching some of Tyce's men prepare for a patrol in the morning's predawn twilight. Braydon was a fit, clean-shaven man who had spent two of his younger years in the service. He still showed the snap and pop, wore a clean uniform, and kept order among his deputies, but he also seemed to be keeping a suspicious eye on Tyce and his men.

The chief was the first to speak, "Did your men ever link up with that special forces unit?"

Tyce stopped mid-sip "What special forces unit, Chief?"

"The guys training in the woods." The chief looked over at Tyce but could see he had no idea what the chief was talking about. "There's a training base about two miles out of town."

"Are you serious?"

"I thought you army guys knew all this stuff. Don't you all talk? I mean, I'm . . . well, I *was* in touch with all the surrounding police forces pretty much daily. We were integrated on the Web for arrests, warrants, etcetera."

"Well, for the thousandth time, I'm a Marine, Chief.

And I thought I told you I was stationed in Quantico. We only come over the Blue Ridge to some do big training exercises."

"Oh, everyone knows about the classified special forces training camp." The chief looked at Tyce, smiled, and shrugged his shoulders. "There ain't much up in these hills that stays a secret for very long."

The chief put the squad car in gear and started driving them out of town. In minutes, they were whizzing past thick stands of tall pines—driving in silence, the Cheat River sparkling in the moonlight. Tyce turned on the radio and flicked through the channels. Nothing but static.

"We didn't get many stations back here before. Looks like the Russians stopped even the few we did get."

The chief braked suddenly as he rounded a bend in the road and his headlight caught two men in dark camouflage uniforms. Both had M4 carbines, which they leveled and aimed at the car. For what seemed like minutes, both groups stared at each other. Then, before Tyce or the chief had made a move, there was a figure at the passenger's-side window rapping on the glass with the point of a pistol.

Tyce rolled down his window and peered up at a balaclava-clad individual pointing his pistol right at Tyce's forehead. The men in front and two others visible in the rearview mirror closed in on them, and then the man with the pistol spoke in a calm voice. "Hey, fellas. Gonna need you all to hop on out of the car."

Tyce began to speak but thought better of it as one of the men in front turned on a laser sight. Tyce saw the laser beam cut clearly in the cold, misty dawn. It was trained through the windshield and right onto his chest.

* * *

They were instructed to dismount the squad car and proceed on foot. Their hands were bound behind their backs, and they were led over hills and through dales. It was a full hour before Tyce and the chief had passed through all the guards and wards the special forces men had established. Overwatch positions, booby-trapped roads and trails, several kill zones set up so the entrant would have no idea they were in deep trouble until it was too late to escape alive. Tyce felt like a fish in a tidal fish trap for most of the way. Then for the last five hundred meters, both men were blindfolded.

Finally, they arrived in a small cave, and their blindfolds were removed. The dimly lit room looked like a clubhouse for Boy Scouts. A soldier in one corner was weightlifting metal rifle cases like they were simple barbells. Weapons and ammo were neatly stacked. In one corner, a soldier worked on a set of night vision goggles and repaired a rifle scope. Yet another had a copy of a girly magazine propped up on his knees and was playing a harmonica.

A man entered and sat opposite from them across stacked ammo crates in place of tables.

"So," said the man, who had an army captain's bars and a paratrooper tab, "what unit are you with?"

"I'm Major Tyce Asher. Company D, 4th Light Armored Reconnaissance Battalion."

"You were nabbed by my boys pretty easily for a Marine recon-bubba."

"Well, for the record, Marine Light Armored Recon . . . Oh, never mind. Are you the OIC for this unit?"

"Commander, yes, I am the officer in charge. *Vy govorite po-russki, tovarishch?*" said Ned.

"No, I don't speak Russian."

The weightlifting soldier snapped, "You answered the commanding officer's Russian pretty quick, for a Yank."

The soldier working on the NVGs chimed in. "Yeah, and what's a Marine doing way up here in the mountains? All this way from the ocean and beach, even?"

The captain chuckled and turned back to Tyce. "Maybe Sergeant Porso has it right. What is a Marine doing this far from the coast, anyhow?"

It was clear to Tyce that the captain was at least fairly confident that Tyce was on the level and was now just having some friendly service rivalry fun at the Marine officer's expense.

"Okay, look. We can spend all night trying to prove I'm not a Russian, but we could really use your help."

The captain smiled a broad grin, and a solid gold tooth sparkled out from the front where an incisor should be. He stuck out a hand at the end of a heavily muscled arm. "Captain William Blake, sir. Everyone calls me Ned, or call sign Comanche-six. What can the 19th Special Forces do for you today, Jarhead?"

Tyce indicated that he'd shake the man's hand back, but he was still zip-tied.

"Ah. Montana, untie the men," said Ned.

After a few moments, Tyce rubbed his sore wrist and shook Ned's hand.

"What's been happening, Major?" asked Ned. "We lost all radio comms yesterday, but we've been watching foreign aircraft overhead. We set up shop here, hoping we'd get some word from upstairs, but nothing. What's the scoop?"

"Russian invasion. Total invasion. Looks like it caught everyone with their pants down. As best as we can tell, they wiped out whole reserve army and Marine units. A few as they showed up at their bases for muster. Nuked some of them and fried some of the spots where the Second Amendment weapons were being stored." Eyebrows went up around the cave, and Tyce noticed a few men leaning in to hear the news from the outside world. "You guys really haven't heard anything?"

"No, total blackout. We suspected something, but we didn't want to alert anyone to our presence. Figured we could use it to our advantage. Only our higher HQ knows we are here."

"Where's your HQ?"

"Draper, Utah. Heard anything from that far west? A lot of the guys have families."

"No . . . but we did see a huge wave of bombers headed west. They must have been loaded for bear and aiming to take out a lot of the midland bases."

"Where's our mighty air force?"

"Lots of it is was forward deployed to counter that Iran stuff. Hopefully someday, they'll come back and kick the Russians around for us, but most of the reserve and National Guard air forces were nailed on the ground. We saw only a few of them get airborne, and there's no telling if they had anything to come back to once they were done dogfighting."

Ned rubbed what looked like a few days' worth of beard stubble, thinking for a minute. "What choo got for fighting forces? I mean, you ain't some kind of troop admin pukes, are you?"

Tyce sighed. "No. We're a fighting battalion. A severely understrength battalion."

"Straight-legs?" asked Ned, using the slang for a regular infantry unit.

"Elements of my company. Delta company, Marine Corps 4th Light Armored Reconnaissance battalion. Call sign Dragoons."

"LAR, I've heard of them. Don't the straight-legs call you all *Lazy Ass Recon*?"

Tyce ignored the comment and continued, "Then we have men from B Troop, 150th Cav—"

"The armor guys?" he interrupted, "I know 'em. Good unit. Call sign Second West Virginia, right?" Ned was starting to seem impressed.

"No, they switched to 'Iron Horse,' for our exercise."

"Do they have any of their Bradley Fighting Vehicles?"

"No, unfortunately not," said Tyce with a frown, "most of the Brads were destroyed in the opening minutes. Hit by Russian attack jets while they were being trucked back up on flatbeds from our training exercise down south. We have two left. But they guzzle so much gas that their acting commander, Lieutenant Zane, put them all in Humvees and on foot. We hid the last two Brads in the woods in case we find a whole shit-ton of gas."

"Or you get in a shit sandwich. Right, sir."

Tyce was starting to get a picture of this guy. Squared away, tough and motivated, and just a bit too cocky, like most Army SF.

"And you, sir? Are you the boss man, or is there a colonel or a general or something?"

"Well . . ." said Tyce, rubbing his wrists, "That part's kind of tricky. We had a National Guard colonel in charge of our mixed-unit training. Exercise Ridge Runner."

"I've heard of the exercise. Who is the colonel?"

"An officer named Colonel David Nepo."

"Heard of him, too. Not much good, though."

"Yeah . . . well, he's missing, presumed captured. He drove into Morgantown just as the Russian paratroops assaulted the National Guard headquarters."

"The Russkies have paratroopers?" Ned smiled. "Hey men, hear that? The Marines found us some genuine Russki Spetsnaz to fight." Then he turning back to Tyce. "Sir, I've heard enough, we're in."

"Not sure I invited you yet, but—"

"Yeah, listen, sir, you're gonna need my guys. Almost all of them are card-carrying combat infantrymen. Whatever you're up to, we're glad to get out of the defensive and onto the offensive." Ned got down onto the dirt floor and cranked out twenty quick pushups, and his men hurriedly fell to the ground and followed their leader, all counting off together every third pushup with a loud "Ranger!"

He caught Tyce's amused look. "Hey, sir, if we ain't killin, we're either prayin' or workin' out, or f—"

"I get the picture, Ned," Tyce interrupted. "And . . . thanks. We could definitely use a hand."

"Okay," said Ned. Ned seemed to be big on shaking everyone's hand. Tyce took it, in spite of the fact that pebbles and small stones were still sticking to it from the special forces man's quick demonstration of bravado on the cave floor.

"If you can lead me and the chief out of here and back to Parsons, I'll have my operations officer fill you in on more of the details. I'm presuming you have your own rides?"

"Yup. We are low on fuel, though. Can you hook a brother up?"

Tyce looked over at the chief, who had been too stunned by the whole affair to speak, and now just nodded.

* * *

Tyce was worn thin by the series of seemingly unending days spent going nowhere. He sat in the corner and stared at the maps of the area his men laid out for him. Some were simple Michelin maps; others had been printed on Chief Braydon's printer, then taped together. He had to hand it to his men—they were nothing if not innovative. Still, he had a lot to consider.

It's only a matter of time, he thought. *They will want to try to get their eyes on any resistance that might be organizing. Eyes on us.*

Tyce listened while his headquarters Marines read Ned's special forces men in on the latest situation, pointing to spots on the map and discussing the small bits of details beyond their own little valley. Mostly rumors, but Ned and his men were very eager to hear any news.

While he listened, Tyce considered the overall tactical picture. The city of Parsons commanded a strategic location with its two bridges over the Cheat River and, perhaps more important, three large roads coming in from Virginia and leading through the mountains down into North Carolina. The main roads of West Virginia would, of course, be completely blocked off, so it was just a matter of time before the Russians started to explore the secondary and tertiary arteries and the country roads up into the backwoods. Parsons would be a logical starting point for these explorations. Tyce slowly tipped his stool back against the wall, all the while pondering what kind of trap they could set for a Russian scouting party.

After the briefing was over, Tyce pulled Chief Braydon aside.

"Hey, Chief. Do you have anyone who knows the local

landscape really well? Or better, a kind of fixer type of guy? Someone who is good at getting things."

"You mean like information, or stealing something?" replied the chief.

"Well, both, I guess."

"Thought your boys were masters of reconnaissance."

"Yeah, not the kind I'm looking for. I need a civilian. But someone who can think on his feet."

"What did you have in mind?"

"Kind of a one-man reconnaissance. I want someone to infiltrate the National Guard base in Morgantown."

"Okay. Got it. Your guys would be too obvious, and one of my mountain men might also be too obvious. A yokel poking around Morgantown would make about as much sense as a Marine eighteen-year-old with a high-n-tight."

"You got it."

"Hmm . . . Well, I think I have just the man for the job."

"Excellent. When can I speak to him?"

"Hmm . . ."

"If he's too far away, I can send some of my men to get him."

"No. He's not far. In fact, he's right here."

"Here in Parsons, excellent. Why the reticence?"

"No, he's right here in my headquarters."

"Oh, you mean you, Chief?" said Tyce, a look of incredulity on his face. "We'd be privileged to have your assistance, but I thought you were committed to the town and couldn't leave for military purposes."

"No," the chief smiled. "Not me. But he is right here in my station. In fact, he's right downstairs. In my jail. Caught him with a load of weapons and explosives. We were going to charge him with looting, but you're welcome to use him,

I suppose. I guess I'll have to help you break him out of my own jail . . ." he trailed off, an unhappy smirk on his face.

Tyce's expression fell, too. A jailbird. Not quite the bona fides he'd been hoping for.

CHAPTER 15

Tyce and SSgt. Diaz followed the chief through the police department HQ, their garage, and down to the Parsons jail. SSgt. threw her machine gun over her shoulder, a belt of ammo hanging out, her muscles bulging. "Hey, sir, follow my lead with this guy. I've dealt with prison types before."

"You've been to prison, Diaz?" he asked, but from her expression, he immediately regretted asking. As her boss, he shouldn't worry much about her past. "Sorry, probably stuff you don't want to talk about."

"Nah, I don't care. Just brings back some sour memories of my days before the Corps straightened me out. I've been to prison more times than you can count."

Tyce eyed her up. Obviously, there was a lot he still didn't know about his troops.

She smiled. "Not me personally, sir. Though, I've had more than a few, ahem, brushes with the law. No, my ex went up the river."

Tyce looked at her quizzically.

"Oh, I forget you don't know shit about New York. 'Up the river' means Sing Sing."

"Sing Sing? The prison? I thought that was just in the movies."

"Nope. It's a state pen. Those electric fences hold back

some of the worst criminal minds in New York. And it's very much open for business. Bursting at the seams, in fact. Or at least it was last time I checked. Hopefully the Russians keep the guards. You don't want my ex, or any of his gang, or even guys like him out of jail. They belong in the hoosegow. Trust me, if they let those guys out, we'll have a lot more to worry about than the Russians."

When they got to the basement, the chief unlocked the big steel door and pointed to the back. The only man in the detention cell was lying on his side, his wrists bound, his back to them.

Diaz approached first, lowering her weapon to her hip in a menacing fashion.

"Hey cell warrior, heard you got popped with some hot swag. Where'd you strap the dinner gongs?" Diaz's rapid switch to full street demeanor coupled with a renewed emphasis on her Big Apple accent, Tyce was surprised to find he could barely understand her.

The man didn't turn, but he responded in a deep Southern drawl. "Took 'em off a dead Russkie, Bronx. He didn't need 'em no more, and I fig'red I could find a good use for 'em," the man said, as nonchalantly as if he were retelling an old war story in a bar.

Tyce had seen the man's mangled motorcycle in the garage before coming down to the basement. It was riddled with bullet holes and badly crumpled, and the man himself looked like he'd hit the pavement. *This dude is damned lucky to be alive*, thought Tyce.

"Did you bitch and run?" asked Diaz.

"Nah. Russians popped some caps. Did you see my bike?"

"So, you bitched out." teased Diaz further.

Tyce gave her a look as if to tell her to knock it off and get back to their purpose.

"Anyhow, I ain't talking, unless you gonna buy me a new cycle?" the man said. Obviously the motorcycle had meant a lot to him.

SSgt. Diaz knelt down beside him, pulled out her combat knife, and cut the zip tie free. Tyce looked on dubiously. She kept her weapon toward the man as he slowly rose up from the steel bench, eying them both.

"What's your name?"

"Wynand."

"Just Wynand?"

"Yep."

"Okay, Wynand. Just how handy are you on motorcycles?"

"Been riding one since I was fifteen." Wynand rubbed his skinned elbows and looked SSgt. Diaz up and down, then over to Tyce, "What's with the She-Hulk? She actually in the military, or do you just keep her around to chew nails and spit horseshoes?"

"*She* is most definitely in the military," Diaz spat out. "Has been for over thirteen years."

Tyce glanced at SSgt. Diaz, who glared angrily at Wynand and fingered the trigger of her weapon. Many still didn't believe females could serve in the infantry. SSgt. Diaz was not just an exceptionally fit Marine, though; she also thought quickly on her feet and employed her machine gun section with precision.

"Look," Tyce interrupted. The gang-like posturing was not going anywhere, "I'm going to cut right to the chase. I need a scout. Someone who can think and act quickly, who can go below the radar and get some information for us."

"I didn't escape your dragnet, boss man. What makes

you think I can help you recon the baddies? Assuming that's what you're after."

"Call me a good judge of character. I need someone who can get in and out and get me the lay of the land in Morgantown. Mostly, someone to find out if the Russians have arrived in strong enough numbers that they can start pushing their forces into the mountains to look for the likes of us. Would you be willing?"

"Depends."

"Ah, yes. You probably want a new motorcycle. What would you say if I got you a nice BMW cruiser from the police impound lot?"

"I'd say forget it . . . I only ride 'Merican-made iron. Harleys."

"Okay, make it a Harley, then."

"Dyna or a Fat Boy. I won't take anything smaller than twelve hundred CCs." Even incarcerated, Wynand seemed pretty slick at sniffing out a deal.

"Deal. In fact, just to make sure you don't run off with your new ride, I'll even give you the Russian weapons back when you return. And maybe even a little more."

"Wait. You're sending me to recon Russians with no weapons?"

"Yup."

Wynand scratched his head, contemplating the deal. Tyce couldn't be certain, but it looked like he was also plotting how he'd get away from Tyce and Diaz as soon as possible. Tyce hoped he'd settle on the best, most logical conclusion: do the job, get some free stuff, and *then* run.

"Okay. I'm in. Where do I pick up the wheels?"

"You can ride with me to the impound lot. I'll brief you on the way and show you what we know about the

Russians, but more importantly what we still really need to know about their composition, disposition, and strength."

"Planning on launching an attack?"

"Well . . . that's need to know, Wynand. But if you have the stomach for it, I could use you beyond just reconning the Russians."

"Got it, boss man. I'm in . . . for a bit. What's say you lemme have some heat. A shotgun, a pistol. Something for my own protection."

"For your sake, I think you'd be better off unarmed. If they capture you with a weapon, especially with one of the Russian weapons we caught you with, I'm pretty certain they won't be as understanding as we were."

Just then, one of the men, Corporal Keller raced in, practically out of breath, "Hey, sir, the eastern blocking force has a few military vehicles stopped."

"Okay, good. We could definitely add some more fighting power to our ranks." Tyce thought rapidly. Maybe it was Colonel Nepo finally coming to take back charge of his unit. "What kind of vehicles? Trucks? Anything with some armor would be a welcome surprise."

"Uh, no, sir. They said it was a couple o' ambulances."

"Ambulances? What—military hospital ambulances?"

"Yes, sir, and that's not all. The head . . . uuuh . . . person in charge is ordering the men around at the checkpoint. Yelling at them and such. They say it's . . . like, a navy admiral."

"What the hell. Navy hospital personnel . . ." Tyce shook his head in disbelief.

Wynand spoke up, "Looks like your troubles are just starting, my friend."

"About right. Let's go get you over to Gunny for a briefing, and I'll go check out the latest crisis."

* * *

Tyce arrived at the eastern blocking force in less than ten minutes after dropping off Wynand, but looking through his Humvee windshield, he could see things were still pretty heated. Three personnel in U.S. Navy utility uniforms were lambasting his men. For the most part, the men didn't seem to be standing up for themselves, and in short order Tyce could tell why. Their leader was a curvy female in a well-fitting uniform who not only had her fiery temper on display in full force, but was also completely disregarding his men's orders to get back to her vehicle. She was forcefully and effectively holding off their attempts to zip-tie her and put her and her sailors in the containment area as they were ordered to do with any new arrivals.

Tyce walked over, and before he could speak, she took notice of him and pushed one of his Marines aside. "Are you in charge of these . . . these . . . infants? 'Cause I'm here to tell you, this is some real bullshit. Have you not trained your men to recognize and respect a U.S. Navy uniform?"

Tyce saw the rank insignia of a U.S. Navy lieutenant commander on her collar, the equivalent of Tyce's Marine Corps rank of major. He held up a hand to wave back the men, who were still trying to get her and her sailors to comply with the roadblock and vehicle search procedures.

"Lieutenant Commander . . ."

"Remington," she said, pointing to the name tape on her breast pocket. Tyce refrained from looking down at her name tape and tried to maintain eye contact.

Instead, he replied, "Look. We've had a lot to worry about in the last day or two, and you can't fault my men for being cautious. Now, what, can I ask, is a U.S. Navy medical team doing up here in the woods?"

"Haven't you heard?"

"Heard what?"

"D.C. is . . ."

Tyce's eyebrows went up, shocked he was talking to someone who might bring news from the capital.

"Yes?" he said, mentally preparing to hear that D.C. had been nuked.

"Captured. Taken over. The Russians have seized D.C. and the Pentagon, the whole area, and are installing the secretary of state as the new President of the United States. They were rounding up all the troops, anyone in uniform. So I . . . we . . . well, we fled. We figured there might be some kind of resistance forming, and we aimed to make ourselves useful."

Tyce was shocked but not surprised to hear that D.C. had fallen, but he still had more pressing concerns. He figured someone else would have to deal with D.C. With the Russians on all sides of the Blue Ridge Mountains, Tyce was virtually surrounded. It made sense though. Of course they would seize D.C. Probably used some of their best troops for that.

That gave Tyce a thought, though, *It might mean the troops in Morgantown were not their best. Hopefully bottom-of-the-barrel leaders, too.*

After all, there were about ten or twenty other military bases, state capitals, and other industrial centers Tyce could think of—just off the top of his head—that were more important than their little neck of the woods. That might just be their greatest advantage. As he contemplated the situation, things gradually become clearer.

"Okay," Tyce started, "you can join us. We could very

much use some medical assistance based on what we're planning to do."

"Wait," she said, hands on hips. "Who the hell said I wanted to *join* you?"

"You said you were looking for the resistance. Well, I'd say you found them . . . us."

She gave Tyce a derisive look from head to toe. "You? You're the resistance?"

"So? The U.S. Marine Corps isn't good enough for you, Miss?"

"So, it's Commander, Dr. Remington, or Victoria to my friends. Which you are not."

Tyce sighed. He could use less of the sarcasm, but he was becoming used to it. That made two women who seemed very quick to try to put him in his place. Unfortunately for him, both seemed to have succeeded.

Last thing I need, he thought, *more fiery women who would rather banter than focus on more pressing matters.*

Even in times of war, the military keeps up a jocular banter, sometimes harshly so—whether to keep sane or to ensure the pecking order was still intact, constantly challenging those in leadership seemed to be a caveman-like response. It was just as present here as it was in locker rooms and athletic fields around the world.

"Okay, I get it. You are one tough cookie, but I have a regiment of Marines and soldiers . . . at least, what's left of one. For what it's worth, we are ready and armed, and we intend to take the fight to the enemy."

She eyed him again, this time with dubious pursed lips and furrowed brow. "I guess I was expecting, like, a general, or a tank commander, or something."

"Tanks wouldn't be of too much use up here in the

mountains . . . Vicky." Tyce smiled. He had absorbed enough heat, and thought he'd better toss a bit back.

"Definitely never Vicky . . ." She glared.

"Look. I think we can help each other." Tyce glanced past Victoria at her two medical Humvee ambulances. "Are those fully stocked?"

"With a full field surgery," she said proudly.

"Do you know how to work a full field surgery?" now it was his turn to be a little dubious. She certainly didn't look like any surgeon he'd met. Most navy surgeons were stuffy old men who wore beady, odd-color-framed glasses and had little in the way of a bedside manner, or even any real people skills. She seemed quite the opposite.

"Yes. And I've taken care of plenty of your *boys* down-range in both Iraq and Afghanistan."

"Good enough for me. Let's cease fire. Saddle up—you and your troops follow me to our headquarters."

She motioned for her sailors to mount up, but couldn't resist one more barb. "*You* have a headquarters?" A phony skeptical expression on her face.

Tyce was deciding whether to ignore the remark when a Marine radio operator ran over with a yellow canary—a sort of military callback slip for radios. It was from Gunny: "Mr. Wynand has been briefed and given detailed instructions of zones where we need intel in Morgantown. Request permission for him to depart friendly lines."

Tyce nodded to the radio operator. "Affirm. Tell Gunny permission granted."

Tyce watched Victoria order her sailors around. They were cooperating. Now that the dust had settled, she even looked to be getting some help from some of Tyce's Marines.

What am I getting myself into, bringing in noncombatants? A navy medical officer and her sailors. And now sending a civilian into harm's way. Tyce thought. He was getting in deep, and that made his stomach crawl.

He had considered sending one or more of his men to recon the city and roads in a civilian vehicle, but as far as he knew, everyone was still playing by the rules. He wasn't about to be responsible for being the first to break the Geneva Convention, getting his men publicly shot—or worse, hanged—for conducting reconnaissance out of their uniforms. And likely cause a lot of other rule-breaking from the Russians in response.

Later, they just might have to break the rules, but for now, it would be stupid to even show up on the Russians' radar. As far as they knew, he didn't exist. They were ghosts in the hills, and he needed to keep things that way for the time being. He knew that the enemy had tremendous firepower, while he was struggling just to get ahold of some more ammunition.

Not exactly in the Marine Corps playbook, but war is war, he thought. *And Wynand has a better chance of developing some useful intelligence than any of my Marines or soldiers.*

CHAPTER 16

Parsons

"There's no doubt about it, boss man. They are coming. And if my guess is right, their main force will be here in about ten or twelve hours. Can't be sure, but there were some smaller groups, too. Look to be sweeping through all the mountain roads." said Wynand.

"All in military vehicles?"

"Best I could tell."

"Armament?"

"Jeep-looking things, rifles and machine guns. A few mini tanks with wheels."

"BTRs . . . " said Tyce, thumbing his chin and lost for a moment in thought.

"They don't look like they 'spect much. Just cruisin'."

Tyce and the others gathered around a big map of Tucker County on the sheriff's office wall. Their group included a few of the new additions—Captain Ned Blake and his senior troops. The operations staff had stuck little red pins representing the enemy into the map based on the last spot Wynand had given them. The intelligence officers had been calculating the rates of march of each of the various trucks and Russian armored cars. From Wynand's report, it sounded like their main vehicles were the GAZ

Tigr, similar to a Humvee, and the BTR-90, a fearsome armed and armored car with a big 30mm cannon.

The intelligence chief looked up at Tyce and nodded. "That's about right. Twelve hours if they're scanning and searching, ten if they're hoofing it."

"Okay." Tyce looked around. "Captain Blake, I want to slow them down. Give us time to prepare. We set up an ambush to the south." Tyce pointed to the likely road they'd take based on Wynand's reports, "Dig in and hit them hard from the flanks. Something akin to what the Taliban used to do to us in Afghanistan." Most troops in the makeshift HQ, except the youngest who had never been deployed to war, nodded their understanding.

It's good to have some battle-hardened warriors in the mix, thought Tyce. *We have some instant understanding and standard operating procedures from our shared experience of fighting counterinsurgency all over the Middle East.*

Tyce wondered if they would be too overbearing for the local constabulary. The police chief and the town's sheriff had never really dealt with this many troops before.

Let alone actual combat, Tyce thought.

Gunny leaned in. "What are you thinking, sir?"

"Hmm . . ." said Tyce, foreboding thoughts of getting citizens to work with soldiers shattered for the moment. "I'll tell you what I'm thinking. Draw them in, then double ambush. One outside the city, about a mile and a half north. Just something to whet their appetite. I want them to get a taste, but then I want them to send in a lot of toys for the second ambush. Something deep in the mountains." He pointed to a spot on the map. "This valley. Harman Valley. It has good roads and good woods. The first ambush will also delay them so we can set up a shitstorm at the second. They won't fuck with us for a while if we can whip 'em good."

"If they don't send in a whole tank corps to deal with us."

"The mayor's not gonna like a plan that drags her town into a lot of death and carnage, Major," said Chief Braydon, who was sitting nearby and listening as Tyce presented his plan.

"Well, I don't see we have a choice. We can see this as an opportunity, or we can see this as a problem. In either case, the Russians will most certainly come to Parsons."

"I'll be honest with you all. We don't want any Russians here, and we don't want you here, either. We can manage just fine by ourselves. Off the grid and unnoticed is our preference."

"Chief, unless I'm missing something, we're at war. We have been invaded. We're all already involved."

"And so now it's martial law?"

"I didn't say that."

"But that's what you're implying. I think if you intend to turn Parsons into a war zone, Mayor Susanna needs to be informed."

"We won't fight in the city. And that's fine, you can inform her once we've worked through the plan. We don't have a lot of time to sit around talking about it, though. In ten hours, Russians are going to be crawling all over the place, and I don't think they'll treat you all any different than they'll treat us."

"Why don't you leave that kind of figuring up to me and the mayor? You don't have a right to endanger the citizens of the town."

"Damn it, Chief." Tyce's blood was boiling, and in a rare display his temper flared. "What are you not understanding? We are at war. Our country has been invaded."

"That's so. But it sure as shit ain't every man's duty to fight back. We ain't all warriors."

"But we are all at war—"

"Is that it? That's what you want, Major? Citizens dying left and right?" He shook his head and looked around the room at some of the citizens who had now joined Tyce. "You can have your mix 'n match army. Just remember, some of us are here to serve the people, not to serve in war."

"First, that's not the implication, either, Chief."

Wynand interrupted. "You want a free-for-all, Chief?" He pointed to Tyce. "How about you, Major? Because that's what's fixin' to happen." Wynand laughed a wicked laugh. "Suits me just fine. Every man for hisself."

As things started to heat up, three of the chief's deputies came over from the dispatch room to listen in. Tyce's Marines and soldiers started to pull to one side of the room, some with unslung weapons. This didn't go unnoticed among the deputies, who also pulled back to the side of the large office, their hands instinctively going to the tops of their holsters. Even Trigger seemed to know they had a bit of a Mexican standoff, and he started barking and growling at the chief. This made matters worse.

"Control your mutt," the chief shouted.

"He's not a mutt, you asshole. He's a combat fighting dog, and apparently he's got bigger balls than you." said SSgt. Diaz.

The chief snarled and started to unholster his pistol.

Tyce could see things were quickly escalating out of control. This would end badly for all. Knowing full well he needed public support, and certainly support from the town of Parsons, he sighed heavily and took a different tack.

Holding up his hand and pushing his carbine around behind him in a disarming gesture, he said, "Okay. Look.

We are in this together. We, meaning Americans, have a duty to our country. Your duty is different from mine and my men's duty, but we cannot allow the Russians to win the day by taking over the city of Parsons and forcing all of us to retreat farther into the mountains. Sheriff, there are no good paths forward. The war is about to come to your fair city, like it or not. But I have an idea. What if we set up for a hit-and-run?"

"What good does that do? You're still planning on killing Russians in my backyard, and you can't tell me that they won't hold me and my citizens responsible for your actions."

"Not if we do it right. I just might have an idea on how we can both get what we need from our initial encounter with them."

"I'm all ears, Major, but whatever we decide, it's still gotta go to Mayor Susanna before I say yes."

"We have some time. Let me go over the idea. If you and the mayor don't like it, me and my troops will ske-daddle from Parsons, and you won't have to worry about us. The Russians, yes, but not us."

"Okay, but it better be a big ol' whopper of an idea."

The tension in the room seemed to ease, and the troops and the deputies returned peacefully—albeit still a bit on edge—back to the board to hear Tyce's plan.

CHAPTER 17

Parsons

Three minivans stopped abruptly about two hundred meters in front of a checkpoint the Marines and police had set up on Route 72, just north of Parsons, to query local traffic. The Marines stiffened and moved to cover, but the police deputies, inexperienced in warfare, moved too slowly. When the first burst of 7.62mm rifle fire blasted into their midst, everyone dove behind their hasty barricade of cut logs and abandoned cars.

One deputy wasn't fast enough and took two rounds as he dove for cover—one to the thigh, and the other to his neck. He was dead before his body hit the ground. The gun battle that followed was fierce and fast. Not having anticipated this confrontation, two of the three vehicles accelerated backward and hightailed it back to the north. The other was riddled with bullet holes. Wisps of grey smoke indicated something was smoldering under the hood.

The sudden sound of gunfire was audible all the way back in Parsons. The chief and Tyce jumped to their feet. A few frantic moments followed as the radio operators tried to establish communications. It was only a few minutes, but it seemed as though time passed in slow motion, like a lifetime before the firefight ended.

Tyce was about to bolt out to his Humvee to check for himself when the radio call finally came in. It was a weary-sounding Marine. Tyce glanced at the duty roster they had drawn up on the chief's dry-erase board to see who it was. The whole board was covered with names of seasoned NCOs. Men he and the others had trained alongside for a good bit, and now were getting to know by name. The report was two casualties: one killed in action, a police deputy, and one Marine wounded in action.

Tyce grabbed the radio handset. "Did you get all of them? What was their disposition and strength?"

The NCO's weary voice came back again. As with many of Tyce's men, this was his first real gunfight, and he was apparently suffering from the immediate fatigue that overcame most once the shooting stopped.

"No, sir. We got one carload, but the other two got away."

"Damn!" said Tyce, looking at his watch. It had only been four hours and they just weren't ready. "They found us already. No time for anything fancy. We gotta punch 'em hard."

The chief stared back at him in wild-eyed disbelief. Maybe he never actually expected the Russians to materialize in any force. He certainly didn't expect them to be there before the time line they'd predicted.

Tyce was a little more resilient to the ever-shifting tides of battle, "Possibly a routine forward reconnaissance patrol checking the roads, but damn it," Tyce said again to the chief.

He calmed his tone, then got back on the radio. "Okay, copy. I understand two enemy vics escaped and are now headed north along your route . . . Route 72?" Tyce said.

"That's affirm, sir."

"Vics?" asked the chief.

"Short for 'Victor.' It's a military term for 'vehicle.'"

Tyce turned to the chief's ready reactionary force. They had consolidated two half belts of .50 caliber rounds and about half a magazine of M16 ammunition for each of the four-man vehicles. The quick reaction force, called the QRF, included a police deputy squad car with two deputies. Tyce would add everyone else he could get ahold of at short notice. He hadn't seen Ned's men in a while. He sent someone to track him down and send him to the command post.

"Chief, I want to send out the QRF and anyone else we can grab. Nothing too willy-nilly or we'll overwhelm ourselves with confusion, and we'll brief them on the fly. You got any thoughts?"

"Let's send 'em. But I want to go with my officers. This is all new territory for them . . . and for me. Just in case they're actually some crazy-ass civilians, you'll want me there to calm the thing down."

"Agreed. There's bound to be something coming to investigate what we did to their men. We need to try to overpower them and buy us some more time. I'll go with my vehicle. If you take the lead, I'll take middle. I'm betting you and your boys know the roads a hell of a lot better than we do. Especially at night."

The men grabbed their flak jackets, rifles, and helmets.

"Men, get ready, right now. Hasty ambush. North side of town."

Captain Blake rushed in and Tyce pointed at him, "You ready?"

"Born ready."

"Find me an ambush site, trooper. Someplace north of

town that favors us. I'll pin the Russian reactionary unit down, you close with them and destroy them, copy."

"I'm good, sir. Me and my boys can handle it," answered Ned.

Tyce grabbed Gunny and gave him instructions to get ready to pack up the whole show. Whatever happened next, there was one thing for certain; their rest and recuperation time had come to an end.

The chief's men had riot gear, and what they still needed, especially flak jackets, Tyce supplied. They were equipped and out the door in less than three minutes. A few minutes later, every man had checked his guns, mounted up, and they were off. Tyce hoped to hell it wasn't just a bunch of locals taking advantage of the situation to settle some old scores. The last report was not very reliable, something about gun-toting minivans was about all that he understood.

"Well, Major, looks like you got your ambush. And a lot sooner than you wanted it, and on the wrong side of the city. I sure as shit hope you don't blast half the town away in the process. Mayor Susanna will have your ass in a wicker basket," said the chief as they departed the station.

The Russian captain watched the first of his vehicles taking the mountain curves with speed and a smooth precision. It had taken him less than forty-five minutes to get his men moving, and another two hours to close in on Parsons. In the lead was an armored personnel carrier called the BTR-90. He could see the BTR's turret, its 30mm cannon on top scanning the hillside ahead for trouble. He highly doubted there was anything in these backwoods that could stop a BTR, one of Russia's premium assault vehicles.

The captain in charge of this reactionary force was actually a sapper, one of the engineers that was supposed to go find mines or plant them. The West Virginia district command had sent out an alert when one of the reconnaissance patrols had called in that they'd been shot at. Not exactly what they thought they would be doing during the American invasion. But hey, at least he wasn't sitting in their headquarters—the West Virginia University Coliseum—building shitters and mess tents, waiting for something to happen.

As for all the soldiers in his distributed battalion from the 30th Sappers, the invasion of America and Morgantown was boring. The town was squeezed between rivers and a low mountain range, and there hadn't been much action yet. No real resistance. The only thing they'd done since they'd off-loaded from the transport aircraft at the municipal airport was a few patrols and a lot of sitting in the Coliseum waiting to be called out to assist any of the infantry units that were in the process of rounding up potential dissidents.

Now, finally, it looked like something might have happened. The intelligence provided by their combat operations center said there might be a few overly patriotic cops or some rogue U.S. Army reservists in the hills. Someone got in a shootout and one vehicle was missing. Although from the confused reports, it was more likely the missing vehicle and soldiers had gone too far into the hills and outrun their radios and their fuel. It had already happened a few times, causing unnecessary excitement back at his HQ.

Fuel seemed to be scarcer than they had been briefed in their planning. They'd been told all they needed to do was to go find "the guy with the keys" and they could use the fuel everywhere. Trouble was . . . most of the fuel guys were in hiding, and the gas stations they were able to break into didn't have enough for their thirsty military vehicles. So much had been used up just driving around the confusing U.S. city streets and country roads. So far, America was a *lot* bigger than the captain had expected.

Suddenly, a light flashed ahead, around the bend. Looked almost like a lightning strike at first, but then came the familiar *pop-pop* of gunfire.

Ah, so the hillbillies and woodsmen want to play, huh? Thought the captain with a disparaging smile as he reached down to unlatch his AK-74 rifle from its holder. With his other hand, he grabbed the radio and transmitted back to base.

"Headquarters, headquarters. This is reactionary element leader. I'm at sector *ekho*-three," he glanced at his map which had been broken into zones, "correction, *ekho*-seven and have sight of some resistance. We will sweep it aside and radio back."

"We understand. Do you need any assistance?" the response was weak and barely audible, such was the height of the mountains blocking his radio transmissions, but he got the gist of it.

"Nyet." He'd fought some pockets of resistance before. Twos and threes with shotguns, mostly. Mountain men who thought they could put up a good fight, but once they received the withering fire his men could lay down, they surrendered or ran in fear. "It is more of the American hillbillies. I will establish better communications once we are mission complete."

Night became day as the BTR sprayed the opposite hill with 30mm, high-explosive incendiary cannon fire. The volume of fire was impressive. Tyce watched as red and yellow bursts slammed into rocks, sending flashes of sparks that sprayed into the pines and set them on fire. Four more vehicles raced up, one troop truck and three GAZ Tigrs, and formed a line beside the BTR. Each vehicle was up-gunned, and the Russians in the turret ring began spraying the hill with their own machine guns. The Marines and soldiers on the far hill slowed their rate of fire, and then ceased altogether as the incoming Russian fire became too much for them to answer.

The radio in Tyce's Humvee came to life. "Um . . . Commander, Commander, this is Main." Tyce's first thought before answering was *I organized things at my temporary command post pretty well, but I am not the commanding officer of the 150th regiment, nor have I been assigned a call sign across the units, so no one knows what to call me on the radio.* But since his was a composite unit, he was, for all intents and purposes, the acting commander of the regiment. At least, until the colonel could be found.

"Main, this is Dragoon-six, send your traffic." He erred on the side of using his usual call sign from his old Marine reconnaissance unit versus making the assumption that he was, indeed, the regiment's boss. He figured that some of the army guys might take offense at a Marine simply assuming he was their commander, and not just in the interim. He knew that there were egos involved and protocol to deal with, in spite of the ongoing Russian attack.

Anyhow, not a lot of time to worry about these things, he thought, *but no one will know who's-who in the zoo if I don't figure it out.*

"Copy, Dragoon-six. The hospital . . . um . . . commander is here, and she wants to know why she wasn't informed about the inbound casualties."

The radio went silent, then Victoria's voice came on the radio. "Hey, Racoon six. This is some real fucked-up bullshit back here. Need to know the nature of your casualties so we can get the operating room ready. Your main CP here tells me you have one fallen Angel and one priority medevac, is that correct?"

Tyce realized in his haste that they had indeed neglected to let Commander Remington and her navy surgery team know anything they were up to, including the inbound wounded man. He'd have to remember to keep her informed in the future. Men could lose their lives if the medical personnel were not prepped for action, and keeping them up to date was firmly Tyce's job. He also made a mental note to try to teach Commander Remington some radio network etiquette, or "netiquette," as it was often called affectionately. She seemed to enjoy using profanity and was pretty liberal with the jokes. Maybe she thought it made her sound tough, but it was not how Marines spoke on their radios. As the old saying went: "Just the facts, ma'am, just the facts."

"Copy, our Main should be able to fill you in. We'll keep you better informed. We are setting up now. Dragoon-six, out."

"STP six copies." Victoria was using the call sign "STP" for shock-trauma-platoon and the number "six" which was used to designate a particular call-sign as the commander, in this case, Victoria.

Makes sense, thought Tyce. *Lots of protocol I'll have to sort out with her later.*

But right now, he was trying to hang on to the dashboard as his Humvee driver, seemingly determined to hit every bump and pothole, raced behind the chief's cruiser.

Maybe it was a combination of the chief's knowledge of the roads, or maybe the initial firefight had damaged their vehicles enough to slow them down, but just when Tyce considered giving up the chase, the chief radioed from the front.

"Hey, Marines. We've got two vehicles coming around the bend in our headlights. Gunny says we should hit them with the sirens and the searchlight. I suspect they'll try to accelerate or open fire. Now's your chance."

"Okay. Once you light them up, pull right onto the shoulder and get into some cover."

"What about the squad cars?"

"Sacrifice the cars, save your men." Tyce practically shouted through the radio.

CHAPTER 18

Parsons

Tyce's radio came back to life after what seemed like an endless pause. He couldn't get to a spot to see without turning around the bend and exposing his group to the oncoming Russians.

"Dragoon-six, Dragoon-six, this is Dragoon-nine-nine," said Gunny, using both of their military call signs. Tyce could hear explosive rounds detonating in the background. Then, a second later, the sound of the bursts echoed across the valley.

"Nine, this is six, send it," said Tyce.

"Roger, they've got us pretty well pinned down. The squad cars are a total wreck, all on fire . . . my Humvee, too."

"Copy, we'll get you a replacement. Keep everyone low. Gotta hit 'em now. Break, break." Tyce took his finger off the handset and paused for a fraction of a second, then keyed again. "Assault element. You are clear, attack time now!" It had all been so hasty, Tyce began a small prayer that Ned had done what he'd asked and more, used a little battlefield intuition to maneuver.

Captain Blake's voice came over in a clean and crisp but hushed tenor. "Copy. Here we go!"

Tyce dismounted from his Humvee and he and his men

crawled up the small rise and watched through night vision goggles just as Captain Blake and his soldiers stepped out from behind cover and sprinted toward the BTR-90, truck, and Tigrs. Thankfully, all seemed fixated on the police car lights and were blazing away. It had all been a cheap and hasty attempt to focus the Russians and Tyce had banked on the Russian commander being too inexperienced to keep an eye on his "six," or his backside.

Blake and his men were essentially soundless; the continuous chatter of the Russian machine guns and the booming of 30mm cannon as they reduced the cop cars and Humvee to smoking hulks muted their entire approach behind the Russians.

Just as Tyce had calculated, in their lust to attack what they believed were a pocket of mountain men and cops, the Russians had posted no rearward security, and Blake's men crawled the ten-meter distance in a few seconds, completely undetected. It was an extremely risky endeavor; they were completely exposed, none of them were wearing body armor, or even helmets. Captain Blake said the protective gear would slow them down too much. Tyce expected one of the Russians to turn at any moment and spray Captain Blake and his men with machine gun fire, but no, the Russians were too intent on covering their own men's advance against Gunny's forces on the hillside.

Tyce watched through his night vision goggles as six grenades' pins were pulled and six high-grade kerosene Molotov cocktails were lit, and all were lofted high into the air. The cloth wicks of the Molotovs traced yellow streaks up into the night air. Ned's men didn't wait around to see them land. They sprinted back like wide receivers with clear paths to the safety of the end zone.

Tyce clenched his jaw as he watched the plan unfolding.

"Hurry, *hurry*," he breathed quietly to himself, pumping his fist. His other hand held his carbine steady against a fallen log he'd jumped behind for cover. Even though he was now Ned's commander, he still felt the urge to share the danger experienced by his men.

Captain Blake and his men hurled themselves the last few meters, diving for cover just as the Molotovs burst, spilling their flaming liquid onto and down the turrets of the Russian vehicles. A moment later, the grenades detonated one by one up and around the Russian vehicles.

The out-of-breath voice of Captain Blake came over the radio. "Dragoon-six, we're clear."

Tyce didn't respond over the radio, instead yelling "Open fire!" at the top of his lungs.

Next to him, SSgt. Diaz and her machine gun platoon had just made it into position and opened up with the two .50 caliber machine guns and two M240 medium machine guns. Each gun had only one belt of about sixty rounds. It was their only remaining machine gun ammunition.

Tyce shielded his NVGs from the huge flare as the explosions briefly turned night turned into day. Putting the M4 carbine to his shoulder, he and the other riflemen down the small hillock began picking off individual Russians as the machine gunners raked the vehicle crew's cabs. In the small valley below, it looked like the earth had opened up into a volcano of fire. Vehicles and humans burned, ammo and fuel detonated, adding to the tumult and cacophony of battle. Ricochets from the heavy guns tore chunks of concrete from the road. Splinters of steel from the shredded vehicles cartwheeled in the air, dealing multiple death blows to the Russians.

Almost as soon as it had begun, the firing slowed down

to a few sporadic shots as the warriors next to Tyce and
Ned's men picked off individual targets with their rifles.
Tyce looked over, and in the flicker of the fires from the
burning vehicles, he could see SSgt. Diaz racing between
her four machine guns, checking them over and assisting
her section. Tyce hoped they had spared a little ammo, but
he was pretty certain in the rush of battle, they'd used it
all. They needed to be sure they killed the Russians down
to the last man.

Dead men tell no tales, thought Tyce as he watched a
burning Russian take two bullets to his torso and collapse,
still on fire. *A gruesome death, but they wouldn't have afforded us any better. War is hell, in so many ways.*

Suddenly, the BTR started moving. Its engine whined at
a high pitch, presumably stuck in a lower gear. Three of the
tires were burning, but it looked like none of the kerosene
from the Molotovs had made it into the crew compartment,
though a few of the .50 caliber rounds must've caused some
slight mechanical damage.

"Shit! Shit!" shouted Tyce, his voice, louder than he'd
intended, echoing over the suddenly silent valley.

"I've got it, sir!" yelled SSgt. Diaz from down the way.

Tyce looked over to see SSgt. Diaz sitting behind one of
her machine guns. Looks like she had saved some rounds
for just such a contingency after all, and she opened up with
perfect accuracy into the rear of the vehicle. Tyce and the
rest of the men stared at her, illuminated from the sparks
of her muzzle flashes, her biceps quivering as she fired
round after round into the BTR. About half her shots
seemed to be having an effect. At any other angle they
probably wouldn't penetrate, but Diaz clearly knew where
to hit the vehicle and make it count. Wisely, she fired at the

flat sides that presented themselves instead of the sloping sides, which would increase her odds of a ricochet.

In spite of this, after a few bursts, SSgt. Diaz stopped firing. She looked at Tyce and shook her head. She was out of ammo. Still, the hits had an effect. The vehicle's driver, in a frenzy to get away and unable to steer, his vision possibly blinded by multiple fires atop his vehicle, plowed willy-nilly into the burning Tigrs and trucks, running over everything in his path, including a few still-burning Russian soldiers. Rubber tires on fire, the BTR blazed a path toward Gunny's position, but then skidded down the ravine and crashed sideways into the icy waters of the Cheat River.

Gunny and his men had been keeping low to avoid getting caught in the crossfire, but now he came over the radio and asked permission to pop up. Tyce ordered a cease-fire on his side of the valley since they were facing a little too directly toward Gunny and told his men to stay down. After a short time, the top of the BTR opened. It must have been flooding with water, and the survivors inside had made the choice to die a freezing, drowning death or take their chances against the Americans.

Three men from the back and the driver leapt from the BTR and shot wildly in Tyce's direction, possibly disoriented from the crash, or possibly still thinking that the wrath of SSgt's machine gun was an ongoing threat. The Russians each got a few rounds off. Gunny, chief and his men rushed forward and responded with precision shots, taking each of the enemies out with one or two accurate bullets. The last man fell into the river with his finger apparently stuck on the trigger, bursts of 7.62mm still firing as he fell off the vehicle and continuing once he dropped facedown into the water, sinking rapidly in his heavy gear. Tyce could see the chief standing up on the embankment above the river firing his pistol into the BTR and anything else that caught his eye.

Didn't take him long to 'get some,' thought Tyce.

He'd seen it a hundred times before. The rush of adrenaline in a battle made some men cowards and other men conquerors. At least until the adrenaline wore off and they realized what they'd done.

A gruesome end to the battle. All of it remained hellishly illuminated by the Molotov-induced and still-burning gas and tire fires on the Russian vehicles.

Tyce lifted his head up from the trench, picked up the radio, and transmitted to his troops, "All stations, all stations, this is Dragoon-six. We'll go in and check the area. Gunny, keep us covered, but watch your shots. Once I give the all clear, I want everyone picking up any serviceable weapons and all the ammo you can find."

Looting the dead was frowned upon. American weapons and ammo were not compatible with the Russian weapons. But one or two working AKs and some ammo would greatly benefit Tyce's troop in future firefights. Tyce judged that they had used more than seventy-five percent of their ammo on the ambush, and without a resupply, they were no good to anyone.

Tyce made his way down the steep slope, holding a few saplings to steady himself along the way. From the road's edge, he surveyed the carnage. Military vehicles twisted and burned beyond recognition. Fires still burning everywhere. The occasional cook-off of ammunition inside the burning truck seemed to be the last remaining threat. Captain Blake and SSgt. Diaz's troops carefully picked their way through the wreckage.

Tyce watched them for a moment and reflected on his own combat experiences. Now that all appeared to be safe, a shred of doubt—or was it some remorse?—set in.

Nope, he thought. *They are invaders, and this is our duty to our country.*

CHAPTER 19

Outside Parsons

Something in the river caught Blue's attention—movement out of the corner of his eye. He walked down to get a closer look. He hadn't seen anyone in days, so he wasn't taking any chances. He crept to the edge of the woods and looked into the river's heavy rapids. There, pinned against the rocks by the current, were two Russian soldiers floating trapped in a swirling eddy. Their faces were ashen white and ghostlike against the dark waters, but they looked to Blue as if they'd only been in the water about ten or twelve hours.

Floated from upstream, thought Blue. *Good. If someone else is killing Russian soldiers, then it's upriver I go.*

He checked the bandage on his throbbing shoulder, then painfully pulled the mountain rucksack back onto it. His legs wobbled a bit from days of hiking, wounded and without sustenance, through the woods. But he had remained hidden, not knowing who to trust . . . yet. The dead Russians were his first sign that there might be someone fighting back. Some kind of organized resistance.

And they just might have need of a good shot, he thought. Placing the custom, wood stock .460 Weatherby Mk V over his shoulder, he picked his way back carefully to the deer trail he had been following toward the city of Parsons.

Tyce felt like he was getting an ass chewing from a colonel or general.

"So you actually thought that by wiping the Russians out down to the last man, they would not come looking to find out what happened?" said Susanna in a tone that she might have reserved for bad dogs or misbehaving children.

"Look, Mayor, we did what we needed to do to win." Tyce glanced at the Chief of Police, but he remained stony-faced. Tyce was on his own, "This is how combat goes. Not all of it is predictable. And the Russians aren't just going to pack up and go home anytime soon. By the looks of things, they are here to stay. They've annexed America, and if we don't do some—"

She interrupted him in a low and slow condescending drawl, her head cocked to the side. "Well now, let's just see if we can remember. Wasn't it a man bearing a striking re-semblance to you who told me yesterday that his whole plan hinged on the last of the Russian vehicles pursuing you out of town to make them think you had no affiliation with Parsons?"

"Well . . . yes, that was the plan, but . . ." Tyce heard himself stammering like a schoolboy. "We had a chance to take them all, without losing any men, and we took it. That I don't regret, Mayor."

"That's an admirable thing, Major. I just wonder how many of my citizens need to get killed when the Russians follow up with a larger force and start interrogating . . . say, my gas station attendant, Ron. Do you think he has the training or resolve to last under a Russian interroga-tion?" She glared, both of her deep blue eyes boring a hole into him. "Any explanation besides just that dumb look on your face will do, Major Asher."

"Look, Mayor, I promise we can get the Russians to leave you and the town of Parsons alone."

"How do you intend to do that?" she asked, her tone both skeptical and stinging.

Tyce had been working on an alternate solution ever since last night's firefight had ended a little too well. The initial plan called for leaving a few Russians alive, then racing out of town to the south so the Russians could plausibly believe an explanation from the town that he was not intending to make Parsons his holdout. It was not the best plan, but it was just feasible enough, and Tyce had counted upon the Russians not being willing to harm civilians. That plan had gone to shit thanks to an extra belt of API, armor-piercing .50 caliber rounds that SSgt. Diaz had saved and used on the BTR. When the Russians inspected the vehicle and found the back and side looking like Swiss cheese, plus no fewer than six dead Russian soldiers in the back . . . well . . .

"The Russians are keen on signals intelligence."

"Explain."

"We have plenty of army field radios. We are going to retreat south of town and set up a radio site. The Russians will suspect it's our headquarters."

"What happens when they attack you with all sorts of missiles and stuff?"

"That's the beauty of the radio transmissions. We can set up the antenna and a dummy HQ in a barn or something. But the relay wires, the actual radios, we can have miles away."

"Like remote control or something."

"About like that."

Tyce tried to sound convincing, but in actuality, he

knew very little about how to establish radio retransmission sites. What he did have was several communications men who had been to school for just that kind of thing. Radio fakery in combat was nothing new, but he was counting on the Russians concluding that he and the other reserve and guard forces had the same equipment as the frontline troops still in Afghanistan and Iran.

"So where is the barn, the site you intend to fake out the Russians?"

Tyce pulled out the Michelin map he'd been using. "Here." He pointed to a Y-intersection in the road about twenty miles south and east of Parsons.

Susanna drew closer and squinted at Tyce's map. "Harman?"

"Yes, the town of Harman," Tyce tried to sound convincing though he was making this pretty much up on the fly now.

"Town . . . it's more like a village." She was near enough now that Tyce could smell the scent of lilacs and cloves. Her shampoo or perfume, he guessed. After smelling sweaty Marines for the past few months and after the stench of last night's battle, it smelled kind of nice. Tyce wondered if that was all a part of Susanna's thing.

Does she use everything available to her to negotiate, even her femininity? Tyce didn't have a lot of time for such things, but clearly dealing with civilians was going to be a part of his new world order and he'd better get used to it.

As she spoke next, her voice lost its air of authority. "Well, I guess that's far enough away from us that it might work." She looked up at Tyce. In spite of her commanding presence, Susanna was shortish, no taller than five-foot-five. She touched him gently on the arm. "You be careful now, Major. I just might have a use for you before this thing is all said and done."

As much as Tyce liked being on her good side, he still couldn't shake the feeling he was being manipulated.

Oh, well. Better to owe some favors to a small town, he thought. *After all, what's the worst they could end up getting into?*

Tyce was sitting in his vehicle, feet propped up, staring at the jumble of tourist maps and trying to make sense of is all, when one of his Marine sentries walked in.

"Hey, sir, we caught a guy poking around the perimeter."

"Okay," Tyce waved him away impatiently. He had NCOs who could take care of curious passersby.

"He was carrying this, sir." The Marine lifted a beautiful .460 Weatherby Mark V Deluxe with walnut stock and a Leupold VX-3i hunting scope. An exceedingly accurate, custom-built rifle. It would only be found in the hands of a very skilled rifleman, Tyce realized instantly.

Tyce sat bolt upright. "Where is he? Was he speaking English?"

"Oh yes, sir. He's an American for sure. Might be a bit . . . you know, slow. I think he's some kind of backwoods mountain man. He's a big ol' boy."

"Okay, bring him over."

"Got it."

The man started off before Tyce stopped him. "And Marine . . . leave the rifle."

Tyce smiled a bit. He knew if he had wavered on that point, the rifle would get "lost" very quickly among his ranks, likely ending up traded to one of his snipers for something of high value.

"Ah, no issues, sir." The man feigned indignation for being called out.

In less than half an hour, four Marines escorted the rifle's owner over to Tyce's command vehicle. All four stood around, more than a little curious about how things would transpire between the newly captured man and their boss.

"What's your name?" Tyce asked, putting his hand out in a friendly gesture.

"It's Blue."

"Um . . . your name is *Blue*?"

Some chuckles from the gathered Marines.

"Yup. That's what my Momma called me. She named me after the mountain flower."

More chuckles. Tyce angrily waved the men off. He didn't expect much trouble from this gentle giant.

Tyce held up the Weatherby. "You do much hunting with this?"

"All my life."

"You any good?"

"Yup."

"Look, I can see you are a man of few words. But maybe you've seen what's been happening around us. I don't need to spell it out."

Tyce thought about how ridiculous that sounded. After all, with Blue's heavy accent and soft, dumb looks, maybe he did need to spell it out. He found himself speaking in a slower meter and choosing simpler words almost unintentionally. "Our country has been invaded. By the Russians. And I intend to . . . ah . . . resist."

"I understand," Blue said.

"Well . . . then, would you consider joining me . . . us?"

"Thought I already did?"

"What?"

"Your men asked me to come on over."

"Okay," Tyce said, not quite sure how the two things connected, but it appeared to Tyce the man was willing to lend his rifle to support the mission.

"So, you'll join us, and you have no problem . . . um, well, fighting?"

"Killed two Russians already, so I guess not. Wasn't much harder than downing a cougar."

Tyce didn't want to pry much more, and he wasn't sure he was going to get more than a few words that he couldn't exactly make sense of in response anyhow. It sounded like the big man was ready, willing, and able, so Tyce just decided to roll with it.

"Okay, here's your rifle back. You have your own ammo, I'm guessing."

"Yup."

Tyce signaled for his men, who had stepped away but remained within earshot.

"Gents, take Mr. Blue here over to the sniper section. Tell the NCOs he's now a part of their organization. They are responsible for his, um, well-being. They need to ensure he's cared for, you know, doesn't get lost in the military . . . system. Could be confusing for some."

The head NCO smiled. "We get what you mean, sir. I'm sure the snipers will be glad to have another mouth to feed, or two . . . or even three." At their last words, the men led Blue away.

Tyce tapped his pen against the map, thinking about what a motley crew they were becoming.

Strength in numbers, strength in the diversity of skills, he thought, *that's the American way. Nation of immigrants who wanted to fight for something bigger and better.* Someone had once said something along those lines in a U.S. history class. He just wondered if he could get these civilians to work in and among his ranks while he tried to conjure up fight-and-flee plans that would make big problems for the Russians.

CHAPTER 20

Harman, West Virginia

There were plenty of barns—hay barns, tobacco barns, barns for cows, corn, and soybeans—to pick from in the broad valley of Harman, West Virginia. The problem was convincing the farmers and townspeople to let him rig it up to look like a phony combined Army and Marine Corps command post so that the Russians would blow it up. No one believed him when he said he'd get them compensation after the war was over. They were patriotic, but they didn't put much trust in the government—any government.

Tyce was beginning to realize that maintaining civil order while requesting support from citizens of a state that already had a deeply depressed economy, especially in the middle of winter, was not going to make him any friends. Thankfully, word had gotten out from the town of Parsons that Tyce was a square and honest guy, not to mention the story of how he and his unit had smacked the Russians down to the last man by the river bend near Parsons. Folks had begun treating him a bit like a Robin Hood, a reputation he liked and one he now needed to live up to. At each farm, folks invited him and his men in for hot soup or coffee, then asked him for news about everything. Rumors abounded but with no Internet, TV, or radio, stories seemed to be getting more and more outlandish.

One nice older couple invited all the men in Tyce's Humvee section inside their front parlor, eager for news. Ignoring the few who courteously offered to wait outside, the couple insisted that everyone squeeze inside their warm farmhouse and wouldn't let them go until they finished off two whole pots of coffee laced with farm-fresh milk and served with warm biscuits slathered with homemade butter. After three days of military Meals Ready to Eat, or MREs, the home-cooked food was heavenly.

Tyce finally extricated himself and his men and moved on to the next farm while the rest of the men gathered in the forest, cleaned weapons, handed out three rounds of rifle ammo per man, and traded Russian knives and pistols. They were three quarters of a regiment, near completely out of ammo, living like vagabonds, with the Russians sure to come looking for them any day now.

It was getting toward dusk, and Tyce was almost ready to give up. One more farm. One more ask. Near the northern edge of town, the old farmer finally agreed. They could rig up his barn as long as they found him another place to live. His assumption was the Russians were going to blow up his barn, so what was going to stop them from blowing up his house?

"Here's the way I see it, Major," said the old farmer. "This house isn't a family heirloom, but I have ten head of cattle and two horses and twenty-eight acres of good land. If I move the livestock, I'm going with them."

Car headlights in the distance informed Tyce that his men, stationed on all roads leading into the valley, were coming to check on his progress. After Parsons, his HQ posted men on all quadrants of the compass as lookouts without being told to do so. As the two vehicles pulled up to the farm where they were negotiating, Tyce recognized the lead Humvee as Gunny's but didn't recognize the big Ram 3500 pickup in the back. He shouldered his weapon, told the farmer he'd find him a place right away, tasked SSgt. Diaz to continue listening to the man's lengthening list of requests, and walked out to Gunny's vehicle.

"Hey, sir," Gunny said, hopping out of his Humvee. "How goes it? Anyone willing to let the Russkies blow up their barn for freedom and democracy?"

Tyce grinned. He needed that. To Tyce, ever since their slow retreat from Morgantown things felt as if they slowly deteriorating, and he'd have to think seriously about saving the men's hides instead of trying to go on the hunt. Gunny always had an easygoing attitude, as if to say, "It's all fucked, but we'll figure it out."

"Yeah, well, I just asked SSgt. Diaz to take over negotiating, if that tells you where we're at."

"Shit. It's so bad that you gotta call in the Latina Rottweiler herself, huh?"

"We might be about there, but we'll see."

"Okay, sir. I brought you someone. Or, more like *someones*."

"Who?" said Tyce, looking inquiringly back at the Ram pickup. "I was just coming over to see who was driving into our little trap."

"You're not gonna believe me, but I've got a full-blown army general in there."

"What? Are you serious?" *It would be too much to ask for him to be a Marine general*, he thought, *but anyone of high rank and combat experience would be good*. Then he could slip back to the role for which he thought he was best suited: second-in-command, or maybe running operations.

The pressure that had been building seemed to be lifting and, for a moment, Tyce's heart lightened.

"Well . . . he's not that kind of general," said Gunny, as if sensing Tyce's thoughts.

Tyce looked sideways at him.

"Uh . . . it may be best if you follow me, sir." Gunny led him back to the pickup.

Tyce came up to the passenger's-side window. The door opened, and Tyce saw two men inside. The driver spoke first, in heavily Native American–accented English. "I'm Bill Degata, and this is General Lawton Custis." He pointed to the passenger, a short man with a half-crown of grey and a flat top that ended in a big bald spot. He stepped out of the vehicle still carrying his back bolt upright, looking fit for an older gentleman.

When he crossed into the Humvee headlights, everyone took a half-step back. It was the general's eyes: stark-white pupils with no visible iris. The surrounding skin was reddened, inflamed, puffy, with watery lines trailing out from his eyes.

"He's blind, by the way," said Bill, seeming to relish the shock his late remark caused the gathered troops. "He looked straight into a nuclear blast down at the city of Danville, Virginia. We keep the bandages on them, except in the cool air. He says it soothes his eyes a bit."

"The Russians nuked Danville?" Tyce asked, incredulously.

This time, the general answered. "Let me guess, you boys have been holed up in the mountains since this thing kicked off, and you don't know much of what's going on?"

"No, sir, we don't," said Tyce.

"You don't gotta call me sir, Marine. I retired a while

ago. But that doesn't mean I can't lend you all a hand. I understand you got Russian soldiers breathing down your neck, and you want to shake 'em."

Tyce glared at Gunny, who shrugged. Tyce was going to have to make up some rules for the men on what information they shared, and with whom. His troops were likely to be in close contact with civilians, and they needed to watch what they said. At the very least because it could endanger the civilians' lives. In war, information could be just as valuable as a fistful of ammunition or a suitcase worth of explosives.

"That's about it, General," said Tyce, continuing to use the respectful term. He figured there was no reason a retired general couldn't give them a few pointers.

The general sat—ramrod straight—in a wooden chair in the old farmer's barn, listening to Tyce describe the lay of the land. Dr. Remington finished placing specialized chemical bandages over both his eyes, then taped them on gently. Tyce watched her work as he spoke. She moved fluidly, deftly, with the skill and precision of someone who had done things like this a million times before.

Where in the world did she treat blast- or flash-burned eyes? He thought. Then the realization hit him: she'd been treating wounded Marines, badly burned in combat by roadside bombs. Her stock went up a full measure in Tyce's eyes, and he vowed to tolerate her short temper a bit more in the future. It was clear she was a very good doctor.

Above them, Marines and soldiers crawled among the rafters and wired radio cable to men on the roof, who were cutting holes and installing radio antennae.

"So tell me again. The valley is shaped like an upside-down Y?" asked the general, patting Victoria on the arm as she finished trimming the ends of the tape.

"Yes, basically. Broad valley in between," said Tyce.

"Farms all around—mainly livestock, or some grains or fruits?"

"Both. Mainly livestock."

"And the mountains? If I remember my geography of the Monongahela National Forest in the Allegheny Mountains, we're near the tallest peak at . . . Spruce Knob. I think I remember it's about 4,800 feet above sea level. Vegetation is pretty much all coniferous trees?" the general asked—or at least, it sounded like a question, but Tyce was pretty sure he already knew the answer and was just confirming his facts.

Tyce glanced at the Michelin map, confirmed the altitude, and agreed. "Yes, 4,863 feet to be precise, and mostly pines."

The general tapped his chin and pulled out a pipe bag. By feel, he filled and lit the pipe and started to puff. Tyce smiled a bit. He was already starting to like this guy.

"Have you ever heard of the Battle of Kings Mountain?"

"No. No, sir," said Tyce, a bit puzzled about where the general was going with this.

"Okay, sit a minute."

Tyce leaned against the edge of the barn table on which the maps were spread out.

"On October 7th, 1780, American patriots defeated a larger British force by goading them into an ambush in a large valley, then retreating before British General Lord Cornwallis could arrive with reinforcements."

"You think we can pull off another ambush? We survived the last one unscathed—but only with a bit of luck and by the hairs on our collective asses. We lost a lot of time trying to prepare the last one, too, then got caught flat-footed. I was hoping to just do a hit-and-run."

"Well, as Vernon Gomez always said, 'I'd rather be lucky than good.'"

"That's a pretty good quote. Another one of your dead generals?"

"Nope, that was Vernon 'Lefty' Gomez, the pitcher for the New York Yankees in the 1930s. But I think he was on to something. Planning alone can't solve all your problems, Major."

Tyce smiled. At least the general had a good sense of humor. "I was thinking of just using the radio ruse and getting the hell out of here and deeper into the woods. Live to fight another day and draw them farther away from Parsons."

"You have reasons for not wanting them in Parsons, I assume? Made a deal with the locals, I guess? Keep them relatively out of harm's way?" asked the blind general, puffing on his pipe. The sweet scents of black coffee and whiskey filled the air.

"Yes, but I think we're running out of time. I don't imagine the Russians will wait long to mount a search for their missing company."

"Attack is the secret of defense; defense is the planning of an attack," Lawton said cryptically, then added, "Ever read any Sun Tzu, the ancient Chinese guy?"

Tyce cleared his throat uncomfortably. He had read Sun Tzu, the ancient Chinese military strategist and philosopher, but couldn't remember any of it just now. "Not in quite some time, General."

"Well . . . I suppose you boys needed to fight counter-insurgency, and some of these old quotes wouldn't have helped you. You all had a tough fight over there. I may know a few things, but your knowledge of the insurgents you fought in Iraq and Afghanistan is how we'll eventually beat the Russians."

Although he felt off guard in the general's presence, oddly, the general's wise tone and his all-seeing but blind eyes gave Tyce a great deal of comfort. Lawton seemed not only judicious, but worldly, and maybe even a bit fatherly, too. For a moment, Tyce imagined him like Colonel Potter from the TV show *M*A*S*H*. Tyce understood that Lawton had probably forgotten more about military tactics and history than Tyce had ever known.

Time to shut my mouth more and listen, he thought.

The general cast his blind, bandaged eyes up at the men working aloft and puffed some more.

"It's all clear to me. All war is based on deception, and we're gonna need plenty of that." He turned to face Tyce. Then, realizing he might be tossing out too many quotes, he went on a little more conscientiously, "More Sun Tzu, I'm afraid . . . but you can learn a lot from brilliant men who conducted war hundreds or even thousands of years ago. Though the weapons may have changed, the battle of wits and human behavior haven't changed much."

"What do you propose, General?"

"What do I propose?" Now it seemed the general's turn to be caught off guard. "Well, I might just have some ideas, but Major Asher, you are the one who needs to make the decisions. You know these men and women better than I. What they are capable of and what they'll do under pressure."

"Hardly. We've only been working together for a short time. A few months."

"A lifetime," said the general. "Did you know that at the battle of New Market during the Civil War, Breckinridge defeated Franz Sigel with less than two-thirds the forces? Breckinridge's men were mostly raw recruits. Boys from the Virginia Military Institute." The faraway tone of his voice made it sound like he was reliving a distant memory. "Breckinridge was just better at leadership and rallying the men. He didn't have a better strategy or even better ground. He just used what he had to his advantage."

"They may have won the battle, General, but last time I checked, the South still lost the war."

"Well, let's just count on changing some of the parts of those equations. Learn from what worked and avoid what didn't." He reached out and patted Tyce on the arm, somehow sensing his distance from him perfectly. He smiled. "Also, I think I can help. I heard you were a little short on ammo and firepower."

"That's an understatement, General. I really don't think we have the ammo to engage what I assume will be a larger unit this time. We expended a lot of our ammo just taking out a Russian platoon. And while I'd love to hear more ideas on tactics, all of those battles you mentioned, at least the two sides had equivalent weapons. If the Russians arrive with anything larger than they had last time . . . I don't have anything that can even deal with a single BTR, let alone anything heavier."

"Oh, no," said the general. "They won't bring armor. Not yet, at least. It would take them two days to get it up here, even if they weren't searching for traps behind every rock. No, no. They will send fast, light, and experienced infantry. Well led, too, I imagine. Mixed with a few BTRs. Yes . . . if we're to defeat a reactionary force, this is the place." He puffed on the pipe and looked around as if he were looking through the walls of the small barn and surveying the entire valley before him. "We'll defeat them with their own human nature and add in a healthy dose of deception. And, as I was saying . . . I just might be able to help in the firepower department." The general's face broadened into a knowing smile.

He leaned in closer to Tyce. "To be honest, I *do* have a *few* projects to suggest. But it's your leadership that will win in the day. No battle was won with even the best equipment if the men didn't trust their leaders, and the men seem to trust you implicitly. Keep your men setting up this radio flytrap; it will be the center of our deceit. But we're going to need a bit more if we're to get inside the enemy commander's mind. It's inside his head that we will eventually win. I have a list of things we need, from Molotov cocktails to fuel bombs. I think I smelled a gas station on the way up here. In these backwoods, fuel may be your most abundant resource—let's use it. Plus, a few of the enemy dying a horrendous, burning death tends to make commanders a bit jumpy. You'll see."

"You make it sound like you're not sticking around. Doesn't exactly make me trust in your plan, General."

"Yes. I have to hit the road for a bit. And one of the details I'm going to give you will be exceedingly tricky. I need you to find some tungsten."

"The metal tungsten? How the hell am I supposed to find that?"

"Son . . . remember what I said? You have to use what's around you. My boy, you are surrounded by America's Ruhr Valley."

"Come again?"

"You are in the center of America's mining heartland.

Every ferrous metal known to man is harvested from these hills. And if you look in the surrounding valleys, you will find some pretty advanced metallurgy shops doing what men and miners have done here for generations. They take metals from the hills and shape them into things. I expect if I give you the specifications, it'll only take them half a day, or maybe less."

"How much time do you think we actually have, General? It sounds like a pretty tall order."

"It is, it is. But trust me, no plan hinges on one thing. It's the effect inside the commander's head that matters." Lawton tapped his temple, emphasizing the point.

The old general's ideas and knowledge were admirable, but Tyce was the one about to commit the men to another battle. One so soon after their last, and likely more dangerous. Right now, the men were flying high on their last victory, glad to have defeated a numerically inferior but well-armored enemy with fewer rounds of ammo and few casualties. But Tyce also knew what defeat looked like. He had tasted it more than once in Iraq. He was hoping to keep the men's spirits high until they reached a safer spot. Somewhere they could let their guard down and relax for a little bit.

"Where, and how, should we set up?"

"That 'where' is easy, the 'how' will be a bit more complicated. You must start with your map of the valley. Then think like the enemy. Be the Russian commander and see the valley as he sees it. Where would you position your forces if you were the Russian?"

"Well . . ." Tyce began reluctantly, the audience of all his troops making him slow to answer with any real commitment. "I might approach from the north. Especially because it would shorten my supply lines back to Morgan-town."

"Good. What else?"

"I would have a reconnaissance element out forward," Tyce said, growing bolder.

"Light, vehicular-mounted scouts with full comms," interjected Lieutenant Zane sheepishly from the sidelines. He was obviously entranced by the back and forth.

"Keep this one around, he'll make colonel for sure," said the general casting a pleased smile toward the young officer, "Okay, but what would they be searching for?"

"I . . . not sure. Us, I guess," Tyce answered.

"Yes, but where?"

"In defensive positions?"

"Is that a question, Major Asher? Because it sounds like you are still thinking like the American commander. That will never do. Be the Russian commander. He will search you out using all of his senses."

Tyce felt a little like a lieutenant going over his first field problem, but he realized he had to get over it. The general was right. If they were to plan a good ambush, they had to keep in mind the fact that the Russians were a think-ing, seeing enemy. They had to be careful about what the Russian commander would see on the battlefield in order to make him respond the way they needed him to. "Well, I would give him something to see. Possibly some dug-in defensive positions. Something to draw in his fire. He will want to shoot and maneuver."

"Excellent. That's his sight. What about taste, smell, and hearing?"

"I don't follow—how will he taste or smell us?"

"It's a metaphor, Major, stick with me. Start with hearing."

Tyce glanced around the barn. His pack of leaders seemed to be really getting into the general's line of thinking. At the very least, it was a great way to think through the upcoming battle.

"I guess he'd hear with his reconnaissance and his radio intercepts."

"Good, so give him what he wants. Let his reconnaissance see prepared defensive positions, and let him hear you blasting radio transmissions from this very barn. It's called confirmation bias. If he sees a defense and hears intercepted radio chatter, what will he do?"

"He'll test his intelligence further before committing," said Tyce, beginning to see things from the enemy commander's perspective. "He will send his reconnaissance to find the flanks of the defense, then he will pin us down in the defensive positions and try to use his better mobility and his BTRs to maneuver around us or to our flanks."

"Very good, Major Asher. Now, you see, he begins to feel across the battlefield. One that you have shaped for him, and when he feels what he expects—fixed frontages guarding a headquarters command barn—he will start to taste his own success. He will pounce."

"So we let him attack us?"

"In a way. But just when he thinks he has won, you spring your final move. Then he is finally defeated where it counts. Not on the battlefield, but in his own mind."

Tyce hated treating combat like a game and committing the lives of his men to possible death like they were just some kind of chess pieces. But really, any ambush they performed had to accomplish two things: get the Russians away from Parsons and give the Russians a big bloody nose. Enough of a bloody nose to get his men in the hills, where they could take the time to lick their wounds, calculate their next moves, and reconstitute their firepower to fight some more.

Tyce looked at Captain Blake, Gunny, and SSgt. Diaz, then he looked back to General Lawton, who stood at the table, a smile visible under his bandaged eyes and face. He seemed happy at the planning table and truly at home in front of the maps. Tyce was most comfortable out in the field, away from the radios and in the trench with his men. The rest of his leaders seemed to be reflecting on the same things as Tyce. Maybe they had a bit of doubt that this whole thing would work, but also, Tyce thought, they might have some hope that they could pull the whole thing off.

The general seemed to read everyone's thoughts. "Don't worry, you all. If we can give them a bloody nose and a big fat lip, you'll get some breathing room to plan another attack. Might even get some time in the coming winter to gather more weapons and men."

He really has forgotten more than I have ever known about tactics, Tyce thought.

He looked around the troops gathered in the cold barn, flickering bare bulbs and Humvee headlights illuminating them as they worked, quietly and quickly, to get the antenna up and radios working. The general had good ideas. Really good ideas. But the rest was up to Tyce, and he knew something the others didn't. He had frozen in combat at the worst possible time. This had cost him the lives of several of his best men. The memory still woke him at night. He looked around the barn at everyone's faces, eerily illuminated by the low light. Some looked down from the rafters, smiling through the tobacco smoke at Tyce and the general.

A few looked back at him as if weighing his leadership, measuring Tyce against the task in front of them. They were listening to every word.

Tyce's felt his stomach tighten as he fought to control and hide his own fears and doubts.

And now they're counting on me again, he thought, and in his mind, he saw the trusting faces of the men he'd lost the last time he took a great risk.

CHAPTER 21

Harman Valley, West Virginia

Tyce's temporary command post was on the west side of the Harman Valley and tucked into the deep woods. His position had practically no visibility of the valley itself. An old logging route nearby gave the regiment the only possible escape route once they'd finished their ambush. Mr. Bill Degata had woken the general, and the two had left hours earlier on their unknown mission.

In the command post, preparations had renewed at a fast and steady pace. Tyce picked the three locations on the map from which to spring the ambush based on what he thought the Russians would do. He chose three leaders—Lieutenant Zane, Captain Blake, and Gunny—and told them to go to the coordinates on the map, to each inspect the area, and then to come back with recommendations.

No more than half an hour had passed when Lieutenant Zane, from the northern ambush spot sent a runner requesting to move his spot to conform better to the terrain and permission to establish an OP, short for observation post. Tyce approved the move and had the HQ men place the pins on the map to reflect the changes.

Captain Blake, in the position they named simply "Center," sent a runner saying he was all good to go at his location. Gunny Dixon sent word from the South ambush location to tell Tyce that the spot worked well, and he was ready to construct the back door. Tyce looked over Gunny's location on the map with respect to the other two positions, then approved it through another Humvee runner.

We better find a new way to communicate, thought Tyce, *or we're going to run the valley out of gas*. With winter approaching, he didn't need to rub another town the wrong way. He discussed things over with his communications sergeants, but besides turning on their radios, they were stumped.

"Hey, boss man," said Wynand.

"Yeah," Tyce answered, a little startled to see Wynand appear out of nowhere.

To everyone's surprise, Wynand hadn't left yet and had been lurking around on his new motorcycle and earning a reputation as a scrounger. He had been chased away from Commander Remington's medical station on no fewer than three occasions while pretending to be sick. Commander Remington had caught him eyeing up her scarce medical supplies, so she gave him some Motrin and sent him packing. When that didn't work and he returned, she had issued him some ipecac, which she had relabeled as cough syrup. He'd been heard barfing his guts out all night and had been laying low ever since. So Tyce was a little surprised when he spoke up from the headquarters shack's darkened corner.

"Do you have point-to-point, closed-loop phones?"

"Field phones? Yeah, we have them." Tyce looked at the communications sergeants, who nodded. They had been lugging around a full regiment's suite of communications, although most of it could not be used out of fear that the Russians were in charge of or monitoring everything from the American satellite network to interceptor gear for their military band radios. "We don't have enough slash wire, though."

"Slash . . . what?"

"The wires to connect them. It's miles between the three ambush locations."

"I don't know nothin' about no slash wire. But did you see the phone lines crisscrossing the valley, boss man? Can't you just tie into those?"

A surprisingly good suggestion. The comms guys spoke up: It was feasible. They'd get right on it. Tyce thanked Wynand, but still got the impression the man was just doing whatever it took to ingratiate himself with whomever was in charge. Tyce had a feeling his true colors were a bit darker than he was letting on. In the meanwhile, however, he was useful. Useful for finding intelligence, and maybe later Tyce could find a use for him in scrounging up something they needed.

Tyce really had no idea how long it would be until the Russians might find them by chance, but he knew that as soon as he threw the lever on the radios, they'd be there pretty fast. The general had called the radio ruse a Venus flytrap, and that had caught on with the men. Now, though tired to the bone, they were talking about how they were going to lure the Russians in and then smoke them. Maybe it was the lack of sleep, maybe it was the pressure, but it was hard for Tyce not to get a little giddy along with his troops.

"Sir, just got a runner from attack position North. They have all their positions in the forest dug in and camouflaged. The lieutenant is asking for you to come and inspect his positions." One of his headquarters operations men handed him a Yellow Canary.

Tyce had been using runners in Humvees to pass messages between the three ambush positions to create complete radio silence. In addition, he had his leaders post air sentries. men who watched the skies and called out for everyone to go to ground when aircraft were spotted. In Tyce's estimation, an abundance of caution would give them the most time before they were inevitably discovered.

"Got it. What's the news on positions Mid and South?" said Tyce.

"South is dug and set. Center is having some trouble. Seems one of the local farmers is not having any of it. He refuses to let them make the oil pits along his farm. Says it'll poison the groundwater for years to come."

"Okay," said Tyce, removing his Kevlar helmet and running his fingers through his sandy blond hair as much out of consternation as to feel how dirty it was. Flakes of sweat-caked dirt fell free. "He's probably right, but unless we kick these Russians out of here, they'll soak the soil with a lot more than just burning oil."

"Like what, sir?" asked one of the headquarters sergeants.

"The blood of patriots, to start," Tyce said, giving the sergeant a sardonic smile and a wink. Combat had hardened many of the men, but Tyce wasn't about to start treating the citizens' backyards like his own personal military proving grounds. That's how a tyranny was formed—he knew enough of history to know that. And if even one citizen got hurt in his clash with the Russians, he could count on word spreading, and that would mean less and less support from any of the other valleys in the future. Who knew how long this conflict was going to last before they kicked the Russians out? What he did know was that it wasn't going to be soon, and he needed to be as close to the people he was defending as possible.

"Sir, it's not as if the EPA or the health department are

going to check up on it, and without the fires, we won't be able to blind their thermal and night optics."

"Not sure of the health effects on us. The guys in Center section are liable to get a few lungsful of that stuff, but it's a bit better than getting a boot put into our spine and a bullet in our backs, which is what the Russians have in store for us."

As if on cue, Tyce spotted Commander Remington making her way through the woods toward the small group clustered near the hunting shack. She had taken off her navy camouflage uniform shirt and was wearing a Marine Corps green sweatshirt to stay warm. It looked good on her. More notable, though, were the bloody nitrile gloves. Tyce turned to walk to the dirt logging trail where his Humvee was parked, hoping to make it the ten feet before she arrived. The last thing he needed was more confrontation.

"Nope! I see you, Major Asher," she barked. "I heard you were back at the CP, and I need to speak to you."

Tyce turned toward her and put on his helmet, both because he was about to mount up and because he knew there was a possibility of a storm brewing between him and Victoria. The men had warned him she was looking for him, and he'd purposely avoided her.

"Dr. Remington, I presume," he said, attempting some humor.

She gave him a small smile but put her hands on her hips defensively. "I just finished working on your man, Sergeant Carson. I saved the hand, but he needs time to rest."

"Vick . . ." Tyce started, then corrected himself. "Commander Remington, I'm not sure you fully understanding the situation here." His curtness relayed some of his own fatigue. "If I don't get every swinging Richard in the field, engaged in making this ambush site perfect, you will be needing to save a lot more than Carson's hand."

She grimaced. "Okay, buster, here's the deal." She poked him in the chest. "At least give your men time to wash up. They are all filthy, and that will compound my problems immeasurably *if* you start taking casualties. The surgery is as ready as we can make it, but if the men don't clean themselves, the infection rates among your wounded will kill far more than I can save with my surgical skills."

She had a really good point, but Tyce wasn't about to halt everything to let the men take showers. "Got it. I'll tell the North, Mid, and South ambush leaders to let their off-duty men clean up."

"Not good enough." She shook her head. "Either you order the men to hygiene, or I'll go directly to them and issue the order. We may be the same rank, Major, but in combat and on medical concerns, I outrank everyone, *capisce*?"

By the tone of her voice and the fire in her eyes, Tyce could tell that she was dead serious. The way she said *capisce*, not the American "capeesh," made him think that maybe she had some Italian heritage. Interesting. Against his better judgment, he was beginning to like her. She was right about the infections and disease. Tyce had seen it in ill-disciplined units. It started with things like jock itch and laziness in shaving. It ended with serious illnesses that put many men in the hospital and out of action for months.

"Okay, Commander. I'll pass the word."

"Good. And while you're at it"—she scrunched her nose and waved her hand—"maybe do something about yourself, too. You smell like a horse."

Tyce didn't reply, instead pivoting and walking to his

Humvee to go inspect the three ambush positions. He was smiling.

A day and a half passed without rest, everyone working to make the ambush positions, and Tyce could see the weariness in the men's eyes. As he and Trigger were making the rounds, he stopped by one of the machine gun nests at the North position. The men had dug fighting holes big enough for two men, then covered them with pine logs and branches. The effect was a blend of cover and concealment. A narrow slit about the width of a cereal box was all that was visible.

Trigger, by now a happy sight to all the troops, wove his way among the fighting positions, finding even the completely camouflaged ones easily. Tyce hoped the Russians didn't bring any dogs with them or the attack was over before it began. In each bunker, the men patted the dog and scratched between his ears. Each squad and platoon usually found some hidden treat for the frisky—and always hungry—Belgian Malinois. Gunny had put Trigger on a diet, but when the dog ran around with Tyce, the diet was ignored. Trigger seemed to know Tyce was a softy and often jumped into his Humvee, knowing he'd be spared the dry dog food diet that Gunny enforced.

Tyce squatted down by Lieutenant Zane at the North position. "How's it coming, Chad?"

The lieutenant looked up from where he was hacking at the sidewall of his underground dirt dugout with a pickaxe. He hopped out of the hole and shook Tyce's hand. "Hey, sir," he said with a smile. "We're pretty much done. We're rehearsing drills to get into and out of the positions with speed."

"Yeah? Sounds good. You feel you can get out of the positions quickly if you need to E and E?" said Tyce, using to the common military shorthand for "escape and evade."

"We're good, sir. Our fields of fire are clean but concealed. We're ready to shut the front door when you signal."

"Good." Tyce was very concerned about the North troops getting surrounded and cut off and was about to speak over his concerns when one of Lieutenant Zane's radio operators ran over waving a Yellow Canary.

"Major Asher, Major Asher."

"Hey troop, what's up?" The man was a soldier, not a Marine. Tyce needed to mix and match soldiers and Marines to make up for gaps or to add technical expertise where needed. It was always painful for subordinates to add or subtract men they had trained with, but keeping unit integrity was less important than right-sizing each of the three ambush sites to fit the mechanics of the coming fight.

Tyce read the message. It said three unidentified, military-style vehicles had been spotted approaching from the east. They were moving slowly. Two of the snipers had them under watch. They were asking permission to fire.

"Where's your field phone, Lieutenant?"

"I have it over in the command post, back farther in the woods. But I don't think that came over the field phone."

"It didn't come over the radio . . . I hope. Everyone should still be exercising radio silence."

"Oh no, it's okay, sir. The men have just been using the Motorola squad radios, not the big military radios," Lieutenant Zane said with a smile.

"Please tell me you're joking." Some of the color evaporated from Tyce's face.

"Umm . . . well, no, sir, I'm not. But they only work point to point. They cannot be detected beyond the valley. Their signals are too weak. One of the guys back in your headquarters said it'd be all right."

"Crap," said Tyce "Stop using them. Immediately! They can still be detected and intercepted by aircraft. How long have you been using them?"

"Uhhh . . ." stammered the lieutenant. "A few hours, I'd guess, sir. We got a radio call from the observation post this morning about zero eight hundred hours. Then folks started using them between the three ambush positions instead of wasting gas driving a runner."

"Shit." Tyce stared at the lieutenant while he thought about how many Russian aircraft had overflown their position in the last four or five hours. He was pretty sure they had been increasing in frequency, although at high enough altitudes that they'd been relatively less unusual. He'd have to query his intelligence officers, but he knew from instinct that at least a few of the lower-flying aircraft were probably absorbing every signal band on the hunt for any stray troops foolish enough to use their radios.

"Okay, pass the word. Use the radios one last time, if necessary. Tell everyone to remain off even the small hand-held radios."

"Copy, sir, WILCO," he said, using shorthand to mean *I will comply.* "Where are you going to be?"

"I want to see who we have headed our way. I'm not sure Center is as prepared as you are yet, Lieutenant Zane, and those three vehicles are headed right for them." Tyce dashed over to his Humvee and headed to Harman High School, which sat at the middle of the intersection going through the ambush area.

* * *

The big Ram 3500 pulled up to where Tyce and SSgt. Diaz were standing on the road to intercept them. Pulled behind the truck was something covered by a large square of canvas oilcloth. Two pickups behind the first were likewise towing something large and wheeled—and even covered, it appeared to be military.

Bill Degata jumped out of the driver's seat and pumped his fists skyward. "Hey, Major. Like the Magi, we come bearing gifts."

General Lawton exited on the passenger's side and, feeling his way around the truck, listened for Tyce's voice.

"What the heck are those?" asked Tyce, still staring at the big canvas-draped hulks being towed behind the pickups.

"Come on back, Major," said the general, leading the way by feel to the back of the truck. "Bill, can you do the honors?"

Bill undid some straps and pulled the cover back. Underneath was some kind of big gun that Tyce didn't recognize.

"What is it?"

"That, Warrior Leader, is a German 88. The anti-tank gun made famous in World War II."

"Well . . . that looks good, but what are *we* going to do with it? I thought you were maybe bringing us something . . . I don't know, modern?"

"Modern don't mean better," said Bill Degata, glaring at Tyce.

"Right. How do we employ it?"

"That depends. Did you get guys to shape the tungsten to the specifications I asked for?"

"Gunny did. Frankly, I've been so busy running around inspecting positions, I kind of forgot to look it over. I think he said he got eight."

"Eight is better than none. Let's get all of these up into the gun position."

"Agreed. Why don't you ride with me, General? I'll need to get a briefing on how we're integrating them into the ambush."

"Everything else going according to plan?"

"No," said Tyce as they boarded the Humvee. The general shook Tyce off when he tried to help him in. "We've had some setbacks, and we've had a breach in radio silence."

The general looked at Tyce with his white eyes, a look of concern over his face. "How long ago?"

"As best we can tell, about a few hours ago. But continuous use till now—I just discovered it. It was the handheld radios."

"Still detectable," said the general, trailing off.

"I know." Tyce could see some worry lining the general's face.

"We have less time than we needed, then," said Lawton. "Probably they'll attack tonight. But we can still make things work, just gotta act fast getting these 'presents' into the southern positions."

"What's behind the other pickups?"

"Behind the Ford is a Quad-50. Another present from dubya-dubya-two. Have you heard of those?"

"No," answered Tyce bluntly, a little concerned about whether to trust the World War II tech.

The general couldn't resist a little smile. Clearly, he took some comfort in his vast knowledge. "It is a four-barrel, .50 cal machine gun. Excellent against low-flying aircraft. Especially helicopters."

Though the general couldn't see it, Tyce raised his eyebrows. "It sounds great, but what about ammunition?"

"No need to worry about that. I have some friends who own a gun store. I have enough to supply the Quad with at least a few squirts. Enough to drive away any close air support the Russian ground guys might try to use. Believe me, as wide as the valley seems to us on the ground, up in the air, it's a tight, narrow little box. And when that little baby gets a-rockin' . . . Let's put it this way: we might be able to level the playing field if we bring it back down to a ground fight. But remember, it's not what we do to the enemy, it's the simultaneous effect of the whole ambush on the Russian commander's mind that matters most. If we don't cause a radio helmet fire . . . well, let's focus on success. That's your department."

It was the first time Tyce had heard anything approaching doubt from the general, and it didn't sit well with him. "I definitely have use for it. Probably on the hill near the command post. It's the most centrally located, nearest to Center but can support all three positions. Most of the valley, even. Do you think they'll use aircraft?" Tyce had considered it, but maybe wishful thinking had given him doubts the Russians would bother using what scarce air support they had against a bunch of wayward mountaineers and some lost troops. The conflict hadn't been long enough for the Russians to have brought in too much of their own attack aviation, yet.

"No doubt in my mind, Major Asher."

"Okay," said Tyce as their Humvee pulled off Route 33 onto the farm road that lead to the hunting shack serving as a command post. "I guess . . . thanks are in order for the toys, General."

"None necessary, my boy. We're in it to win it. And this is more than a little bit personal for me and Bill."

Tyce didn't press the general any further, instead asking, "What's behind the third truck?"

"Heh, heh. Well, that'll be my and Bill's little surprise. Call it an early Christmas present if things go south."

Tyce stared at the general for a moment as they pulled into the command post. He hadn't really realized it before, but they had placed almost all their trust in this funny little man from nowhere and his toys. And while he had instantly earned his and everyone else's trust with some wise words, Tyce couldn't help but wonder, *What if he's wrong—or worse, just some nuts old man with delusions of grandeur, the keys to a World War II museum, and a lot of quotes from ancient history?*

CHAPTER 22

Harman

Lieutenant Chad Zane gazed over the dark valley through his night vision goggles, shivering constantly. The bitter cold air chilled him to his bones. He'd looked at his watch about every two minutes, and he knew it was just after two a.m. Route 32 ran parallel and directly next to his hidden bunker. Without any vehicles on it and from his position, low among the weeds, he could barely see over it. But so far, there was nothing to see. He was about to turn off his NVGs—batteries were scarce, since they had run through most of their stock during the monthlong exercise—when he heard the slight whine of a distant vehicle engine. It wasn't increasing in volume rapidly. Whatever or whomever was coming was taking their time.

The military radio, silent before now, burst to life. It was Zane's observation post, stationed a kilometer up the road in a small hamlet called Dryfork. They had broken radio silence, speaking in a low tone: "The enemy is en route to your position." A short pause, "Composition follows. Sixteen BTRs and three GAZ Tigrs."

Even in the wintry air, a thin bead of sweat broke out on the lieutenant's brow. Sixteen BTRs was a *lot* more than they had planned for.

"Copy. Keep the reports coming, and when the last

enemy vehicle passes, prepare to close the front door," he said. His voice quavered a bit over the radio. He was unable to completely suppress the fear in his voice. He looked through the narrow slit between the logs over the valley and Route 32. He knew soon a lot of Russian vehicles would pass right by him. With luck, they wouldn't see any of his men's positions. They were completely camouflaged from the north, and the only thing visible from the south was the narrow slit. But there was no turning back now.

Tyce listened in as his field phone operators received reports.

He glanced over at the general. It felt good to have him back. Although Tyce was still a bit dubious, he took some comfort from having the old man in his headquarters. Tyce wasn't necessarily buying all these historic quotes, but the effect on the men was palpable. It was like they had a wise sage on their side.

The general sat in an old wooden chair, the flickering candlelight illuminating his bandaged eyes and face. He showed no emotion. He sat still puffing on his pipe while his buddy, Bill Degata, described some of the features on Tyce's regimental battle map. Tyce's men were in charge of what was called "running the board," which meant tracking the battle with little pins in the map. But they gave Bill Degata and the general a wide berth, and when either asked a question about positions, weather reports, etcetera, the troops responded quickly and respectfully. They had seen how Tyce and the other senior leaders treated him, had heard the stories of his past and blinding, and word had even gotten around that he was the mastermind behind the ambush. They treated both with a bit of reverence. Tyce was glad for it.

The troops' enthusiasm for the mission had only increased with the general's additional know-how. But Tyce knew the ambush was going to have its drawbacks, its flaws, and worst, its casualties.

Tyce walked over and picked up the radio handset. "Copy position North. Make ready. Understood enemy headed to your position. Ensure everyone is underground. They will most certainly be using thermals," he said, referencing the Russians' ability to use thermal imagers to see in the dark. Any source of heat could be observed against the cold winter backdrop. Inside their little log dugouts, they should be generally safe from view until the time was right.

He rekeyed the handset. "Center, Center, report your position."

There was no delay; Ned Blake's voice came back over the net. "Position set. All troops are in their positions."

"Copy Center position. Break, break." He unkeyed then rekeyed, as was procedure when calling a different unit. "Position South, position South, report status."

Captain Blake's voice came back, loud and clear. "All set, six," he said, assigning Tyce the respectful call sign for a commander. The number "six" was the number designator for a unit commander regardless of their rank or service. It was a universal way of acknowledging someone's leadership, and Tyce was instantly appreciative of the confidence—especially given over the radio, when everyone could hear it, and from his army special forces commander.

"Copy South. Break, break." He unkeyed, then rekeyed. "All stations, all stations. We have reached go criteria for the ambush. Get ready. Center, you will initiate the ambush when the middle vehicle passes into your kill zone. Acknowledge."

"Acknowledged," came the simple, one-word response from Ned.

There was nothing left to do but wait while the Russians steadily approached.

CHAPTER 23

Harman

The Russian colonel tuned his radio to better receive his reconnaissance element leader's transmission. The report was clear: they had spotted several figures in the woods.

He grabbed the handset and barked out his orders. "Bypass them, reconnaissance force. They are merely an observation post. Main force, you will bypass them, too. But be mindful that this means we are about to cross into their ambush zone. Trail force, hold back and wait. The enemy observation post will pull out of their position after I cross with main force into the Harman Valley. You can kill them once we are set to proceed south and commence our attack."

The Russian BTR-90 command-and-control vehicle was cramped, but he had all of the headquarters men he needed packed into the space.

His intelligence officer turned to him. "Sir, radio intercepts coming in. This is what you were looking for. It's an enemy stronghold. At least four . . . five enemy radios are broadcasting."

"Understood. Reconnaissance, pick up your speed and move out."

"Sir, you cannot cross into the valley without tripping off the ambush."

"I am aware, Captain. The reconnaissance element will be our eyes and ears. Focus on the intelligence and specific locations our sensors have provided you. When we halt at the mouth of the valley, you will confirm the three target clusters. Then we unleash hell."

Tyce's 150th Cavalry regimental HQ was a hive of activity. As everyone now understood better from their previous snafu, all the regiment's radios could be intercepted. So, in short order, the communications men had designed an elaborate system using military field telephones tapped into the old civilian hardwired phone lines. It was working beautifully, but the lines were susceptible to being cut, either on purpose or from detonations or shrapnel in battle. So far, it was doing fine and would zero the Russians in on the one spot that was transmitting loud and clear: the barn in the center of the valley with the unmanned remote radios.

"Sir, Lieutenant Zane at North says his listening post has observed the Russian vehicle forces splitting into units. A lead element, looks to be a reconnaissance force, and a second element, which looks like the main body and has a lot of BTRs in the mix." Tyce raised an eyebrow as the radio operator continued. "He's getting a firm count on the total number now. The main body is halting on the edge of the woods and not entering the valley. The reconnaissance force is moving out rapidly, but they are not using the roads. They seem wise to a trap and are heading out into the farmland. Lieutenant Zane wants to know if you have any special instructions."

"No. Tell him to hang tight and remain patient," Tyce said.

Instinctively, Tyce glanced at the general, almost as if for validation that things were unfolding as they should. The split of the Russian forces and the lead reconnaissance element going off-road was a change from what he'd expected. Still, there was no change on the general's expression. He sat there puffing on his pipe, patiently listening to the radios and everything happening around him like the calm at the center of the storm.

The Russian captain looked through his long-range night optics. In the dim moonlit valley spread before him, he could see trees, hills, and the tops of some houses. It was the perfect place for an ambush. But that didn't bother him. There was nothing in the remnant American army that he feared. The reports had been good. They had captured all the major arsenals practically intact. The invasion had been a complete surprise. This was just a few scared soldiers holed up in the hills with little or no ammunition.

Still, a cornered rat can be dangerous, he reminded himself. He'd seen more than a few battles himself and had been handpicked to wipe out this little nuisance before they showed up on the Russian maps in the captured Pentagon.

They had tortured a few citizens in Parsons, who had all but told them that there were about a hundred men in the Harman Valley. Battlefield interrogations always brought the best intelligence. He seriously doubted the rabble could inflict any real casualties on his own forces.

* * *

"To the Russian and American tanks, it was the scourge of the war," said the general in a hushed tone as he, Tyce, and Bill Degata arrived at the Center position.

"I think it's more like the scourge of *my* war," said SSgt. Diaz. "I never saw so much gun grease in my life."

"Well, you just wait, SSgt. All that maintenance, oiling, and cleaning on the 88 and the Quad-50 will pay off."

Tyce rubbed his hand across the barrel of the big gun, his red lens flashlight showed the shiny, oiled mechanisms. He could clearly read the German word "*RHEINMETALL*" stamped down the side. He was going over the motions he would use as the weapon's new loader, and he wanted to see the breech mechanism one more time. Things were all unfolding as best they could and now he would have to do his part in the dark. He wondered if some German kid on this very gun had done the same thing eighty years before, his gut twisting in knots as he awaited a different kind of Russian tank in a war that now seemed long ago.

"The Russians were so scared of it, it's said they nick-named it *nozh dlya masla*, or the 'butter knife.' Its high-velocity shells were designed to send a flak round up in the air to shoot down American and British bombers. The Germans learned early in the war that if they gave it a good shell, it could slice through most of the tanks on the battle-field. They later mounted it on their heaviest tanks, the Tiger and King Tiger."

"Let's hope it slices through *these* Russians like butter, too," said SSgt. Diaz.

The nighttime critters had come out. Tyce and the men sat on the edge of the breastwork they had dug for the big cannon just above their log cabin command post. They were all tense inside, but the evening's sounds were familiar and put them at a sort of ease. These were the sounds of their homeland.

"We'll see," said the general. "I've been sitting on this historic stuff for many years and always thought about what I would do in an invasion. When I heard through the grapevine that there was some resistance popping up, I knew I had to lend a hand one more time. Let's just hope those shells we made under the Russians' noses are worth a damn. Without the time to craft some fins or sabot petals, we're relying on the guns' sheer might."

"What are sabot petals?" asked SSgt. Diaz.

"Well, they allow us to make the shell into a sort of dart. The way we had to make them is more like a bull—"

"Dragon Skewer, this is North," came a crackled but hushed voice over the radio. It was Lieutenant Zane.

The general had named the German 88mm gun position "Dragon Fire" to inspire the men in the coming battle. Only no one could pronounce it in German, *Drachen Feuer*, and kept saying "Dragon Skewer" instead. Tyce heard the latter was supposedly the name of some Japanese anime character. "But she's hot," the soldiers had said, "and she carries this really, really big battle-ax." From then on, there was no turning it back; the nickname was now officially "Dragon Skewer."

He had also given the men's positions, dug in and concealed across the valley, the names Kursk-North, Kursk-Center, and Kursk-South. Kursk was the name of a famous Russian tank battle from World War II.

The Russians had won the battle of Kursk, and when he briefed the men on it, he got a glint in his eye as he channeled some of the general's energy and described how the Germans had been too bold and had been defeated by the Russians piecemeal, just like he intended to do. The

Russians had lured them in, then hit them hard in their advancing flank.

He explained that the tables were now turned, and this Russian commander they were facing was also too bold, just as their German counterparts had been over seventy years before.

So they would steal the name of one of Russia's glorious battles and use the same tactics against them. The trap they had laid, and the gun they were going to use, deserved some historic references, Tyce thought. The history lesson and the motivation of tying their smaller valley fight in Harman, West Virginia, to that of a larger, massive, famous tank battle was just the ticket. The "Kursk" thing hadn't worked, either.

The men liked that Tyce was trying to tie in history and had learned tricks from previous wars to use against the Russians, but ultimately the duty of regimental historian was probably best left to the general. So Tyce stuck with inspecting every last detail, motivating his men and manning a whopping big gun.

"North, this is Dragon Skewer, go ahead." said Tyce.

"Roger, sir, I see dismounted movement ahead. They are about a platoon abreast, coming into the tip of the Y now."

"Roger, I copy. Report once they have hit the trigger line." Tyce was well aware that North was in a dangerous position. But that's why they had the best camouflage. Their position, by design, was about to be overrun. The men would have to remain completely undetected in order for the plan to work.

"Dragon Skewer, this is Center, I can confirm. I now see about twenty-four dismounted Russian infantry. They are already on both sides of the river. The main force looks to be just behind them. I think I can make out one of the BTRs," said another hushed voice. It was Sergeant First Class Garrison from Lieutenant Zane's B Troop Bradley section.

"*Skewer* copies all," said Tyce giving in to the new name.

The waiting was killing Tyce, but there was no other way. If the plan worked, Tyce and the men would make their smaller force appear much larger and stronger to the Russians. But first came the surprises.

The minutes ticked by.

If things worked the way they had planned and rehearsed it, there would be radio silence for just over ten minutes.

At the thirteen-minute mark, Tyce began to worry.

"Hope we don't kick off at unlucky thirteen," said SSgt. Diaz, who had come in behind them and was shielding her watch to check the time.

Tyce was about to tell her to go down below and check on her machine gun fighting section once more when the radio quietly came alive, breaking the still air.

"Dragon Skewer, this is Center . . . clear to fire . . . the enemy has crossed phase line red!"

SSgt. Diaz was looking through the AN/PAS-13 thermal sight system they had rigged onto the old German cannon.

"Major . . . I can confirm . . . I can see the targets. Just where we predicted. They are at max range, er . . . it's on phase line red."

"Roger. Fire when ready."

Diaz took a second more, carefully turning the small adjustment wheels on the underside of the big 88mm gun. Diaz had oiled and lubed the gun as the general had instructed, and the excess grease on the camouflage-painted gun made thin, shiny rivulets down the cold stamped steel in the glimmer of the moon. SSgt Diaz, as a heavy gunner herself, was a natural to fire the weapon.

"Time to find out if those rounds you loaded were worth a crap," said SSgt. Diaz, a big grin barely visible as she jerked the handlebar trigger.

Boooom!

The cannon let out a tremendous roar, followed by a loud clang as the barrel jerked backward and the spent copper shell casing fell from the gun onto its metal out-riggers.

The still of the night was broken, and the Russian infantry and the lead BTRs started firing—more out of alarm than anything, because none of the fire was directed at them. It seemed to be wild shooting.

"Dragon Skewer. Center. You sure got them going, as you said they would. Missed by sixty meters. The BTR is now stopped. But your fire came extremely close to some of the dismounted Russian soldiers. So no up or down adjustments required, just go right about sixty."

SSgt. Diaz was back up in the gun quickly making and fine-tuning the sights with the adjustment given. She turned the small dial on the gun six clicks and then pointed at Tyce. Tyce grabbed another shell. They were down to seven 88mm projectiles. Tyce was glad Diaz couldn't see him in the darkness. He was starting to perspire heavily, and his prosthetic leg was beginning to wobble. They didn't need the whole attack failing because he dropped a round or lost his leg hobbling around to grab rounds in the dark.

"What the *fuck* was that!?" yelled the Russian colonel into the radio.

"Sir . . . it flew over the lead vehicles' heads. It sounded like a high-speed shell. A heavy artillery piece of some kind."

"Fucking impossible," said the assault colonel.

The vehicles opened up their guns on the hills. No one had seen a muzzle flash, so they fired blindly toward anything they thought might conceal a high-velocity gun. A clump of trees, a darkened farmhouse, anything to stop this new threat.

The colonel ordered the men to cool it and only fire at identified targets. With all the noise, their outgoing fires were preventing anyone from hearing any incoming shots and identifying its location.

"Find and destroy that fucking gun. But no wasted shots." he yelled into the radio.

"Up," said Tyce as he slammed another 88mm shell into the big gun's breech. The back hatch closed onto the shell automatically with a heavy *clack*.

Without waiting, Diaz pulled the handlebar a second time, and with a boom, the mighty gun fired the second tungsten penetrator downrange.

Since Diaz and the gun had no real armor-piercing rounds, the tungsten they were able to craft in the middle of the night at the metal foundry was essentially just a really hard bullet. Like a big steel fist, it would slam into the target, but at over two thousand feet per second. There was no way to tell if it would succeed, and nothing to do short of doing what they were doing now: trying the impossible and hoping for the best.

Spaang! came the sound of high-speed metal on metal.

They both looked at each other in the dark, a look of pure glee across their faces.

"A hit!" Tyce said, overjoyed and giving Diaz a high five.

Boom! Boom! Boom!

Their momentary celebration was interrupted as three 30mm rounds struck the trees they were standing under and sent searing-hot shrapnel in all directions. It was probably just searching fire, because no more rounds followed, but it was enough to knock Tyce backward. He was blown literally off his feet and momentarily stunned by the concussions. Diaz was not as lucky.

Tyce shook his head and crawled over to where she lay motionless. A three-inch piece of steel stuck from her arm, and even in the darkness he could see she lay in a pool of her own blood.

CHAPTER 24

Ned's Center position was manned by a small group of twelve of his special forces soldiers. The rest of his men had set up a defensive position at Tyce's actual HQ. They'd redistributed a bunch of their ammo to the other positions, but kept a few AT rockets and had crafted a lot of improvised explosives. They were dug into small fighting holes that were only thirty feet off the east side of Route 72, near a green highway sign that read DAVIS 19 MILES. They peered anxiously through their NVGs at the green silhouettes of the BTR-90s who were firing occasionally into the hills trying to find Tyce and the German 88.

"They seem pretty well distracted," he whispered to the soldier in his dugout. "I'd say part one of the plan is working."

The nearness of the enemy's armored vehicles made their adrenaline pump. But they were ready. Major Asher's orders had been tight. They had done no fewer than three full battle rehearsals, and so far, the route the enemy vehicles had taken was consistent with their predictions. As they had guessed, the infantry passed right by them fixated on whatever their vehicles were firing at, and were now about 150 meters in front, reluctant to get too far off the road in the dark pine forest. They appeared not to be really checking the area over much, and they also looked like they had no night vision. The vehicles' drivers were clearly more anxious, bounding swiftly from cover to cover. The sounds of Tyce's gun seemed to have increased their pucker factor.

The second German 88mm round had scored a hit. It hadn't penetrated but had ricocheted right off the front slope of the armored hull. From the sound of it, it had hit with tremendous force. Enough that the vehicle stopped just in front of Center's position while its crew, stunned, tried to make out what had just happened.

"Go," whispered Captain Blake.

Captain Blake watched his men. A specialized sapper team he'd hand selected, led by his trusted Sergeant, Sergeant Dean, followed closely by two corporals, Franklin and Miller. The three leapt from their small fighting hole and ran toward the parked BTR-90.

They got within a few feet, and Sergeant Dean's NVGs flared up when Corporal Miller lit his Molotov cocktail. As the alcohol in the old Jameson bottle burned brightly in the otherwise dark night, Sergeant Dean's NVGs washed out, and he ripped them off and pulled his carbine to his shoulder to cover the other two.

In the moonlight, the big silhouette of the BTR-90 was now plainly visible to the naked eye. Dean's stomach churned as he realized they would also be visible to the dismounted Russian infantry just in front of the vehicle.

Corporal Franklin jumped onto the vehicle and threw a huge homemade grenade down the open hatch. It was crafted from an empty 10-pound can of pork and beans, the gunpowder left over from making the 88mm high-velocity shells, and a fistful of heavy horseshoe nails from the farm. The boys had nicknamed the thing "the Whopper."

As it tumbled down through the turret, Franklin could clearly see the BTR-90's commander inside illuminated by "the Whopper's" sparking fuse and the red vehicle lights, still trying to assess the damage from the German 88 hit. Franklin then motioned to Miller, who handed him the lit Molotov. When he looked back inside, he saw a commotion as the crew scrambled to douse "the Whopper," as he threw the Molotov behind it, jumped off, and didn't look back.

As the two men ran back to their fighting hole, a loud but muffled explosion took place behind them, followed by a grisly gout of flame blasted twenty feet straight up from the top of the BTR's hatch like the tail of a comet. Then began a series of detonations as the ammunition inside the BTR began to explode, lighting up the entire valley.

The three men pulled their carbines up, watched the raging flames, then looked at one another, awestruck and silent, then back to the fire.

"Fuck me!" said the Russian colonel aloud. Frantic radio reports were now coming in from multiple vehicles simultaneously.

"Sir, vic 2 just got hit. It looks like it was anti-armor. I heard the round. It sounded like a high-velocity shell. Sir, it must have penetrated. Vic 2 is burning. I can't see anyone getting out. The rounds are cooking off inside. It looks like they're all dead . . . burned," came the report.

"Okay, okay. No death reports on the radio. Why are they shooting over the lead vehicles? That means they can see all our lead vehicles and troops. Now listen, we have to advance. No more slow searching. The enemy is somewhere in the hill to our frontage. The middle of the valley splits at the end. In the middle is a hill mass. That hill has some heat spots on it. Sight in, and continue your attack now. Weapons free. We will have reinforcements soon."

He knew none were coming, but he could hear the men's voices wavering, and he couldn't take a chance that they would lose their nerve at this critical moment.

"Dragon Skewer, this is Center. They have taken the bait. They are continuing past my position in force and headed right toward South. They are advancing rapidly now. The dismounted troops are moving at a fast jog, too." said Ned.

Tyce crawled over to the radio. His head still felt like it was filled with a hundred buzzing bees, "Copy all . . . Continue as planned," said Tyce thickly, his tongue stuck to his mouth and the words coming slowly, "Call the headquarters . . . confirm South is all set up."

"Roger, you all good to go up there, sir?" asked Ned.

Tyce couldn't concentrate well enough to answer again, and he ignored the last transmission. He crawled back over to SSgt Diaz and shook her. After a few seconds, a deep moan came from the hefty woman. She rolled over onto her back, sat up, and stared at Tyce blinking, her face covered in dust and dirt.

"What the fuck was that, sir?" she said in a dopey voice.

"We got hit." Tyce managed to squeak out.

She looked at her arm. "Would you look at that!" She pointed to the shrapnel and blood pumping from the wound and pouring down her arm. "Fuck me."

"It's going to be OK, Staff Sergeant." Tyce tried to re-assure her.

"Doubt it." she said and proceeded to rip the chunk of metal free from her flesh. Tears of pain flowed down her cheeks leaving streaks in the dirt, "Ow." she said quietly.

Tyce's wits were starting to return, and he could think a little more clearly, "Anyhow, I don't think they have our position. Otherwise they'd be pumping more rounds at us.

The radio squawked up again, "Dragon Skewer. This is Center. Another two vehicles just passed. I say again, two more BTRs crossing phase-line Red. They're in your kill zone, sir. Need you to blast them. Do you receive me?" Ned's voice sounded a little more desperate.

Tyce grabbed the radio, "Roger, Center," Then turned back to Diaz, "We have to get the gun back in action. Are you OK to keep firing?"

"Don't think so," she said tearing off part of her shredded uniform sleeve and wrapping it twice around the bleeding wound. "My right arm doesn't seem to want to work."

"Okay." Tyce made a move toward the gun, then halted himself, "What about loading? Can you still carry the rounds to me?" They had staged the rounds in a little dugout pit covered with logs a good twenty meters back. It was common military practice to keep the ammo and the gun separate so if one took a hit it didn't destroy the other.

Diaz didn't reply, she just stood up, ran over, and grabbed one of the heavy 88mm rounds and hobbled back, her wounded arm dangling by her side.

"Well, what are you waiting for, sir? An invitation from the Russians?"

Even more impressed by her bravado under fire, Tyce pushed himself up and manned the gun. He'd watched the general instruct Diaz on its operation, but was still a little unfamiliar with the jerry-rigged night vision equipment they'd strapped to it. Diaz hefted a round up to the gun with her good arm, then kicked it into the breech with her foot. The mechanism snapped shut while Tyce was dialing the closest Russian targets.

Boom! went the old German gun followed quickly by a distant *spaang* as the shell hit its mark.

This time, the vehicle was hit clean down along the left side, right along the midsection. The BTR had been caught in an open field, bounding from its position and toward the cover of a copse of trees.

The heavy round didn't penetrate the armored hull, just skidded right along its side, but the damage was still immense. The screaming ball of tungsten going two thousand feet per second hit the BTR, ripping three of its four tires to shreds and tearing into the steel road wheels. The left wheels jammed, and that side locked up, but the right wheels were still going full speed. The vehicle spun violently on its axis, carving a deep semicircle in the field before coming to a full stop, tipped half on its side and facing the wrong direction.

The BTR's commander, who had been up in his turret scanning for targets, was tossed free from the vehicle at close to fifty miles per hour, landing in a twisted pile, his arms and legs contorted in impossible positions.

"Colonel, vic 4 just went down . . . hard. We're being bracketed, sir. Gunner says he thinks there might be several guns, sir. We still cannot identify. They have us in their sights, down the long axis of the valley. What are your orders, sir?" There was a serious tone of panic in the man's voice.

"Calm down! Everyone, stay off the radio and continue to *advance*, damn you!" shouted the colonel.

In the firelight from the first burning BTR, the colonel was near enough to see and hear the impact. By the sound, he was certain his commander had been correct, it was definitely high velocity and not just one of the U.S. infantry's shoulder-fired rockets. Beads of perspiration broke out on his brow.

Crap, crap, crap, he thought.

An out-of-breath radio operator popped up from their HQ in the woods below. "Sir, Gunny radioed for me to come check on you . . . and we heard the hits up here." in the dim light the Marine could see both Diaz and Tyce sweating profusely and racing back and forth frantically trying to work the gun and its heavy ammo.

"Get over here, kid! Help me load these rounds." yelled Diaz.

"No, go get the lady doctor." yelled Tyce, his eyes still fixed in the gunsight eyecups.

The young Marine stood fast. For a brief second, he seemed to be weighing whether to obey his commander or the giant, angry, and bleeding staff sergeant.

Before he could obey either command, a shout came from the woods "It's fucking Commander Remington." Even over the chatter of the battlefield below and their own noise and haste, they could hear her sprinting up the trail.

"We don't have time for that crap now," said Diaz lugging another round over to the gun.

"Yes, you do have time for that crap!" said Victoria as she burst into the clearing. "And it's called medicine. We've been practicing it for thousands of years now, you idiots. Now, shut up. Both of you. Do your job and fight. And let me do mine. Where the hell's Diaz?"

She searched around with her hands, her eyes still becoming accustomed to the dark, then finding her, she immediately set about working, opening a medical back-pack and dragging the big SSgt down to the ground, where she lay the wounded arm flat across her knees. Diaz protested a moment, then sat down hard and let Victoria do her work.

No more time to waste. They had to fire, now.

Tyce slammed the half-loaded round into the weapon, the breech mechanism closed, and he pulled the hand lever.

Boom! went the old gun again, the big metal breech dashing back, the pistons slowing the recoil and putting the weapon back into battery.

Immediately came a radio call from Ned, "Dragon Skewer, this is Center. Another good hit. That one pene-trated. The vehicle is burning."

Tyce looked over the broad, flat valley of Harman. The report of rifles and the many muzzle flashes in the valley told Tyce what was happening. Each accurate shot sent the Russians into a tizzy and probably against orders for fire discipline, they began fighting ghosts, much like he had in Iraq and Afghanistan. An unseen enemy is the most un-nerving. Only now, this was his homeland and he was pleased to be the one destroying the foreigner from the shadows.

If we make it out of here today, thought Tyce, *I'll re-member this. We can be successful if we put our minds to it and use some ingenuity.*

Gunny's voice came over the radio net. "Dragon Skewer, this is South. The lead BTR is turning onto our obstacles and crossing the trenches. He's at phase line blue and almost on me. Permission to kick off our surprise."

The Marine radio operator loaded another round and Tyce sighted in another BTR while yelling back to where

Diaz was being treated by Victoria, "One of you get on that damn radio and tell Gunny to wait for my command. We need the Russian commander all the way in the kill zone."

Boom! went another round.

"I've got it." yelled Diaz, pulling the radio close to her by a wire while Victoria dug smaller pieces of metal from her arm and protested her every move.

"Another hit!" yelled Tyce.

Diaz couldn't resist pumping her arms while she balanced the radio receiver between her ear and shoulder relaying the message to Gunny.

"This is not helping me save your damn arm, Staff Sergeant."

"Colonel, we've spotted that gun position. Firing now." came in one report, quickly followed by another, "Sir, we can see the enemy trenches in front of us. That headquarters barn is right behind them, just where you told us it would be. Permission to surge forward."

"Granted!" radioed the colonel firmly. Finally, the tide was turning. It was time to strike at the heart of the beast.

He watched two of the BTRs pumping rounds into the trees on an adjacent hill. It looked accurate, about where he'd have placed a gun, too. With the enemy gun effectively suppressed, all he had to do now was close the final distance and wipe out their command. After the hard battle, he was practically licking his lips in anticipation. He didn't relish reporting the few losses to these hillbillies, but clearly, they'd bitten off more than they could chew.

* * *

The trees came alive with exploding 30mm cannon fire. The entire area lit up from the showers of sparks. Tyce and the others dove for cover. The crack of detonations and whizzing shrapnel filled the air. They had found his position. There was no way to man the gun now.

Tyce fell flat on his belly and crawled back to check on the others as the Russian cannon fire continued to pound their position. Victoria and Diaz had made it back to the ammunition dugout. The radio operator must've been caught in the open when the rounds first began to impact. He lay atop an 88mm shell, his body sliced to shreds. Tyce grabbed him by the arm and dragged him toward the ammo pit. It was the only shelter available.

Victoria stopped, pulled away from Diaz, and checked the radioman. She shook her head at Tyce. The three of them lay low under the pine logs as rounds continued to burst all around them. Huge limbs, metal shrapnel dust, and debris flew all around them, making communication and even rational thought next to impossible.

Under the logs, they were relatively safe. But that's when Tyce realized they were sitting atop the remainder of the 88mm high-explosive shells. One piece of shrapnel, and they were all going to go up in a blaze of glory.

CHAPTER 25

Tyce crawled over to Diaz, the 88mm rounds cold against his stomach. He tugged on her shoulder. They could not hear one another above the din of the incoming Russian fire, though it had slackened a bit.

They are probably on the move toward Gunny, he thought.

Tyce held his thumb and forefinger up to his ear like a telephone. Not particularly effective, but Diaz got the point and pulled the radio out from by her feet where she had dragged it when the firing started.

Tyce tried to cup the handset tight to his mouth and transmitted, "Gunny, fire now!" he yelled. He could not be certain the Russians were all fully in the trap, but based on his best guess, it was time to take back the initiative.

In seconds, brilliant and enormous flashes of white and yellow illuminated the whole valley. The Russian cannon fire on Tyce and the gun position ceased immediately. All three sat up, their ears still ringing, and looked out over the valley below. Even through the thick pines, they could still see the enormous blaze as propane tanks and gas drums erupted like volcanos from the middle of the earth. Next, the fuel dumped in the trenches lit up, creating rings of fire around the advancing troops and vehicles.

Several of the explosions detonated with enough force

that the nearby Russian infantrymen were coated in burning gasoline. None of the improvised bombs provided enough force to penetrate the BTRs, but liquid gas flung into the air poured back down through the open hatches and over the engines of those caught in its radius.

Two Russian BTR crews jumped off, their jackets and helmets on fire, abandoning their vehicles and sprinting to the rear on foot panicking all nearby. Seeing this, many of the dismounted infantry also began a general and disorganized withdrawal. Until now, many hadn't even seen who they were fighting against, and this was too much for them to bear.

A third vehicle, awash in burning fuel, gunned it into reverse hoping to escape the incoming flames. With the constant *pings* of bullets still impacting them from all sides, the crew remained inside. It looked like they were not about to give up the protection of their vehicle or were hoping to activate their fire extinguisher systems and at least get back far enough to dismount out of the danger of the fire and constant small arms. But it was too late for them. Enough fuel had entered the cabin and found the stored ammunition. Sparks, flames and heavy smoke began to erupt out the hatches, like a slow-to-start Roman candle. Even worse, the throttle was jammed in reverse, so the burning vehicle backed across a plowed field dripping red gobs of ignited fuel all the way.

The exploding gas tanks, the lit trenches, all of it was such a spectacle that for a heartbeat, the entire battlefield ceased fire as every combatant, both enemy and friendly gaped awestruck at the grisly sights. Near the center of it all, the burning ghost vehicle retreated slowly, popping and burning, leaving a long line of lit fuel in its wake.

Not a person watching didn't feel at least a passing bit of sympathy for fates of the crewmen trapped inside. Theirs were hideous deaths on display for all to see.

The Russian colonel's eyes were wide as saucers and tears of stress and anguish flowed freely down his cheeks. He wiped them off quickly on his sleeve, lest someone else see. Then continued to watch in silence, thoroughly overwhelmed by the turn of events. His radios also remained silent. All of his men were now forced into fighting their own small pockets and too busy to report up the chain.

"Fuck this." he said aloud, "All vehicles, all vehicles. The American hillbillies are using IEDs. Button up and pull back on me. Time to hit them with the heavy stuff," said the colonel.

He didn't need to send the order twice. The sheer weight of what had just happened had already fallen on the men's psyches and seemed to pull them back even before the order was given. The awful sight of the still moving and burning BTR seemed to have sounded the retreat from beyond the grave.

As they pulled back, the remaining BTR crews and infantry grew more and more angry and fired willy-nilly. A need for vengeance arose in some and in others a desire to keep the Americans at bay. They sprayed the hills, trees, and anything that they didn't like. The wanton acts added back a bit of bravery that was lost, but the Russians' spirits were now thoroughly broken.

The colonel sighed and looked over at the air officer, "Call them in." he said simply.

* * *

Tyce, Victoria and Diaz all edged to the lip of the gun position and looked out. They had the best vantage to watch the Russian retreat.

"Do you think they'll advance again?" asked Victoria.

"If we give them too much time to think about it, they will. Maybe not willingly, but their boss will rally them if he sees a chance. He doesn't want to return to Morgantown and face his superiors empty handed."

"Should we hit 'em again?" asked Diaz.

"Most certainly." came a voice from the wood line. The sonorous voice of General Lawton surprised them all, "But for the moment now I'd say you have thoroughly defeated the enemy commander. At least in his own mind." Bill Degata towed the general over to where the trio was half sitting, half kneeling. "Did you break my gun?" asked the general. "It's on loan, you know."

A thundering roar resounding across the valley, two Mi-24 Hind Russian attack helicopters raced down the valley from the north, their 30mm cannons blazing.

"What now, boss?" asked Diaz.

"Call Gunny, tell him to kick into phase three."

"And we'll help load another few rounds." said Bill.

The gun was covered in branches and debris, but looked okay. Bill and Victoria together hauled over another round and the one-armed Diaz helped them load.

"Aim for the vehicle that looks like he's ready to advance again, son." said the general as Tyce eyed the retreating vehicles through the sights, "It may not be their commander, but you want to reward whomever takes the first step toward bravery. The rest will then reconsider."

There were many to choose from, but with the helos closing fast he needed to fire. If he waited too long, the helo would see them and they were not likely to survive a direct attack from the elevated position the helos could provide their own 30mm cannons. Sweat broke out, and he could hear the whispers of the rest behind him goading him into action.

Shit, he thought, there was so much smoke and so much cannon blasts from the BTRs obscuring his vision. *Wait, there—* One of the vehicles had halted its movement. It began to inch forward. The beginning of a rally, Tyce could feel it in his bones. He took careful aim, sighted in, and pulled the hand lever.

Boom!

The cannon jerked back on its carriage, a tungsten round on its way.

Spaang! the round hit the BTR right against its side. It ricocheted, but the impact seemed to change the vehicle commander's mind. His vehicle began to reverse again, and those near it hastened their withdrawal. If they had forgotten about their enemy's cannon, the reminder that the gun was still in action spurred them on.

"Now, give the command to the Gunny for your final surprise." said the general.

The Russian colonel nodded to his air-liason officer, "Have them strafe that damn tree line. That gun is back in action. Is the Il-20 picking up any other radio transmissions? Have the other hit their HQ. We might not be able to get there, but if they can take out their HQ we can begin our advance again."

"Yes, sir. They report a massive spike from a barn over there on the next hill. It's glowing in the thermals, too. The Il-20 reports that from the amount of signals coming from that barn, it *must* be their command post."

"Okay, tell him to hit that spot with everything he's got."

The Russian air liaison returned to his station at the bottom of the vehicle, where he lay down on the steel floorboards. He had the handsets held to his ears and was trying to coordinate the helicopters on to the radio hot spot that the Il-20 surveillance aircraft had detected with its direction-finding gear. After the sounds of the 88mm gun ricochet, he refused to come off the floor.

The Russian Mi-24 pilot acknowledged the spot and said it was hot in his thermals, too. The colonel listened to the Mi-24's blades make a groaning whine as it pulled a hard right to circle back south toward the barn on the hill.

Additionally, reports were coming in from all his men that the American small-arms fire had virtually ceased. Either they were cowed by the arrival of his helos, or they were running low on ammo. It didn't matter to him much either way.

Ah, good, thought the Russian colonel. *Finally, the tides of war are turning back in my favor.*

"*Na, vykusi!* Eat fire!" the Russian pilot yelled into his radio set.

From afar, he had zeroed almost immediately onto the enemy barn headquarters. It was a superhot spot in his thermals. He listened to the radio as his wingman still searched for an anti-armor cannon that was playing havoc against the Russian ground forces.

The pilot was too young to have fought in Afghanistan, but he had heard the famous stories of *Comrade* Mi-24s being of great assistance to the brother infantry, and so he was elated to finally take out—what had the ground commander called them? Ah, yes, "hillbillies."

The pilot dipped low and fast into the valley, pushing thrust to get on target, then pulling back and leveling so the weapons officer could maximize all his weapons on the target.

"Now, Vassily." he ordered through the intercom.

The whoosh of the rockets firing off the wing mounts and the shudder of the 30mm told him Vassily was going to be right on the mark. The barn was quickly ripped to shreds, and the big, lurching Mi-24 started up its forward momentum again, ready to go assist his wingman.

Gunny had to sprint back to the Quad-50 from the cover of his trench once he got the radio signal. The gun had been placed away from the trenches with the best view of the sky, which unfortunately meant he had to cross twenty meters of open ground to get to it. He watched the helo's rounds blast into the barn next to him as he ran, ripping the simple wooden structure to pieces. Wood spans and framework danced through the sky.

Behind him, from their trenches, the men yelled encouragements, "Go, Gunny, go!" and "Hurry your fat ass, Gunny!"

He closed the last few meters and slid like a baseball player coming into home, tumbling into the ditch around where the Quad-50 had been dug in. He had only a small window when the Mi-24 crossed over the treetops on its attack run, its nose dipping toward the barn. In the gun position the helo passed directly above him, its 30mm cannon dropping heavy shell casings all around him. Gunny wasted no time ripping the canvas cover off the quad-50.

He sat down hard on the bare metal seat and furiously worked the hand cranks to rotate and elevate the machine.

No one had known exactly which side of the valley the enemy aircraft might come from or even what kind of aircraft might come for them. Tyce and the general had been insistent that they'd wait until the time of most need to race in air cover. That was when Gunny was supposed to unveil their final bid for success. Without it, there was always a chance the Russians would overwhelm them.

The big bird filling his sights, he cranked down on the trigger with all his might.

Tak-tak-tak-tak-tak!

The Quad-50's four barrels blasted heavy-caliber bullets directly into the helo's nose and underbelly. The Mi-24 pilot hit his thrust and tried to jerk up on the collective in one last desperate attempt to climb up and away, but the volume of fire from the machine guns was too great.

Chunks of his airframe ripped loose. The pilot couldn't see a thing through the torrent of bullets slamming his helicopter cockpit. The windscreen exploded, sending a thousand shards of glass into his and the weapons officer's faces. The fat Russian bird yanked sharply upwards, tracing a smoking, flaming arc up into the sky. Then it seemed to simply run out of power and hung in the air, suspended at its zenith for the briefest of seconds before it began a lazy death drop back to earth, its nose still pointed up. The bird came crashing tail first down into the tall pines. A big black and red orb of fire and smoke rose skyward as all of its remaining aviation fuel burst into flame.

The second Mi-24 was still attacking and looked like it had a narrow approach on Tyce and the 88mm. It began an attack with a rocket run.

Gunny wasted no time. He cranked the hand wheel as fast as he could to a point that would account for the almost 1,400-meter distance to the second helo. Using the firing Russian rockets as a reference in the dark sky, he said a Hail Mary and gently squeezed the trigger.

For a second time, the M45 Quad-50 reliably hammered out four white hot jets of .50 caliber bullets. The gun's rate of fire was nothing short of spectacular. In World War II, it had earned the nickname "Meat Chopper," and today it would add to its reputation as its rounds screamed skyward and made contact with the other Russian chopper.

The distance and the lack of clear visibility put him at a distinct disadvantage, but the second Mi-24 stopped firing, and he could hear the *whop-whop* of its heavy blades as it flared up and pulled away. Out of rounds and losing sight of the rapidly departing aircraft against the night sky, Gunny stopped turning the hand crank and just stared into the open darkness, and panting heavily.

Still riveted to his seat, Gunny watched thick smoke rising from the four barrels when a cheer rose up from the trenches behind him. It started small, but then came like a wall of thunder. All the men had watched his spectacular display of heroism and bravery.

"Gunny, you da man!"

"Holy shit Gunny, you killed 'em."

"Fuck ya, warrior!"

The shouts were joined by war whoops, rebel yells, and shrill sports arena whistles.

Gunny flopped his head back, gave a huge sigh of relief, and allowed himself a giant grin as the men continued to hurl encouragement and genuine cheer.

CHAPTER 26

Harman

Tyce couldn't stop smiling. The ambush had worked. The Russians had a few tricks up their sleeves, but by using the general's advice and sticking to his own, well-rehearsed plan of successive ruses, the Russians had been beaten. He grabbed the radio and congratulated the men at each of the three ambush points and told them to break their positions and come up the hill to his actual HQ. The phony HQ still burned brightly in the valley floor. Even that ruse had worked.

After sending out orders, he pulled out his canteen and gulped the whole thing down in just a few chugs. He glanced around the small gun position and patted the lightly smoking beast as if it were a dog that had done its master proud. He reached over and pulled SSgt. Diaz to her feet, checking over her wound.

"How's it feel? Hurt much?"

"Nah, feels fine. I'm ready to go, sir."

"Atta girl," Tyce heard himself say, instantly regretting it. He was so used to having only male leaders, but now both SSgt. Diaz and Victoria glared at him in the partial moonlight. Then all three broke into an uneasy and fatigued laughter.

Bill Degata looked at the three of them in confusion, "What's so funny?"

"Nothing, Mr. Degata," said Tyce, still chuckling. "Let's get down from here and go see how everyone else is doing. I'd like to see if we took any casualties." They all gave Bill and the general a hand down the dark trail.

Once they were gathered around the hunting shack, Tyce had his Humvees brought up the logging trail. Victoria went to her ambulances and started treating the wounded as they arrived. All three ambushes started trickling in a bit at a time. Tyce greeted each column of men, eager for some news. One by one, the units reported in. A few shrapnel wounds, a lot of scrapes and cuts—but then came the fatality reports, fifteen KIA. Tyce's heart sank. It all seemed now to be a Pyrrhic victory. His spirits down, he walked over to confer directly with his leaders as they arrived.

The general walked over to Tyce as he sat on his Humvee hood, quietly listening to the details from Lieutenant Zane, Captain Blake and Gunny Dixon.

Everyone turned toward the general when he couldn't suppress a few dry coughs, but he covered his mouth with a handkerchief and managed to croak out, "How'd the Quad-50 do?"

Tyce looked at Gunny, "What'd you think, Guns?"

"Holy crap, sir. That thing might be old, but it sure did the trick." Then, realizing the impact his comment might have on the older general, he said, "But, you know, oldie but goodie."

"I think you need to stop while you're ahead." said SSgt Diaz.

"It sounds like hoorays are in order for the home team,"

said the general before again breaking into a small coughing fit.

"Absolutely. You OK, sir?" asked Gunny.

"Hoo-ah!" said Ned.

"Maybe," said Tyce, a little worried about the old man's health.

The general recovered and sensing Tyce's mixed emotions asked, "Remember, lad, trust your instincts, even when things are going badly. Let the military half of your brain take over, and it will find a way through the madness"—the old man held up a radio—"and maybe trust your men a little. They captured a Russian radio. My Russian is pretty rusty, but we think we heard the name of your opposite number, the Russian commander who took over Morgantown. His name is Colonel Nikolaevich. We're not getting any more transmission, but maybe we can give it a go later. Listen in to them for a change."

Tyce appreciated the captured equipment as well as the words of wisdom. He just still wasn't certain he was doing it right, and their losses seemed to prove it. He was used to having a higher headquarters to call for help in a pinch. The general certainly was providing the spiritual guidance he needed. But that didn't give him the leadership or the support and supplies he desperately needed.

Tyce turned their attention back to business. First, he congratulated them. Even though he took the losses personally, he felt they deserved his personal thanks. Next, he asked for an ammo count. Even with the ammo commandeered from gun stores by Gunny and what little Ned was able to redistribute, the unit was once again almost completely dry. Finally, it was time to go over the next part of the plan.

Tyce had been so absorbed in the ambush that he'd only

given rudimentary thought to what was next. Now, after the hard work and casualties, he wanted to give the men a break, if possible. He pulled out the map and asked them where they thought the best location to set up shop for a while would be. Somewhere they could lick their wounds, get some food, rest, and hopefully find a source of ammunition. Most of the reservists had a better idea of the surrounding areas since they had grown up and lived most or all of their lives in West Virginia.

"Somewhere in the Monongahela National Forest," recommended the general. "It has many entries and exits, and some areas are so dark, even on the brightest of summer's days you can't see inside the deepest nooks and crannies of the forest."

"Why not back at the SF training facility?" Captain Blake suggested, using shorthand to refer to the special forces facility. "I think there might be some ammo there. There's a few bunkers we never looked into, and it's real near Parsons. The townspeople have been good to us, and they were a town worth defending."

"What about melting into the woodwork?" suggested Gunny, who was a family man. "Maybe let the boys go home for a week, see their families, ensure they're safe, then come back renewed and recharged."

Tyce thought long and hard about that recommendation, but his fear was that many would not return.

"Well, some of the reservists and Guardsmen had jobs besides the service," said Gunny.

"True," said Tyce, "but we're at war. The rules have to be different now." He didn't like the words he said, even while he was saying them. He vaguely remembered General George Washington saying the same words at Valley Forge, or some such. Even under an oppressive regime, the American ideals were what were most important, and his home state of Virginia's motto was *Sic Semper Tyrannus*: thus always to tyrants, meaning tyrants would never win. Tyce wondered if he was becoming a tyrant for not letting the men return. He caught himself saying out loud, "W.W.G.W.D.?"

Victoria seemed to get it right away, "George would have probably fought some more, then given his men some furlough after a big fight and a promise of a pay increase, and *then* given them a big speech to ensure they understood their duties to their nation and returned. He still would have lost about ten percent, though."

Behind a phony mean streak, Victoria conceals a very intelligent side, thought Tyce.

"What about the ski resorts?" recommended Lieutenant Zane.

Everyone stopped and stared at the junior man. They were about to scoff at him when Tyce interjected, "Let the man speak."

"Well, sir. The ski resorts all have an abundance of food, warm fireplaces, dorm-style rooms. Good hilltop—defensive positions. Groomed slopes mean easy visibility and good fields of fire for our crew-served weapons."

"Hey, you really got something there," said Gunny.

Tyce pulled out the map and looked to Zane. "Show me. Which ones?"

"Well, I'd recommend . . . here." He pointed to a mountaintop about five miles away, "Snowshoe ski resort. It's a bit far, but at last count, we have over six hundred men. Snowshoe should have enough food and fuel stored up to last us through the winter. Probably some 'chichi' shops with extra Gucci snow gear, too. We could augment the men's equipment and ensure no one gets frostbite before some of the really harsh conditions begin."

"I'm in," said Captain Blake.

"Makes sense to me," said Victoria. "I'll bet they have a fully stocked medical facility, too. They'd have to, dealing with all the breaks and lacerations folks get on the slopes."

Tyce was about to lay down a verdict when a shout went up from the northern perimeter where they'd left men to watch the Russians and ensure they continued their retreat. Word was sent back that something had been spotted in the sky. Tyce had half-expected another air attack but hoped the burning BTRs would keep any high-flying, thermal-detecting aircraft guessing.

A runner came over from the unit that had spotted it. Out of breath from hauling ass to get back to Tyce's command post, the kid heaved a moment while everyone waited for him to catch his breath.

"Sir . . . we see . . . paratroopers."

"Holy shit," said Tyce. They all looked up, and sure enough, even from their spot back in the woods, the unmistakable sight of hundreds of parachutes could be seen by the moonlight.

In moments, the sounds of approaching jet aircraft also rumbled overhead. Tyce had been on the other side of owning the sky in Iraq and Afghanistan and knew that those high fliers were just picking their targets in their thermal sight systems.

The general spoke. "They'll prep the objective for the paratroopers with some fast mover attacks, if they can lock onto any thermal signatures. If you don't get everyone into the deep pines, I'd say we're about to be walloped by attack aviation."

"How long have we got?" asked Zane.

"Probably fifteen to thirty," answered Ned.

"Okay, let's go!" said Tyce to all leaders present. "We go

by units. Commander Remington and Alpha-Med, you stay with and follow my Dragoons. Captain Blake and B Troop, you use your Humvees, and Lieutenant Zane, take your Charlie Company. Pick your own routing and try to stay off one anothers' paths. We have no time to spare, and this is one of those circumstances where trying to clump together in a long ranger file will just make juicier targets for the fast movers. Then those paratroopers will encircle you and pick you off. Get to your units, take five to brief them, then move out!"

"But where to?" asked Lieutenant Zane.

"Snowshoe. Your recommendation was perfect, Lieutenant Zane."

With that, they all raced off to get their units moving.

"What about my guns?" pleaded the general, his voice cracking.

"Sorry, sir. No time to pack them up and bring them down. We're going to have to ditch anything that can't be hauled out in the next few minutes."

And with that, Tyce raced over to his Humvee, gesturing at Victoria to get her ambulances moving and stacked up behind him.

Less than five minutes later, every one of Tyce's units was in the woods and making their way southward under cover of the dark forest and across the cold, desolate Allegheny Mountains. As they departed Harman Valley, a few snow flurries began to fall.

CHAPTER 27

Snowshoe, West Virginia

Tyce struggled to open the door to his Humvee. The howling snowstorm pushed back against him with fury. When the frozen, heavy steel door finally cracked open, snow and chill wind whirled into the vehicle like a frozen demon. For the tenth time in the last hour, Tyce jumped out and cleared the windshield with gloved hands.

He caught himself nervously looking behind, as if expecting a Russian BTR to come tearing through the snow, its autocannon blazing. But through the blizzard, all he could see was a sheet of white and the dim white glow of the headlights of the Humvee behind. No sooner had he finished cleaning the caked ice from the wiper than the windshield was partly covered with snow again. He gave a thumbs-up to the driver, who cranked the wipers and defroster again. Spotting another figure outside the Humvee behind, he trudged through the knee-deep snow toward the figure.

As he approached, he recognized the big form of SSgt. Diaz, with Trigger by her feet and partially under the hood of the Humvee for warmth.

He tried to yell over the wind. "About ten or twelve more miles!"

She looked up at him, her balaclava covering her mouth

and goggles over her eyes. She'd pulled someone else's uniform jacket up over her head to protect her head from the whipping wind. Her lack of specialized winter clothing was yet another reminder to Tyce that they had been woefully unprepared for this. After their exercise, they'd intended to be fully secured back in their barracks in Morgantown by now.

She pulled the balaclava down and tried to yell back. Instantly, wind and snow smacked her chapped lips, making verbal communication near impossible. "I sent my gunner back to count all the vehicles. Every time we stop to clear the snow, I send him back to check to make sure we haven't lost our Tail End Charlies in the snow," she said, using the military terms for the last few vehicles in a convoy that sometimes had a hard time keeping up.

Tyce didn't want to complicate things further and nodded, giving her the thumbs-up and patting her on the shoulder. "Not much farther!" he yelled against the storm, then walked back to his Humvee.

Looking forward, he could barely make out where the edge of the road met the forest. He signaled the driver to follow him and walked ahead as the Humvee followed slowly. He knew he could see the road better than the driver, whose windshield was constantly covered up in spite of the wipers whipping back and forth violently. He longed for the warmth of the Humvee, but he had to get his troops to safety.

He walked a few hundred feet, then went back to the Humvee. They drove even more slowly to keep the road in sight as Tyce warmed himself up, then his Humvee gunner traded out walking in front for a bit.

* * *

Two hours later, with Tyce leading the snowbound convoy and fuel running dangerously low across the group, Tyce thought he spotted something ahead. He approached a little more cautiously. They could easily run into a Russian patrol and not even see them until they were right against one another.

It was a sign. A large, ornately carved wooden sign. It was mostly covered in snow, so he wiped it off with his arm until he could make out the word "Snowshoe" and the carving of a large rabbit, which he presumed was the symbol for the resort.

Tyce let out a heartfelt whoop, which was all but lost to the winter wind but raised his spirits immensely.

He struggled through the snow and back to his Humvee. There, he sent the gunner back to inform the other vehicles they'd arrived at their new base. He allowed himself a few minutes of warmth in the heated Humvee, then he resumed trudging through the snow, leading his wayward band on the road up the mountainside.

CHAPTER 28

Snowshoe

Tyce and SSgt. Diaz returned from their patrol at the head of blue-faced, snow-covered troops, through the doors and into the warmth of the ski chalet. Windy white swirls of blizzard followed. The evening patrol sat waiting with apathy for their turn in the swirling maelstrom, geared up and in an organized, but sleepy line. Gunny barked an order, and the men let out a collective grumble but got to their feet and marched lethargically past their returning brothers and into the snowy dusk.

The returning patrol made a beeline for the huge fireplace, where the navy corpsmen had tables set up with Dixie cups full of hot cider. The troops pulled off ice-covered gear and sank unceremoniously in wet heaps onto the huge leather sofas, their cheeks and hands glowing all manner of red and pink hues.

Tyce and Diaz tramped their feet at the entrance and moved aside from the outbound troops to confer with Gunny. Gunny waited patiently for them to pull off gear, holding two canteen cups of cider. He watched with more than a little interest as Diaz unbuckled her helmet and peeled off her balaclava. A mass of beautiful, tangled, cinnamon-brown hair spilled around her shoulders.

Gunny saw he'd caught Tyce's eye and hastily chirped, "Any sign of the storm abating, sir?"

"Actually, I think it's getting worse." said Tyce unbuckling heavy boots and rubbing frozen toes.

Gunny went back to staring at Diaz as she tugged off her uniform top, her wet shirt steaming in the warm air, and showed off some of her solid but shapely body. "Uh, still nothing from regiment on the radios?" answered Gunny, "We have been hearing some American voices on the civilian bands, but we can't make them out. I've got men on the roof trying to tighten up the signal."

Tyce looked back out the chalet's big front windows and into the blue-grey darkness. Night was coming fast.

"Okay, Gunny, but don't let them tinker up there for long. No more than an hour. I'd say the temp is in the teens. With the windchill, it's probably closer to zero, and dropping." He pointed to the roof. "Up on the tenth story, that wind is going to be killer."

"Okay, sir. I'll get them down in an hour. It would be good to get some outside news, though." Gunny stared at SSgt. Diaz pulled chunks of snow off the ends of her auburn hair for a moment, then added, "The observation post at the bottom of the mountain passed word by phone that they stopped two civilian vehicles, did you hear?"

"Hadn't heard." Tyce narrowed his eyes.

"They're civilians. Probably trapped by the storm."

"Okay, let's triple-check that. I don't trust the Russians not to have co-opted some locals into trying to find us now. I'd figure some folks might forget their patriotism for a full tank of heating oil this winter."

"Never in 'Merica!" Gunny joked. "They're being escorted up here now, sir. Want to meet them when they arrive?"

"Nah." Tyce looked at the troops from his patrol, all

joking by the roaring fire. "Did we get the gas turned on yet?" It was warm and toasty in the main room, heated by an overabundance of leftover chopped wood, but the individual rooms would still be freezing. He supposed it didn't matter too much to the troops. Some camaraderie, a warm sleeping bag, a roof overhead to stop the snow and walls to stop the wind, and they were pretty much okay.

"No, sir. But we did find a few more stocked storerooms. I'm thinking we'll check out the other hotels soon, too."

SSgt. Diaz pulled off her long-sleeved shirt. Her olive drab T-shirt underneath was soaked and clung to her muscled body. Tyce caught Gunny eyeing her up again. SSgt. seemed oblivious to the attention and pushed her machine gun over to Gunny to hold, stretching out tired muscles but showing off her figure even more.

Tyce had known it was inevitable. And as soon as they had found the warmth and comfort of the ski chalet at Snowshoe, his troops were bound to start to get friendly.

"Gunny," said Tyce abruptly, pulling Gunny's gaze away from SSgt. Diaz. "I need you and SSgt. to accomplish two things. Ready to copy some instructions?"

SSgt. Diaz grabbed her gun back, laid the gun on its bipod, and she and Gunny both pulled out notepads and pens.

"Go ahead, sir."

"Okay. Number one, I need you to make sure our sentries at the four corners are alert, weapons trained on the roads and woods, and that they're being replaced every two hours, max. I don't want anyone falling asleep."

"Got it, sir. What else?"

"You and the NCOs make sure you walk around a bit and ensure the troops aren't up to any . . . mischief."

Gunny glanced at SSgt. Diaz as Tyce emphasized the last point. She was still writing, but nodded, then looked up. "You got it, boss," she said, her Bronx accent coming through. She punched Gunny hard in the gut, "No mischief," she echoed.

The captured U.S. Army trucks were perfect for transporting the Russian Spetsnaz battalion. The hardworking, U.S.-manufactured Caterpillar C12 advanced diesel engine provided a lot more power than their own trucks and even gave them a bit of speed in navigating up the steep, snow-covered West Virginia roads. The twelve trucks and two BTRs stopped in the city of Elkins to check the maps and look over their equipment before moving onwards to their attack.

The major watched the men scramble down the side of the huge truck and stamp their feet to ward off the cold. The men wore the heaviest Russian winter parkas, but the West Virginia mountain air was still thin, crisp, and bitter cold. They hadn't had long to prepare. Their commander had been adamant: "Attack at two a.m. If you are late or early, you will not get support from attack helicopters. They will attack the objective building at three a.m., sharp, then your Spetsnaz will mop up what pieces remain."

The comforts of the Snowshoe Mountain Resort made it too easy to let their guard down. Gunny had divided up every two-man pair into the unoccupied resort condos. Complete with kitchen and queen-sized beds, the troops were living large—quite a change from living in a dirty hole in the ground. They still had not gotten the gas and heat turned back on, but the comforts of a clean bed and running water made a huge difference even with the lack of heat.

Victoria walked through the immense great room. A roaring fire in the fireplace lit the room, and the troops were milling around, keeping warm. Soup and cider were being cooked in big pots over the fire. It was clear from the volume of noise and rambunctious behavior that someone had broken into the bar. Victoria spotted a few bottles being handed around.

A murmur of "officer" started up, and all the bottles were quickly hidden when she passed through. She stopped and grabbed two cups of steaming hot soup, glaring at a few of her female navy corpsmen as she went through the soup line, silently admonishing them for fraternizing a little too closely with the soldiers and Marines. She saw Captain Blake, Gunny, and SSgt. Diaz making the rounds.

They'll keep everyone under control, she thought, *and besides, the troops deserve every break they can get.*

Victoria walked down the hall, spilling soup from the two canteen cups. She spotted Tyce through the glass windows of the resort's business center. He and his headquarters staff had taken the offices over to use as planning and map rooms. He sat still, his head in his hands studying the maps and bundled up in a heavy civilian parka, gloves and hat.

After knocking, she entered.

"Hey," she said. "Need any company?"

He sniffed the air as she sat down. "Is that chicken noodle?"

"Who said it's for you?" she teased, then handed over

a canteen cup and a plastic spork. "When's the last time you've eaten anything besides coffee?"

"I've been meaning to go grab some dinner. Heard the sailors were helping out in the kitchen again."

"It's actually about to be breakfast. And we still call it a galley in the naval services, which you are part of." She looked at her watch; it was already after midnight.

He smiled tiredly but didn't answer. However, his stomach answered for him, grumbling loud enough for them both to hear.

She continued, "Gunny found some more storerooms, a few full of food for the resort. He's also found one of the caretakers, who is trying to help him get the giant kitchen going. For now, my sailors are handing out hot broth they're cooking over the fireplace, but once we get the gas going, we'll have steak and eggs for breakfast. Probably in an hour or so."

"A warrior's breakfast."

"A what?"

"It's a naval tradition," Tyce said with a smile. "Since the days of the battle of Iwo Jima in the Pacific, the Marine Corps has been serving troops a steak-and-egg breakfast before they go off to fight." He looked up at her smiling again. "Anyhow, that's what we call it."

A Marine sergeant from their makeshift radio and operations center knocked and entered, "Hey, sir, the guys who took the general back to Parsons just came back in with those two civilian vehicles. They said the general's temp is over 103, but he seemed on the mend. They also said they brought you a few visitors."

Tyce nodded and returned to his maps.

When the Marine exited, Victoria wheeled a chair over and sat down beside him. "What are you working on?"

"I . . . well, I'm trying to look for the best spot to attack the Russian supply lines. They will have to get most of their major supplies by road into and through West Virginia. I learned from fighting against insurgents that you can starve a force by attacking their supply convoys."

"Exciting," she said, trying to sound interested. She stared at the map but felt like she was probably seeing a tenth of whatever Tyce was seeing.

Seemingly reading her thoughts, he began to describe things. "This is a military tactical map Captain Blake loaned me." He dragged his finger down a thick red line that bisected the map. "This is Interstate 79. On either side, you can see the contour lines representing peaks, valleys. The other lines, blue here, are rivers, waterfalls, brown with spikes are caves, square boxes are homes, etcetera."

The highways and streets made sense to her. But the woods and lakes didn't. She threw her arms up. "Dude, I won't lie. It's an indecipherable mess to me."

Tyce chuckled. "Well, in the Marine Corps infantry officers' course, we have to learn everything about maps, compasses, and topography."

"Really? In the navy officers' medical course, we learned which fork to use at formal dinners aboard U.S. Navy ships."

He chuckled again, and she gave him a narrow-eyed glare, mocking his zestful laugh at the navy. She said, "But, I'll bet the anatomy of a human endocrine system would be just as indecipherable to you and your Marines."

He smiled. "Thank God for that. Me and my Marines have come to count on Navy medicine in Iraq and Afghanistan," he said, realizing he'd probably stepped a bit too far.

"Everyone's got a job, Major. If everyone in this mixed crew of yours were a gunslinger, you all wouldn't last long after the gunfire's over." She looked from the map and up to Tyce. "What else do you see?"

Tyce looked at Victoria. Her dark eyebrows stood in beautiful contrast to her pale blue eyes. "If I'm being honest?" He couldn't maintain eye contact and looked back to the maps. "I'm looking over the fallback plans again."

"Well, you've certainly kept everyone busy with your drills, but do you actually believe they'll find us?" She looked around and outside the glass room at the men and women enjoying themselves by the giant fireplace, as if just now realizing how impermanent their new lives were going to be. "Guess it sounds prudent, though . . ." She trailed off unhappily, as if a short stay might disrupt some other of her plans.

Whatever her meaning, Tyce didn't catch it. "Prudent? Maybe. But yes, it's just a matter of time," Tyce said.

"Before they find us?"

"Before I fuck up again." Tyce blurted out the deep truth before he could stop himself. With little sleep and an over-whelming desire to keep everyone safe, plus the comfort of speaking in private, the sudden burst of honesty was inevitable. He covered it with a small laugh, as if he were merely joking.

"Fuck what up?"

"You know . . . lose or injure more men."

She put her hands on her hips, one of her many signs of displeasure. "You know, that's some real bullshit."

"Is that like your catchphrase or something?" He smiled, trying to lighten what he'd inadvertently turned to a dark-ening mood.

She didn't take the bait. "So, what? Suddenly you are the Jesus of war, and you're supposed to know what will happen in every battle?" She crossed herself, then with a wry smile added, "Like a good Catholic girl, I say that with all due respect to the folks upstairs." Tyce noticed that her upper-crust Connecticut accent was tinged with a hint of Italian. An odd combination, but she was an unusual woman.

"Yeah, sometimes I feel like I need to know everything. And if not me, the general sure as hell should." Tyce put his elbows on the map and rested his chin in his hands, "Without his huge brain, I'll admit, I'm not really sure what to do."

"You're taking the general's illness pretty hard. He's only human and humans get sick. He's a little older and he probably pushed things as far as he could for you. Besides, he's just another tool in your toolkit. He may not be here to guide you, but the men trust *you* to figure it all out."

"Do they?" Tyce fired back at her.

She gave him one of her patented, sly grins. "Well, I do. And I'm not so easy to impress, Tyce."

He chuckled, but he also noted it was the first time she'd used his first name since they'd first met.

"Tell that to the men out there." He pointed to the great room, where everyone seemed to have settled down with big grins on their faces. Apparently the steak-and-egg breakfast had arrived. "I'm not sure you'll get the same sentiment. I'm just hoping we get Colonel Nepo or the blind general back soon." He had all but given up on the unit's actual regimental commander returning and now the general was out of the picture, too, leaving all the authority resting on his shoulders. It made him immensely uncomfortable.

Her tone suddenly became serious. "Maybe some might hold you accountable for the casualties, Tyce, but that's leadership. Especially leadership during adversity."

"I hold myself accountable, Victoria," he said. A small jolt coursed through him for being informal, but it actually felt good to use her first name.

"Those young men and women knew what they signed up for. People die in war. It's not as if you killed them."

"My decisions did."

"I don't see anyone else stepping up to take your place, bubba. And last I checked, we didn't do so bad. A mix of soldiers, Marines, and mountain men took out most of a Russian company. Or battalion, or whatever that was." She looked at him, testing him with a cute smile, "And they had tanks and attack helicopters."

"BTRs." He corrected her, "not tanks." But her upbeat mood and dry humor seemed to be having the desired effect on him, easing some of his heavy thoughts on the new burden of command. It was pretty clear he needed a friend. Someone of equal rank to whom he could speak his mind.

The glass door opened. It was Gunny. "Hey, sir," Gunny said, then startled, noticing Victoria sitting close to Tyce. "Oh, hi, ma'am." He smiled.

"What's up, Gunny?" said Tyce.

"The guys tell you we have visitors?"

"Uh, yeah," said Tyce, clearing his throat and dropping his voice back to a gruff Marine growl.

"Well, you won't believe it, sir, but the chief and Mayor Susanna Holly are here. They're looking for you."

"What?"

Police Chief Braydon entered first, his left arm in a cast, both eyes blackened, and his nose taped and obviously broken. Susanna entered behind him. Every finger on both of her hands was splinted and wrapped, and the wrappings were tinged with red. Neither looked very happy to see Tyce.

* * *

The radio call came from the lead BTRs. They were scanning ahead, and even with the heavy snowfall, they reported they had passed the checkpoint at the church and could see the base of Snowshoe mountain. They knew if they went farther, they'd probably be observed by pickets, but they also knew they had the advantage of surprise.

Colonel Nikolaevich checked his watch, zero-one-thirty hours. He picked up the radio handset. "All forces, dismount and get into attack formation. Vehicles, prepare to provide overwatch. Ensure all thermal imagers are running on black hot and call out all targets." Time was on their side, but staring up at the sky it was apparent the weather was not. No matter, he was certain of his advantages and he was ready to attack.

"Chief, Mayor, to what do we owe the pleasure?" said Tyce, trying not to sound surprised.

"We're here on business, Major. Not as friends. First, I need to inform you of the tally of your little adventures in Parsons."

Tyce's face dropped and he, Victoria, and Gunny shut up and listened as Susanna's voice rose and she began a mini-tirade. "We have two dozen citizens taken prisoner, or 'arrested' as the Russians termed it, and taken back to Morgantown. There is now a garrison of Russian troops who've taken over policing duties for our town. Worst, they interrogated a lot of folks, using the boot and the fist. Needless to say, your presence was well known, and now my town is paying the price for it."

Tyce stared at Susanna, unsure how to respond—

especially given that she was obviously one of those who had the worst of it.

"Good. Stunned silence. I would expect nothing less. As I mentioned, you all didn't think very long about the consequences of your actions on my citizens."

Tyce spoke up with a firm and direct tone but softened somewhat by her bitter words. "This Russian invasion has a scope well beyond the borders of your town, Mayor. I'm truly sorry for what happened to the town, and you . . . but this is a war. And war to the end. You have people hurt, but I've lost men. We were forced to retreat after the Russians counterattacked our positions in Harman. What you see here are the living, and we've chosen to fight and die if necessary."

"Very well, Major. But these unfortunate incidents are not why I chose to come find you. I have a second purpose, also business. Because I . . . *we* need you to survive. At least for a few more weeks."

"Oh?"

"Yes. Right now, the Russians have found your positions here."

"Holy shit!" said Tyce standing abruptly, "They've found us?"

"How could you know that?" asked Victoria.

"I have a lot of contacts. And if you listen very closely to people who think they are interrogating you, they say things they don't even know they're telling you. I would imagine there's not much time to discuss it. I hope you have worked out an escape plan."

"We . . . well, we just got here." He stammered. Susanna had a way of stopping him in his tracks, "We do, but . . ." he began, than trailed off as he caught a glimpse of the troops in the great room stuffing their mouths with steak and eggs.

"Good. You're a big boy, I'm sure you'll figure it out. I'm leaving in the next two or three minutes. I don't intend to stick around and see how well drilled your men are."

"Do you happen to know which side? From where, I mean."

"Front door, I believe you all would say. They couldn't be far behind us on Route 219. Chief here knows the roads better than they do. Even one armed, he earned your men and mine a slight head start getting here."

Tyce pointed to Gunny. "Sound the alarm. I'll take over the spoiling force. We evacuate, immediately."

Gunny turned and raced to call the posts and sound the alarm, which was basically just the buildings fire alarm.

Within moments, Tyce had a small quorum assembled with a few more arriving by the second.

"Stick to the plan," Tyce said. "Gunny and Wynand, you're with Captain Blake. Get your half of the troops to the Humvees. Docs, SSgt Diaz and Blue with Lieutenant Zane's half. We leave immediately. Thanks to some advance warning, and if we scoot, we can get everyone out of here." He pointed to the Mayor and the Chief. "Thank you again, Mayor." They nodded in return.

"Don't thank me. Just get the hell out of here and survive. Then come visit me very soon." said Susanna.

Tyce still didn't like the sound of Susanna's threats, warnings, or even her help. Each time it felt like a double-edged sword. Without a word further, she and the chief turned and left.

Tyce didn't wait. "I'm going to check on the headquarters men. They should be destroying everything, and the sentries should be collapsing back into the perimeter. Lieutenant Zane, SSgt. Diaz, if I don't make it to the basement in five, leave. You're on the clock, now move!"

"Aye, aye, sir." They all said. Victoria lingered a second, then she too raced off to organize her ambulances.

Troops scrambled everywhere and runners sprinted out to grab the men and women on patrol around the small ski village. The urgency in the air was just below panic, Tyce could feel it. They had all practiced the evacuation plan, two times a day, but now that it was for real, it looked to Tyce like controlled chaos. Their peace shattered, an unnerving feeling seized Tyce's insides as he watched the men and women prepare to evacuate their happy home.

At least we got a few days' rest, thought Tyce.

The evacuation drill was to ditch everything not already loaded into packs or the Humvees and go. Half the unit was to get out of Snowshoe in the Humvees, the other half to depart by skis. The destination built into the drill was Ned's former SF camp up by the Cheat River, but also close to Parsons. Tyce had forced the small unit leaders to study every aspect of the routing until they'd memorized every dirt road and frozen creek. At least they knew the route by heart, but all from the maps. Tyce fretted over everything.

If Mayor Susanna knew they would be back near Parsons, she would not approve, but it'd all been rehearsed before she dropped the bomb on them about the Russians torturing civilians. But for Tyce, the deciding factor was Ned's firm belief that they could score a big cache of weapons and ammo there and still remain hidden from the Russians. He'd considered going after a bigger base, one full of supplies, but he knew the Russians were now wise to the composition and the abilities of his unit. Their preemptive attack in the middle of a snowstorm proved they were out for blood.

Not enough time to adjust the plan because of the Mayor's news, thought Tyce. It was war, and he knew there were many sacrifices ahead and behind, the Mayor's included. He was also pretty sure she had something in store for him that would require even more sacrifice. She wouldn't have let him off that easy, especially to look at what they'd done to her personally. Tyce shuddered to think about what the Russian occupation of Parsons must have been like.

After checking that the perimeter was coming in and the HQ men had already left by Humvee and skis, Tyce made his way to the ski-out basement of the lodge to join the last remaining troops to leave. He passed the kitchen on the way and spotted rows and rows of steaming eggs and cooked steaks.

No time to even destroy that, guess we're feeding some hungry Russians this morning, thought Tyce.

In the basement, Tyce watched the last men and women scramble to don their gear. He noticed they each had some extra cans of food, and a few looked to have pockets bulging with a bottle of whiskey or vodka. He supposed they knew as well as he did that a few comforts and snacks were going to go a long way in the next 24 to 48 hours. Anyhow, the Russians would take everything so it was better to leave them nothing. Still, he worried all the little extras might slow the men down from the rehearsed evacuation plan time line.

Tyce hastily pulled on his snowsuit and grabbed his

body armor from the hook, then headed outside. There, two groups scrambled to clip into skis, while buddies helped them lift heavy packs. One squad leader got a count, performed a last-minute weapons check, then they vanished into the dark and frosty woods. The wind served to dampen any sounds as the troops departed, and the blizzard would cover their tracks soon enough.

With some luck, it'd take the Russians a while to find them again. Their undertaking was going to be a massive human effort. Even for trained skiers, a cross-country-ski trek with packs through the mountains at night would be difficult. Tyce and the skiing half of the unit were going more than sixty miles. Many of the troops had only ever been on skis during the past few days of practice. Daily ski lessons through a rigorous crash course designed by knowledgeable NCOs had helped, but most of them took it as a bit of fun in spite of their leaders upbraiding them after every failed slalom turn or snowplow stop.

Confident most of the troops had departed, Tyce clipped into his own skis and prepared to wait for the last few men. He wanted to leave with them and ensure all his troops got out safely.

A Marine crashed through the basement door behind him scaring Tyce half out of his wits, "There you are, sir." out of breath, he panted for a second, "Sir, it's the perimeter men. They refuse to go."

"The hell you say."

"They think they can hold off the Russians and gain you a few more minutes."

"They'll die at their posts." said Tyce in utter exasperation. "Take me there." said Tyce pulling out of his skis, ripping off the bulky plastic ski boots and charging through the snow behind his Marine in nothing more than stocking feet.

* * *

Tyce watched through NVGs as a platoon of Russians walked alongside the lead BTR, their rifles up and at the ready scanning the hills. Blue was peering happily through the new night sight Tyce's armorers had affixed to his Weatherby rifle. He hardly needed it. The road was lit by innumerable streetlights and the snow would play hell with the optics. The Russians seemed to be asking for a fair fight. They probably knew as well as Tyce that the best way to fight an elusive enemy was to give him a target, then once he popped up, crush him.

"Gimme the word, and I can take two of 'em boys before they even know what hit 'em," Blue whispered to Tyce.

It was hardly necessary to whisper; the wind was loud enough to cover most noises. Tyce pulled his own NVGs away, the snow and wind stinging his eyes.

"Hold off, Blue. There's dozens more behind them. My estimate is those men are just the reconnaissance element. They're trying to get us to take them on. I'm mostly worried about that BTR. For sure, his thermal gunsights are sweeping over the mountainside right now, and I'll bet behind him are a lot more. Anyone sticks their butts up too high, and he'll see the heat signature." Tyce looked back at the three others, the Marine messenger and two soldiers who'd refused to leave their post. They smiled at him, but Tyce could only shake his head.

"You damn fools." he said, but it was lost to the wind.

He had a mind to court-martial both of them, if they ever got out of this situation. Instead he signaled for them both to shimmy up to he and Blue. Once there, he pulled all four behind the snowbank and made sure Blue could hear him while he kept an eye on the Russians.

"What's the plan, men?"

"Me and Sergeant Copper here are gonna blow the propane tanks, snipe a few, then skedaddle."

"That's it?" asked Tyce, expecting some sort of elaborate delaying tactic.

The one named Copper looked back at his buddy, "No need to complicate things with a lot of fancy maneuverings, sir. Just hose them off and git."

"Fuck." said Tyce, rubbing his frozen feet, "Okay, I'm in. But then we go. What do you want me to do?"

"You any good with that musket, sir?" asked Copper.

"Yes. Maybe not as good as Blue, though."

"Good. Mister Blue, you initiate the hit by taking out the vehicle commander. Think you can drop one into his hatch?"

"From this angle . . . might'n be able." said the big mountain man without taking his eyes off the sights.

"Ok, whomever you can then. Barnes, you hit the propane initiator, then the three of us nail whoever we can. Say, give 'em about one minute of sustained rifle fire. Then we leave."

"Okay. Good." said Tyce.

The sooner they did so, the better. They didn't have long before the Russians reached the top of the mountain, but it was as solid a plan as any. Regardless, he needed to get the men out of here and back to their packs. His decision to ditch the ski boots had gotten him here quicker, but now, with both feet like icicles, he regretted not taking a minute longer to put his snow boots on. He thought he was just going to chew some ass, then get back to his pack and ski off. Now he couldn't help indulging some brave men in a last-chance effort to give the rest of his unit much-needed minutes to melt into the woods and farther on their way to safety.

"I can't see the feller atop that battlewagon," said Blue, "But I can see the guy drivin'."

"Just as good. On three, you shoot him in the head. Everyone got it?"

Some "yeps," and nods of heads.

"Here we go. One. Two. Th—"

"This is bullshit." said a voice from behind them. The four men all spun around to see Victoria and Trigger walking up to their position.

"Commander, I have a lone figure on the hill." said the BTR gunner to his commander over the intercom.

"Just one?"

"Might be some others. Looks like maybe a dog. All behind a snowbank. Three hundred meters. Permission to fire."

"Granted. I'll call the CO and let him know we found these damn Yankees and we're now in the assault."

The gunner had a perfect bead on the figures in the snow. Four heads sticking up peering at them up and one standing up, all clear as day.

"Colonel Nikolaevich, we have the enemy in sight. Attacking, time now."

"Roger, no mercy." came the response.

"Victoria, get down!" yelled Tyce.

Not waiting, Sergeant Copper yelled, "Fire!"

Blue squeezed the trigger.

* * *

The Russian BTR driver had his head up and out of the hatch. Driving while buttoned up in a snowstorm was impossible, so like most military vehicle drivers he'd erred on getting his boss to the objective over the risk of sliding off the road. He had confidence in his bulletproof helmet and that he could close his hatch as soon as the gunner spotted his targets.

That's when a .460 Magnum round entered his mouth, then tore through his trachea and out the side of his neck. In the last seconds before he died, choking on his own blood, his eyes grew wide in horror and his foot jammed reflexively down on the accelerator. Right then, the gunner pulled the palm switch and fired the 30mm gun.

Boom! Boom! Boom!

Came the all-too-familiar sounds of incoming 30mm cannon fire.

Blue fired again. Then all hell broke loose. Bullets, rifle-grenades, 7.62mm machine guns and 30mm cannon fire split the hill to shreds. Trigger began barking uncontrollably. Someone screamed in pain.

Tyce dragged Copper into the basement ski room of the chalet. Blue pulled off the man's body armor, and Victoria tore off his parka. Three shrapnel wounds oozed blood through his shirt. She pulled off her medical backpack, dug out a morphine injector, and stabbed it into Copper's thigh.

"Why are you still here?" Tyce barked at her.

"Waiting for you"—she looked over at the wounded man—"in case something like *that* happened." she yelled back, hastily applying QuickClot and bandages to the wounds.

Tyce watched her work for a moment, helpless as she performed her duty.

"We leave, now." said Tyce. No one argued.

Blue and the messenger Marine helped Copper back into his jacket, onto his feet, and then outside. The Russians were already right up the street just two buildings away. They had seconds left. They all snapped on their skis and helped Copper into his. The morphine must already be taking effect because he now moved as if he felt no pain and started petting Trigger and smiling at the dog.

"Copper, it's you and me, understand? Hold on to my shoulder and we ski together. Victoria, you, Blue, and Trigger, start moving. We're right behind. Go!" they nodded and skied onto the steep ski slope.

Tyce turned to the other two, "You two are rear guard. Watch the top of the slope. In a few seconds, you follow. Got it?"

Both nodded.

Tyce held Copper by the waist and with some difficulty pushed them both off and on their way. He could just barely make out Victoria and Blue. They were a hundred meters ahead. Tyce and Copper had made it fifty yards down the slope when heavy gunfire erupted behind them. Both men skied a bit further, wobbled, then dropped to the ground, but none of the fire was aimed at them.

Lying in the snow, they looked back up to the top of the slope, fighting to rise back up on their skis. They could barely see the outlines of the two men, their rifles blazing away on burst mode at the unseen attackers. Several big explosions lit up the dark resort, silhouetting the two lone defenders and casting their umbra through the falling snow and against the adjacent mountain peaks. Tyce and Copper were unable to tear their gaze away as their men's fates played out before their very eyes. A massive fusillade of tracer fire fanned out from atop the hill across the valley like a hundred laser beams. Then it was all over, and once again darkness shrouded the men.

"Let's go." said Tyce, "Nothing more we can do." his voice wavered, dismal and distant.

Tyce supported a wobbling, wounded Copper to his feet, and Copper, in turn, supported his shaking boss, and together they skied silently into the woods. At that moment, a deeply wounded Sergeant Copper understood Tyce better than anyone who's never personally witnessed their fellow warriors being cut to pieces.

CHAPTER 29

Monongahela National Forest, West Virginia

Sweat streamed down Tyce's face, out his sleeves, down his pants, and into his boots. It turned to small icicles on his balaclava. The fingers of his gloves were frozen together and stuck to the ski poles. Wet slush in his boots stung his feet, and since running around in his socks at Snowshoe, he'd given up ever feeling his toes. He tried to focus on his ski tips as he slid them back and forward and listened to the others panting next to him.

In their last hour of nighttime, the snowstorm abated, then the sky began to turn blue. The first rays of light began to dance atop the pines. In loud *whumps*, clumps of snow fell free from the high treetops, and for a brief moment of exhaustion Tyce's brain wondered at the winter's majesty as thousands of little crystals drifted from the tall pines, through the sun's light and down to earth. Then he remembered the dull, numb ache of his frostbitten feet.

Occasionally, they came to a downhill slope and made two or three miles of good progress. Inevitably, at the bottom of the hills they had to strip off their skis and put on snowshoes. Tyce carefully helped Copper out of his boots, then together they picked their way over a frozen river or cautiously crossed an unplowed road, weapons up and ready. Then began another arduous hike up another steep West Virginia hill and through more dense and unforgiving woods.

Tyce's energy was waning, and he'd only had that cup of soup Victoria brought him nearly twelve hours before to serve as dinner, breakfast, and now lunch. In the past two hours, he'd been running on nothing but fumes. He took some courage watching the others persevere, especially Copper. But he could see the morphine had worn off, and finally Copper asked for a halt.

They had been taking a breather about every twenty minutes, as much to rest as to check on the wounded Copper and to defrost Trigger. On the last stop, Tyce had noticed two big cuts to Trigger's belly. He had probably cut himself when the top of Snowshoe blew up on their final delaying attack. Might have taken some shrapnel. For now, the cold had stanched the bleeding, but when they reached safety, Tyce thought the dog might be in some trouble, not sure what Victoria could do. Trigger's wound could become infected, and if he had lost a lot of blood, hypothermia would set in.

Add it to the never-ending list of woes, Tyce thought as he squatted next to the loyal pooch and pulled snowballs off him. He glanced at the others resting in the snow against their packs. He'd kept the breaks to a few minutes at a time and forced everyone to drink water from canteens they'd stashed inside their snowsuits to keep them defrosted. He pulled out his canteen cup and poured out some water and laid it in the snow. Trigger lapped it up greedily.

He looked back at Copper, who was resting against his

pack, and smiled, "You ready to go, old man?" he asked, trying to squeeze out a little more encouragement.

Copper's eyes and smile remained fixed on Tyce, but he didn't move.

"Okay, no rest for the weary." Tyce tried to put up a good front, but he was as dog tired as Copper and yearned to lie down a few minutes more as well. Tyce walked over to him and pulled his skis out of the ground and laid them next to Copper's boots.

"Here we go."

When Copper still didn't move, Victoria came over and waved a hand before the man's face. She laid her fingers against his throat, then turned to Tyce and shook her head. She closed Cooper's eyes and looked up at Tyce sorrowfully. Tyce called Blue over and not surprisingly, Blue pulled out a Bible and asked permission to say a few words. After their prayer, the other two looked at Tyce.

"What should we do?" asked Victoria.

"Leave him." said Blue, "We can come back for him later." The old mountain man was used to death and didn't see a reason to slow their progress if they didn't need to. He'd killed lots of things in the snow and returned to get them later.

"No," said Tyce, "We take him with us. I'm not leaving another man behind."

No one argued, but Victoria glanced at him as if he were talking nonsense. She knew he was almost out of strength and literally carrying deadweight would slow them to a crawl.

"It's okay." said Tyce, "We'll trade off, but we're getting this man back to his family."

Leaving Snowshoe and escaping the Russians was only half their trouble. Now, fighting across a hellish, mountainous landscape with a wounded dog and a dead man was going to be the other half. In fact, as Tyce snapped back into his skis and hefted Copper's lifeless body onto his back, he realized that escaping the Russians had been the easy part.

Until gunfire erupted from the opposite slope. Someone had tracked them all night and finally caught up.

CHAPTER 30

Monongahela National Forest

For the time being, it looked like they had lost their Russian pursuers. It had been six hours since they were last taken under fire. The fire had been inaccurate and at long range, enough to keep them trekking at an anxious pace and constantly looking behind. Six hours fighting through the snow, but the afternoon and even early evening sun had warmed their bodies and their moods a bit.

Tyce struggled with Copper's body, even rigged up and towed behind on his skis; the added weight was taking its toll. Blue had traded off for many of the hills, but Tyce cheated the time line and took more of his share carrying him. Tyce had ditched almost all of their gear to lighten the load. Both packs were first to go, Copper's body armor and parka, then Tyce's flak jacket and helmet, finally mag pouches, combat webbing, and extra grenades. Now his weary mind kept returning to the possibility of just leaving Copper in the snow. It would be immensely easier and perhaps twice as fast. He was slowing down and endangering the rest of his small, fleeing band.

No, that was exhaustion taking over. He must let his rational thoughts win. He knew they'd never find Copper again. Without a GPS lock or a firm location on his map, it would be a huge challenge to ever find Copper's body.

That is, if wild animals didn't find him first and make him a midwinter snack. Tyce shuddered at the thought of one of his men being eaten.

No way, Tyce thought. *No man left behind. Even if it means sacrificing my own life in the process.*

His men would never follow him again if he treated their fallen with such disrespect.

A crackle of gunfire broke out behind them again, and they sprinted up the last steps of the hill, snapped skis on, and skied as fast as they could down the other side.

Night was coming, snow was whipping up again, and their visibility was reduced to a few meters. Trees became obscured, like a white sheet had been drawn over the forest. Tyce glanced behind, hoping the renewed snowstorm would obscure their tracks. His eyesight was blurring, and the snow obscured more than twenty meters back, but he could still discern neat cuts through the snow that the Russians would surely be able to follow.

"Hey!" Tyce yelled against the storm.

He'd stopped too long and could no longer make out the other two. He looked around; disorientation from the fatigue had taken over. The snow fell even in huge, downy flakes, adding to his confusion. He glanced around and back again, hoping to see something that would at least tell him what direction he was going. Copper's body tied to the skis and laid out parallel to his at least told him he hadn't inadvertently turned. His tongue lolled out and his mouth hung open. He could feel his heart beating irregularly.

"Stop! he yelled, then to himself, "I can't . . . can't go on."

Victoria and Trigger materialized ahead of him through the nearly impenetrable white mass.

Thank God, he thought. Then as Victoria neared, "I . . . where . . ."

"Tyce," she said, pulling down the balaclava and revealing a huge smile on her lips, "Blue went on ahead. He caught sight of something. Let's go."

She held Tyce by the shoulder, and together the four of them forged forward another hundred meters. Then they saw Blue racing toward them and yelling. Ahead a flicker of light, maybe a streetlight or a house, but definitely a sign of civilization.

"Aim for those lights!" Blue shouted to them gleefully, the sound of the wind nearly drowning him out. Victoria turned back, the balaclava around her face and neck thick with ice and snow. She nodded and yelled ahead to Blue something Tyce couldn't hear. Blue came back, grabbed Tyce, attached a strap to him and started to tow Tyce and Copper. Trigger came up and bit Tyce's gloved hand and started to drag him forward. Together, they made it the last full measure.

Several buildings became visible through the snow.

"It's a bar!" yelled Victoria in Tyce's ear trying to encourage him onwards. It worked.

Another twenty feet and they could see people through the glass windows. The place was packed. A generator and the glow of the hearth showed why practically half the town was gathered there. Warmth and power were just about all anyone could want in a storm and during the crisis of an invasion. That, plus some human company to reassure them and, of course, a little bit of alcohol to make the invasion a bit more digestible.

Tyce crashed through the doors. Blue came next, dragging Copper's body inside with him. Victoria and Trigger came next. Tyce tried to say something, but collapsed down to the floor. Victoria removed Tyce's skis while Blue pulled Tyce to his feet, Copper's body still tucked under his other arm. The entire bar crowd pivoted and stared at the three snow-and-frost-covered figures. There was a brief moment of uncertainty as Tyce surveyed the place and the locals stared back at them. The last thing he wanted was to involve the locals in his battles, but he and the others could barely stand, Tyce most of all.

"We're U.S. military, there is a Russian assault unit just behind us. They've followed us all day and night. They're going to kill us, and we're out of ammo." Victoria said through numb, blue lips.

There was no response, just vacant looks.

"Does anyone here have a Goddamned gun?" Tyce managed to squeak out.

A chuckle started in the corner of the bar. An older man in overalls with a huge, flowing white beard started a big belly laugh, then those around him joined in, and in moments, the whole bar erupted in laughter.

"He's serious!" said Blue, "There's Russians just behind us."

Tyce held his carbine up, shrugged his shoulders, pulled the magazine, and stared into it. Looked like about four more rounds. He turned his back on the bar, propped himself up against Blue, and prepared to fire at the next thing that came through the doors.

The man with the beard stopped laughing. He casually slipped off his bar stool and walked up to Tyce. He came in front of him and looked him right in the eyes.

"You all look exhausted. Why don't y'all just sit this one out?"

At which point, he pulled out a Smith & Wesson 45 silver long barrel that glinted in the firelight. "We can take it from here." The old man motioned to the lady bartender, who poured three coffees, then added a liberal amount of whiskey to top them off.

One by one, the men and women in the bar pulled out pistols and hunting rifles, donned their coats, and patted or saluted Tyce, Blue, Trigger and Victoria on their way out into the blizzard. No one seemed to be coordinating their movements, but Tyce watched through the snow as they set up just in front of the building. Blue dragged Tyce over to a bar stool and plopped him down heavily, then put the hot coffee and whiskey drink in his hand. Victoria sat next to Tyce and Blue next to her and all three sat and stared like they were watching an evening's action flick on the TV.

In less than a minute, muzzle flashes blazed from every corner. The blizzard muted most of the weapons' reports, but it was all over before the trio even fully realized what had happened. In ones and twos, the town reentered the bar, some reloading lever guns, others dumping out brass from wheel guns, and still others replacing spent AR magazines with fresh ones. They each went back to their seats and their drinks, drained them in one gulp, and called for refills while discussing amongst each other if there would be more Russians coming and whether to leave the bodies in the snow or not.

The man with the beard was the last one back inside; he and another man carried a third, who had been wounded. Blood was running down his leg, but you would have barely known he was wounded to look at him. Either he had had enough to drink to dull the pain, or he was just made from the tougher stock the West Virginia mountains seemed to be known for, because he had a huge grin plastered across his face and kept chanting, "got me two of 'em," holding up two fingers like a peace sign—"Got me two"—and collecting cheers as they carried him over and laid him on top of a big oak table. Several others gathered up some bar rags and a bottle of whiskey—careful to grab some of the cheapest the bar had on offer—and poured it on the rags, then wrapped it around his bleeding thigh. He winced in extreme pain, but yelled out, "Got two of 'em, the bastards."

Victoria pulled off her snow jacket, grimacing at Tyce as she watched the men perform their drunken triage. She grabbed her medical bag and stomped over to bring the men's field medicine back into the twenty-first century.

The old man with the beard came over to Tyce and shook his hand. "Drink up, soldier, you ain't got no Russian problem no more." And he pointed to Tyce's whiskey and coffee.

"There'll be more. They'll come looking." He managed some sips of the hot beverage. It was over-the-moon tasty.

"Probably, but the snow will cover them over for now." said the old man, feeding Trigger bits of beef jerky. Trigger's tail thump-thumped against the bar. "And later we'll go out and recover the bodies and give them a Christian burial in the woods behind the chapel."

The warm room and whiskey, coupled with exhaustion and an empty stomach, started to make Tyce's head swim.

The bearded mountain man smiled again and clapped Tyce on the shoulder. "You just take a rest, Major Asher. We've got you all settled now."

Tyce was about to ask how they knew his name, but all he could manage was, "Where are we?"

"You in the free city of Davis, West Virginia, boy." said another local.

CHAPTER 31

Davis, West Virginia

Tyce awoke with a start and sat bolt upright. Completely disoriented, he looked around the room. Wood-paneled walls, a worn woven throw rug displaying a hunting scene, old wooden crossed skis on the wall. A warm fire in a fireplace. The place smelled like pine, and the warm glow was inviting. All this added to Tyce's confusion.

He tried to pull his arm from under the blankets to check his watch, but it obeyed him only slowly and with great effort. He cringed. Nearly twenty-four hours on skis had caught up to him. Dull, throbbing pain in both arms from dragging Sergeant Copper and pushing ski poles. His thighs throbbed, and a different, sharper pain stabbed at his fingers and toes.

Frostbite? he thought.

The pain jogged his memory. Clouded thoughts returned. A long trek through a blizzard, a risky firefight, townspeople killing their pursuers. What time was it? A window—it was dark outside. Nighttime. But how long had he been out? Hours? Days? He'd lost all sense of time.

Surely there are Russian reinforcements coming. They have a unit missing, he thought.

A cold, prickly sweat swept over him, and he reached around for his M4 carbine. When he didn't feel it by the bedside, he took a moment to steady himself. Then, with great pain, he pulled his knees up toward him and half-rose, half-rolled out of the bed. His feet touched the warm floor, but his ankles and knees gave out, and he fell in a heap onto the hunting rug.

The sound of footsteps scurried toward the room. He turned his head toward the door to see Victoria looking down at him with the usual disappointed curl to her pretty lips. He was too pained to get up.

"Well, if that isn't some real bullshit. You are supposed to stay in bed," she scolded him, then sat down in a chair and looked him over. "But since you're finally up, we've been hard at work while you've been laying down on the job," she gibed at him. "Some of the townsfolk and I did some calculating. Do you realize we skied almost sixty miles? And you carried Copper most of that whole way."

"Who . . . I mean, how . . . ?"

"Don't worry. I sent Blue away when I undressed you. And also when I dressed you back up again." She smiled. "I had to look you over for injuries and frostbite. You went down pretty hard. You should be glad I managed to save your fingers and toes . . . and other extremities. I warmed them slowly, so you didn't lose anything. And I promise, I didn't look . . . much." She giggled.

"I'm in no mood for joking, Commander—"

"Okay, can we just go by first names again? After all, we're the same rank, and we're also in private, and we have some time."

"What about—"

"Blue and Trigger are fine. And the town took Copper to a cellar. He'll be buried in the morning."

Tyce heaved a sigh of relief. "How long have I been out?"

"About eight hours."

"What time is it? Shouldn't we get going?"

"It's about four in the morning, and no, you need to rest. We can get up and move again in the morning after a hearty breakfast. The bar we were in last night said they'd serve us up some bacon and eggs tomorrow."

Tyce's stomach grumbled loudly at the thought of food, and Victoria giggled again.

"I brought us some snacks, just in case you woke up early. Be right back."

She hopped off the bed and returned with a plate of cheese and bread and a bottle of red wine.

"The bread is good carbs, you need them. The cheese, too—some dairy will be good for your empty stomach."

"And the wine, doctor?" said Tyce, a hint of humor returning.

"The wine . . . well, that's for me. A reward for dealing with a stubborn old goat of an infantryman."

Victoria had been busily answering Tyce's rapid-fire questions, but now she locked eyes with him. The look lasted just a second too long for two workmates, and a heartbeat too long for two friends.

"Should I pour us some wine?" She reached over him and grabbed the glasses off the nightstand, her arm brushing against him and her chest coming close to his face.

"Why . . . I mean. Victoria, it's not right. I have a mission . . ."

"This isn't about you, Marine. It's about me. I'm tired of racing around. I want this. No, I need this." Tyce, as tired as he was, was more than a little taken aback by her forward nature. "And quite frankly, I'm tired of listening to your self-doubt. Maybe a romp in the hay will do your damn machismo some good. You're a combat leader, for Christ's sake. Act like one."

"That's not fair. You only know me—"

"I know you plenty. I know you through the eyes of your men. I know you in the way you look out for them every day, even when they don't notice. I knew you the first time I laid eyes on you. You are what our nation needs in a time like this. You are what the Corps made you—"

"Ha!" It was Tyce's turn to interrupt. "The Corps tossed me aside a long time ago. When leaders in the infantry—men I looked up to—said I wasn't worthy. A medical board. With doctors like you. They said I wasn't . . . that I wasn't a whole . . ."

'Oh, bullshit. More self-pity. You're here, aren't you?" She took a long sip of wine and then put the glass up to his mouth. Tyce sipped at it, reluctantly. He took the glass from her. He needed the drink. He downed the glass and felt the wine warm him inside and quiet his mind. She smiled and poured another. She drank some, gave him the glass, then kissed him full on the lips. It felt good. Too good. Tyce shook his head.

"I've . . . I've just killed a lot of men."

"That's what warriors do."

"I mean *my* men. They died. Because of me, my decisions. And it's not just them. The mothers, the families. The blame."

"So, it's your fault? The enemy played a role, Tyce. Those that blame, those that hate. They need something to affix their anger to, and they can't yell at the Taliban, at ISIS." Victoria shook her head. "Tyce, there's no room to dwell on the past. You are in command of your own destiny. Combat is bloody. Combat is tragedy after tragedy.

Your job as a leader is to make sense of the things you can." She pulled him close and kissed him again.

She opened her blouse a little and pulled his hand up to her neck, then reached over and started slowly unbuttoning the flannel shirt she'd dressed him in only hours before. "And you deserve this, and I deserve you. Be here. With me, for a time. Have the courage to enjoy one fucking thing in your life before you let the world dictate who you are supposed to be."

"What about—"

"What?" She stopped and stared into his eyes. "Your leg? Or your . . . other parts? I already checked, you've got everything where I need it tonight. So just stop fucking thinking and kiss me, you total idiot, before I lose patience and go find Blue."

"You wouldn't dare!"

"Ha!" She laughed the most beautiful and coquettish laughter Tyce had ever heard, "Gotcha. Knew I could break that unbreakable, gruff Marine exterior."

Tyce let his hand drop to her open shirt, and this time, he leaned in and kissed her, his lips against hers. It felt wonderful.

Rays of sunlight peered through the cabin windows. Tyce rolled over and touched the far side of the bed, but it was empty. Had he dreamt the night before? No, he could still smell Victoria on the sheets, and he smiled to himself. She was a gorgeous and intelligent woman. More important, she understood something of the trials and tribulations that made him tick. He stretched, but his muscles barely responded. He was still paying for the—what did she say?—*sixty-mile* ski trek.

"Well, good morning, sleepyhead," came Victoria's gruff and tough voice from the doorway. "I have coffee in the other room."

"Mmmmm . . ." said Tyce.

"That's about all you said last night, too. Must mean you didn't mind it too much."

"Mmmmmmmm!" he said again, louder, as he tried to stretch his exhausted muscles.

"I have some Motrin for you to take with your coffee. And better, I have some good news. We'll be extracted from here and back to Parsons in an hour or so."

Tyce sat up in bed. "Really? How—"

She ignored him and continued, "I also got word from Gunny that he has everyone accounted for over in Parsons. It's a small Christmas miracle. Besides a few cases of legit frostbite and some ditched and broken Humvees, they all made it. You were right about one thing, though: they are after us. The Russians have wanted posters up for us all over. Well, you, mainly. They have your picture posted in nearly every small town with a reward of six tanks of propane for the winter to the person who steps forward with info about your whereabouts for the Russians. The townsfolk showed me a copy. It's a pretty good likeness. Looks like you in your dress blue uniform. You look handsome. Still . . . six tanks of propane would go pretty far this winter. A pretty good offer, but I'd need at least seven." She rubbed his chest to warm him up and flashed him her sly, coquettish smile.

"How did we get word? Do they have a radio here?" said Tyce eagerly, already thinking of the things he needed to radio over for Gunny to do in his absence.

"From Gunny. In fact, I was just coming to try to wake you. When I called over to the mayor's office about an hour ago, I got ahold of Gunny, SSgt. Diaz, too. She wanted to ask permission to go on a foraging run to get some machine gun ammo. Says Captain Blake still thinks he knows some hidden ammo bunkers. Guess the Mayor let everyone weather the storm back in Parsons too, at least until we can get the SF camp."

"Called over?" said Tyce, suddenly sitting upright and staring at her.

"Yeah. The town told me this morning that the landline phones were up and running again. Another miracle. You should be proud of me—I've been taking the initiative to make this resistance of yours happen while you slept the night away. Or maybe I was just that good," she said with a note of glee, pushing his hair back over his forehead and leaning in for a good morning kiss.

Tyce pushed her aside, much to her annoyance. "We have to get moving." His tone was urgent. "Now!"

She tried to push him playfully back into bed. "No, we're fine. Relax. Gunny has two camper vans on the way to pick us up right now. Should be here in about an hour." She glanced at her watch. "So you just lay down a bit longer." Then, in a husky tone, she added, "Doctor's orders."

"No!" he said, pushing her away.

Her expression changed to irritation at his rebuff of her advances and his lack of acknowledgment for what she figured were some top-rate, infantry-style decision-making skills.

"We must leave immediately," he croaked out.

She seemed about to object more, but he held up his hand and clutched his throat. He was completely dehydrated. "The Russians . . . they'll be here very soon . . ." A haunted, shaken look came back over his face.

"No, they won't." Victoria was completely shocked by

his sudden change in attitude. "Wait, what do you mean? They couldn't."

Victoria filled up a glass of water from a pitcher by the bedside and handed it to him, staring at him with frustration. He gulped it down greedily, some of it sloshing down his face and neck.

Then he croaked, "They did it. They turned the phones on."

He paused, sipping more water, his throat starting to clear. "They wouldn't have turned the phones on if they weren't monitoring. Every word."

She stared at him, a look of mixed shock and horror growing with the realization of the truth of his words.

He nodded as if acknowledging her fears. "If you called an hour ago, the Russians will be here in no time. We need to get out of here. And let the town know to get ready. They'll have to blame us for the dead Russian platoon. They'll have to tell them we killed the troops and left or there will be reprisals. The Russians will likely kill half the town."

Tyce looked up at Victoria. His words had shattered her newfound feelings of safety and security in the town and their brief sanctuary in the cabin.

"Oh my God, Tyce," she said, the horror of her own actions finally dawning upon her. "I screwed up, big-time." Gone was her usual self-assured attitude, and she bit down on her lip. Staring into his eyes, tears beginning to well up in hers.

Tyce continued, "We need to find a way to warn Gunny. He'll drive right into them."

"I . . . oh . . . oh no. I'm so sorry, Tyce. I thought that . . . I tried to do everything I thought you would do. I would never have guessed they'd tap the phone lines."

"They control *all* the infrastructure now, Victoria."

His heart jumped a little. Her usual tough exterior, her strong bearing, had cracked, and she was deeply upset. She had just wanted to prove to Tyce and the troops that they could count on her. That she had a use in this new world order, and that she would fight for Tyce and to regain their nation. That she could heal *and* do a spot of organizing when needed. Now she stood motionless, her confidence gone.

Though he knew there was no time for such things, he realized he'd hurt her feelings. And he also realized he cared for her, deeply. They had only moments left, but he needed to make sure she was not stunned into immobility. He'd seen that before on the battlefield. When greatly shocked or distressed in combat, some troops just sat still in true shell shock.

"Stop. No time. You could never have known."

It was painful, but he tried to soften his tone and his expression some. "Let's just get to a vehicle and scoot. See if the old man can get us a car." He stood up painfully and looked around the room for his prosthetic leg and his rifle. "I'd rather not hike over another mountain, if we can avoid it."

He found them both resting in the corner and hopped over. He hastily buckled on his leg, then grabbed his rifle and the stack of rifle magazines while Victoria watched him. He was all business again. The cold, hard warrior was back, and the man whose chest she'd rested on so comfortably all night was gone. She had hoped she'd bought them a little peace and quiet. She'd thought if she helped and did the right things, there might be a chance for more intimacy. A closeness she needed in the chaos and worry of this stupid war. A feeling she had yearned for.

CHAPTER 32

Morgantown

General Tympkin's plane touched down with a hard bump. The small, commandeered American twin-prop Beechcraft C-12 wasn't well suited to the snowy and windy conditions of West Virginia, and Colonel Nikolaevich knew the general was going to be in an even darker mood than usual. Nikolaevich had his staff all turned out, their grey winter overcoats flapping against the chill wind and the rush of air from the propellers.

The general stepped onto the rickety metal stairs shoved next to the plane and, upon spotting Nikolaevich, narrowed his eyes. Tympkin looked at his footholds coming down the ice-covered rungs, and Nikolaevich made a quick trip to the base of the stairs and called his staff to attention, then pushed a heavily gloved hand up to his brow in a salute.

"Good morning, General. It is indeed—"

"Cut the shit, Nikolaevich, and lead me to your office. We have matters to discuss, and because of you, there is now an urgency . . . from the top."

"Yes, General."

Colonel Nikolaevich half-led and half-followed the general to the third story of the Morgantown reserve center.

* * *

The colonel's office was pretty much as the former occupant had left it, minus the decorations, trophies, and awards. He ushered the general in and took his coat, then handed it to his aide. Before Nikolaevich could even get his coat and gloves off, the general had sat in the colonel's chair and behind his desk.

"Comrade Colonel . . . what am I to do with you?" he sighed.

The colonel had been practicing his opening defense in his head for several days and began quickly. "General, with the resources at hand . . ." His well-rehearsed speech trailed off. General Tympkin's gaze turned to a scowl and scared him to death. He tried to began again, "General, Insufficient assets—"

The general slammed a fist against the wooden desk, making pens jump and paperclips scatter from their holder. "Maybe I am not being clear. You will stand. You will listen. I will tell you what to do, and then you will do it. At no time will you speak unless addressed. Am I clear?"

Colonel Nikolaevich leapt to attention, "Yes, General." He felt rivulets of sweat drip uncomfortably down his back, into his trousers, then down his leg.

"You have three days. And I will never hear again from you about 'assets' and 'resources.' The American 10th Mountain Division, whatever was left behind when they deployed to Iran, were assessed to be only mechanics and support personnel. The American version of our undesirable units. Hoodlums who have been caught doing drugs, failing their fitness tests, or just too attached to Mommy to deploy. This assessment came from the highest levels. It was wrong. So right now, the battle in the highlands of New York at a place called Fort Drum is consuming most of our reserve forces. Meanwhile, a little place called

Camp Lejeune and another called Fort Bragg are quickly becoming smaller versions of the quagmire that has become synonymous with Fort Drum. And that's just the American East Coast. Do you get the picture, Colonel?"

"I do, sir." Sweat was now beading on Nikolaevich's brow, threatening to turn into a full-blown faucet and drench his face, but he did not dare remove his gloves or coat at this point in the general's speech.

"Good. So maybe you're not a complete idiot." The general let the harsh nature of the words sink into his subordinate. "Now, here is the part you must pay very close attention to, Colonel. When Comrade President Kryptov came to the Pentagon, he stared at my maps for about an hour before speaking. After an hour, he turned to me and pointed to the red markers on the computer screens over the hills of West Virginia and asked me a remarkably simple and straightforward question. One which I will now pose to you." The general leaned forward and placed both palms flat on the wooden desk. "How . . . the . . . fuck . . . ?"

Nikolaevich stared into Tympkin's eyes, then began to answer in a dry voice. "Comrade general, it is hardly a failure—"

"Ah," interrupted Tympkin. "You see. You should be proud of yourself. You already got out more words than I'd have expected before I wanted to bash your nose in." He leaned back again and smiled, but it was a sinister and completely unforgiving smile, the kind that churns men's stomach into a pot of gastric acid.

General Tympkin stood up and called outside the room for the aide to bring his greatcoat and gloves, then turned back to Nikolaevich.

"You have three days. Then I return to hear your plan. I will bring my staff. You will personally brief a full and organized plan to pacify your assigned region. And if I hear 'more resources,' I will demote you to private and send you into the ranks of our 8th Guards Division who, right now, are fighting and dying outside Fort Drum. Maybe then you will provide some use in our struggles. At least you can give your life and die for a team that is currently winning their fight with blood and courage."

With that, the general turned, put on his greatcoat and gloves, and walked back to his plane.

CHAPTER 33

Parsons

Tyce was dirty from head to toe. Caked in mud, soaked to the core, and stinking like a horse. How had Victoria even tolerated being near him? he thought, but he figured she must have been filthy too, so it hadn't mattered.

Susanna had kindly offered the troops the use of the police chief's locker and shower rooms. She then offered Tyce the use of her own shower in the mayor's office. He questioned her motives for a second, but after getting a whiff of his own scent, he quickly accepted.

After finding nothing but women's bath products in Susanna's shower, Tyce came out smelling like lavender but loving the clean feeling. Toweling off, pleased with himself for not stinking, and scratching at his freshly cleaned hair, he looking forward to a hot-water shave.

He entered Susanna's vacant office, where she had said he could store his things, to grab his shave kit from his rucksack. At least, it had been vacant when he went in to take a shower. As he entered, whistling the Marine Hymn, naked and with the towel slung over his shoulder, an older man sitting in the office chair coughed uncomfortably.

Susanna sat at her desk and looked at Tyce from head to toe, letting out an amused sigh. "Mac, I want you to meet Major Tyce Asher. He's the Marine whose *assets* I've been describing to you," she said with a grin. "Hero of the West Virginia mountains."

Tyce hurriedly covered himself with the towel and smiled. Susanna had done it again. There was clearly never going to be a time when he could turn his back to her.

"Major Asher, this is the governor of the great state of West Virginia. The honorable Mr. Ted MacIntyre. We just call him Mac."

"Honored, sir," said Tyce, continuing to clutch the towel around his waist. After another awkward moment of hesitation, he stepped forward and shook the governor's hand.

Tyce had been so flustered that he hadn't noticed two men at the window.

The governor spoke. "Major Asher, I'd like to introduce you to the Vice President of the United States and the secretary of energy."

Tyce had partially recovered his composure after being surprised out of the shower by the governor, but this was a lot more to bear. His expression went flat, and out of the corner of his eye he could see Susanna's face light up in a crafty smile while he stared at the men by the window. Her ploy was now complete. Tyce was left speechless.

The vice president, a tallish man, greying at the temples, could see Tyce's distress. He walked over casually and shook his hand. "Major, we've heard quite a lot about you." He beamed.

Apparently, Susanna couldn't resist one more punch and added, "And now you get to meet him . . . in the flesh." The typical charismatic luster returned to her smile, and she stood up from her desk. Tyce noticed most of her fingers were still wrapped and splinted.

The governor gave Susanna a disapproving look and said, "Major Asher, we've caught you at a disadvantage.

Why don't you finish changing and come back in? What the vice president and I have to say to you is of the utmost importance."

Tyce nodded, grabbed his uniform and pistol belt off the back of the chair, and headed back into Susanna's bathroom.

In a few minutes, Tyce was back, and they all gathered at the big, round table in Susanna's outer office.

The governor spoke first. "Major Asher, we have a mission for you. A mission of national importance. You have done some hard work in the hills of West Virginia, and now we have a mission that is above and beyond the call of duty."

Tyce, now recovered from the earlier shock of being buck naked in front of the vice president, was still reluctant to speak. It was more than a bit of an ambush, and he figured this was what Susanna had been grooming him for all this time. Possibly seeing if he was made of strong enough stuff to even do the job. Testing him to see where his loyalties lay. *So,* he thought, *old Susanna is actually quite a patriot at heart.* Enough so that some kind of civilian underground had sought her out and entrusted her with the lives of the last remaining members of the U.S. government.

The VP spoke up. "Major Asher, as you probably already know, the president has been missing. There is little we can do to find him, if he's even alive. D.C. is the new center of Russia's power over our country. I suspect it will take more than your unit to dislodge their forces, and they are bringing new troops in on a daily basis through the seaports, through BWI and Dulles airports, among others in the occupied territories. The situation in the East is grim, and getting worse."

"I follow, Mr. Vice President. What about our active units deployed against Iran in the Middle East?"

"It's a good question. We don't have any command and control over our forces, so I wish I could tell you we could order them back and have them attack and repel this invasion. But here's the thing I do know. The Canadian government has offered, through secret comms, to help us reestablish command and control over all our forces."

"Well, that's the best news I've heard since the damn Russians invaded. But I'm not sure what I can do to help. I mean, I barely made it this far without losing the whole regiment. We are low on ammo and weapons, and we don't have any of the considerable advantages in technology we once possessed. No satellites, air-cover artillery, or armor."

"Yes, we're aware. All those assets are now in Russian hands. But I can get you a small stockpile of ammo. In fact, one of your attached leaders, Captain Blake, was training on the site just recently. We've had training ammo out there for the SF units for some time. Radios, batteries, some anti-tank equipment. All in limited supply, but I understand you could use it."

"That would be a very welcome surprise, Mr. Vice President."

"But it all comes with a catch."

"Okay, you have my attention, sir."

"I need you to seize Yeager Airport and get the Cabinet and myself aboard a plane—"

"Two planes, sir," interrupted one of the Cabinet members, who Tyce recognized as the secretary of state.

"Correct, two planes. We'll split the Cabinet for survivability into two aircraft and head north. If only one aircraft makes it, mission accomplished."

"It sounds like a very good idea. There would need to be a lot of planning. I don't imagine the Russians at the airport will roll over. In fact, Yeager is one of the most defensible airports in West Virginia. Has to be—it houses some of the West Virginia Air National Guard's biggest commands."

"Exactly why we think it's the best for our needs. U.S. aircraft will still be there. Our best intelligence suggests the Russians didn't destroy much of it at all and are cross-training their pilots on our captured aircraft. And why wouldn't they? It's basically a free air force, with all the parts and fuel reserves they'll need to comb fighting men like you in the hills for years."

"It sounds like it's at least the start of a plan, but it begs my biggest question. How the heck am I supposed to fly you to Canada, Mr. Vice President? All my men are infantry, reconnaissance, and support specialties."

"Ah, that's where Mark and Gene come into play. Gentlemen."

Two men in civilian attire, whom Tyce had assumed were Secret Service, stepped forward.

"These men are actually the source of much of our intel. They are both pilots from the 130th Airlift Wing. You get us there, and they'll fly us out."

"Is this a direct order then, Mr. Vice President?"

"No. Does it need to be?"

"I've always been told to steer clear of volunteer missions, sir. They are usually the ones that leave a lot of men dead," Tyce answered flatly. He'd watched a lot of good men get cut to pieces, and he did not relish going on some fool's crusade if it didn't accomplish one of his two goals: hurting the Russians or taking care of his troops.

"I understand. May I call you Tyce?"

"Yes, sir, but it doesn't bring me closer to agreeing to

put my folks' lives on the line again. They have been through a lot, and we're finally getting up on our feet a bit. We've stuck a knife in the Russians' side, and I intend to keep twisting that knife until we take back what's ours."

The VP smiled at the governor and Susanna. "I think we have the right man," said the VP. "Tyce, the mission will ensure the continuity of our government. Your government and the last duly elected government by the people, of the people in the United States before it was crushed under the boot of a foreign invader. This isn't my mission, Tyce, this is the mission of the uniform you wear and the people it represents. Will you do it?"

Tyce scratched at his three days' worth of beard growth. In all the excitement, he had yet been able to take a razor to his face. "Well . . . I'm not sure how I could turn that down, Mr. Vice President. Any way I look at it, it becomes a necessity. A duty. If we don't get you out, the Russians will eventually close in and find you. With both the VP and the president in their grasp, I suspect the Russians will declare all their policies lawful. Whereas right now, with you missing—well, almost missing—once you show up in Canada, the whole Russian invasion loses any sense of legitimacy."

"That's right. I'll add something else if it helps you make your decision, Tyce. You can have anything you can drag or grab from Yeager Airport. Finally, I'd like to use my powers as the vice president to promote you to lieutenant colonel for your bravery in fighting thus far, even if you don't accept the mission."

"No, sir."

"No, you won't do it?"

"No . . . I mean, yes, sir, I will do it. We will do it. But no promotions. That looks like a bribe to get you out. Not only does it turn my stomach, but the men would see right through it and think I was on some kind of quest to make rank. Using their lives as fodder. No, sir, if we do this, we do it because it's our duty to preserve the nation we love."

"Okay, we are in your hands, Major. You may have everything you can take from the armories in the SF training grounds east of here. Distribute it to your troops as you need. I imagine you need some time to do some planning?"

"Yes . . . yes, sir," said Tyce, looking over at Susanna. "But I'm going to need you to authorize me to exert some power over the local establishment. The police . . . and the mayor."

"Granted. Whatever you need, within reason. You have full autonomy and military authority over the region and whatever matériel you need. We must preserve the Union."

"Good. Thank you, Mr. Vice President." He turned to the door and called for Gunny, who arrived from the adjacent shower looking clean and fresh. "Gunny, grab the usual suspects. We've gotta figure out how to save America."

CHAPTER 34

Morgantown

General Tympkin eyed Colonel Nikolaevich but listened patiently as the colonel went over his plan to fight the resistance in the mountains. The briefing consisted of ways in which the Russians intended to work with the local population and help them increase their crop yields, and by doing so win their hearts and minds. Much of the plan centered around reeducating the people to the ways of the Russian Federation—to the ways of communism.

Colonel Nikolaevich personally briefed them on what he believed was an excellent overview of the ills of democracy, how, according to his well-educated thinking, they could convince the American proletariat to surrender the things they didn't need and come to understand the excellent advantages posed by a collective system. No more superrich bossing them around, they would be free to enjoy the fruits of their labors, to farm and live off the land.

The colonel and his staff droned on for over an hour. Finally, General Tympkin showed his annoyance and stopped the briefing.

"Colonel Nikolaevich, send your people to go get some dinner. I wish to speak with you in your offices."

In the colonel's offices, the general proceeded to rail

against Colonel Nikolaevich and his overly nuanced plan to fight the hillbillies.

"Do you not understand that these remnant elements of the former military are determined to defend their homeland? Before you even have an opportunity to reeducate the local farmers, you are going to have to get off your ass and fight what's left of their army. Get in the hills and root them out. I need you to be ruthless."

Colonel Nikolaevich was scared stiff. Since the general's last visit, he'd pulled out all the stops and worked up what he considered to be the plan Tympkin would want. If this wasn't good enough, he had no other ideas. There were two reasons Colonel Nikolaevich had been sent to the sleepiest part of America: No one ever expected resistance in the mountains of West Virginia, and maybe more apparent to General Tympkin at this very moment, Nikolaevich had graduated at the very bottom of his officers' course.

"You have one week, Colonel Nikolaevich. One week to get after an opponent that, right at this moment, is sharpening their blades and searching for your throat. Mark my words, these men want to defend their homeland and will resist anything you do to stand in their way. They care little for collective farms and the ability to exchange their wares. They want freedom."

"But General," the colonel interrupted, still not understanding the signs the general was giving. "Once we teach them about our system of free education and show their minorities the Russian system of true equality, they will gladly relinquish any hold their system has over them and relish the wonderful workers' system that we provide them."

The general listened, nodding without interest, and stood to go, then reemphasized his point. "One week. Then it's Private Nikolaevich in the assault-breaching element of the 8th Guards." He marched out and signaled General Kolikoff to follow.

On his way out, Kolikoff pulled Nikolaevich aside. "Old comrade, let me know what I can do to help you. I'm in the new center of power, the American Pentagon, and we have many assets available in the area that are not tied up in fighting the former regime at their old bases. We still have some reserves. Do not go at this fight alone. Let me help. But also, I have seen General Tympkin at his best, and at his worst. He means what he says, comrade. And he is not a man to be trifled with."

Colonel Nikolaevich stared at him vacantly, and then General Kolikoff hastened off for the flight line to fly back to Washington and the Pentagon.

CHAPTER 35

Parsons

"We only have one choice," Tyce said as he finished up the attack briefing and looked around at his leaders.

Gunny was the first to offer up anything. "Sir, what you're asking for is basically suicide, running directly into the mouth of the enemy like that."

Tyce rubbed his face with his hands. His Marine Corps instructors in college had always told him "Never let 'em see you sweat." Fine advice for some deodorant commercial, but it was one of those stupid phrases of the day that everyone repeats over and over, trying to sound pithy. But just at this moment, it resonated deeply with him, and he finally understood what they had meant with their cheesy pop-culture mantra. The men didn't like to see their leader frustrated or in doubt. But it was hard to hide his feelings from his men in such constant close quarters and under such critical circumstances.

"Look, I know I'm asking a lot—"

"Boss, you're asking everything. You're asking them to go right into the teeth of the bear," Wynand interjected.

It looked like Victoria was about to burst, and she blurted out, "It's all how the men understand it. Ty . . . I mean, Major, if you say it's necessary, if you tell them they are the last hope to keep the vice president alive. If you tell them they are the last gasp of a democracy not just under fire, but *on* fire and with only one elected official still alive at the top . . ."

She stopped just short of finishing her thought, but Blue, in a rare instance of speaking in public, finished for her. "Then we'll all follow you to the gates of hell, Major. You've got my rifle at the ready."

"And we'll need it, Blue. You stick with the snipers, see if you can't teach them a thing or two."

Even the sly Wynand interjected. "It's the best way, boss—hit 'em where they least expect it and let them hit us where we ain't. Think I might be able to get some eyes on the lay of the land, too. Got a bud up there who does the sewage trucks for the airfield."

"I'm not gonna ask—it seems you know a lot of folks. If you can find out where the flight-worthy birds are, though, we sure could use that intel. It would be murder to get all the way into the perimeter and find the aircraft have no fuel."

"Or be missin' an engine." said Wynand.

Tyce looked at Ned. "Captain Blake, what do you think?"

Ned chuckled. "Sir, I'm still trying to get used to you and your Marines' tendency to lead by consensus. Me and the men of 19th Special Forces are here to do the job. Maybe we can even prevent you Marines from just becoming cannon fodder, as you all seem determined to do."

Tyce and the rest laughed a bit, but the last words also stung some—as they were intended to. Since Ned was only one rank below Tyce, and was a card-carrying special forces Ranger, he had the chops to take the occasional poke at the boss.

"Okay," Tyce said slowly. "We do it. Ned, you're the bait. Commander Remington, you need to get all your sailors who can walk and every bit of medicine you can scrounge. Gunny, have all hands ready to move out at twenty-two hundred hours. It'll take at least four hours to get there."

As everyone scattered to go get their men prepped, General Lawton tugged on Tyce's sleeve. He'd had a rough go, and everyone just assumed he'd beaten a bad fever. Victoria told Tyce in private she though it might be something far worse. He might have radiation poisoning.

"Good work, son."

"Thanks, sir. Means a lot coming from an old salt such as yourself."

"Old salt . . . hmmm, I have some miles on me, but just you remember, wisdom and judiciousness are friends at the same party."

"And which dead general is that quote from?"

"Well . . . let's just say, he ain't dead yet."

CHAPTER 36

Parsons

Captain Ned Blake stared through his night vision binoculars at the approaching convoy. In any other scenario, against any other opponent, the approaching Russians would have gone unnoticed until they were directly on top of their quarry. That was, in fact, exactly their aim. But Ned's men of the 19th Special Forces were not an ordinary opponent.

Ned's men hadn't just spotted the approaching Russian convoy as they made their way across the frozen and snow-covered West Virginia landscape. True, the Russians had traveled the forty miles under cover of total darkness with blackout lights to conceal their travels over the highway. But Ned's men had used an RQ-20 Puma, a low- to no-light military drone, to covertly observe the Russian soldiers as they rolled out of their racks at one a.m. They had watched the Russian officers muster their troops on the snow-covered cement outside the former National Guard barracks, and even watched them lazily go to the chow hall to eat breakfast before the NCOs performed weapons inspections by flashlight, then mount up and head toward Ned and his troops. All this before the drone had to return due to its battery limitations. If Ned's men were the bait, they were the kind of bait that looked like easy prey, but turned out to be anything but.

Still, Ned was taking no chances. He reached over to his pack and fished out his thermal vision binoculars. They took a moment to warm up, but after a few heart-racing seconds, he was rewarded with a clear image of the vehicles stopping on the next rise over. He watched patiently as they dismounted, their NCOs quietly and efficiently getting them into their assault formations. The light artillery, two small field guns, might actually have gone unnoticed. Ned's drone had come back to charge up before the light artillery had been spotted.

They must have mustered and departed from a different part of the base, Ned surmised. But at least two of the "gun bunnies," as the Americans called artillerymen, seemed to have an unquenchable smoking habit. Ned watched the cherry-red embers at the ends of the smokes dangling from the lips of their men through his thermal vision as they unpacked and set up their gun.

Well, one thing's for sure, thought Ned. *They are ready for the day*. Ned was more than a little envious of the Russian's battle array. He could see medium and even heavy machine guns.

He smirked a bit and leaned over to one of his senior sergeants. "Here we go, brother. Tell C Company to prepare to unleash all hell on my command." He locked and loaded his M4 carbine.

Just like Ned's team was doing outside Parsons, Tyce looked through his night vision goggles. But Tyce wasn't playing defense to the Russians' offense. He and the rest of the 150th Cavalry were one hundred percent on the offensive. And if he played his cards right, the Russians at Yeager Airport near Charleston would be nowhere near as ready as the Russians attacking Ned. Or, more accurately, falling into Ned's trap.

Blue slid across the snow on his belly up next to Tyce, his military-issued snowsuit keeping him dry.

"Major, I've done all I can with your HQ folks. Given them all the Russian positions we reconnoitered. I'd like to ask permission to head back to your snipers' positions and help out there for the battle."

"Sure, Blue. Keep sending back reports as best you can. I know they're glad to have your rifle in their mix."

"Don't know about that, Major, but one more long gun can't hurt, and I'm no good to anyone back here at your HQ."

Tyce was experienced enough to know that Blue meant no offense by the remark, but Tyce also knew he'd be spending almost the entirety of the upcoming battle up on this very hill overlooking the airport. It pained him more than a little. As a Marine, he wanted to be where the action was, but as an officer, especially a field-grade major, and the commander of the unit, he knew his place was orchestrating the meticulously planned pieces, taking in the ebb and flow of the fight, and shifting forces who were heavily engaged or spurring on the groups that were meeting success and encouraging those that inevitably were not. As the old militarism went: "all plans fall to shit on first contact." Tyce hoped to make today an exception.

Tyce's short-range radio headset sparked to life. It was Gunny Dixon.

"Dragoon-six, this is Dragoon nine-nine."

"Go ahead, nine-nine," Tyce whispered into his mic.

"Okay, six, I've got a final count. But you're not gonna like it."

Tyce's stomach fell a bit. If something had piqued Gunny's masterful instincts, it sure as hell wasn't going to sit well with Tyce. "Send it," said Tyce shortly.

"Okay, in addition to the dozen attack helos and up-gunned Tigrs Wynand reconned, he also reported two new additions. Probably arrived in the past twenty-four hours, but thank goodness Wynand spotted them."

"Yeah, what did he spot?"

"Two Russian main battle tanks. Just piecing together what he and his buddy described, it sounds to me like T-90s."

"Shit . . ." Tyce said under his breath. Then he keyed the mic. "Copy, nine-nine. We should have expected it. As the Russians open up the seaports, there's gonna be more and more of their big stuff coming ashore. Break, break," he said, using the familiar military term to signal he was now going to reach out to another unit. "Heavy, heavy, this is Six."

"Go for heavy-guns," came SSgt. Diaz's familiar thick mixed Bronx Spanish accent.

"Okay, heavy-guns, if you were listening, nine-nine has spotted two pieces of armor near the entrance. You got any-thing in that kit bag of yours that can help?"

"Hey, six, I copied that. But if I shift them rockets over toward those tanks, B Troop and Dragoons are gonna have a tough time with those GAZ Tigrs once they react to their attack through the wire."

Tyce sighed. These were the difficult decisions of com-mand, even right on the cusp of battle: a commander had to shift his forces to meet changes in the enemy's ranks. "Roger, heavy. A tough fight just got tougher, but if we don't take out those tanks on the opening salvo, the companies won't last under their tank main guns. A 125mm smoothbore cannon against infantry is a bad combo. They've got sufficient medium machine guns and ammo to do the job. So you just take out those tanks before they can move, and then hightail it back to the line companies."

"Six, I copy all. Acknowledged and WILCO," she said.

Seems Ned and Zane's army lingo is rubbing off on the Marines, Tyce realized. *Not necessarily a bad thing. Perhaps even the best sign of a cohesive unit.*

Whoosh. Boom! Boom! Boom!

The sounds of four AT-4 rockets launching splintered the night air, followed by three concussive blasts—the American missile men were rewarded with three detonations, and three Russian GAZ Tigrs went up in flames. Immediately, Ned's soldiers opened up from their positions on a berm, and the clatter of machine guns and the arcing red zigzag of tracer fire filled the air.

Ned watched the Russians race for cover in surprise at the American counterattack. Ned could just imagine what was going through the Russian commander's head. Only a split second earlier, the Russians had been the aggressors, creeping in on what they'd been told was a sleepy band of unprepared guerillas on the outskirts of Parsons. It wouldn't take long for them to recover, though. These were the Russian special mountain forces, and though the blast and gunfire set them back, the effect was momentary.

The remaining Tigrs opened up with their own up-gunned and heavy-barrel machine guns. These were not the small-caliber, standard Russian 7.62mm. These were much bigger, the so-called Kord-12.7mm machine gun, and the effects were immediate and devastating. Huge clods of frozen earth blasted from the front of the berm, while others skipped just off the crest. There was nothing B-Team could do but hunker down and await a pause in the Russians' heavy gunfire.

Ned watched everything unfolding, a slightly uncertain confidence filling his gut.

It was time to pull the rug out.

He keyed his mic. This time, there was no use whispering. The deafening sounds of battle all around them would drown out any but the loudest voices. With what soldiers and Marines call a battlefield voice, he yelled into the radio, "All stations, all stations, this is B Troop Six-Actual. One-team is pinned, two-team, time to make your move. Three-team, stay covered, but stay ready."

All three teams acknowledged the order. Ned watched from his concealed perch on the adjacent wood line as two-team unleashed a withering, accurate volley of fire directly into the Russian flank. The Russian advance halted immediately; they were caught, out in the open, and stunned to be receiving a whole new barrage of small arms.

Ned allowed himself a slight smile. As much as Ned's special forces men had been the bait to draw off the largest of the Russian forces hunting Tyce, being a target that knew what was coming had a distinct advantage. The Russian disorientation didn't last long, though.

Their confusion and Ned's grin both melted away as the Russian light artillery began a lightning barrage against two-team. Well drilled, the Russians fired with speed and efficiency. Ned watched round after round burst into the trees, raining deadly shrapnel down onto his forces. Now both one- and two-teams were effectively pinned.

Ned tried to reach two-team over the radio. Four, five, six times he called over, but the only sounds he could hear were the not-so-distant blasts of the Russian light artillery crashing through the trees.

Crap, thought Ned, wondering whose plan would win the day.

CHAPTER 37

Yeager Airport, West Virginia

Tyce rubbed his frozen hands together and yawned, his jaws popping from the cold and fatigue. He knew the men were as exhausted as he was—maybe more so since many had low-crawled through the snow to get into their positions. Things were looking like they were falling into place. The critical factor had been getting into their positions without being noticed. No radios, no headlights, virtually no signatures that they had crossed the mountains with heavy gear and equipment and not stopping until they'd reached just outside the normally bustling Yeager airport.

Tyce surveyed the airfield's fence line. Mostly quiet, a few vehicles drove around the inside of the perimeter. Guard towers—manned with heavy machine guns, no doubt. Tyce walked the short distance over a rise and into the woods, then pulled the heavy blackout tarp covering his command post aside and instantly felt the warmth of all the bodies inside.

Inside, bathed in red light, his radio operators and, in fact, a whole miniature and portable command post was abuzz with activity. Field phones, their ringers turned off, buzzed. Men pushed pins into maps as the scouts called back with position reports of the enemy. The snipers were hard at work, still struggling to get into their positions while simultaneously trying to map out the enemy vehicles and men.

Gunny handed Tyce a cup of coffee. "Now all we have to do is sit back and let the boys and girls do their jobs."

Tyce glanced at Gunny. Both of them knew it was never that simple. As the old saying went, "If anything can go wrong, it will go wrong."

Wynand was in a corner, smoking a cigarette. Seeing Tyce, he walked over. "Boss, I was almost fifteen minutes inside the perimeter when I got that old feeling. One of the patrols seemed to be suspicious of our sewage truck driving around the planes, so I lost 'em and got out before they could nab us. Still, I gave your flyboys and Lieutenant Zane the locations of the Hercs you wanted me to find. Those C-130s are pretty huge airplanes. No idea how you plan to get them up in the air without someone on the Russian side noticing."

"Thanks, Wynand. Your intel, as always, is spot on." Tyce couldn't help but wonder what would happen if Wynand went rogue and turned to the highest bidder. The Russians would pay a lot for the information in that ex-con's mind. No telling if he hadn't already given them the goods. Tyce still remained suspicious of the hick's motives.

A radio operator interrupted his thoughts. "Sir, report from Comanche-six, Captain Blake's C-Company men. He reports: 'The bear is in the trap, the bear is in the trap.'" The young radio operator spoke his message twice and with a twinge of glee—partially because the transmission from Ned's radio operator had said it twice, which was standard protocol to ensure the message was clear, but also because important words carried more gravity in combat when repeated. Maybe he also liked bringing his boss some good news. Tyce sure could use some.

"Copy. Hand me the hook." Tyce reached out for the radio handset and keyed the mic. "Comanche-six, Comanche-six. Understood all. Do you need any support? How's it looking?"

Tyce realized his words were futile, given the distance between the two units, but he said them more to give confidence to everyone listening. Pretty much every leader would be able to hear Tyce's side of the transmission. A few might get some bits and pieces of Ned's transmission, but without the powerful, amplified radios Tyce had in his command vehicle and tents, they would only hear half the conversation. Still, Tyce knew getting wind that Ned's people were doing well would likely give the men with him at the airport some small comfort that things were unfolding according to plan.

The response from Ned came immediately. Ned was obviously planted next to his radios, running his fight much as Tyce was about to run his own.

"It's all going to plan, Iron Horse-six." For the mission, Tyce had decided to stop using his "Dragoon" call sign and instead allow himself the battlefield promotion to "Iron horse-six." It still sounded weird to him, but to the troops it symbolized an ascension of sorts, to the boss and commander of the unit, and not just another company commander.

"Good, copy." Then Tyce decided he'd better add, "I've got great confidence in you and your men, Ned." It sounded cheesy once he said it, but he knew he had always appreciated when his superior officers spoke to him like that on the cusp of a difficult mission, and he hoped it would have the same effect on Ned.

"Copy all," was the only response from Ned, but in the background, Tyce could hear the continuous staccato of machine gun fire.

Tyce felt his stomach clench. Was he condemning his men again? Was he just sending more boys off to the slaughter? There certainly was nothing he could do now to help Ned and his men. Maybe he'd spent too much time trying to keep the Russians off him and hadn't paid enough attention to Ned's battle. It sure sounded like a hellish fight.

Fuck, he thought. *Is there any aspect of senior leadership that's easy?* He already knew the answer. A few seconds later, that fact of warfare was reinforced again.

While Tyce was talking to Ned, he'd been somewhat aware of General Lawton. He still coughed occasionally and was listening in on the captured Russian radio in the back of the LAV C2 vehicle with Bill Degata, his chin in his palms.

"Hey, Major," said the general. His gravelly voice always carried some gravitas, but it bore an even more serious tone now.

"Yes, sir?"

"We may have a problem."

"What now?" asked Tyce.

"My Russian is still pretty rusty, but I'm listening in on a conversation between the Russian West Virginia commander, that Colonel Nikolaevich, and the Russian installation commander down below us. They . . . well, actually, it sounds like the entire Russian 8th Mechanized Corps just went on alert. I'd guess from the urgency in both men's voices that they are tracking Ned's battle over in Parsons pretty well. They're trying to decide whether to come to the rescue of the base commander, or to go reinforce the troops attacking Captain Blake."

"Okay," said Tyce, his brow furrowing. This was the deciding moment. If Ned's attack looked like it was bad, they'd send reinforcements to Parsons. If not, they'd come south to Yeager Field. He'd have to trust Ned to stick it to them so hard that they were at the very least stuck in the dilemma of the decision.

Gunny's next words put even more pressure on Tyce. "Here comes Murphy, sir," he said.

Tyce glared at him again. He thought for a few seconds. He could feel every man's eyes on him as he stared past their small command post into the dark, cold gloom.

"We attack now," he said.

Shocked looks and a gasp went up around the command post. Moving up the time line for the attack would cause some real problems, not the least of which was that SSgt. Diaz hadn't yet moved her anti-tank rocketmen toward the front gate. Also, if they took the airfield too early, the Russians would send reinforcements south.

The general dismounted from the vehicle to come over to talk to Tyce in confidence. Gunny turned his back toward the rest of the men and spoke in a low tone before the general walked over. "Sir, could I caution against going early—"

Tyce was not having any of it—not the general coming to counsel him like a coach coming to the mound or Gunny's muttering. He interrupted both loudly enough so everyone in the command post knew it was his decision. "Stop. We attack now. Believe me, I know the consequences. But right this very moment, Russian soldiers are waking up in their barracks. If we give them even ten minutes to organize, we'll be facing hundreds more alert and ready troops. I'm not risking them hardening their defenses."

Tyce's tone was harsh enough to get the radio operators

chattering again. Without needing to be told, they knew what was coming next, and they sent transmissions to all the forces to kick off the attack more than an hour early.

The general and Gunny, undeterred and each about to advise against Tyce's new course of action, still sidled closer to Tyce. But Tyce forestalled any further discussion. "Gents, I know we will cause frustration and some bit of chaos among our own men if we kick off the attack now, but giving the Russian commander even ten minutes means the force we're about to attack will double in strength and build up his lines to near impenetrable. We attack now. Do you hear me? We attack now, or we doom our men to what will be catastrophic odds. We'll trust Ned to fight his battle and siphon off some or hopefully all of the reinforcements. We just have to force the gods of war onto our side by taking initiative before circumstances are decided for us."

As if presaged by Tyce's command, one of the radio operators spun around and yelled out, "Major, Dragoons is reporting that one of the tanks is moving. Looks like they're headed to the back side of their perimeter, right toward B Troop."

Tyce looked at Bill, Lawton, and Gunny. "It's go time, Gents. Put your game faces on, because we're out of time to think. It's time to act." Each man nodded assent. Tyce turned to the radiomen. "Order the assault. All stations are to kick off in the exact sequence per the order, but to do so right now!"

None of the four radiomen even turned to look at Tyce. They all just transmitted the order.

CHAPTER 38

Yeager Airport

SSgt. Diaz's left hand played mindlessly, building little snow castles, while her right hand flicked the safety on and off her M2 .50 cal. Her right arm was still sore and bandaged, but she wasn't going to let it bother her. She looked down the line at her other machine gunners; they were likewise sitting restlessly in their assault-by-fire positions. She had watched her missile men slink into the predawn darkness half an hour earlier. They were all but invisible now. Nothing remained but long furrows in the snow, where they had slipped off to their new positions.

She didn't like dividing her forces. Once divided, they lost a lot of their punch, and they became more open to flank attacks. She looked at the snow castle her left hand had built, then squished it flat.

"Fuck it," she whispered, making little ghosts with her breath.

Diaz reached up to her helmet and flipped her NVGs down over her eyes. She still couldn't see her missile men, which was a good thing—it meant it was very likely the Russians hadn't seen them, either. Even though she'd told them to hasten their way into their assault positions, she was growing more and more impatient with every passing second.

She could see the Russians, though, and in greater numbers than before. They were a swarm of activity, even in the predawn hours. Their defensive positions in the guard towers and slow patrolling along the airport's perimeter access road network had increased. She mainly watched the taillights of the Russian tank as it drove through the base toward the back of the perimeter. There was nothing she could do about it; even if it had been in range, it was now at long, long range, and it was very unlikely her men could hit the thing. She just made a mental note that sometime soon, a piece of Russian armor would be joining the fight and making things a real bitch.

Seconds clicked by. The tension grew. She watched the remaining Russian tank through her NVGs. Their men had only recently begun clambering about the tank. They had likely all been sleeping at their posts when the alarm went up.

If we attacked even three minutes earlier, she thought, *we would completely surprise the Russians.*

She hoped it still wasn't too late to gain some momentum during the Russians' confusion. They may be getting up and to the alert, but since no one was shooting at them and they'd never been attacked on this base before, they probably still felt pretty secure.

Her short-range radio headset came alive. "Attack, attack, attack. Commence attack," came the word from back at the major's command post.

About God-damned time, she thought at first, but then, wasn't this early, like really God-damned earlier than planned? *Well, as the boss always said, all plans turn to shit on first contact.* Looked like this one was turning to shit *before* first contact.

Her eyes were fixed on the piece of terrain where her rocket and missile men should be. They would have adjusted to the best position suitable without the need to ask her, but they'd be in the same general area.

Her stomach was doing cheetah flips. Every additional second felt like a minute, every minute felt like an hour.

She glanced back at the Russian tank. It'd been joined by two GAZ Tigr gun trucks.

Crack—Crack!.

The blast of two rockets split the night. Two streaks of fire arced through the darkness. The first, an AT-4 rocket, zipped past the tank, narrowly missing the mark and impacting the side of a building with a loud smack.

The second shot, a Mk 153 SMAW rocket, skipped off the front glacis of the Russian T-90, but detonated on the tank's turret. The nose cone must have hit at a wrong angle and been bent, because it looked like it did little to no damage to the tank's turret. Through the NVGs, SSgt. Diaz could see the glow of lights coming from inside the tank. They were spinning the beast up.

Uh oh. Here comes trouble.

No more time to think about it. The firing of the rockets was the signal for everyone to kick off the attack and advance. SSgt. Diaz knew her part. She depressed the butterfly trigger on her Browning, and a burst of heavy .50 caliber rounds sang through the air, striking the two GAZ Tigrs. Her other three machine guns opened up in a throaty roar, and all guns joined to create a dense haze of bullets impacting in and around the front gate.

Metal struck metal, and sparks flashed all around, adding to the mayhem. Chunks of metal, mirrors, pieces of the GAZ tires, and glass flew in all directions. The

Russians caught in the open as the crossfire began were immediately blasted to the ground and churned into chunks; such was the force of the heavy rounds.

Like a lumbering giant, the big T-90 began to move. The driver, eager to get into the action, or just blinded by SSgt. Diaz's withering incoming fire, ran over one of the pinned Tigrs, and likely several of their wounded comrades. It crashed through the front gate and headed directly toward the Dragoons as they emerged from behind the hill, racing into the Marines' oncoming assault on the front gate.

Blue was surrounded on both sides by Marine snipers. Six of them, plus himself, had been lying in complete stillness, embedded deeply in the snow.

"One thing certain, you men sure are quiet," Blue whispered to the nearest one. The man nodded. He and all the other men's eyes were fixed forward through their special night vision optics. Their white camouflage and thermal-reducing ghillie suits made them almost completely invisible to even the best Russian equipment. Blue, on the other hand, was wearing Duluth Trading Company flannels and an old mountain parka that had been painted white for him by the men.

He smiled. The usually uncommunicative man suddenly seemed to have the urge to talk. "You boys know when we supposed to start?" he whispered.

The nearest man next to him patted him on the arm and put his fingers to his lips in a shushing gesture.

Diaz's rockets fired. The noise, even from Blue's position a few hundred meters away, was immense, but Blue had been told to expect it, and he didn't move.

Then her machine guns opened up. The halo of the

bullets left streaks with their tracers, bright against the darkness and illuminating the white snow. The fiery impacts and noisy ricochets were even more impressive to Blue. "Whoa. You boys ever seen somethin' like this before?"

The Marine next to him grinned, then whispered, "Now."

All six Mark 13 Mod 7 sniper rifles and one .460 Weatherby Mk V Magnum fired simultaneously. They pierced the night like assassin's daggers. Unlike Diaz's heavy guns, the Marine's rifles used no tracers, gave no muzzle flash, and the targets they struck gave off no sparks. Six of the seven targets fell silently into the snow from their guard towers or back into their Tigrs without a whimper or a word. Most were struck across the chest, the wind literally sucked out of them as the round opened up a nickel-sized hole and tore through their lungs and split their hearts.

But Blue's designated target was a single Russian guard half-outside his tower, his rifle up and still staring in the direction of the rocket fire. The Marine snipers had given him a "can't-miss target," about three hundred meters away and a small zone near the front gate. But Blue had spotted something else by the tracer fire at the last second: a Russian officer standing way back by his vehicle, cigarette in one hand and the radio receiver to his ear in the other.

At least Blue figured he was an officer; *He's standing there all cocky-like. As if he owns the joint.*

Blue figured the other snipers just hadn't seen the man yet, or they would have probably told him to shoot the officer and not just some dopey guards.

Seems a better target, he thought.

Blue really didn't relish disobeying orders, so he'd tried to tell someone. But they all seemed to be too intent on their own primary and secondary targets.

The trouble was the officer was well behind the lines, about twelve hundred meters away and mostly obscured behind an armored vehicle door, wearing a steel helmet. He was not controlling the action at the front gate through the radio but was about to jump in the vehicle and move off. Probably someplace where he could better control his troops against Blue's U.S. boys. But Blue wasn't about to let that happen.

Blue wasn't classically trained like the Marines who had spent years learning to aim their high-velocity rounds directly into the middle of the chest at center mass, or longitudinally through the soft spot under the arm or even through the arm and into the chest. No, Blue just did what seemed best and aimed for the impossibly tiny target he had available to him and well beyond the rifle's intended maximum range. He trusted the Lord and his father's .460 Weatherby Mk V to hurl the huge, fat, rhino-stopping Magnum 450-grain bullet at more than 2,660 feet per second, which would close the distance before one full beat of the target's heart. Or as Blue always liked to think of it: *most lickety-split.*

Bang!

Blue squeezed the trigger. The rifle jumped in his hands. He didn't miss. The round tore directly through the Russian's face and came out the back side of his neck and kept on going into a building another few hundred meters farther on. The officer's head exploded, his arms flailed wildly into the air, and then his torso slammed up against the vehicle. The vehicle crew stared at his carcass in horror.

Blue said a quick Bible verse to himself: "These things I have spoken unto you, that in me ye might have peace. In the world ye shall have tribulation: but be of good cheer; I have overcome the world."

Then he figured he was still obliged to kill the target

he'd been assigned, the tower guard. He worked the bolt, loaded another, and fired, killing the man with another face shot. Then loaded again and switched to the Tigr's top gunner, killing him. Then loaded another and shot a man working a machine gun near the gate. The man's head knocked back, like it'd been swatted by a baseball bat, and the gun superelevated, firing harmlessly into the air and over the mountains. Then Blue took two men in rapid succession, midstride running to reinforce their companions at the gate, knocking them both flat to the ground.

"They jus' keep on comin.'" said Blue chancing a glance at the others. All six of the other snipers stared at Blue, eyes wide at his incredible shooting skills.

"Sorry," Blue said. "Did I kill some of your'n? I'll stick to them Russkies in my zone." And Blue went back to killing more targets in the zone he was assigned.

Ned had to admire both the Russians' courage and their ability to rapidly shift under the tough combat conditions Ned's men had meted out to them. With each move, and even with all Tyce's preplanning, they were able to fight with tenacity and a certain hardheadedness.

Well, that was all fine, but now it was time to deal his last card.

"Three-team. Go!" said Ned.

"On the way!" yelled the three-team leader back into the radio.

And with that, in one swift combined action, two-team launched into the Russians on a third flank. Three-team had been hidden directly next to the light artillery. Ned hadn't known the Russians would park artillery there, but he had given them a nice flat, protected piece of land and expected they probably would use it to park something soft and squishy. He had been hoping for the Russian leader's command post, but the man was as tenacious as his troops and had advanced in respectable fashion with his men.

The skirmish—more like an execution—was over in just a few seconds. Three-team fired their rifles, then overran the artillerymen's positions, spraying each Russian multiple times. The special forces men's assault was swift and merciless, and then they moved on farther, toward the rear of the advancing Russians.

The Russians continued to advance on three-team's positions, thinking they had two-team properly suppressed in the wood line with their light artillery. Suddenly, they faced fire from two sides again. Three-team sensed their slackening fire and popped up on the berm again from the Russian front. Two-team, no longer driven deep into the dirt from the artillery, low-crawled back onto their machine guns at the edge of the woods and began laying waste to the Russian left flank.

With the Russians trying to defend on three of four sides, they quickly withered and died, unable to keep up a steady enough fire to prevent Ned's men from advancing slowly into them. One by one, they were given a choice on how to die: stay in place and be mowed down by two-team's machine guns, advance and be picked off by one-team's rifles and now grenades, or retreat and run smack into three-team's cautiously advancing men. The firing angles on the Russians were tricky, but Ned's men were careful to prevent fratricide.

Ned himself lobbed M203 rifle grenades into the dwindling Russian mass. The 40mm explosive dropped a deadly fan of light shrapnel, putting steel into the pockets of Russians but also crushing what Ned thought might be an attempt to mount a comeback.

Some men on the right side, clustering around their brave but foolhardy leader, seemed like they were going to try to make a run for the woods. At least, it looked like there was some attempt to get out of the bloody kill zone. Whatever order the Russian commander was giving to his men died in his throat as Ned pumped more 40mm rounds at him, and the last of the Russian special forces suffered well-aimed shots and death by tiny cuts from a hundred steel shards.

Ned had walked down the hill at a fast, firing walk, emptying a magazine at medium range while on the move and trying to coordinate over his throat mic radio. Halfway, he took a knee and slapped a new magazine into his rifle. It had all ended so quickly. Spotting his first sergeant, Ned waved him over, still surveying the carnage.

"Hey, sir. Helluva fight." The first sergeant knelt by Ned. "We took twelve wounded. I'll get them back to the navy medical folks the commander left us. Glad she did— that arty was worse than we'd bargained for. If three-team hadn't attacked when they did . . ." he shook his head. "Anyway, two wounded, Morgan and Colvin from two-team. Looks like they'll need more than what the docs here have. We'll need to get them to the commander ASAP."

Ned couldn't suppress a brief smile, expecting a worse tally from the first sergeant. "Could have been worse—"

"No, sir, not finished," interrupted the first sergeant, still a little out of breath from the fighting. "We also have ten Angels." Everyone dreaded hearing that term on the battlefield.

Ned and the first sergeant pulled off their helmets, wiping their brows. In spite of the below-freezing night-time temperature, both men were near exhaustion and overheating. Their adrenaline was crashing down, leaving them sweaty and drained.

"Copy," said Ned. "What . . . who?"

The first sergeant pulled out his notepad. "Bishop, Cruz, Gibbons, Mendez, and Morris from two-team. Barnes, Cameron, Dillman, Harper, and Houtz from three-team.

"Harper? Harper . . . Harmonica Harper?"

"The same, sir."

Behind them, shouts and sporadic rifle fire echoed across the clearing as a wounded Russian made a move toward his weapon and was cut down.

CHAPTER 39

Yeager Airport

The Dragoons began their assault with four LAV-25s tearing up and over the last ridgeline just two kilometers from the perimeter fence of Yeager Airport. They gunned the heavy Detroit Diesel engines, which roared, dominating the early morning and partially drowning out SSgt. Diaz's still blazing guns.

The vehicles bounded across the frozen fields. Two vehicles sprinted ahead as the other two provided covering fire, then they switched roles, maintaining a continuous leapfrog in this manner and keeping up a continuous volume of fire. Directly behind them, six Humvee gun trucks followed, firing .50 cal, and behind that, three five-ton troop trucks were taking up the rear. The trucks were unarmored, but still, they advanced just behind the assault wave, ready to release their Marines, attack the gate, and seize a foothold.

They hadn't gotten more than two hundred meters when their lead vehicle spotted the Russian T-90 tank careening headlong through the front gate right for them. For a moment, all four vehicles paused, slowing almost to a halt, like adolescent hyenas who had just spotted a full-grown lion bearing down on them. Then the Humvees slowed, and the trucks in the back stopped dead in their tracks.

Across the entire Marine front assault line, the momentum stumbled and hesitated. In their planning and rehearsals, they had never counted on tanks. Moreover, even though the tanks had been spotted and reported a few minutes earlier, not everyone had heard about them yet. Those who had, mostly the unit leaders, had been told Diaz's rocketmen could take them out in the opening salvo. But as each vehicle crested the rise and their men saw the tank blasting at them, they all braked.

The attack was breaking. Even the able, eight-wheeled LAVs, excellent in their assigned role of raiding, scouting, and reconnaissance, were completely unprotected against the tank's 2A82-1M 125mm smoothbore main gun's fire.

Everyone yelled over the radio at the same time, "T-90 is still up. I say again, the tank is still operational!" The tactical radio nets were jammed from platoon to company and up to Tyce, with the report that the big steel beast yet lived.

Inside the turret of hull number 11, the lead LAV, SSgt. Casillas, barked over the intercom, "Gunner! Tank! Direct front, eight hundred meters. AT, fire *now*, God damn it!"

The young gunner, a corporal, was too shocked to reply to the command. He had also spotted the tank in his gunner's sight and started panicking, even before being given the command to fire. The enemy tank filled almost his entire sight. The tank stood out in complete contrast to the cold night in his thermal imagers, and the mighty T-90's silhouette was unmistakable. He had committed it to memory in gunners' school. He squeezed the trigger and prayed.

Thump—thump—thump.

Cannon fire shook the inside of the turret, filling it up with hot gases and thickening the atmosphere in the already tense, sweaty, and cramped quarters. HE rounds blasted the side of the tank with no effect other than to cause a neat shower of sparks. The LAV gunner fired six more rounds of HE, watching the effect through his sight.

SSgt. Casillas, who had sunk into the turret and was watching the gunner's actions through his own commander's sight, kicked at the gunner with his free foot and yelled, "God damn it, Corporal, I said fucking AT!"

He grabbed the gun's palm control switch, overriding the corporal, and screamed, "From my position." meaning the turret and its 25mm gun were now slaved to his controller.

He then began a milliseconds' long preparatory ritual, born from living, eating, and breathing inside the turrets of LAVs since joining the Corps almost fourteen years prior. Through prickly-hot stress-induced sweat, his heart beating out of his chest, he concentrated fully on the Russian tank in his gunsight reticle, and the electric turret motor whirred in response to the deft movements of his wrist. He clicked the thumb selector to AT, then swung the gun in a G-shape, slowly zeroing in on a tiny gap, a chink in the enemy's armor.

The gunner panicked some more. "He's firing, Staff Sergeant!"

There was a loud boom, and behind them one of the troop trucks disappeared in a cloud of black shrapnel and hot fire. More than a dozen men had just gotten evaporated off the battlefield.

"I know," said the SSgt, recognizing that he had only one chance, and he'd better make it count or the tank would pick the troop trucks off one at a time.

He was looking for a gap on the tank turret. Since the inception of modern tank warfare, this gap had been called the Hull-Turret Separation. But a trained gunner just knew it as the chink in the armor, the sweet spot, on most heavily armored tanks. He could hear the blasts of the other LAVs in his platoon firing away. He could see the sparks of their shots against the tank as he aimed, all of his brothers' shots went erratic, all wild, all panic fire. There was little to no room for error. He took careful aim and pulled the trigger.

Boom—boom—boom.

Three 25mm depleted-uranium shaped, fin-stabilized penetrators hummed toward their target.

The first was a quarter inch too high and ricocheted harmlessly just like his fellows' shots, which continued like bees stinging a single-minded bear. The second round peeled back an inch of metal on the turret, but likewise had no discernable effect on the gargantuan beast. But the third struck its mark, passed through the tiny gap between the hull and turret just where he had aimed, and penetrated into the skin of the tank. On the outside, it left only a bright red mark, looking a lot like a fluorescent cherry through the gunsights. A bright white puff of smoke billowed from the hole.

Everyone across the Marines' advancing line let out a sigh as, a second later, the top hatches of the T-90 blew off and a jet-white spout of flame blazed skyward like a blow-torch.

God bless those men, thought Casillas, sitting back in his seat.

"Your gun," he yelled to the gunner, who relinquished his own palm switch, "And don't ever do that again."

The LAV men were not tankers—far from it, they were infantry and reconnaissance men. But they understood perfectly what kind of death those five men inside had just experienced.

"They would have given us the same, if we'd have let them," said Casillas through the intercom, reading his men's minds and popping up on top of his turret to polish off some Russians with his pintle machine gun.

Casillas and his three wingmen closed the rest of the distance to the front airfield gate in under eight seconds, their throttles wide open. There wasn't much left of it after the withering rocket, 25mm rounds, and Diaz's machine gun fire. The Russians who still resisted had nothing but small-arms fire, which couldn't penetrate the Marine LAVs. Casillas and the others switched back to HE and laid waste to the surviving vehicles and sandbagged positions, sending shrapnel spiraling through the area in a web no one could escape, killing the remaining soldiers.

The LAVs breached the threshold, then drove right through the perimeter, finally stopping their lightning charge and in control of the position. Then the trucks and Humvees disgorged their cargo of infantry, each one eager to get the hell out of the vulnerable canvas-covered vehicles and into the fight. A few glanced back at their stricken truck, now burning voraciously—sorry for its fate, but thankful for their own.

Casillas's LAVs then turned their turrets toward several more distant guard towers, which fired sporadic and harassing, long-range automatic weapons on the Marines. Turrets swung over, one vehicle to each tower, and pumped out accurate fire. Two towers splintered apart, wooden boards, sandbags, and fragments of ballistic glass flying through the air. A third tower, silenced by the snipers moments earlier, was blasted to pieces, just to be safe. The fourth blew sky high, ripping the top off the tower and commenced a spectacular display that continued through the next ten minutes of battle.

Everyone in and near the airport, even those far away, looked toward the immense, rolling explosions. Both friend and foe alike turned instinctively from their own skirmishes to see the fireworks as they lit up the sky. Those closest saw the most sickening spectacle, as two men, both literally engulfed in flames, chose to leap the forty feet to their deaths rather than be burned alive.

Morgantown

A banging on Colonel Nikolaevich's door woke him from the deepest slumber. The last radio transmission from his men attacking the insurgent stronghold in Parsons suggested things were going very well and according to plan. They had crept up to the enemy's positions and were going to: "pound them to dust," promised their commander. So the colonel had turned in for some much-needed rest.

"What the hell is it?" he shouted, more out of surprise at being woken than actual anger.

"Colonel . . . Colonel, there has been a . . . a . . ."

It was Nikolaevich's normally mousy adjutant. Nikolaevich was hardly about to wake up for some administrative tidbit better left till morning.

"Yes, yes," he called out, yawning, "I will sign the TM-44 requisition documents in the morning, Mikhail. But give me some rest. I just need a few hours. And tell the duty officer that I should not be disturbed unless there is a real emergency."

To the colonel's surprise, his door flung open, bathing him in the bright lights of the outer hallway. Nikolaevich shielded his eyes and somewhat modestly covered his new flannel PJs with a blanket.

"What the hell—"

"Colonel," Mikhail continued apologetically, "I was sent here by the duty officer. He is down in the ready room, and he sent me to wake you, immediately. There's, um. That is . . ."

"Mikhail, get to the God-damned point. What is so urgent that you burst in here?"

Mikhail shuffled nervously from foot to foot. He was not used to being this forward with his commander, but the duty officer had been insistent, even grabbing him by the uniform collar and yelling into his face.

He played with the brim of his army-issue cap. "I, uh. Well, it is not certain. I mean, you understand, Colonel, I do not fully understand the tactics of the matter, I am only an admini—"

"Mikhail, you worthless bastard, get to the fucking point." Nikolaevich's patience with his adjutant was always strained by the man's circumspection, but at two a.m., his fuse was instant.

Unable to contain himself, Mikhail blurted out, "Colonel, Charleston has been invaded!"

"What?!"

Colonel Nikolaevich grabbed the glasses off his night-stand and leapt from bed, pushing his adjutant aside and racing to the operations room. Mikhail followed, stammering about how none of it was his fault and other unintelligible objections. He stopped short of reminding the Colonel he was still in his pajamas.

CHAPTER 40

Yeager Airport

The timing was imperative. The assault by fire and attack to seize the gate had to dominate the Russians' attention, and Lieutenant Zane's mobile assault force—now the hammer punch—needed speed, surprise, and momentum. Tyce watched the occasional machine gun tracer fire hitting a few positions deep in the airfield: a Russian in a window, or a vehicle's movement on an adjacent road suppressed by Diaz or wiped out by Blue and the snipers.

He allowed himself a tiny bit of joy when the HQ men around him cheered as the call from Dragoons came over the radio. "Front gate is secure."

The route appeared to be open, but there was no time left, and only those truly ignorant of warfare let themselves be fooled by small tactical successes. Reversals were common in combat, and small victories were fleeting. If they didn't send the second wave of the attack now, they could expect a strong and swift counterattack. Although General Lawton was back in the woods, Tyce could almost hear him saying some such thing, recommending caution while also being quick to seize the opportunities his attack had created.

Tyce grabbed the radio handset and barked out the next command. "B Troop, commence your attack."

Lieutenant Zane, who had clearly been waiting on his radio for his chance, was quick to respond. "Copy, sir. Attacking now."

Everyone in the small, hastily dug and snow-covered trench glanced to the right, looking toward B Troop's concealed positions on an adjacent road network.

Twenty Humvees burst from the woods, racing forward. They were joined by Zane's last two operational M3 Bradley Fighting Vehicles, brought up on two flatbed trucks through windy back logging trails at great effort. They nearly hadn't made the journey. Mayor Susanna had found Tyce two logging truck drivers who were more than willing to embrace the cause. With their heavy treads clanking, the Bradleys now advanced in the middle of Zane's pack of Humvees.

They look just like a pack of wild dogs, thought Tyce.

The Humvees were loaded with Zane's scouts, whose critical piece involved securing the two aircraft they needed. The M3 Bradley Cavalry Fighting Vehicle amounted to Tyce's last remaining surprise. He had no other card tricks to play. Zane's force at full strength was three platoons, packed with four Brads apiece. But the Russian strafing attack on his column, coupled with a huge lack of both maintenance men and the parts required for the heavy machines, meant Tyce's surprise force would not be the overwhelming force it could have been. Still, it would have to do.

It looked like Zane and his boys didn't care. Being a lighter force had its advantages, too, and Zane knew it. Every Humvee-mounted machine gun was thumping away, and the Bradleys' cannons were lighting up the darkness with accurate fire directed at two guard towers in their sector of the perimeter that were blocking their access.

The two Russians here had either been too surprised to fire back or too focused on Tyce's diversion at the front gate to show much resistance. They popped off some small arms and shot a shoulder-fired rocket-propelled grenade at the Brads at long range. All of it impacted in and around the rapidly advancing vehicles, but none did any damage of note.

Zane's men returned fire on any targets that showed themselves with a zest and audacity that the National Guard scouts were known for.

All the better, thought Tyce, *just business.*

The Russians' conduct against civilians at Parsons crossed his mind briefly, but there was never time in a fighting man's heart for retribution. Rage, payback, reprisal— these were all words for combatants who fought without thinking. That type of approach might win a battle or two, but eventually, that steam wore off. A larger purpose was what galvanized an organized troop. Still, against his better nature, it felt good to get some wins.

Ultimately, Tyce knew, the thinking dog won the day, and right now Tyce had unleashed the hounds. Zane's hounds. He peeled back his NVGs; they were not necessary to see the right flank, such was their volume of fire. The Bradleys were going to town. Almost uninterrupted, their 25mm cannons devastated the towers, then zeroed in on the few GAZ Tigrs bold enough to show themselves.

Tyce's assault positions were now officially supporting one another. *Excellent, there's no stopping this momentum!* he thought jubilantly.

He was wrong.

Parsons

Ba-Boom!.

It was impossible not to look at the source of the incoming fire. The second Russian T-90, still masked by several outbuildings on the interior of the airfield, looked like it had turned back toward the gate when Zane's men attacked. The driver had decided or been commanded to address and halt Zane's advance.

Tyce's stomach fell to a new low, and for a brief moment, he thought he was going to actually, physically retch. The tank had caught B Troop at the worst possible moment of their advance: completely in the open, in a barren field, and exposed from all sides and guilty of a high, perhaps too high, level of confidence, which had overtaken Tyce as well. Tyce had picked that sector on the map because he had estimated all reinforcements would be headed to the front gate. But the Bradleys, like their wheeled LAV brothers, were no match for the T-90 that turned to face Zane's forces.

"Jesus Christ!" yelled the commander of Bradley hull number 727 through the intercom.

It was all instinctual language—language he rarely used. He was a religious man, but he blurted it out as he felt his hair stand on end and his muscles collapse.

"Motherfucking tank. T-90, direct front, eight hundred meters. Gunner open motherfucking fire!" he yelled.

The first rounds ricocheted harmlessly off the front glacis, the sloped armor meant to deflect incoming projectiles. But then it was the T-90's turn. He was loaded and ready.

Boom!
Spaaang!

The incoming 125mm skipped off, up, and over the Bradley. But the noise of the impact inside the Brad was unbearable rattling their brains and causing popped and bloody eardrums and noses. Unfortunately, Sergeant First Class Garrison, 727's commander, knew that the Russians had just fired an HE, or high-explosive round, probably what had been loaded to deal with the dismounted Marines he'd been advised were attacking the gate. The next round would most assuredly be a AT, or anti-tank, round. This took the Brads' survival chances to less than five percent. It was just a matter of time before the Russian gunner got his ammo and range correct and peeled the Brads open like tin cans.

SFC Garrison flicked a switch to extend the batwings, the mechanical arms that held two anti-tank missiles. The BGM-71 TOW anti-tank missile was now his best chance, perhaps his only chance, of survival. Driving while firing the TOW was less than optimal—in fact, the handbook said it wasn't to be done. If they didn't hold the vehicle steady, the gunner couldn't track the wire-guided missile all the way to the target. As the missile jetted over the terrain, a tiny copper wire would spool out behind it, and the gunner had to guide it in flight like a remote-controlled car on a wire. This was hard to do for most gunners, even sitting while static on a training gunline. Right now, 727 was moving at its max speed of forty miles per hour.

"Gunner, fire TOW!" yelled SFC Garrison.

The gunner was too preoccupied to respond. With a *whoosh*, a TOW missile fired and the whole turret shook. The gunner's face was still buried in his optic, trying hard to keep the stabilized turret firmly locked on the enemy tank while the vehicle bounced over the field.

Garrison pressed his face into his own gunsight and watched the missile fly toward the tank. It spiraled through the air, popping up and down as the gunner struggled to keep the seven-hundred-mile-per-hour thirteen-pound warhead flying toward its target.

Below both men, to their front and left, the driver had heard the orders and felt the missile launch, and was now fighting the wheel and throttle. He'd been trained to keep the vehicle steady when the gunner fired, and he used every bit of concentration on his own job to keep things steady— a challenge, given he could barely see the landscape at their speeds, but he dare not slow down or they would become an even better target for the T-90. The whole crew had to work as a team on a nearly impossible task. Melded with their machine, they were going to live as one or die as one.

"Almost there," said the gunner, whisper quiet into his intercom. "Almost—"

But it was a miss. Both SFC Garrison and his gunner let out a bitter sigh as the missile struck the high chain-link fence between them and the tank. The warhead flew a second farther, pulling the fence along with it, then nosed into the tarmac and detonated, leaving a gaping hole in the fence.

At the very least, it had opened the fence for their next shot. It was a slim consolation, as the T-90 would respond before they could take that shot.

Inside the Russian T-90, things were just as chaotic as inside their counterparts' turret.

"*Chert voz'mi, zagruzchik*, God damn it! Get my fucking gun reloaded, you simple son of a bitch!" yelled the tank commander. He'd seen the enemy's missile launch, and he knew the capability of the TOW missile. It could kill them.

"*Zagruzhen!*" shouted the loader to inform his commander that it was reloaded. He grabbed another round in expectation and clicking the foot switch to close the hatch on his ammunition storage rack.

"*Zagruzhen!*" the commander yelled in response.

"*V doroge.* On the way . . ." the gunner barely breathed into the intercom, not wanting to shout and lose his concentration, keeping his face buried in his own sight.

The big 125mm cannon roared, the breech ramming back into the turret and locking open.

Before the round had even struck its target, the commander yelled into the intercom again. "Load HEAT!" A high-explosive anti-tank round would surely cut through the American vehicle like butter.

The loader already had the next round cradled in his hand. He jammed it into the waiting breech assembly and tapped his foot to close the ammo door.

"*Uurah!!*" yelled both the gunner and commander as they watched the high-explosive anti-tank round blast into the Bradley.

The Russian HEAT round burrowed into the Brad's one-inch-thick laminate armor, boring a thumb-sized hole through. The commander knew that inside the Brad, the shaped charge created a murderous mass of molten metal. The chunks would spin and tumble throughout the vehicle, passing directly through men and equipment with no remorse.

The Russian gunner saw smoke out the top hatches and the gun port.

"Target destroyed, slewing onto the second *Amerikanski*." and he wasted no time jamming the turret hard to the right to get his optic on the second Bradley.

* * *

"Fucking hell!" said 727's driver, looking through his periscope vision blocks. He watched their brother Brad in front grind to a halt, smoke and flame visible from its top. "They just killed 728."

Garrison didn't waste breath to tell the driver to shut up. They had all seen what had happened to their lead Brad.

"Fire second TOW," he said.

"On the way," responded the gunner, pulling the trigger.

The second, and last remaining ,TOW catapulted off the Bradley's launcher. They had now closed to within four hundred meters of the perimeter fence and six hundred meters from the T-90. The time of flight for the missile would be shorter, but the terrain was still rocky, and holding the wire-guided missile on target was once again proving challenging.

The gunner's face was plastered so tightly into the eyecups that when the driver hit a big ditch, he felt his nose crunch, breaking immediately. The cartilage sliced through the skin, and blood began to pour down his face. In spite of it, he remained fixed to his sight. On the other side of the ditch, he saw the missile's tail fins and bright white exhaust gases, still visible.

"Motherfucker . . ." he muttered to himself, watching the TOW, a death grip on the controls, guiding it toward its target, his face and sight now a mess of dripping red blood. Each new bump and every twitch of his palm control cut his broken nose even deeper.

The missile traveled the remaining distance to its target like lightning, the gunner keeping it steady all the way. SFC Garrison let out a war whoop as the missile closed, but he stopped his victory cry as he saw a puff of smoke from the T-90's barrel.

The driver saw it too and yelled, "We're dea—" but a Russian-made, 125mm tank round entered directly into his compartment, the red-hot metal cutting short his last words and killing him instantly.

The Russian tank crew let out a war whoop of their own as they watched their round penetrate the second, and the only remaining, enemy Bradley. All that was left now was to mop up the Humvees charging willy-nilly at them. The commander thought perhaps they should switch over to their coaxial 7.62mm machine gun to conserve some of the tank's main gun rounds. No telling what other surprises the Yankees might still have in store for them.

More than a little confident and pleased with his crew's performance, he stuck his head up through the top hatch to get a better view. The main threats eliminated, just as they had practiced in tank school back in the No-vocherkassk Armor Academy, he could now take a little time to enjoy the fruits of his men's labors. He still felt the cold, prickly sweat dripping down his spine.

A harrowing adventure, to be sure. I cannot wait to brag about it to my buddies up in Morgantown, he thought. *Now, let's not waste time. Maybe I'll personally take out a few of these pesky Humvees with my 12.7mm Kord machine gun.*

He propped himself against the top of the turret, the frozen air now burning his nostrils as he gripped the Kord and prepared to sight in and fire on the approaching Humvees.

That's when the TOW missile burrowed into and through the front armor of his turret. In his last moments before death, he could actually see the fins of the enemy TOW missile just before it struck. The inside of the T-90 blew to pieces, ripping apart the gunner. In a millisecond, the powerful American penetrator reached the tank's magazine, detonating the stored rounds like a volcano and blowing the commander up and out of the turret. His body was ejected over two hundred feet, parts of it glowing from the hundreds of embedded and burning metal chunks.

SFC Garrison looked at the burning tank through his sight a moment longer, glanced at his gunner, who was gingerly touching the broken end of his nose, then pulled himself free from his turret. A choking smoke was emanating from the driver's compartment.

"Gunner, switch back to the 25 and keep scanning. We're immobile, but we can still act as a fire-support pillbox and assist the lieutenant's advance."

"Roger. Scanning now," came the bone-weary response from the gunner.

"I'm up and out. Gonna go check on Phillips." he said, referring to their dead driver, "Warn me if you're firing."

"Roger."

Both men's voices betrayed their emotions and the post-combat crash. The adrenaline had gushed to all corners of their bodies when the battle began, literally firing every twitch muscle in their bodies for perfect control. But now the adrenaline had ebbed away, leaving Garrison physically exhausted and his gunner light-headed from blood loss.

SFC Garrison stepped onto the cold metal turret, kicking spent 25mm casings off the vehicle as he made his way over to the driver's top hatch. He opened it up, and white smoke billowed out. From what little he could see, burning chunks of red and yellow metal were still stuck like glue to the sides of the driver's compartment, and just below lay Private Phillips's corpse, gutted and unrecognizable.

Garrison tipped his crew helmet back and stepped away

from the smoke pouring out of his driver's hatch, then watched Zane and his Humvees advance pell-mell through the hole in the fence his Brad had helped make. They drove directly past the burning T-90 and made their way toward the central military airplane hangars.

"Fuck me . . ." Garrison muttered.

At least they had helped turn the tide and might now be able to get the vice president out of here.

Mission accomplished, he thought, *but at quite a cost. Hope that asshole appreciates this.*

He heard muffled shouts from the gunner inside. "Hey Sergeant, better get back in. There's activity out on the flight line."

Garrison hopped back into his turret and snapped his crew helmet back into the intercom.

"What do you see?"

"Unsure, but it looks like there's some helos trying to take off."

SFC Garrison gulped and took a look through the gunsight himself.

"Jesus . . . those are Mi-24 Hinds."

"Fucking what, sergeant?"

"It's a Russian armored attack helo," he said. He flicked the switch on his radio to broadcast his spot report of a new enemy contact. "All stations, all stations, this is seven-two-seven, I've got a SPOTREP. And you ain't gonna like it."

CHAPTER 41

Yeager Airport

Tyce heard the short, intense fight and could see dense black and white smoke rising high into the morning sky, lit by flickering flames from the other half of the base. The reports from Lieutenant Zane were ill received. If correct, one or more Russian helicopters were about to be airborne. Most important to Tyce, it greatly increased the risks. And meant more casualties.

Do I call it quits? he thought. *When is this thing over and I admit I've lost?*

There it was again, the creeping self-doubt he'd worn like a terrible demon on his shoulders since his fight in Fallujah, Iraq. He thought over what General Lawton had said to him at Harman: "Trust your instincts, even when things are going badly. Let the military half of your brain take over, and it will find a way through the madness." Words to live by, and he pondered them a second.

And what about what Victoria had said? He could re-member it perfectly. But thinking of her, his mind went to other thoughts. He remembered her soft skin, warm and pressed up against him. What had she said? Ah, he remem-bered, "Tyce, there's no room to dwell on the past. You are in command of your own destiny." All comforting words, but still just words, and they didn't seem to be helping him think of a solution when his assault was about to fail.

Tyce was struggling not to call Lieutenant Zane constantly to get the latest information on the helicopters. The sun was just beginning to light up the morning sky, hints of blue wiping away the greys. He'd be able to see them himself soon enough. He pulled out his binoculars, but the lights across the service apron still shielded everything on the other side of base from view.

He heard a rustle from behind him. Someone was asking to be directed to his position. He couldn't take his eyes off the battle to look. A few seconds later, he heard the vice president speaking behind him.

"Hey, uh, Trooper, looking for your commander."

Crap, not now, thought Tyce.

"It's me, sir," said Tyce, reluctant to look up for even a moment to acknowledge his new commander in chief.

"Oh, hey there," said the VP, coming forward to stand next to Tyce. "We know you told us to stick back behind the woods for safety, but we heard the positive reports back at your command Humvees and wanted to come up and congrat—"

He was interrupted by the whooshing noise of rotor blades and the renewed chatter of machine guns, followed by tracers careening high into the still darkened sky. A few stray rounds chirped and buzzed as they passed over Tyce's small forward command post.

The VP looked up, his mouth agape in wonderment. His silhouette fully illuminated by the battle and against the wood line, "Oh, is that—"

Tyce grabbed the VP by his borrowed flak -jacket and hauled him down into the small fighting hole.

"Wowzers. Guess we should duck. Heh heh. I'm new

to all this, you know." The VP was clearly wanting to talk to someone in the know, but he couldn't have picked a worse time.

"Mr. Vice—" began Tyce, but the helicopter sounds were growing louder. Then a call came over the radio.

"Sir," said Tyce's radio operator. "It's the B Troop commander. Lieutenant Zane wants to talk to you." The radio operator tried to pass the handset to Tyce, but the VP, who was still new to the heavy body armor and was clambering about to catch a glance of the happenings, got tangled up in the pigtail cord.

"Sorry." said the VP.

Tyce extracted the handset and keyed the mic, his frustration clearly evident in his tone "B Troop-six, B Troop-six, this is Iron Horse-six actual, send your traffic."

Oblivious to the urgency, the VP continued talking loudly, and Tyce couldn't hear a word over him. "Should I move? I mean, if I'm in the way, you just—"

Bra-aa-ap!

The loud and continuous sound of a Gatling automatic gun fired a long, full burst. On the far side of the base, a thin stream of light emanated from the sky about five hundred feet up in the air and swept back and forth across the ground like a fire hose.

"Oh, shit!" exclaimed the VP loudly. "Should we do something about that? Or . . . is that our guys?"

Tyce rekeyed the handset, but he knew Zane now had other matters to deal with. "B Troop, this is Iron Horse. Do you need assistance? What's your situation?"

A youngish voice came over the radio. "Iron Horse, this is Private Miller. We're getting raked by fire, one of those Russian 'copters made it into the air and is firing at us. We've spread out and taken cover in the hangars. Three

Humvees are burning. Including the lieutenant's vehicle. He's on fire. I don't think—"

But Tyce didn't hear the rest of the transmission. The handset was ripped from Tyce's grasp, again caught awkwardly on the VP as he pulled his body up to get a better view.

"God damn it, sir!" yelled Tyce. "Get the fuck back to where I put you until this fight is over!"

The VP turned to look at Tyce, a look of shock and anger across his face.

"Hey, you can't talk to me—"

"Sir." Tyce's face was tightened into a menacing scowl, "if you don't get the fuck back to the woods and out of my CP, I will pistol-whip your fat ass out and throw your unconscious body behind us where it can't get in the way."

"You . . . you . . . " the VP pointed at Tyce, but recoiled in fear as he did so, "don't you dare threaten—"

Tyce pulled his pistol out of its holster. There was zero time left for this kind of thing. "I'll shoot you my-fucking-self before you cause us to lose this fight."

"Listen here—"

Tyce pulled the receiver back and put a round into the pistol's chamber.

The sheer rage and anger emanating from Tyce was enough, but the addition of threats and now a loaded pistol spurred the VP to scramble out of the hole. He bolted back toward the woods without looking back, still caught in the radio wire, the handset bouncing behind him.

Tyce looked at the radio operator who stared back at him with a newfound sense of admiration for his boss, "It's okay, sir, I'll hook up another in a jiffy."

Tyce could waste no more time. With Zane dead or out of the picture he needed to personally take charge of the situation before things spun out of control. Fortunately, the radioman had the spare hooked back up in seconds and handed it to Tyce, again watching him with admiration and maybe even a touch of fear.

"Okay, copy all B Troop, here's what needs to happen. Do you still have comms with your remaining Bradley?" said Tyce.

"We do, sir."

"Good. You all go to ground. You can't fight that helo alone. See if you can get your Brad up on your internal radio-net and try to talk him onto that helo when it comes back. He'll be firing at long range from his perch on the hill, but that 25mm cannon should cause havoc. At the least, it might make him pull out and reconsider. Maybe give you all some breathing room. I'll have the LAVs do the same on this side."

"What should we do about getting the Hercs?"

Tyce thought about it a second, tapping the microphone against his helmet chinstrap. Things were slipping, and he was getting that sinking feeling again.

He keyed the mic, "Halt the mission to secure the C-130 Hercs, for the moment. Just keep a few guns trained to the skies in case that Hind comes back and keep the men under cover. If you can, go ahead and blast every Russian aircraft still on the ground with your .50 cal or anything for that matter. At the very least, let's make sure nothing else tries to get airborne."

And there's nothing remaining but scorched earth when, or if, we leave, thought Tyce.

"This is B Troop. We copy all and WILCO." came a new voice.

Good, he thought, *glad to have Private Miller run the*

show, but also glad for someone in B-Troop with some more experience quickly getting to a spot to take charge.

Tyce handed the mic back to his radio operator. He breathed a sigh of relief and looked down. He still had the loaded pistol clutched in his right hand. He holstered it and hopped out of the hole, but staying low, he made preparations to leave, donning his equipment and grabbing his carbine. He summoned one of his HQ sergeants and passed instructions to relay any vital messages to him in his Humvee.

"Aye aye, sir. We'll run the radios from the HQ and pass the vital stuff," said the man. Tyce caught him staring with incredulity. He clearly couldn't contain himself and blurted out, "Holy shit, sir. You do realize you just threatened the Vice President of the United States with a fucking loaded pistol."

Tyce grimaced at the words as he buckled his equipment belt and grabbed his grenade pouch. That was sure to come back to haunt him, but there was no time to worry about it now. He turned to his Humvee crewmen in an adjacent fighting hole. "Go grab the Humvees, we're getting into the fight. And call Dragoons. Tell them to peel off two of their LAVs to go with us. We're going to need 'em.

An LAV crewman heard the call and raced up, "What's your intent, sir?"

"We're gonna go secure those fucking aircraft and get the Vice President of the United States the fuck off my battlefield."

On the way toward the front gate, Tyce called Victoria on the radio. Tyce had already learned the hard way that he needed to keep her informed, and he still expected her usual temper would be in rare form.

"Alpha-med, Alpha-med, this is Iron Horse-six."

Her smoky, loud, and brusque voice came back instantly. "Okay, so what the hell is going on. . . um, six?"

"Copy, need you to send your ambulances up to the front gate. Dragoons will send someone to escort you there. Then, you need to strip off a section and send them into B Troop's breach point to render aid. Zane has been the hardest hit."

"Say again your last transmission, Major. I'm trying to copy all this down, and my driver has us all over the road." A pause, then—"Slow the fuck down, Murray!" she yelled at her driver, forgetting to unkey her radio. "So where exactly am I going, Asher?"

Tyce actually sighed in frustration, waiting for Victoria to unkey the radio and finish her transmission. Tyce actually thought for a moment he'd rather be back in Fallujah, Iraq, where it was just combatants fighting and cross-talking over the radios.

"Alpha-med, use call signs. Everyone else is on this radio, too. And I say again, Dragoons will guide you to the front gate. Just be prepared to treat my wounded."

Victoria rekeyed and spoke in an even, monotone said, "Alpha-med copies." Then, still failing to unkey the handset, Tyce, and everyone else with a radio heard her talking to one of her other docs, "You know, this is some real bullshit. We barely even know what the fuck is going on, the grunts don't tell us shit, and that asshole thinks we can find our way in the darkness . . . who's he think he is treating us like that . . . I'm going to bust his fucking face open, later."

Tyce actually felt his face flushing red, but he quickly

regained control as they arrived at the front gate to the airfield. Burning wreckage greeted them, and Marines tucked behind cement barricades, weapons pointed both outboard and inboard.

Good, thought Tyce, *they took the initiative. The threat is just as much external as it is still internal. If the Russians go for Ned, we've got some time. If they don't go for the bait . . . well, we have a hell of a fight coming.*

As yet, the Russians had mounted no internal reactionary units. He supposed most of the experienced Russian infantry on the base had been wiped out in the initial assaults, but they couldn't be too cautious. The Hind had been driven skyward, but it would return. Tyce was sure of that.

In minutes they had the two LAVs and two ambulances assembled, and together Tyce guided them all headlong into the base and toward uncertainty.

CHAPTER 42

Yeager Airport

B Troop was still spraying grounded Russian aircraft when Tyce arrived. He didn't believe in retribution, much . . . but he hoped they were getting it out of their systems. It seemed like some small recompense for their fallen boss, as the National Guardsmen were shooting at everything in sight. Tyce had some worries they might hit the U.S. C-130s he needed for evacuating the vice president and his entourage. When he arrived at their sector, though, his worries were alleviated. Zane's platoon sergeant was there to greet him.

"Did you leave anything that can fly?" Tyce asked the combat scout.

A smile crossed the man's face when he saw their indomitable leader. "Hey, Iron Horse-six. We hope not. Good to finally see you this far forward on the front lines. The Army has gotten you this far. Figure you can get us the rest of the way?" Tyce had half-expected a good-natured ribbing, especially after what B Troop had just experienced.

"Any sign of that Hind coming back?"

"No, sir, but as you directed, I've got SFC Garrison scanning the skies overhead with his thermals. Maybe they moved off."

"I very much doubt it. The Hind crews are pretty proficient and will take care of their aircraft. That is, if they all got aboard before you started spraying the place. They'll touch down and get the flight crew to look over and repair any damage they might have taken. They usually even carry a mechanic aboard."

"We got a few pieces of him—I saw some chunks fall off—but he kept on going."

"Yeah, Roger that. Keep the perimeter secure, and I'll bring in the pilots so we can get the VP the hell out of here. Any word on your boss?"

"Yes, sir. We got 'im. What's left of him, I mean."

"I'm sorry for that, Trooper." said Tyce, his gut sank from the deadly reminder of their mission's risks.

"Sir, if it's okay with you, I want to put the L-T, that is, Lieutenant Zane in for a Bronze Star with combat V." he said, referring to his lieutenant, "He was a young kid, but still a fantastic leader. Also, SFC Garrison. His section of Brads won the day."

"Okay, I'm all in. But for the moment, game faces, okay? This thing ain't over until the fat lady sings."

"Guess that makes the Hind the fat lady then, sir."

More than fifteen minutes later, Tyce was beside himself with worry. It had taken them over an hour to completely secure the airfield, and they were just now beginning to get the big Lockheed turboprop planes fired up.

Too long, and no more word from Ned. We'll see that reactionary force very soon, Tyce thought.

He checked, double-checked, then triple-checked the men on the perimeter lines, but everything appeared to be in order. Meanwhile, he'd brought all his forces down and into the Yeager airfield including his mobile HQ.

Better to have a everyone inside a consolidated perimeter, he'd thought.

So far, not a hint of more enemy had reared their ugly heads, but time wasted on the objective was now Tyce's worst enemy. The Russians had shown time and again that they possessed all the manpower necessary to sweep Tyce's token forces aside. He'd mounted a daring raid, but his small team was no match for a calculated Russian response.

Victoria had set up shop inside one of the hangars, and Tyce wanted to see how his wounded men were faring. Just as he had directed his men to do, he raced from one hangar to the next, not wanting to expose himself for long—especially now that the sun had come up and they were visible from all around.

A hail came from the rafters of the hangar. Tyce looked up and saw Blue and several snipers. A long, three-story ladder had afforded them access to a series of crisscrossed gangways where several cranes and other electronics were housed, and they had set up a modified sniper hide position. They had punched some holes in the siding and seemed to be pretty happy with their vantage.

"How's the view up there?" Tyce yelled up.

"Not bad, sir," came the response from the team leader. "You all look like ants from up here."

"Okay," yelled Tyce. "Just be careful you squish the right ones if the time comes."

Two Humvees drove into the hangar and stopped near Tyce. The Marine driver leaned out of the Humvee.

"Hey, sir, the C-130 crews worked really hard and fast, but say only one of the planes is operational. The other must have been damaged by some crossfire or something."

Crap, thought Tyce. They had been planning on increasing the survivability of the government guys by splitting them between two aircraft, just in case. If the planes were detected by the much more maneuverable Russian fighters, at least they could have split up, and one of them might make it. In any case, it was all very risky, but at least they still had a chance with one plane—and their luck had held out so far.

"Got it," said Tyce, "So we're ready?"

"No, sir. They just asked that we stay out of their way while they go through their preflight check."

Tyce waved the men off and gritted his teeth. Everything was taking too long. Why even do preflight checks? *Don't those stupid flyboys know they have a bigger chance of getting shot down, especially with the time they're wasting, than having a small fuel leak?* Tyce had never been big on flying, and after a few crummy experiences downrange, he tried to grab a Scotch or a few beers before taking a civilian flight. But right at that moment, routine safety was the least of his concerns.

Right as the Humvees turned to head back out, one of the sniper rifles above barked out a flat report, which resonated loudly throughout the metal hangar.

"Hey, sir," came a shout from above as Tyce sprinted a short distance for cover, tumbling behind a stack of aviation tires. "There are a few guys probing the perimeter. Looks like the same guys we fought before. At least, the uniforms look like Russian air force." There was a slight pause. "One less of 'em now," the voice said cheerily.

Bang!

Another of the alert snipers had fired.

"Make that two . . . but they are looking for a weak spot. We'll keep them at arm's length. 'Bout how long ya figure?" This time, it was Blue's voice. Looked like he was still keeping himself gainfully employed.

Tyce put his helmet back squarely and wiped himself off. Since Iraq, the sound of a sniper's bullet still made him jump—both incoming and outgoing sniper shots. Tyce tried to stand, but his prosthetic had come off when he had leapt over the tires.

He yelled up to Blue, "Hopefully soon." Then hopped over to retrieve his leg. He saw Victoria approaching him from the corner where she had set up her ambulances. She wore her usual scowl, but it softened the instant she saw him hopping around for his leg.

Embarrassed, Tyce tried to get over to the leg before she reached him, but she misread his intent and hustled over to help him.

"Hey, Tyce," Victoria said, as she helped him buckle the prosthetic back on. Her hands and arms were covered with dark red bloodstains.

Tyce looked her up and down. He was embarrassed for being a cripple and needing someone's help in battle but even more angry at himself for noticing her again as a woman. But she looked all the more beautiful to him after performing her duties saving his men's lives.

"How are we doing?" he asked to cover up his embarrassment.

"You mean, how many have we lost? None on my operating table," she answered with a medical provider's firmness while snapping the last buckle on Tyce's leg. "But I can't account for those still out on the battlefield. I tasked several of your men to guard some of my corpsmen, and they are out there right now recovering the . . . fallen." Her voice choked up a little.

"You haven't lost anyone?" Tyce said incredulously.

"No, but there are four of your men who will need prosthetics. I took three arms and one leg. They are recovering in the back of the Humvees, if you want to visit with them. Though I doped them heavily on morphine drips."

"Yeah, I'd like to visit with them. See how they're doing."

Victoria looked Tyce over, as any medical officer would, then rubbed some dirt off his cheek.

The moment was nice. But just as before, it was interrupted—this time by the sounds of an LAV engine. One of the two LAVs Tyce had sent to keep a good, roving eye on the perimeter shot into the hangar, its turret pivoting on a distant target as the vehicle spun around and tucked just on the inside of the huge metal sliding door. The commander was up and out of the turret and waving Tyce over.

Tyce ran over to the LAV and climbed aboard. The commander caught Tyce by the hand, hauling him aboard like an old cavalry movie. Tyce grabbed the crew helmet handed to him and squatted behind the pintle-mounted 7.62mm machine gun on the top of the vehicle.

He keyed the intercom. "What's up, guys?"

"Hey, sir, that Bradley said he's spotted the Russian helicopter. He said he just caught a piece of him through the thermal sights running behind the ridgeline to the east."

"Okay, understood. What direction was he traveling?"

"South."

"Crap," said Tyce. "Means he's probably spotted SFC Garrison's Brad. Where are your other vics?"

"Two still at the front gate, and my wingman is near the edge of the hangars—"

Wham wham wham wham!

The hillside around the remaining Bradley lit up. They heard the *whop-whop* of the huge Russian helicopter, but the pilot had chosen his approach wisely. He had stayed below the shelf that the airport was set on and now, by the sounds of things, was maneuvering between or slightly above the giant, three-story hangars.

As they moved more out into the open, Tyce could see a huge brown cloud of dirt near the stricken Brad.

Tyce flicked the control lever so he could transmit over the radio. "All stations, all stations. Mass fires on that damned chopper. Don't give him a second's break."

There was no response over the radio, but Tyce knew at that moment, everyone in the unit was looking for their chance to pepper the aircraft. Sure enough, the sounds of small arms came from all around the camp: the familiar *pop-pop* of rifle fire, *kerplunk* of 40mm grenades, and the *buk-buk-buk* of 7.62mm machine guns. It sounded like everyone who'd spotted the threatening helicopter, no matter how small their window of opportunity, wanted to give it hell.

Rooooar!

The enemy helicopter flew right between the two hangars and directly over Tyce's LAV. Tyce felt like he'd just had a minor heart attack. It was so close, he could almost have reached up and touched it. Instead, he opened up with the pintle-mounted machine gun and gave it a heavy burst from the weapon. The effect was minimal. It looked as if all the rounds bounced off. If nothing else, though, at least the bulky aircraft was having to keep moving to avoid getting shot from every angle.

The LAV crew were talking, trying to get an angle, but the aircraft was too swift and their turret too slow to get off a good shot. Tyce knew the 25mm would surely make a mark where the smaller arms couldn't.

Tyce shouted through the intercom, "Get us out in the front of the hangars. If that Brad is still alive, he can cover over our heads and we can cover over his."

"Copy, sir. You sure it's worth the risk going into the open? That bird has some anti-tank missiles that will chew through our armor."

"It's worth a shot, and we're doing no good stuck between these buildings. If we sit here, eventually that damn flying tank will pick us apart piece by piece."

The LAV bounded out to the front side of the hangars, the tall buildings still preventing them from seeing west, but they could easily see out east to where the Brad was. Tyce instantly lost confidence in his own decision when they saw it, though. There were huge plumes of white smoke coming from the Bradley.

"Hey, sir, he's a goner. Best we go back between the hangers. Without his cover on our blind side, that Russian will make short work of us."

"No, let me try to raise him. You call over to your wingman and pull him over near us. Have him cover southeast, and you cover northeast."

Tyce clicked over to the battalion net and tried to raise the Bradley. After several calls with no response, he was about to give up when a faint call came, barely audible above the noises from the vehicle.

"Iron horse, Iron Horse, this is two-seven-two."

"Hot damn," said Tyce. "Hey, copy. Glad you're alive. How you holding up over there?"

"Driver bought it, but me and my gunner and scouts are alive. I had them set fires all around us to confuse the helo's thermals."

"Well, it confused us, too. Interrogative, your main gun working? Are you up for some work"

"That's an *affirm,* and if it means gutting that fat Russian bird, absolutely."

"Can you cover over our heads?"

"Yes . . . yes, sir, I see you right out in the open. Shouldn't you get some cover, six?"

"No, we're going to make a fighting triangle. Need your gun to cover our backs. We'll cover yours. This pilot is good. He's gone to ground a few times and popped up in different spots. I think he's using old Russian anti-armor doctrine. We just need to get some good, clean shots off at him."

"Roger six, makes sense. We're locked and loaded here. What if he has missiles?"

"Then I need you faster on the trigger than he is."

The waiting game proved to be even more unnerving. After the last bursts of gunfire, the Hind had disappeared again. The gunship was swift enough and had enough terrain to hide behind to pop up again anywhere.

Tyce listened to the whirr of the turret as the LAV gunner scanned. The commander, Tyce, and even the LAV driver were atop the vehicle and searching the skies.

"Iron Horse, Iron Horse," came a radio call.

"Go for Iron Horse-six."

"Roger, this is Tower. The C-130 Herc crew wants to know if they are clear to taxi?"

Tyce had been so intent looking out for the enemy aircraft, he had almost forgotten about his primary mission. His men had hastened up to take over the airport's control tower on their own initiative. *Great thinking, boys!*

"Okay, that's a negative," Tyce said with maybe a bit too much force, revealing his thoughts. If the C-130 were to pull out now, the helicopter would most certainly blast it before it could even make it to the runway.

"Tower copies," came the response.

Tyce thought for a second. "Hey, Tower, can you spot that helo on your radar?"

There was a brief pause, then another voice came over the net. It was Gunny. "Negatron, boss. This is Gunny. We took the tower, but it's just us infantrymen up here. I couldn't tell you which one of these switches was a radar and which one launched the nuclear strike."

At least it gave them another vantage point. "Okay, keep your eyes peeled."

"That's one thing we can do. Also, the Herc pilot wants you to know that he's spinning up now, he has to get the engines fired up and check throttles and fuel feeds or he's a negative for takeoff."

Crap, thought Tyce. *Double crap crap!* If the C-130 spun his rotors, the helicopter was sure to see his engines in its thermals. The four turboprop engines would stand out against the cold air like white hot embers in a fire and probably leave a plume of snow.

"Hey, sir, this is Tower. He says it's now or never. He's gotta warm up those engines."

"Okay, have him spin up, but tell him to wait." Tyce found it immensely ironic that only half an hour before he had been trying to speed everyone up, and now he was begging for just a few more minutes.

The LAV commander came over the intercom. "If the C-130 pulls out of his parking stall, engines at full rev, wouldn't that draw the helo in?"

"It might . . . I'm not too comfortable using the VP's plane as bait."

"Why not, sir? We're bait."

Tyce ruminated on that point a second more. It was insanity, but he was out of options and way past being out of time.

"Tower, tell the Herc to rev his engines all the way up."

"Roger." Came the response and in seconds everyone

heard the Herc's big engines throttle up and a massive plume of white snow crystals rose above the base.

A few more minutes and Tyce was just about to give up when the now familiar *thump-thump* came distantly to their ears. It came from the northwest, right above SFC Garrison's Bradley.

The Hind poked its head up from behind the hill, taking the bait. It raced forward, aiming to make a run on the Herc, Both LAV gunners locked on it and started cranking out rounds at a rapid rate even though they were beyond their maximum range. None hit, but the Hind immediately knew it was being fired upon from somewhere. Still, the Hind Pilot remained fixed on the Herc.

"Don't hit the Brad," yelled Tyce.

Spotting the LAVs in the open, the Hind turned its nose for a moment and fired a barrage of rockets, then a second and a third, then went back to diving at the Herc. Thankfully, the continuous, but inaccurate LAV fire caused the Hind to juke and dodge making the rockets land wide. A cluster of them blasted the ground around Tyce and the LAVs, blowing huge chunks of asphalt into the air. Tyce felt like a sitting duck.

It was extremely long range, but Tyce couldn't resist opening up with the top-mounted machine gun and joining in, his anger rising. As he did so, he heard everyone else on the base firing, too; the snipers, small arms, and Diaz's machine guns joined in again.

Good, keep him on edge, thought Tyce.

As it neared the field, enough 25mm shots were now hitting the Hind that it finally seemed to change its mind. Switching focus from the Herc to fully committing to attacking the LAVs, the pilot turned his helo and now raced directly for the LAVs.

"He's coming for us. Get ready for a heavy rocket and gun run." yelled Tyce.

It was a good idea—take out the threat, then go for the Herc—but the pilot neglected one fact. SFC Garrison and his Brad were still in the fight. In its eagerness to smash the two LAVs in the open, the Hind passed directly over him. Garrison's Brad waited until the Hind was directly in line, then opened up with the 25mm at extreme close range.

One, two, then three rounds hit the tail rotor, bursting the blades. Four, five, six rounds made contact with the massive helicopter's armored body and it started to smoke.

Now at a closer range, the LAVs' cannons found their mark, slapping into the fuselage, tearing pieces of metal framework, and shattering glass from the pilot's and copilot's bubble windscreens. The Hind started to spin, slowly at first, then more and more rapidly, gradually losing altitude and descending toward the airfield.

A testament to the aircraft's design, the bird slammed into the ground but remained relatively intact. It heeled over, the rotors still spinning rapidly and tossing up great chunks of earth and snow. No one let up, they all unleashed hell, tearing the grounded beast to pieces until it finally caught fire.

Tyce thought of the pilots—soldiers just like him and the rest of the men. Then he remembered they had never asked for this war, and the Russians were invaders and occupiers. Against his better judgment to try and stay dispassionate, he fired another few shots at the aircraft, then tilted the barrel back and keyed his radio, letting out a series of rapid orders.

"Tower, tell the Herc drivers to taxi. Main, send the

Humvees with the VP and cabinet to the runway. Alpha-med, collect all casualties and prepare to leave."

In minutes, Tyce and Gunny stood outside the Herc, its engines whining. Three Humvees pulled up, and the VP and his cabinet jumped out. He took one look at Tyce and smirked. He wasn't soon going to forget Tyce had almost killed him.

Tyce stuck out his hand. "No hard feelings, Mr. Vice President. Just gettin' the job done."

"No hard feelings, Major. I understand. Though maybe next time you could just ask me to move back a bit before you lock-n-load on an old civil servant."

"No can do, sir. If there is a next time, I'll need you to stay out of my and my troops' way."

The VP pulled in closer to speak directly into Tyce's ear. "Would you really have shot me, son?"

Tyce smiled. "Next time you're on my battlefield, we'll have to find out."

The Herc crew chief shouted at them from the open side hatch to get aboard.

"Good luck and Godspeed, Mr. Vice President. I hope you and the rest can do the right thing by the American people from up there in Canada." The VP nodded and then he and the what remained of the government of the United States scrambled onto the C-130.

The Herc pushed the throttles to full, released the parking brakes, and jerked forward rumbling toward the runway. For a brief second, Tyce held his breath as the pilot, eager to finally get airborne, took the turn onto the runway too fast. The wheels skidded off the taxiway, its wingtip practically scraping a snow-covered gravel berm, but it righted, and in moments it throttled up and dashed down the runway. It ascended into the air, but remained no higher than a few hundred feet, staying within the valley for cover, and headed north.

CHAPTER 43

Yeager Airport

SSgt. Diaz knelt down, opened the feed tray cover of her machine gun, and began wiping it down with gun oil. The barrel was still hot and made a hissing sound. Wisps of smoke rose up from it. Tyce and Gunny were still watching the last hints of the C-130 as it soared off just above the treetops and through the canyon, but SSgt. Diaz seemed uninterested and continued to wipe down her weapon.

Victoria walked over to the gathered leaders of the 150th Cavalry Regiment. She was still wearing her bloody latex gloves. "Are we sticking around here until the Russians mount a counterattack?"

Her question seemed to jolt the rest of them out of their moment of victory. They all realized their gains had been temporary. It was time to get back to the business of their own survival.

"What's next, boss?" asked Gunny.

Tyce looked around at the mayhem, the still-burning tank hulks and the crashed Russian helicopter. For a brief moment, they owned the entire base, but Victoria was right; it was just a matter of time before they were going to have to fight again. They might not have turned the tide of the war today, but they sure as hell had shown that the Russian invader was fallible and could be beaten. For now,

Tyce needed to gather Ned's force, then find a place to hide out until it was time to thrust the spear into the Russian side again.

"Back to Parsons?" asked Blue, still a bit out of breath after climbing down from his sniper's perch.

"No, let the indomitable Mayor Holly rebuild her fair city." said Victoria.

"I fully expect that when next we meet, she'll be in control of the northern half of West Virginia," said Gunny.

"No doubt," said Tyce. "I want to give the troops a bit of a break—they've earned it. Not sure how long it will last before the Russians find us again, but I'd rather set up a solid base of operations than go out on the road. I think we find a new HQ. Someplace with an abundance of chow, fuel, and maintenance parts. Plenty of space for the troops to wash up, and where we can slink off into woods. You know, someplace where we can do some classic hit-and-runs, like the insurgents used against us in Iraq and Afghanistan."

"Kind of like insurgent Americans?" asked SSgt. Diaz.

"Nah, that has a bad ring to it."

"Rebels." said Wynand.

"No, that means were rebelling against the legitimate government. Last I checked, it's the illegitimate government we don't support."

"Freedom fighters?" asked Blue.

"Well . . . that's already taken. You know, 'a Mountaineer is always free.'" said Tyce quoting the West Virginia state motto.

"What, then?" asked Victoria.

"How about just the 150th Cavalry?" said Tyce.

"Ha, giving yourself a promotion, sir?" said SFC Garrison, who was now mountless and needed to share a ride with Tyce.

"Well, I heard the position of commanding officer of that unit was at least temporarily vacant," and he patted the day's hero on the shoulder.

Tyce's motley band chuckled, then locked and loaded their weapons with what little ammo they had remaining, collected their wounded and dead, and boarded their vehicles, slipping quietly back into the woods, unseen by any but some West Virginia mountaineers—who would surely never tell the tale of what they'd witnessed there that morning.

EPILOGUE

Omni Homestead Resort, Virginia

"**S**anto c-c-c-cielo! Holy crap!" exclaimed SSgt. Diaz, her peanut butter–coated tongue twisting her Bronx Spanish accent even more than usual. "This is the best f-f-frickin' PB&J on the whole God-damned planet."

Tyce laughed openly at the spectacle of the giant woman sitting cross-legged on the floor and taking enormous bites from the sandwich, her ever-present machine gun laying across her legs like a kid's favorite toy. It was gone in four or five gulps and washed down with a swig from a can of Coors Light. She looked around to see if anyone else was going for seconds, when no one did, she grabbed another from the platter of sandwiches Victoria and her sailors had made for everyone. When no one was looking, she took a third and slipped the PB&J over to Trigger, who downed it in one bite and, licked his chops loudly and happily.

Captain Blake stepped into the luxurious lobby area of the Omni resort in Hot Springs, Virginia, looking around the room. Spotting Tyce, he walked over and pulled him aside. Ned was practically the only one still in full-camouflage uniform with his helmet and flak jacket on. The rest had augmented their uniforms with civilian clothing.

"Hey, sir."

Tyce put the beer can on the side table and looked over the notes Captain Blake handed him.

"Sir, here and here." He pointed to the map he held up for Tyce to look over.

"Okay, Ned, those look just fine." He clapped the special forces soldier on the shoulder. "Now, how many men can you spare to come to the party? They deserve a break along with the rest of us."

Ned smiled back at his leader. "Sir, business first. You gave me a mission to secure this outpost, and I take that seriously." He turned to leave, seemed to fully take in the fun going on around him, and turned back. "Just make sure you swabbies save some beer for us working dogs, sir."

"You got it, Ned."

"And none of that Coors Light. Don't they have any IPAs in the root cellar here?" He looked around a bit more at the lavish appointments of the four-star resort and hotel Tyce had commandeered as the headquarters of the 150th with its leather couches, double-sided fireplaces, and chandeliers made from antlers.

For a moment, Tyce felt guilty for keeping men on duty, but he was going to have to get over that. From now on, there was no way they could ever all relax until the Russian hordes were gone.

Gunny interrupted the conversation. "Hey, Captain Blake, if your boys only drink the froufrou junk, I'll make sure there's some set aside. And do the special forces expect them to be served in our finest champagne crystal? Wouldn't want your men to have to sink to the lowest level of the workingman's beer."

Both of the men laughed. While he was giving Ned a good ribbing, Gunny was simultaneously pouring himself what looked to be a fairly fine Scotch into the exact crystal champagne glass he was mocking.

"I think I'm finally getting used to the Marine Corps type of humor," said Ned. Then he walked out to oversee the construction of the new observation posts.

At the tail of the conversation about alcohol, Victoria walked back in wheeling a luggage cart stacked with cases of beer, eliciting more laughter from Tyce and Gunny. Pretty much everyone was now dressed in some kind of stolen ski resort wear. Tyce had all but demanded folks try to relax for a bit, but Victoria had apparently selected the most form-hugging gear she could find. Tyce found it hard not to stare at her figure.

"So, you wanna let me in on the joke? Or is this just more navy *shaming*?" asked Victoria.

Tyce's face turned red, as did Gunny's. Victoria's fury was now well known across the unit, and few chose to cross her path.

SSgt. Diaz, still washing the peanut butter down, now with another fresh beer, looked back and forth between the two men, then over to Victoria. "Well, ma'am, if these two are too pussy to tell you, I'm glad to fill you in. You look like a frickin' sorority sister going to do her workout at the fashion studio. Maybe no one told you—we ain't in Connect . . . Connecti . . . cut, whatever . . . anymore."

Everyone laughed at SSgt. Diaz now, her attempt at a joke falling flat as she stumbled over the word. She took another enormous bite of PB&J and started petting Trigger to conceal her frustration.

Victoria twisted her lips to the side and glared at them all. "This is some bullshit. You Marines are the most sexist—"

Blue interrupted her, bringing a plate of cooked BBQ

chicken wings: "And civilians." Victoria turned to Blue, her eyes narrowing. "Uh . . . hi, ma'am," he said with his gentle mountain man charm. He grabbed a wing and tasted it, then hurried off. They were delicious, but Blue was too wise to stick around and get into the crossfire of Victoria's famous rants.

"Look, you . . . grunts. Just because we're holed up waiting for the next boot to drop doesn't mean we shouldn't stay in top physical shape." She gave a holier-than-thou look. "And as far as me and my sailors are concerned, the workout store selling top brands is open for business at a significant discount."

SSgt. Diaz stopped munching on her PB&J and looked up thoughtfully.

"And they have a full array of weightlifting gear and exercise equipment in the resort hotel's gym next door."

"Hey, copy that, ma'am," said SSgt. Diaz, dropping her sandwich and wiping her mouth on her sleeve.

"Hmm," said Tyce. "Guess we'll have to get used to starting our lives anew."

"And seeing each other as neighbors, too," said Gunny.

"More like patriots and compadres in arms," said Tyce.

Everyone smiled, trying to imagine what the next few weeks or even months would be like. Gunny pulled out the expensive-looking Scotch he'd been keeping close to him, too afraid to set it down lest one of the troops snatch it. He poured everyone a glass. Tyce and SSgt. drank it up greedily, but Victoria sniffed it and put the glass down.

The general and Bill walked over to find Tyce. The general had a large book tucked under his arm.

"Been reviewing a few things about hit-and-run tactics during the German occupation of the western half of Russia."

"General, I'm eager to hear your advice, as always, but

couldn't you take a break with us for a bit? I'm already feeling guilty for leaving Captain Blake's men to do some dirty work while the rest of us take a breather."

The general sniffed the air. "You know, they say the blind start to develop their other senses when they lose their sight, and I do believe I smell some oak barrel–aged Scotch. Let me guess . . . Gunnery Sergeant Dixon?"

"Yes, sir," Gunny answered a little reluctantly. "How'd you know?"

"Ah, if I learned anything in my years of service, it's that the senior enlisted man always knows where to find the good stuff. Pour us a glass."

Gunny poured a fresh glass, then hoisted his up. "We made it. At least for a bit. Here's to living to fight another day."

"I'll drink to that," said Tyce and they all hoisted their glasses and drank.

Gunny looked at the half-empty bottle, shrugged, then filled all their glasses up once more.

SiriusXM satellite radio and even some ham radio repeaters had started broadcasting a Radio Free America channel for the past few days. The main studios for XM in Rockefeller Plaza in New York City had been taken over in the first days of the invasion and were broadcasting calming music and pro-Russian propaganda. Still, one of the XM bands was broadcasting from parts unknown, and everyone with an XM receiver had been tuning into it as a source of real news about the occupied nation of America.

An announcer began the evening broadcast slowly and clearly. The massive global change brought about by the Russian invasion of the U.S. had actually changed the day-to-day tenor of most people. Everyone was a little more uncertain about the world's order with America still an occupied nation.

"This is John Enzio broadcasting for Radio Free America. We have another full broadcast tonight from our new location. First up on the program, word from West Virginia that a group of American citizen insurgents, joined by the West Virginia National Guard and a handful of Marines, has been fighting back. And perhaps more importantly, I am joined now by a special guest for his first interview since making it safely out of the occupied states and establishing the new American government in absentia. Mr. Vice President, welcome and congratulations for maintaining the integrity of the elected government of the U.S. First of all, National Guardsmen and Marines? Am I reading that right, Mr. Vice President?"

"Yes, local citizens banded together with army National Guard and Marine reserve leadership and are fighting back. But that is just one region. We're getting reports across the states of even more citizens rising up to stop the Russian aggressors."

"That's very encouraging. Should we expect more reports like this one? More reports of these . . . citizen soldiers? And, perhaps just as importantly, should we be calling you *Mr. President*?"

"Yes . . . and no. The Cabinet and I hope that stories like those from West Virginia will encourage citizens to do the right thing. Not everyone is a fighter, but some might want to stop the Russians in different ways. Not since the Revolutionary War have we seen an occupier seize and subjugate the American people. And to your second question: no. We still do not know the whereabouts of the president. So while I, and others, are honored to be performing his duties during these grim times, the U.S. government is officially intact, and we believe the invaders cannot have killed the president. Beyond the invasion, the assassination of a U.S. leader would be another tally against this evil and despotic regime. We need the leaders of other nations, our allies, to see and hear what's happened here. It is not, as the Russians have put it, an occupation meant to redemocratize our republic."

"Another tick mark in what we all believe will be a long list of grim atrocities when the final tally is in. Right, Mr. Vice President?"

"Correct, John. We have a long way to go, but the first counterblows have been struck, and the insurgency has risen. An American insurgency against the tyrant occupiers. Speaking of which, directly following our discussion, we have a number of items we'd like to broadcast to our resistance."

"Absolutely. We proudly carry the title of Mouthpiece of the Free Republic. What, may I ask, are we broadcasting? That is, if there's nothing too classified. You know, just the basics to encourage our listeners that the fires of democracy are still burning fiercely."

"Well, of course. The Russians may listen to every broadcast, but we'll speak in guarded terms that won't be of much use to them. Let's see . . . your listeners can't see me looking over my shoulder, but the whole cabinet is standing right behind me. Okay, nods from most: We have a few requests for specific intelligence from our secret agents working inside the country. A few promises to keep with some of our resistance fighters, organizational items for the coming days. Also, I'm honored to announce a few promotions for some of our uniformed men and women still living the harrowing life of leading our resistance."

Yeager Airport

The morning's sunlight reflected brilliantly off the white-crested Appalachian Mountains. Below the Russian Ka-60 Kasatka helicopter, West Virginian farmlands with their brightly painted red barns dotted the peaceful winter scenery. It was picture perfect, almost like a postcard. Inside the helicopter, however, things were anything but calm.

General Tympkin turned back from gazing out the window and faced the two colonels sitting in the helicopter bench seats across from him. Next to him sat General Kolikoff's three majors and his Spetsnaz bodyguard, Captain Shenkov. Not one had so much as moved since their flight took off from Morgantown in the predawn darkness. They knew their destination, and they knew the ramifications of today's trip. Or at least, they thought they did.

General Tympkin checked his watch, then pulled the helmet-mounted microphone closer to speak. His two days without shaving had left his face with a dark shadow, and as he keyed the mic, the first sound was the loud scratching of his unshaven chin as he dragged the mic toward his mouth.

"*Khorosho*," said the general over the helicopter's intercom. "Right. Open the side doors. I want everyone to get a good look at the destruction."

He stared at Kolikoff and Nikolaevich, and they both unbuckled to slide the heavy metal doors to the side. Kolikoff was visibly sweating even after the side hatches had been opened. Nikolaevich stared outside, absently flicking at the rifle strapped across his chest. All three majors sat unmoving, their helmets' lowered sun visors concealing their eyes. They were obviously too intimidated to even look in General Tympkin's direction.

"Pilot, what is our distance to Charleston airport?" the general asked.

"General, we are over it in one minute," came the quick response from the cockpit.

The general peered over the edge, and within a moment the destruction of the base filled everyone's view. Three thick black columns of smoke were the first things visible, dominating the scene of destruction. The pilot yawed the aircraft to afford the men a better view, and everyone except the three majors leaned over out of morbid curiosity or to get a better vantage.

The shattered guard towers and front gates were easily identifiable. The remainder of the tower's twisted support spans stuck out like skeletal hands grasping up from the grave. Everyone's eyes were drawn to the closest source of one of the columns of smoke. Heavy recovery vehicles, likely used by the previous owners for towing aircraft around the tarmac, were hard at work attempting to pull the destroyed Russian T-90 tank from the ditch where it had come to a final halt. As they tugged to wrestle it loose, bright yellow sparks appeared, shooting out the open top hatches. Several pops were audible, even above the rotor blades' downwash.

All three recovery vehicles hastily cut their lines and scampered quickly away from the tank. Ammunition, until now lying covered and undisturbed, began to cook off from the heat and movement. Everyone watched the scene closely, rooting silently for the men to hurry their scramble to safety.

A boom permeated the air as the stoked fire reached the center magazine, blowing the tank's turret into the air and heading straight for the helicopter. Obviously, the plight of the stricken vehicle had distracted the pilot as well; the pilot yanked the controls hard left, mostly out of surprise, but it was an unnecessary reaction to a danger more than two thousand feet below.

The general rekeyed his mic with another loud scratch, then said, "This is the product of failure."

Kolikoff and Nikolaevich swallowed hard.

"Yesterday, our sources tell us the escaped American vice president has officially promoted your opponent. This Marine, Asher. He is now a lieutenant colonel. And gentlemen, I have to tell you . . ." General Tympkin leaned in closer to the men and signaled them to come nearer. "I must tell you, I would have done the same thing. He and his band of merry men are real fighters. The kind of citizen insurgents our grandfathers became in the German invasion of our country in the winter of '42.

"Do you know what else I believe?" said the general, a crafty smile now on his face and an uptick in his voice, as if he were about to reveal the secret to it all. Nikolaevich and Kolikoff shook their heads.

To everyone's surprise, Captain Shenkov grabbed Colonel Nikolaevich by his rifle and pulled him swiftly out of his seat. Nikolaevich, arms flailing about, tried to grasp an edge or a surface as he wrestled against the stout Russian special forces captain. He seemed about to catch onto something when General Tympkin struck his boot sharply against the colonel's forehead.

The boot tipped Nikolaevich off balance, but maybe it was more the shock of his boss giving the coup de grâce. As Nikolaevich fell through the hatch, he gave the most horrendous, bloodcurdling scream over the intercom. Then the cable snapped. Even then, his screams were still audible a second more from outside the helicopter as he plunged to his death.

The helicopter's crew chief looked back into the cabin to discern the source of the noise, but the general signaled him to land, staring at the still-horrified Kolikoff.

"This is now your mess, Kolikoff. Do you understand your new duties and the consequence of any further failure?"

"Yes . . . yes, I do, General," he stammered, nodding violently.

ORGANIZATION OF U.S. RESISTANCE FORCES

150th Cavalry Regiment
USANG
(West Virginia National
Guard)
COLONEL DAVID NEPO

XO and Interim Commander
MAJOR TYCE ASHER*
* "Mr. Wynand"
* "Mr. Georgia-Blue"
* "Corporal 'Trigger'"

U.S. MARINE CORPS

Dragoons,
4th LAR Bn, U.S. Marine
Corps Reserve (now a
captain)
Gunnery Sergeant Dixon
Staff Sergeant Diaz
(Quantico, VA)

U.S. NATIONAL GUARD
(WEST VIRGINIA)

Company C,
2nd Battalion,
19th Special
Forces Group
Captain Ned
Blake
(Camp
Dawson)

B Troop,
1st Squadron,
150th Cavalry
USANG
1st Lieutenant
Chad Zane
(Eleanor,
WV)

U.S. NAVY

**Shock Trauma Platoon–
ALPHA**
JTF CAPMED
Fleet Surgical Team 10
Forward Resuscitation Unit
Commander Victoria Remington
(Bethesda, MD)

AUTHOR'S NOTE

*To be ignorant of what occurred before you were
born is to remain always a child.
For what is the worth of human life, unless it is
woven into the life of our ancestors
by the records of history?*
—MARCUS TULLIUS CICERO

When I was growing up in the 1970s and '80s, we fell asleep to a living nightmare every night. A real, live enemy who lived just over the oceans and who wanted to kill us all in a firestorm of destruction. The seemingly unstoppable *Soviet Bear*.

In a very Orwellian sense, everyone at my school had a common bond. A fairly simple feeling of a vast togetherness through the shared looming and personal deaths we all expected from a nuclear attack. Or, if we survived, through a cold and ever worsening nuclear winter. We all talked about what we would do if the "Russkies" invaded. Calling someone a "Commie," or a "Pinko" was a universal slam. It didn't matter if you loved U2, wore tie-dye T-shirts, and wanted to save the whales with world peace *now*; there was an inevitability to the Soviet threat.

They didn't care about our beliefs, because they believed our whole system was a malfunction and it was their sworn destiny to root out our government, our religions, and our people. While we practiced "duck and cover," we made pacts on what we'd do when the war began. It seemed always on the horizon. We talked about what a post-nuclear landscape would look like. Movies like *The Day After* and *A Boy and His Dog* gave us examples of what to expect.

We made lists of which weapons we would take. I was supposed to bring a Louisville Slugger and a Crosman pellet rifle, a Buck knife, and three boxes of C-rations I'd bought from the army-navy surplus store. These boxes had cigarettes in them, and we learned to smoke as we hiked the mountains. Every weekend was another chance to explore which parts of the Rockies would sustain us for the longest period in extreme weather of summer and winter while we hunted and fished to survive. Our parents had sung protest songs in the '60s, but even they seemed to believe the Soviets were a threat to every American and their allies, regardless of their beliefs. They were too old to make it, we knew, so we just accepted the fact that they'd have to stay behind and deal with a Soviet occupation while we fought from the hills. Then the movie *Red Dawn* came out, and we all now had an example of what to expect and how to fight back and win.

It was a foregone conclusion that we would never surrender to an occupier. It was also a foregone conclusion that we would fight and harass the enemy to the bitter end, even if it meant giving up our lives to do so. We knew nothing about combat besides what we'd read and seen in movies, but that was enough to keep a fire going. That and the simple lessons we got from our government and history classes that America was something great, something bigger than us, and held an ideal that we could not let die. Something our parents, grandparents, great-grandparents, and so on had fought for and, when necessary, died to defend. We had a purpose beyond survival from attack. A duty to ensure the continuity of our way of life. A boyish naivety, to be certain, but it was what we believed.

The numbers of deaths, the gulags, the hellish purges, the men or women who bravely stood up but then disappeared in the night because of their beliefs, the athletes and generals who defected from behind the Iron Curtain—all of them told tales of corruption and oppression. These were enough to ensure we felt righteous and just in our beliefs.

But then, in one remarkable summer, the Russian coup of 1991 ended with the complete shattering of the Soviet Union and the collapse of what most of us saw as one of the most deadly and repressive regimes the world has ever seen. And all of a sudden, we were the world's sole superpower. Righteousness and right had outlasted oppression and intolerance.

In the giddy times that followed, I joined the Marine Corps, believing I needed to do my bit as an American in the new world. Believing it was my job to ensure we remained ahead of any emerging versions of fascism that might arise, and even just to support our new role as the peace broker in an age free from tyranny.

But to all of our amazement and my amusement, I soon discovered that we (the U.S. military) were still training to fight against a Soviet-like army in our military schoolhouses and maneuvers. When the War on Terror (and it *was* a war) began, we modified how we trained and how we fought to curb the threat of a collapsed nation's former military forces and the angry youth of an entire region. Anger at poverty, anger at inequality, anger due to religious perceptions, anger due to history. The anger and the rise of an insurgency was predicted by all, but still we trained to fight a Soviet horde, believing a large-scale army on one or two fronts (China and Russia) to be the most pressing threat to our nation and its allies as a whole.

As a student of history and literature, none of the twists and turns of our new war surprised me. The urgent grasping for solutions to fight COIN (counterinsurgency), the major challenges of logistics, fighting a determined, predominantly civilian-based army, or even the lawlessness of a distributed combat environment in Iraq or Afghanistan. In my early years, I had read widely in military history. I studied great historic battles, watched endless war films, and especially listened to the sonorous and quietly spoken backroom reminiscing of veterans of World War II, Korea, and Vietnam. The visceral shock, the bitter sting at loss and injury, and the gravity of decisions that caused them, were not a surprise; they hurt tremendously, but on some level, I had expected them. But the disconsolate gloom that followed, our constant struggle to fight a faceless enemy, and our seemingly unaware—or even uncaring—public came as a shock.

As Marines, we had a saying we repeated often in combat—one of many maxims that I believe only soldiers, sailors, Marines, and airmen can conjure up when faced with futility, terrible burden of life and death, constant fear, and the inevitability of our own deaths not just on a daily basis, but on a minute-to-minute basis. It went like this: "America is not at war. America is at the mall. The Marine Corps is at war." There was truth in that simple statement. And, I wondered often, what happens when the next war comes?

My officers and men earnestly believed in the new war, one in which we fought in cities and hamlets to expel an ideological equal. This was the way we would fight, they thought, now and forever. And we rebuilt the military schools and thinking to ensure everyone knew how to fight in a COIN environment and could help us win that last war.

The trouble is, we never will fight a last war. Our newly minted Marines, sailors, soldiers and airmen believed this, and that we would never again fight a war on our own soil. They listened to us, the men and women who fought in the previous war, and they felt it a certitude that fighting small but long wars would win over a population. But the truth is, history repeats itself, and there is nothing new under the sun, and time and again, we foolishly believe the pacifist doves that Neville Chamberlain's "peace for our time" is achievable (as we believe the hawks in wartime).

Quietly, stealthily, enigmatically, war will come creeping back to our doorstep. History does not lie. And through all of recorded history, war remains as likely as the clouds above and the dirt below. So we dare not ignore the things that amputees after the Civil War knew, that men with collapsed lung knew after World War I, that men with shell shock after World War II, that men with frostbitten hands knew after Korea, and that men who were spat on after Vietnam knew: you may not want war, but war will find you no matter how deep you bury your heads in the sand.

So what war are we prepared for now? For *some* kinds of war, yes. But if history is our teacher, we are very well prepared for the wrong kinds of battle. Our enemies are always watching us and thinking of new ways to fight. And if we take the last lesson from military history, we would know that our next war will look nothing like the last, and we will remain unprepared . . . until it is too late.